Immortal Muse

Stephen Leigh

DAW BOOKS, INC.

DONALD A. WOLLHEIM, FOUNDER

375 Hudson Street, New York, NY 10014

ELIZABETH R. WOLLHEIM
SHEILA E. GILBERT
PUBLISHERS

www.dawbooks.com

There's no doubt about this one . . .
To my own Muse and live-in Daemon, Denise

Acknowledgments

This book is entirely a work of fiction, although it depicts several genuine historical characters. Let me repeat: this book is *fiction*. Not fact. Please understand (and forgive) that the details of actual people's lives have been taken and seriously bent and twisted: I have conveniently ignored facts that interfered with the story, and I have created incidents and interactions from whole cloth. In *no way* should the reader believe that the historical personages displayed here actually did or said what I have them doing and saying. These characters live only in an alternate reality of my imagination (and yours, while you're reading the book). For the *genuine* lives of these people, please go to actual historical documents and scholarly research—there, you might find something approaching the truth.

You won't necessarily find it here.

Thanks to Dr. David Perry, for helping me avoid egregious historical mistakes in Venice and Rome!

Thanks to my first readers, whose comments helped shape the book (and made it a very different book from the version that they read . . .): Loni Marie Addis, Anne Evans, Anne Gray, Kelly Moffett, Denise Parsley Leigh, Devon Leigh, Megen Leigh, P. Andrew Miller, Bruce Schneier, Justin Scott, Don Wenzel, Kathleen Wilson, and Hania Wojtowicz (and special thanks to Hania for the French lesson, and from France, no less!)

And most especially, I want to express my gratitude to my editorial muse, Sheila Gilbert, for her continued faith in my writing, and for making sure that each book has been the absolute best I could write at the time.

1:
CALLIOPE

Camille Kenny

Today

THE *BENT CALLIOPE* REEKED of spilled beer and desperate egos. The aromatic combination spilled out of the open door, past the bouncer, and onto Rivington Street, wrapping insistent arms around Camille and shepherding her toward the tavern.

"Hey, Ink!" she called to the bouncer, sitting with one ample ass cheek on a rickety barstool to the side of the entrance as he texted on his phone. "Warm enough for you?"

Ink's pear-shaped body leaned back against pallid bricks. The yellow tubes of the *Bent Calliope*'s neon sign glowed above him, lending the man the sickly pallor of the living dead. The hue didn't manage to make his thinning hair, too-wide features, or the poorly-drawn tattoos crawling his arms and emerging from the frayed collar of his plain white tee appear any more attractive. "Too warm," he answered, glancing up from the phone. "Better out here than in there, though." There was no ambition burning inside Ink at all; he had been sitting on the same stool the first night Camille wandered into the *Bent Calliope* a year ago; she suspected he would *still* be there, growing steadily older, heavier, and more sedentary, long after she left.

"I hope the beer's cold, at least."

"When you find out, let me know." He nodded his head toward the door. The white noise of a dozen simultaneous conversations drifted through the rumble of two-decade-old, stale music. "Half your crowd's in there already." There was a subtle, possessive emphasis on the "your."

"Thanks, Ink."

Camille entered the *Bent Calliope* largely unnoticed as she passed through the crowd, one of the advantages of being significantly shorter than most people. Her group *was* there, as Ink had said: in the rear corner farthest from the jukebox speakers, where one could nearly carry on a conversation without shouting. Through the shifting forest of bodies, Camille glimpsed Morris' shaved head gleaming in the fluorescent lights, his dark skin beaded with sweat. Despite an early May heat wave, the *Bent Calliope*'s proprietors had yet to turn on the air-conditioning. Morris seemed to be gesturing to someone to his left—probably Mercedes, who was also one of the regulars.

Camille could feel their pull, an almost physical tug in her head as if emerald ropes were snaking out from them to her, lashing around her and pulling her toward them, and yet . . .

There was someone else here. Someone whose pull was noticeably stronger.

Close to the polished, glass-ringed bar, Camille stopped. A man sat on one of the stools, his left hand cradling a pint glass. He was the source. He stared at her; when she glanced at him, the sense of instant connection made her inhale. A green aura hung around him, so bright that she wondered that none of the customers could see it. As their gazes met, he looked away quickly, guiltily. Camille continued to study him as he pretended to be looking at his foam-smeared glass. She could see the glimmer of a gold ring on his left hand, and her mouth tightened. *Well, there's a problem . . .* Camille sidled up to the bar near him, taking a stool that had just been vacated. "Hey, Tom," she called out to one of the bartenders. "A pint, please." She set a five down on the bar top.

As Tom placed the glass under the Guinness tap, Camille noticed that the man was watching her again, this time via the mirror behind the bar. She could see her reflection also: a woman most people would guess to be in her early-to-mid-twenties; wavy, auburn hair settling just below her shoulders; large green eyes; petite enough that she sometimes still found herself being carded. Again, when he realized she had noticed his attention, he turned back to his glass once more. The feeling of connection remained, the sense of needing to know who he was, what he was. Inviting tendrils the color of spring grass slid from him toward her and she wanted to touch them and taste them, but she did not. She watched and she wondered: he was a painter, she had almost decided when Tom set the Guinness in front of her, curtains of light-brown foam still falling from the head into the darkness of the stout. She let the drink settle. She felt the stranger's intention in the moment before he moved, frowning a bit as he slid from his barstool, circling behind the two other patrons between them. She could feel him at her back, a pressure all along her spine. He enveloped her in his unseen radiance, and it was nearly too much to bear.

She waited, taking a slow sip of the Guinness and licking the foam from her lips. When he still didn't say anything, she turned slowly on the stool. His hair was a sandy brown and longish, scraggly enough that it looked like it had been months since it had last been cut. Strands frothed around the collar of a blue sweater over an oxford shirt; the sweater was rumpled, as if he just pulled it out of an overstuffed drawer and put it on. He had the build of a runner. His height was perhaps six feet or an inch or so taller. She held his gaze for a moment: his eyes were that shade that might be a light blue, a pale green, or even a dappled gray depending on the light, and she liked the faint crinkles at their corners, which told her that he smiled a lot.

She glanced significantly at his left hand. "You're supposed to take that off first," she told him. "Though the white line would still be a dead giveaway. Women know to look for it."

She was pleased to see him flush, and more pleased to see that he made no attempt to cover the ring with his other hand or put it behind his back—though he did glance at her own unadorned left hand. Instead, he held up his hand as if seeing the ring for the first time himself. *No, not a painter, or there'd be pigment under those fingernails . . . Maybe a writer?* "That's not why—" he began, then shook his head. She found she liked his voice, too: a warm, easy baritone.

Why are they always already married? It just makes things complicated. There was no answer to that. There never was.

He gave a long exhalation that sounded more like a sigh. "Look, umm, jeez . . . I don't really know how to say this. It's just . . ."

Camille found that she was smiling in spite of her reservations; his smile in return deepened the lines around his eyes: a genuine smile, an inviting one. "It's just . . . ?" she prompted.

Another exhalation. "I'm a photographer—a professional. That's how I make my living. I was wondering . . . Have you ever modeled before?"

"If that's a pickup line, Mr. Married Photographer, I have to tell you that it's really beyond lame."

He was shaking his head before she finished. "No, no," he said hurriedly. "It's . . . well, you have an interesting face—and an interesting accent, too, I have to say. What is that? French?"

"French by way of Italy and other places a long time ago—though I'll give you credit; most people don't notice it anymore. And, yes, I've sat as an artist's model if that's your question," she answered flatly. "And I don't do porn," she added. "Hard or soft core."

Another headshake. His eyes widened. "Umm . . . Good. I don't either."

"So there are no nudes in your portfolio?"

The color was still in his cheeks. "Well, yes. A few. The human body's beautiful—which is, I know," he said hurriedly, "what every erotic photographer says. But I don't do anything prurient. At least, not to my mind."

"And I'll bet all those nudes are female?" He didn't need to answer; she saw the answer in his face. "Uh-huh." Camille took another sip of the Guinness. *You should get up and walk away. Go back to the ones you've already chosen. You don't need this one, even if his green heart is so interesting. Are you truly ready for what that would mean? Are you willing to take the chance of fouling up what you're here to do?* The tendrils of his soul-heart slid around her, enticing. She felt, also, the dangerous blue strands within it. But knowing what she *should* do didn't seem to matter.

She didn't move to leave, stroking the rim of her glass. "So you do *art*, not wedding shots and not porn." She already knew the answer; she would never have stayed otherwise, would never have talked to him. She would never have noticed him if it were any other way. The connection would not have been there.

"Pretty much. Along with some commercial stuff now and then to pay the bills."

"New York's full of people who call themselves photographers," she said. "The city's positively *stuffed* with them."

"I'm different."

"Of course you are."

He reached into the pocket of his jeans, pulling out a small flash drive, handing it to her. A name—David Treadway—was screened onto the black plastic in bright yellow letters, along with an address, e-mail, and cell phone number. "My business card and portfolio," he told her. "Why don't you take a look at the sample shots on the drive? If you like them, and if you're interested, give me a call."

She held up the drive. "I know your name now, David. Aren't you supposed to ask for mine?"

"Give it to me when you call."

"When? Not if?"

"I'm figuring you'll like the shots," he said. His smile appeared again, a flash of teeth and a crinkling of his eyes. The color of his aura deepened, and with it the feeling of connection, of needing to know this person, became more urgent inside her. Strange colors rode in the emerald, colors she'd seen only a few times before, and that scared her more than the fullness of the energy. "Look, I have to be going," David said. "I really hope you like what you see." He nodded toward the flash drive. "Give me a call. Or e-mail me. I'm serious; I'd be interested in working with you. I can't pay you much, but there'd be something in it for you."

He hesitated, shifting his weight from one leg to the other. She put the flash drive in the pocket of her jeans. "I'll look at it," she told him. "From there, we'll see. Is that good enough?"

"Sure. I'm fine with that." He was staring at her, as if he were trying to memorize the lines of her face.

"You have to go," she reminded him.

"Yeah, right." He favored her with another smile. Yes, the lines at the corners of his eyes folded nicely. "Talk to you soon, I hope."

This time he did turn, sliding between the people behind him and heading toward the door. She watched David as he opened the door of the *Bent Calliope* and nodded to Ink; she *felt* him leaving as well—the creative energy, the potential bottled inside him, the connection, his soul-heart—until the door closed again. She touched the pocket of her jeans, feeling the lump of the thumb drive under the cloth, touching it the way she often touched the pendant around her neck, stroking it as if for reassurance. "Damn it," she whispered aloud. "I don't need this. Not again. Not now."

Now that he'd left, she could again sense the others in the back of the room; they'd been lost in his larger wave. She took her glass from the bar, leaving the change Tom had put on the bar top, and threaded her way through the crowd. She slowed as she approached the group, though. Their energy illuminated the air, like a sun shining through forest leaves, light just beyond the range of the visible, and she could bathe in it and take it in. It would nourish her. Yet . . .

Morris would be talking about his latest project—something properly avant-garde and inaccessible, like the video of his ice sculpture melting in real time that had garnered him some interest in *The Times* last year. Rashawn's forearms would be spattered with paint from her current work. Kevin's hands would be restlessly drumming on his thighs as he sat, as if part of his mind were still attached to the drum kit back in his apartment. Mercedes would be sitting silent and listening, watching, and imagining each of them as a character in her novel. And Joe . . . And James . . .

Artists all. Creators all. And when Camille arrived, they would all turn to her—smiling or dour or somber—and they would all want to talk to her, to pull at her mind, to ask her opinion, to tell her what they were doing . . .

To take what she had to give them.

"Her crowd," as Ink called them. Her entourage. Her lovers, many of them. The ones who fed on her, and she on them in return.

Camille's forefinger traced the outline of the thumb drive through her jeans. "Fuck," she said.

She turned, set her half-full pint on the nearest table, and left the bar.

She took the thumb drive out of her pocket and inserted it into the side of her laptop. A few seconds later, the icon showed on her desktop: "David Treadway—portfolio" underneath it. She double-clicked on the icon, then on the first file in the window that opened.

An urban landscape wrapped in snow filled her screen: the side of a tumbledown tenement building dark against a pristine white blanket. She found herself nodding immediately at the composition, the way that a shadow led the eye toward the lee of the building where a figure huddled, hands shoved into the pockets of a ragged overcoat, the blue trim the only bright color in an otherwise monochrome painting. The man's face was grizzled and his eyes were slitted, as if the light reflecting up from the sunlit snow pained him. The figure was sized perfectly in the landscape: large enough that the canyoned face could tug at the viewer's emotions, yet not so large that he dominated the photograph. She thought perhaps the photo had been taken somewhere in the Bronx.

A moment of poetry seized and frozen by the lens: Camille pressed her lips together and opened the next file.

Black and white, this one: two wild mushrooms caught in strong chiaroscuro, the light molding their forms beautifully, with another gorgeous composition that held the eye. But what stopped the photo from being just a nearly abstract composition was the shadow of a hand, as if some unseen observer was about to snatch away one of the mushrooms. It gave the photograph a tension it wouldn't have otherwise had. The composition reminded Camille of the sterile arrangements by Edward Weston of seashells and landscapes: beautiful composed and technically spectacular. Weston's work had always struck her as aesthetically accomplished but somehow passionless and empty, lacking the "some-thing" that had made his friend and contemporary Ansel Adams a ge-nius behind the viewfinder and in the darkroom. Still, Camille had to admit that even Weston had discovered emotion when he found Charis and started photographing her. . . .

Camille shook her head to rid it of the memories and looked again at David's photograph.

This . . . This had a humanity and emotion that Weston's still lifes often missed, and again Camille felt the pull she'd noticed in the *Bent Calliope*. She stared at the photo for a few moments more before click-ing on the next file.

Black and white again, but a portrait this time: a woman sitting on a chair and staring directly into the camera. The background was in deep shadow, with light coming from the left, enough to the side that her light brown hair cast fine shadows over the hollow of her cheeks. It was the expression in her eyes and the pressure around her lips that caught Camille: a defiance, almost, as if she were daring the photographer to take the picture, or if she were defying the viewer to judge her. The way her hands grasped the arms of the wooden chair increased the tension in the portrait: she looked as if she were about to rise from the seat, per-haps in irritation, perhaps in actual anger. The woman wasn't classically beautiful, but there was a delicate attractiveness to her features, even with the severity with which she stared back at the viewer.

Camille wondered if this were just a model he'd happened upon, or if perhaps this was the wife.

She glanced at the rest of the pictures, which confirmed her initial impression: David Treadway had the nascent talent. He had a vision for someone to mold and bring forth. That *she* could bring forth.

The question was: did she want to do it, yet again? Did she *need* to do it? Did she dare? *That's not why you came here. You're here to find Nicolas and take care of that problem. Once that's accomplished, you can think about someone like David.*

She dragged the folder from the thumb drive onto her desktop and watched the progress bar as it copied the files onto her hard drive. She ejected the thumb drive and pulled it from the USB port. She turned it over in her fingers, looking at the name and the phone number, while her left hand stroked the pendant under her blouse.

She fished her cell phone from her purse. *This is a mistake. If you do this, then you risk having Nicolas find you before you're prepared. You know he's here in the city; you can't let him slip away and you can't let him turn on you. He'll know. He'll feel your presence here and you'll turn from hunter into hunted.*

It's a mistake I've made a dozen times now, and maybe I'll make it a dozen more times, she told the scolding interior voice. *Maybe I have no choice. Besides, if this causes Nicolas to show himself, then I can take care of him, once and for all.* Taking a long breath, she dialed the number printed on the thumb drive. She heard a ring, and another, and another. *A mistake . . .* She started to press the "End Call" button when she heard someone pick up. If it had been a female voice, she would have ended the call immediately.

"Hello?" she heard David say quizzically. There was noise in the background, muffled music and loud voices. She wondered if he was at a party—was that why he'd left in such a rush?

"You really have a wonderful eye for composition," she said. "I just have one question: do you still want to know my name?"

There was silence for a few breaths, then: "Oh! The *Bent Calliope*, right? The ginger with the interesting face and the attitude." He was pleased; she could hear it in his voice. She still liked the sound of him, though. She could feel the baritone tugging at her through the tinny speaker of the phone. "You've already looked at my portfolio?" The artist: always looking for reassurance that they actually possessed some talent.

"Yes. As I said, you have an eye for composition, though I suspect you also know your way around Photoshop."

"C'mon, Photoshop's just a tool," he answered. "No worse than using any of the old darkroom tricks of dodging and burning. It's no substitute for . . ." He stopped.

". . . for artistic vision?" she supplied.

She could almost hear his shrug. "Yeah. I guess. If you want to call it that."

She laughed at his effort at modesty. "My name's Camille. Camille Kenny. And now you have my number, too. It sounds like you're busy right now, so let's talk tomorrow."

"So I can photograph you?"

"I don't know yet. But we can talk about it, at least."

"I'd like that." In the background, Camille heard a woman ask him distantly: "Who are you talking to?" She heard the sound of his thumb muffling his response. *A mistake . . .*

"Look," he said finally, "yes, I'd like to meet with you . . ."

"Tomorrow," she said quickly, before she could change her mind, before the doubting voice could convince her that this was wrong. "You know *Annie's*, half a block east of the *Bent Calliope?* I'll buy your lunch. 1:00."

A pause. She imagined him surreptitiously glancing at his wife. "Sounds good. I'll be there."

That morning, before she met David, Camille was doing what she'd done every morning, in different locations, for a year.

Her butt cheeks were sore from sitting on the concrete planter, and she was worried because the security guard kept glancing at her from behind his desk at the hospital's employee entrance. She touched the pendant she wore under her blouse, as she often did when she was nervous, then burrowed for the remnants of her bagel in the paper bag she was carrying, pretending to watch the pigeons in the little plaza rather than the stream of nurses and doctors entering Beth Israel Hospital.

So far she hadn't seen Nicolas, though that meant little. The Finding spell she'd placed within her pendant that morning echoed faintly around the building, so she was confident he'd been here, and not that long ago. Maybe he wasn't a doctor or nurse; maybe this wasn't his duty time; maybe he was working at some other hospital and had just stopped by here; maybe he wasn't in any of the hospitals at all and had taken on some other identity and profession.

Maybe her guesses and her research and her spells were simply wrong.

But he *was* here in the city. She was certain of that. The spate of recent mysterious deaths—the so-called "Black Fire murders," both female and male bodies that had been found charred beyond recognition by some unknown heat that had consumed them without touching anything around them—all said so, the Tarot cards said so, her intuition said so. She could *feel* his involvement.

Nicolas was here; once she found him, she would kill him.

The security guard pushed his chair away from the desk. He was staring at her, and she saw him speak briefly into the microphone attached to his uniform, his gaze still on her. Camille gathered up her paper bag and slid down from the planter. She started walking slowly away before the guard could leave the building, pretending that she'd never noticed his attention. She didn't want to be stopped, not with the Smith & Wesson Ladysmith .38 revolver that was snuggled in her purse. She had a carry permit, but questions could be embarrassing.

Another wasted morning.

She hoped her lunch with David wouldn't be similarly wasted.

As she walked, she slid her cell phone from its pocket in her purse and hit speed dial 8. The phone rang four times and she was about to give up when she heard the clatter of the receiver and a gruff voice on the other end: "Bob Walters."

She'd hired Walters a week ago in semi-frustration at her inability to track down Nicolas. New York City was simply too big, too vast for her.

She gave Walters copies of the few photographs she had of Nicolas. He looked at them with a raised eyebrow. "These look old," he said. "Like this one . . ." A thick forefinger pinned one of the prints to his cluttered desk. A wastebasket seemed to have been upturned over the desk: papers were scattered everywhere, there were at least three Styrofoam coffee cups, each with black sludge at the bottom, and scribbled Post-It notes were stuck on every available inch of his grimy computer monitor's sides. The investigator himself appeared to have neither slept nor shaved in the last week, and to be running entirely on caffeine. The overstuffed file cabinet behind him looked ready to explode at any moment. "This photo is WWII vintage—the clothing and everything," Walters told her. "In fact, that uniform collar looks Nazi. How old is this guy?"

"He's in his mid-to-late twenties," Camille told him. "But he'll look exactly like that man—at least in the face."

"So he'll look exactly like this guy from over seven decades ago." He made the statement slowly, with a droll lift of his eyebrows. Walters was a retired police detective who had gone into the PI business, and hard luck and decades on the force had carved deep lines in his stubbled face, made his brown eyes weary with sagging, dark bags underneath, and scrubbed away most of his gray, coarse hair, though it hadn't managed to touch the sympathy she saw in his eyes. He looked to be somewhere in his late fifties and was nearly a cliché; all he needed was a dangling cigarette and a half-filled tumbler of cheap scotch, and he could have walked out of a Raymond Chandler story. There was a green soul-heart in him, also, deeply buried and small, but pulsing: it was the reason that Camille had felt comfortable with him. Camille wondered what creativity drove it, what aspirations or avocations the man might have that he kept so well masked. "You give me his grandfather's photo, and you don't have a name for me, either?"

She laughed at that. "He changes names like you change your underwear," Camille said. Walters displayed his false teeth in what looked more like a smirk than a smile.

"No need to get personal, young lady," he answered. "Look, I'll be honest. I'm not exactly cheap, and I think you're wasting your money with this. You give me a bunch of old photographs and say your guy looks like this, and he might be a doc or might not be, but wherever he is, people are likely to have died." Walters sighed. "This is New York," he said. "People die here all the time. And there are more than eight million people in the city. That's a lot of haystack for your little needle who doesn't have a name or a location, or even a decent photo."

"I know," she told him. "But he's here. I'm certain of that, and I need to find him." Walters didn't ask why she was so certain, for which she was grateful. She doubted that hearing that the Tarot array she'd laid out every night for the last two months and the spells she'd cast had told her that, or that she was certain that the current serial killings around the city were Nicolas' doing. "He likes to hurt people, and I'm the only one who can stop him," she told him instead.

And I need to find him before he finds me. That's the race we always have, she thought.

"And you're the only one who can stop him." He sighed. "All right, Ms. Kenny. It's your dime. I'll make copies of these and put it out to people I know. They'll flash it around the hospitals, and I'll check with my old contacts on the force for any new murders that look strange. And what are you going to do if I find him? How are you planning to stop him?"

To that question, she wasn't willing to give Walters an answer. She only smiled. "Find him first," she said. "Then we'll see . . ."

That conversation had taken place weeks ago. She could imagine Walters now on the other end of her cell phone connection, scowling at the cheap prints on his wall. "Hey, Mr. Walters. This is Camille Kenny. I was just wondering . . ."

"Got nothin' yet," Walters said, interrupting her. "My people are checking things out, like I said, but . . ." She could hear his shrug. "It's not like you gave me a hell of a lot to work with. Let me have another week; I got my folks checking all the hospitals and clinics, as you suggested, and I'm running my contacts with NYPD myself. If this guy's as dangerous as you seem to think he is, maybe they have something on him. If I still got nothin' by Monday, then we should talk about whether you still want to throw money at this."

"All right," she told him. "Just let me know right away if you get anything."

"Yeah, sure." His voice told her that he didn't expect to be calling her any time soon.

She hit the "End Call" button on her phone; she glanced at the time on the screen before she put it back in her purse alongside the Ladysmith—she had just about enough time to get to *Annie's* before David got there. She glanced back; the guard was sitting at his desk behind the windows again, no longer looking at her. She kept going out to the street, and hailed a cab.

*   *   *

At 12:50, she was worried he wouldn't show. At 12:55, she was certain of it, and was surprised at the relief she felt. At 1:00, she was certain Fate had intervened and she'd just dodged a huge mistake.

At 1:02, as she was starting to slide out of the booth, David walked in. He saw her, waved, and she was trapped. He slid into the other side of the booth, placing a camera bag on the scarred, glossy tabletop next to Camille's laptop and the condiment tray. "Sorry I'm a little late," he said. "I didn't get out of the apartment when I thought I would."

The wife . . .

In the afternoon light shining through *Annie*'s front window, the lines around his eyes were deepened—Camille decided he must be in his mid 30s, still young enough to have his artistic dreams of fame and glory, old enough to have started thinking that maybe they weren't going to be realized. But the eyes the wrinkles surrounded were clear and kindly, and his smile came easily when the waitress appeared at their table. She handed David a menu, and glanced at Camille. "The usual?" she asked, and Camille nodded. David closed the menu and slid it over to the waitress.

"I'll have the same," he said. The waitress arched an eyebrow and took the menu. David grinned at Camille. "What am I having?" he asked.

"You'll just have to wait to find out, won't you?" she told him.

"How are we going to work together if you're so uncooperative and secretive?"

"We don't know that we *are* going to work together yet, do we?" she answered.

He spread his hands in mock defeat. She could feel the intensity of his creative energy: the emerald aura of his "soul-heart," as she'd come to call them. His soul-heart surrounded and filled him, but only the surface was visible. There was far more of that energy still below, untouched.

She could touch it, if she dared. She could bring it fully into him, so he could tap it. And so she could tap it as well. "You have me there," David said. "But you liked the photos?"

Camille nodded. She slid her laptop to the center of the table and opened it. The picture of the homeless man in snow appeared. "Tell me about this one," Camille said. "Is this a staged shot?"

David shook his head. "No. It's from, oh, six or seven years ago. I'd just bought a new digital back for my Hasselblad, giving up my last vestige of using film, and I was out in the new snowfall checking out how well it worked—I thought that the heavy contrast between the snow and the dark buildings would be a good test to see what kind of dynamic range I could get. I saw that guy watching me, and took a couple shots with him in the frame. Turned out to be the best of the bunch, I thought."

Camille nodded, pressed a key. The portrait of the woman replaced the snow scene. "I like this one, too," she said, watching his face carefully. "The expression she has is exquisite."

There was melancholy in the flicker of a gaze he gave the photograph. He looked more at the table than the screen. "Yeah," he said. "Helen." He looked over at Camille; she noticed him unconsciously twist the ring on his finger. "My wife. I took that last year; it was one of the few times she agreed to sit for me."

"Helen doesn't like being photographed?"

"Among other things."

Camille could feel the undertone in the comment. *So there are problems. . . .* She struggled not to let anything show on her face. "Maybe she thinks the camera steals her soul."

He gave a chuckle that was wrung dry of amusement. "Maybe. She didn't seem to mind so much early on, though." Again, Camille had the sense that there was much being left unsaid, that all it would take was the right word and he'd let the remainder of the bile spill out. She remained silent, waiting. He glanced again at the photograph, pressing his lips tightly together. "What about you?" he asked. "Are you afraid of a camera stealing your soul?"

"Not a camera, no."

His eyes held hers for a long breath, unblinking, and she felt again that inner, insistent pull toward him, the connection waiting to be made. She let her gaze drop, deliberately. "Then you're willing to let me photograph you?" he asked.

"Not yet."

"Why not?"

"I still don't know you well enough."

He spread his hands wide. "What do you need to know? I can give you references if you'd like. You can check 'em out. I promise I'm legit."

She closed the laptop's cover on Helen's face. She could feel the hunger already, even though she tried to deny it. The gnawing was not in her stomach, but in her chest and in her head. *The green soul-heart . . .* "Why were you in the *Bent Calliope* last night, David? I've never seen you there before." *And I'd have known if you'd been there.* The thought made her smile to herself.

He lifted a shoulder. "I don't honestly know. I was supposed to meet Helen at a party one of her coworkers was giving, and I was a little early and—frankly—I wasn't much looking forward to the evening. I saw the bar, and I've heard a bit about the Calliope Group of artists in the last year and thought I might drop in to see what's going on; thought it might be a good place to have a beer before I went to Helen's party. Maybe two. Or maybe I just wouldn't go at all . . ." He stopped. "Sorry," he said. "You didn't need to know all of that."

"Strange how whenever a woman gets hit on by a married guy, their marriage is always in trouble, or it's a sham, or they're separating, or they have an 'understanding.' Which one is it for you, David? No, let me guess. I'm going to say it's the 'trouble' gambit."

He didn't get angry, only shook his head and reached for his camera bag. "You really have the wrong idea about me," he said. "Y'know what, I guess this was a mistake. I'm sorry."

A mistake . . . The hunger and the need for caution warred within her as he started to slide out of the booth. She felt the tendrils of green heart recede from her. As he started to rise, she reached out, putting her hand on his bare arm. The warmth and softness of his skin reminded her of other days, other times. "Stay," she said. "I'm sorry. The problem's not you. It's me. Every time . . ." *When I let myself get close,*

I put the other person in danger. Every time, Nicolas feels it, too, and until I deal with him, finally . . . But David wouldn't understand any of that. For that matter, Camille wasn't certain she did herself. She stopped the words, giving him a smile. "I'm sorry," she repeated. He was staring at her hand on his arm. She felt muscles slide under her fingers. "Besides, you don't know what you ordered yet."

He smiled then, and she felt him relax. He pushed the bag back toward the condiments and settled himself again. "Let's start over," he told her. He held out his hand toward her. "Hi. My name's David."

She took his hand. "Camille," she told him. "It's good to meet you, David. I take it you're a photographer?"

After lunch, she walked with him down Rivington and onto Pitt, moving leisurely toward the Williamsburg Bridge. David had plucked his camera from the bag—not a Hasselblad, but a Canon SLR—and occasionally snapped a picture as they walked, though she noticed that he was careful not to place her in any of the shots. She watched him as he crouched down and focused in on a battered wooden sign on the door of one of the storefronts, so close that the grain and the flaking, painted curves of the letters made an abstract canvas.

" 'Anything that excites me for any reason, I will photograph; not searching for unusual subject matter, but making the commonplace unusual,' " Camille said, and David straightened.

" 'Making the commonplace unusual,' " David quoted back to her. "I've heard that before. Is it Ansel Adams?"

Camille shook her head. "Edward Weston. In some ways, a better creator of aphorisms than a photographer."

"Ouch!" David said. "So have I made the mistake of asking a photographer to sit on the wrong side of the lens?"

"No. Mostly I . . ." She shrugged. "I paint a little, do a little singing, and dabble in chemistry." She leaned across his arm, looking at the picture on the screen of the camera. "If you crop in along the right and bottom to get rid of that blue edge that's sneaking in, then I think the composition will really pop."

He stared at the image on his camera screen, tilting his head. "Huh. I think you're right. Should I have heard of you?"

"Not me. Some of the people I've known, maybe."

"The *Bent Calliope* Group?" he asked.

She let that go; if she told him the truth, he wouldn't understand it. "Yeah," she said. "Them. I'm . . . I'm part of the group."

"Then I'd like to see your work."

"Maybe one day you will," she said automatically.

"That's a gorgeous cameo, by the way. Is it an antique, or something new?"

Her hand went to her breast; she realized that when she'd leaned over, the pendant had swung out on its chain from under her blouse. The oval of carved sardonyx, wrapped in a band of gold petals, glinted brick-red and ivory-white in the sunlight: a woman's profile carved into the white layer, her hair—in the upper layer of red—coiled on top of her head and bound in a swirl of ribbons. "It's an antique, yes," she told him. "It's very old. Been in my family for generations." The lie came easily; she'd practiced it often enough.

"May I?" He held out his hand, then pulled it back. "But if it's something private, then . . ."

His politeness and concern fed her nascent hunger even more. *He could be so much more for you than mere sustenance.* Wordlessly, she slid the chain over her head and took his hand, placing the cameo in his palm. She watched him as he turned it in his fingers, knowing he didn't understand how much her gesture had meant. He nodded, finally, and gave the piece back to her. She quickly slipped the chain back on, tucking the pendant under her blouse again. "It's exquisite work," he said. "I think I can see a resemblance to you: in her nose and the shape of her chin. The color of the hair's about right, too—too red to be brown, too dark to really be just red."

"Other people have suggested that," she told him. "Look, David, I . . . I have to think about all this a little more. I'm sorry."

"Don't be," he told her. "We don't have to push anything or rush.

Take your time. If you want, I could send you my standard model release, so you could look it over . . ."

She was already shaking her head. "I don't need the release."

"Then you've already decided?" The disappointment in his voice was palpable.

"No. If I trust you enough to model for you, then I'll trust you enough that I won't need a sheet of paper to protect me. Would you . . ." She looked away for a moment. *If you do this, then you're taking the first step toward more. You know it. You won't be able to stop, not if he's anything like you suspect him to be.* "Would you like to swing by the *Bent Calliope* again on Friday, maybe around 9:00 or so? You wanted to meet the Calliope Group, right? Well, I can introduce you; you might like them, and we can talk some more."

He was already nodding before she'd finished. "Sure. On Friday. I'll call you if anything changes."

They'd reached the corner of Delancey Street, loud with the hush of taxi and car tires on asphalt, the air scented with exhaust. New York was like all large cities she'd been in recently: full of movement and sound, and fragrant with the aromas of people and ambition. "Okay, then. I'm going this way." She pointed westward. "It was good talking to you. I'll think about this, and maybe I'll have an answer next Friday."

She was already feeling awkward. Had he been anyone else, any other of her friends, she would have hugged him and maybe kissed him; but he wasn't, and to do anything else seemed wrong. She smiled at him instead. "Next Friday," she said before he could say anything else. Then she turned and began to walk away from him, glancing back once to see him still standing at the corner watching her. The yearning hunger surged inside her, and she forced it back down.

Not yet. Maybe never. It's too dangerous right now.

But she already knew.

INTERLUDE ONE

Perenelle & Nicolas Flamel

1352 – 1370

Perenelle Flamel

1352

PERENELLE HAD EXPECTED to be happy with her second marriage. She'd hoped for a wonderful new start to her life.

Life, it seemed, intended to disappoint her.

Rue des Saints Innocents was a noisy chaos as Perenelle approached the market square. The shop ledges were down in all the windows along the avenue as curious passers-by examined the proffered wares; the banners above the market stalls fluttered in the desultory (and sadly fragrant) breeze off the Seine. Ahead of Perenelle, a crowd gathered around a young man with a dancing bear. The man looked handsome enough in his scarlet tights and broadcloth tunic, a battered viol propped up in a case at his feet. The bear appeared to be ancient and arthritic, its muzzle silvered with gray. The creature snarled as its owner struck it on the snout with the viol's bow, and Perenelle saw that the beast was missing most of its teeth. The poor creature's coat was scabrous; islands of scaly patches created a painful map on its flanks and the creature's fur was gone entirely under the spiked and thick leather collar. Flies seethed around the open sores. The bear's claws were brown and cracked, dulled from scrabbling on the cobbled streets. Still, children screamed and ran when the man struck the animal with the bow again—across the front paws this time. The bear roared in irritation but reared up. On two unsteady legs, the beast took several mincing steps as the owner scratched out a poor tune on the viol and sang in a warbling baritone:

"Je puis trop bien, Madame

Comparer a l'image que fait Pygmalion"

Perenelle shook her head at the poor bear and the poorer performance, but tossed a denier into the viol case—maybe the coin would mean the bear would be fed that night. She walked on, listening to the calls of the merchants. It had rained the night before, and she skirted the pools of water and the piles of offal in the street's central gutter, lifting up the hem of her dress. The two maidservants with her followed, chattering to each other and giggling as they cast their gazes back to the dancing bear—or more precisely, to the young man. "He has a lovely bum, don't you think?" she heard the older of them, Marianne, say to the other; Marianne was fourteen, and (Perenelle suspected) rather too interested in what men and women did in their beds. Perenelle *tsked* and frowned at the girls; they ducked their heads with a last glance, hiding their faces under the brim of their wimples, and hurried after her.

The market was crowded with throngs of Parisians, which was a delightful change from three years before, when the terrible pestilence afflicted the city. That appalling spring and summer, it was whispered, over 700 people within the city walls had died each and every day. In those horrible times, the stench of death stretched black tentacles through the streets of the city and those who could fled from the terror.

Perenelle remembered those days too well; they still haunted her dreams. She had been married to Marlon then, but her husband had been taken by the pestilence like so many others, his body racked with fever while horrid, dark mushrooms of stinking pustules sprouted from his armpits, neck, and groin. Perenelle's father, Cosme Poisson, had been an apothecary and alchemist; she'd learned some of the craft from him in her childhood—her mother had died birthing her; her father had never remarried, and Perenelle had taken on the role of helpmate for Cosme until he'd died, five years before. By the time Marlon became sick, most of the physicians had either died or fled the city with the others, and there'd been no one to help. She'd mixed potions to take the fever from Marlon's body, to ease his breathing, to reduce the swellings.

She might ease his symptoms, but she could not cure him.

Marlon's eventual death had been a blessing given his suffering, but she hadn't witnessed his passing. The fever had taken her, too, though her symptoms had been less severe and she'd eventually recovered, but long after Marlon's body had been taken from the house. She didn't even know in which of the several mass graves outside the city walls he'd been buried.

For months afterward, she'd lived with the guilt that she'd survived while he'd died. It wasn't that Perenelle grieved horribly for Marlon; she'd married him, a mere musician, in the heat of a youthful infatuation and against her father's wishes. After the initial fire had faded, she found that while she liked Marlon, she also didn't truly love him, but there was no good escape from the iron bonds of marriage. Still, she'd been with him for eight years before he was snatched away by the plague, and she liked to believe that it was her presence and her support that had helped Marlon rise within the court before his untimely death, an entertainer whose ballads were often requested, even by the king.

But in a Paris seemingly half-emptied by the horrors of the pestilence, she found herself lonely and lost. She'd thought that she was essentially already dead: twenty-eight, widowed and childless, her parents gone, her red hair already beginning to turn brittle—though her body stubbornly insisted on breathing.

Then she'd met Nicolas Flamel. He'd courted her hard, used every advantage he had with her. He'd gained first her trust, then given her what she'd thought—again—was love.

And maybe it was love. Maybe that's all love ever was and ever could be, despite the grand tales and stories. Maybe love was something that bloomed like a bright flower in spring, only to inevitably wither away and eventually pale into a withered, brown husk: a mocking reminder of what it had once been.

But now, with love a barely-remembered and colorless stem, she carried another gift for Nicolas . . .

"Madame, here, you must smell these!" A peppercorn seller thrust his wares under her nose, bringing Perenelle back to the present. The astringent smell wrinkled her nose and nearly brought back the nausea that struck her every morning recently. "Fresh, and ready to spice your supper. Only six deniers for the lot, just half a sol. You won't find a better bargain anywhere in the city."

Perenelle hefted the bunch. "Two deniers," she said. "They're small and so old that they barely have any smell at all, but I might be able to make some use of them."

The man's eyebrows sought to reach the eroding shore of his greasy black hair. "Two deniers!" he nearly shouted. One of the dogs wandering around the stalls glanced up at them, then continued sniffing the ground as it searched for dropped food. "Why, Madame must wish my children to starve and be cast out in the streets. The very least I could accept is five deniers, and even then I'm barely paying for my own costs."

They eventually settled on four deniers, and Perenelle tossed the peppercorns to Marianne, who placed them in her basket. They continued walking the stalls, buying fish, vegetables, and wine, and stopping in the nearby boulangerie for bread. With the servants sufficiently burdened, they walked back down the street toward home.

The houses of the rue des Saints Innocents leaned against each other like gossiping washerwomen or old men crowded around an ale-spattered tavern table. Nicolas' house—Perenelle no longer really had any belief that it was at all *her* house—nestled among the others, three stories high, with Nicolas' store taking up most of the ground floor. The sign, *Nicolas Flamel: Scrivener & Manuscripts,* was nailed above an open stall window stuffed with scrolls and flyspecked parchments bound in frayed leather. Rust stains from the nail heads flowed in static red rivulets over the gilded scrollwork. Perenelle saw Telo, Nicolas' apprentice, a thin boy of eleven, sitting on a stool in the open doorway.

"Where's your master?" she asked him as the maidservants slid past him, taking their baskets into the kitchen at the rear of the house's ground floor.

He lifted his chin. "In his laboratory, Madame," he said. His voice was high, still that of a child. "I'm to call him if we have any serious customers. Otherwise, he said not to disturb him until dinner, as he's working." He ran a finger under his nose, smearing snot across his upper lip and cheek. "There's been naught but idlers, though even that's terribly hot work today." He sighed dramatically.

"Go on to the kitchen," she told the boy. "Tell Marianne to give you some wine, cheese, and bread, and you may bring it back here. I'll watch the store while you're gone. Hurry back!"

Telo jumped down from the stool, bowing his head. "*Merci beaucoup, Madame,*" he said, and ran off. Perenelle watched him go and leaned against the doorway of the house, her hands rubbing her stomach. She imagined she could feel a swelling there, though it was far too early for that. Still, it was enough to cause her to smile; maybe this news would help with Nicolas. Maybe the flower of love could bloom again.

Nicolas . . . She'd met him in the winter of 1349 after the death-scythe of the pestilence had passed, at this very shop. Without any source of income except for the rent that came to her from her father's house, Perenelle had come here looking to sell her father's old alchemical manuscripts. She was surprised to see how young the owner of the shop was—younger than she was by several years, yet he had the sophistication and the knowledge of a much older man; in that, he reminded her of her father. His fingers were stained with ink, he smelled of old paper, and there was a severity in his thin face. Yet his dark eyes were alight, and the way he swept his hand through the unruly mass of his hair as he leaned over the parchments she'd brought was disarming. It was apparent that he also knew alchemy, claiming to be a student of the art, and that also softened her toward him.

"This is a copy of the papyrus *Graecus Holmiensis*," she told him. He only nodded, his lips pressed together. "And this is one of Jābir ibn Hayyān's manuscripts—an original."

"You're familiar with these?" She could sense doubt in his voice, but he tempered it with a faint smile.

"A little," she told him. "Like you, I'm a student of the art, though a poor one. I helped my father with his work. I made a copy of his experimental notes also, if you'd be interested in that. He was working on chrysopoeia."

"Weren't they all? *You* are the copyist?" The smile broadened. She liked the way his eyes crinkled as he grinned; that, too, was like her father. The somber air about him vanished with the expression. "So you can write, as well."

"*Oui, Monsieur*; my father schooled me. I'm keeping the original for myself."

"To conduct your own experiments?"

"Perhaps." She shrugged. "I haven't yet decided."

That was how it began. Nicolas asked for time to look over the manuscripts, and that evening he escorted Perenelle to a tavern, where they ate and talked. She found it wonderful to converse with him: he was full of energy and ambition, doing well enough with his business, and had aspirations of doing more. He was fascinated with alchemy, yes, but he claimed to be even more interested in spells and incantations held within the ancient manuscripts. That first evening, he showed her how he could, with a single word, cause a small flame to appear on a wick. But he didn't, as so many other men did, try to dominate the conversation. She noticed even then how Nicolas listened intently as she talked about her father and his work, coaxing her with gentle questions to say more. She thought it flattering then.

This attraction was so very different than what she'd felt with Marlon, whose face and easy manner had managed to capture her, but who didn't have a serious or ambitious bone in his body. She thought this was the way it was *supposed* to be between man and woman. She was quickly infatuated with Nicolas for his mind and for his passion.

Six months later, he asked Perenelle for her hand in marriage. He gave her a golden ring as a token. "One day," he told her, turning the ring in his fingers and placing it in her palm, "you and I will make these by the hundreds from nothing but base metal . . ."

That was Nicolas' alchemical quest—the search for transmutation of elements; beyond that, he had little interest in what chemicals and potions could do.

"*You helped me become what I am,*" her father had told her, not long before he had died. Cosme touched her hair as he had when she'd been a child, lifting the red-orange tresses that seemed to flame in the sun. He'd always told her that the brilliant color of her hair showed up in their family for one person a generation, to mark someone who would have a special life. "*And after you helped me, you took that handsome but mediocre musician as a husband—against my wishes, as you know—and I must grudgingly admit that you have made him a passable example of his craft, if still nothing exceptional. Maybe that's your gift, daughter. Maybe you are a muse, a new Calliope or Clio. My very own daemon.*"

She could do the same with Nicolas, she thought. He was already talented and successful; perhaps with her at his side he could become famous. She thought she'd discovered a kindred spirit in Nicolas, and so she took his ring and his name.

Now, she was no longer quite so certain.

She was somehow held in a gilded prison with open doors, and now a new shackle had been added . . .

When Telo returned, Perenelle left him to his task. She first went to the kitchen to make certain that the trout she'd purchased at the market was being properly cleaned, and that Marianne wasn't stinting on the salt while curing the portions that were not for the night's supper. After seeing that the kitchen work was satisfactorily underway, she walked up the stairs to the third floor, which was Nicolas' laboratory. The smells became stronger as she climbed the final flight: bitter, metallic scents tickled her nose and coated the back of her throat; sulfur lent its distinctive stench to the mix. She could hear the clinking of a glass vial and the faint, almost cheerful bubbling of retorts over their fires. Nicolas had his back to the door as she entered, bent over a manuscript with his forefinger tracing the line of words.

He didn't seem to notice her arrival. She watched him without saying anything for a few minutes, her hands unconsciously cradling her stomach. She had agonized over when to tell him that she was pregnant—certainly not before she was absolutely sure herself. But she had missed her second monthly bleeding now, and her stomach was unsettled every morning. Two days ago, she'd gone to the *sage-femme* three streets over; the woman had nodded and congratulated Perenelle after her examination. Already, she could imagine that she felt a faint stirring in her womb, the quickening of the child.

With Marlon, even after eight years, there had been no children. She'd prayed for a child, often, to both God and the Blessed Virgin, but neither deity had ever answered. She'd thought that she would never hold her own baby in her arms or suckle her at her breast. Now, after less than a year with Nicolas, the miracle had happened, but she wondered whether he'd share her joy.

The somberness that she had sensed in Nicolas from the beginning enveloped him now. During their courtship, he had talked about them working together, but he rarely let her do so. He'd ignored her pleas for a workshop of her own, a place to do her own experiments, seeming to find that concept amusing. When he came to her bed of late, there was little affection in him; he topped her as if he were performing a duty: his face serious, his release quick. Now that he had the entire library of her father's old manuscripts to work with, all his attention was either on his efforts in the laboratory, or on his attempts to make the magical spells he'd found in the ancient manuscripts actually work—even his scrivening and manuscript-selling was ignored unless a customer insisted on attention.

Perenelle wouldn't have minded any of it had she felt that Nicolas wished her to be his partner in this enterprise. Her father Cosme had been single-minded in the same way, but Cosme had shared his passion with her. Nicolas did not; over these several months, he had made it increasingly clear that he found any suggestion she might make to be both intrusive and irritating. There had been arguments, each angrier than the last, and a few times, she'd been afraid that he might strike her, though he never had. During their disagreements, he had become increasingly vulgar and abusive toward her, and while he hadn't touched her, he had destroyed nearby objects in his fits, or thrown things about.

But she was married, and that left her with little choice. Some of the neighboring wives gossiped about far worse abuse that they or others they knew endured each day. They told her that it was the way things were between men and women, and that she should pray to God and thank Him that Nicolas provided for her well enough. She talked to the parish priest, who told her that marriage was a bond that could not be broken, and only fervent prayer would help her. Her situation could be far worse, he said.

Despite what the society and the priest said, she could have left him—she *should* have left him. Her father would have told her to do that, she knew, though a woman on her own had few resources. She had nearly made up her mind to leave Nicolas and accept whatever consequences followed when she missed her first bleeding. She stayed, thinking that perhaps the cold she'd had the week before had caused it, but then the morning illness had come and the second bleeding had been missed, and she knew.

That changed things, especially if a child could repair the rift between them. Perenelle hoped that the announcement would ease the increasing tension.

Her cordwain slippers hushed across the wooden floor. Nicolas glanced at her as she approached him and grunted. He turned back to the manuscript, which she saw was one of her father's. In her worst thoughts, she wondered whether those manuscripts were the only reason he'd married her: so that the property she'd inherited from her father would become legally his without his needing to buy them; so that her work in translating them would also be his. In front of him, the retorts chortled over the blue flames from small charcoal braziers. She glanced at the jars in front on the table and suddenly frowned. "Nicolas," she said, "you're not doing this correctly. The powdered iron shouldn't be in this mix at all, and sulfur is a component of vitreous earth, not the fluid, and so you shouldn't be using it in the retorts."

Nicolas craned his head back to glare at her. "You should be silent, wife, rather than demonstrate how little you understand."

Perenelle shook her head. "I'm sorry, but I happen to know this experiment very well. I helped Father with it several—"

She stopped. Nicolas slapped the table so hard that the retorts chimed in their iron holders. "Be *silent*, wife," he roared. "I don't need to have your nonsense filling up my ears while I'm working."

"It's not nonsense—" she began, but even as she started to speak, Nicolas' hand drew back and slapped her hard across the cheek. Perenelle gasped and staggered back, her hand to the burning redness on her face.

Now she took a step away from him as he scowled and lifted his hand again. "Nicolas, please! I only wanted to tell you—" she began but he slapped her again, harder this time, and she stumbled, nearly falling. She sobbed. "Have you gone mad?"

"Be *quiet*, woman!" Nicolas roared. "I want no more nattering about that idiot Cosme Poisson. Your father was a dabbler and a fool, and you've inherited his stupid, *stupid* foolishness." Spittle flew from his mouth as he raged. He advanced on her, pushing her, and she fell to the floor. Trying to break her fall, she felt her left wrist collapse under her and she cried out in pain, sobbing. "Stop that wailing!" Nicolas shouted at her, and he kicked her. She tried to shield her stomach; his boot struck her in the side just at the ribs. She doubled over, and his next kick caught her in the face. White fire exploded in her vision as she heard her nose crack. Blood was dribbling down her face and smeared her hand when she put it to her face. He drew his foot back again as she stared at red-stained hands.

"Nicolas! Stop! I carry . . ." She tried to draw a breath, but that sent fire stabbing through her side and nose. She shrieked, forcing out the words. "I carry our child."

His foot stopped in mid-strike. He looked down at her through slitted eyes. "Liar!" he hissed, but his eyes held sudden doubt.

She shook her head desperately. Droplets of blood spattered the floor in front of her. She cradled her left wrist to herself; it was already

His chanting stopped, and she heard a tap on her door. "Perenelle," she heard Nicolas call from behind the wood. "I would speak with you, wife."

She didn't answer, didn't know how to answer, confusion running through her head. She was shaking her head silently when he opened the door. She looked down to her knitting again as he came toward her, the clack of the needles loud in the stillness. His clothing reeked of the lab: chemicals and potions and fire. She felt more than saw him kneel at the side of the chair. His hand touched her arm, and she dropped the needles into her lap. She closed her eyes.

"I'm so sorry, Perenelle," he whispered to her, his voice rasping and penitential. "I don't know what deviltry possessed me, but it was wrong. I've shrived myself to the priest and begged for God's forgiveness, and now I've come to you, to ask the same. My wife, I should never have raised my hand against you, and I promise you that it won't happen again. You . . ." She heard him swallow; she still couldn't look at him. "You are my inspiration, my helpmate. Since you've entered my life, I've come so much farther than I could have believed . . ." He stopped, his fingers tightening on her sleeve. "I really wish you'd speak to me, Perenelle."

She did look at him then, if only to force him to see her battered face. His gaze moved away guiltily. "I'm with child," Perenelle told him; she wasn't certain why—she'd intended to give him only silence. But the words came, tumbling out from her mouth as if she were afraid that if she didn't say them now, she might never have another chance. "That's what I'd come to tell you, but you were working and I saw it was one of my father's experiments and you'd made a mistake, and so I spoke and you became so angry when I'd only wanted you to be happy that our child was growing in my womb. Our child . . ." As quickly as they'd come, the words turned to dust in her throat. She swallowed.

Nicolas was staring at her. "I know," he husked. "I heard you when you said that to me, after I struck . . ." He stopped, taking a long breath. "You're certain of this?"

She managed a nod.

"Perenelle, I'm so ashamed." He sounded sincere, as sincere as when he'd told her that he respected and loved her, that he wanted her to marry him. "Look," he said. "I had this made for you." He placed a small paper packet on the knitting. "Open it."

The packet was heavier than she expected for its size, and when she folded back the paper, a piece of jewelry slid out from the envelope into her hand, a golden chain pooling around it: an oval pendant of sard-onyx, a woman's face carved into the multicolored layers of glistening and polished red-brown and white. Tiny leaves of gold held the stone. The face was carved in profile, her hair bound up in the Roman fashion. The carving was incredibly detailed and realistic, and even in profile she knew the face; she had often glimpsed it in the small mirror in the hall. Despite herself, she gasped at the beauty of the piece, and at what it must have cost.

"I gave the artisan the sketch of you I had the street artist make last year at the Hot Fair—you remember; the one we put in the front hall—and told him how to best shape your features. I had him depict you as a Muse, and I think he's caught you perfectly. Don't you? This is my pledge that I won't abuse you again that way. Please, tell me that you forgive me."

She thought of the bag in the chest, of her plans to leave. "I can't, Nicolas," she told him. She looked at the pendant gleaming in her palm. "This is beautiful," she said, "but it doesn't change what happened." She held out her hand to him, giving him back the pendant.

He let it dangle from its chain for a moment, then draped it over her head before she could move. "This is yours, no matter what," he said. "It holds my promise to you. I want you to wear it forever."

With the words, with the placing of the pendant around her neck, she felt her old feelings for Nicolas rise up as in response. Her fear of him was still there, but it felt blanketed and dim. The resolution to leave him felt foolish against that old pull, that old attraction. She wanted to stay with him, wanted to make this work. A part of her inside rebelled against this new compulsion but the rebellion was faint. She fondled the pendant in her hand, rubbed her fingers over its smooth surface. *Nicolas* . . .

He rose to his feet again. Reaching down, he stroked her bruised face and she found that she didn't flinch away from his touch. She was frowning, but she allowed him to caress her cheek. She closed her hand around the pendant but didn't look up at him. "Wear the pendant always," he said.

And with that, he left her. She nearly called out for him to stay, but the words fought against the disbelief inside her, and he was gone before she could speak.

She stared at her carved image on the pendant until she heard the great bourdon bell, Emmanuel of Notre Dame on the Île de la Cité, toll the Angelus.

Then, wondering at herself and her change of heart, she pulled the bag from the chest and took out her clothes, placing them back where they belonged.

That night, she kept the pendant on under her nightclothes. She would do that every night thereafter.

~

Perenelle Flamel: 1358

THEY WERE TALKING POLITICS AGAIN. Politics was a dangerous subject: that was a topic that nearly always sent Nicolas into a towering rage.

That was a topic that, in many places in France at the moment, could cause someone, saying the wrong thing at the wrong moment to the wrong person, to be killed. And had.

Perenelle passed the door to the study where the men had gathered on the way to her tiny laboratory—the best aspect of their new, larger

house on the rue Saint-Denis. Perenelle had sent in Marianne with refreshments an hour ago; the maidservant had left the door slightly ajar.
Perenelle paused at the jamb, listening to the voices inside.

". . . Provost Marcel will bring us down with him." That was Benoît
Picot, a minor *bourgeoisie* official, and also a banker in the *cité*. "He
might claim to have the Third Estate in mind, but I tell you that he's
become mad with his power and he *will* overreach. I have it on good
authority that he's in discussion with the king of Navarre, and that he's
also spoken to the English about opening the city gates to them. He'd
give us over to the filthy Black Prince himself."

"I agree," she heard Nicolas interject as other voices grumbled their
agreement. "The Provost urged the mob to murder Marshals de Con-
flans and de Clermont, and that has turned Dauphin Charles and the
nobles against him. The court is now set against the Provost, and so he
turns to Navarre and supports the Jacquerie in their rebellion. Neither
of them will save the Provost, but I worry that he'll get *us* killed in the
process."

"What do you propose we do about it?" Picot asked.

There was a long pause, and Perenelle started to pass on when she
heard Nicolas clear his throat. He spoke in not much more than a whisper, and she had to lean toward the crack of the door to hear him.

"I propose that we do to Étienne Marcel what he did to the Marshals," Nicolas said.

Perenelle nearly gasped aloud at that. Afraid that Nicolas might
have heard her, she hurried on down the narrow, dark-paneled hallway to her laboratory. She started to shut the door behind herself, but
stopped, seeing two other people in the small room.

"What's wrong, *Maman?*" Verdette looked up; she was seated on
the floor just inside the door, her dress pooled around her on the oaken
planks with her dolls set between herself and her nursemaid Élise, a
young woman of fifteen whom Nicolas had hired a year ago. Élise was
blonde, comely, and large-busted, with wide, flaring hips and a plump,
sensual mouth. Perenelle knew what the entire household knew: Nicolas had hired the girl for more that her skill with children. Nicolas and

Perenelle had slept in separate beds since Verdette's birth, and he only rarely came to her bedchamber at night, though as if in penance, he'd given her the laboratory she'd wanted all along now that they had moved into a larger house.

Perenelle vastly preferred her laboratory to Nicolas' presence in her bed. Élise could take Perenelle's place under his un-tender ministrations; in any case, he'd tire of her soon enough, as he had the others who'd preceded her in her position. The passion of affairs was a flower that withered even faster than that of love.

She hated that Nicolas had his mistresses, but she found herself unable to speak out to him about them. Whenever she tried, she could hear Nicolas' voice in her head, and her doubts and fear vanished like snow on a warm spring morning.

Perenelle touched the pendant around her neck. She did that often; as it always calmed her.

"Nothing's wrong, my *petite alouette*," Perenelle told her daughter, crouching down to stroke the girl's curls. At five, Verdette still had a bit of her baby pudginess, but that was rapidly fading, and Perenelle could see Nicolas in her dark, sharp gaze and in the set of her mouth. Perenelle glanced more harshly at Élise while still talking to Verdette. "I thought I'd told you not to play in here," she said. "The chemicals here are dangerous."

"I'm sorry, Madame," Élise answered. "The door was unlocked, and she ran in here with the dolls. I wouldn't let her near the chemicals or your experiments. We've been very careful."

"That's not the *point*, you silly goose," Perenelle said, exasperated. "She's not to come in here at—" She stopped, seeing a scrap of parchment peeking out from under Verdette's frock. "What is that?"

"I found it in Papa's library," Verdette said, pulling out the scroll. She unrolled it; Perenelle recognized it, one of the papers that interested Nicolas far more than her: spell incantations in Greek, illustrated with drawings of fantastic, grotesque monsters with clawed hands, cloven hoofs, and barbed tails. Perenelle and Nicolas had engaged in long discussions about this, even before their marriage. Nicolas believed the

way to the greatest power lay through incantations and spells; Perenelle
believed that it was via the alchemical formulae and recipes.

On the scroll, the monsters writhed in terror and agony while lightning snarled around them; a wizard stood to one side, hands extended
while the lightning flared from his fingers. Letters were written in Greek
underneath the illustration, but the manuscript itself was brittle and
riddled with brown-edged lacunae; the text was incomplete. "It was out
on his reading desk. See how pretty it is, Maman?"

"I don't care, Verdette. You can't touch these—they're very precious and rare. Élise, if you can't control her, I'll have to—"

"You'll have to what?" The voice came from the doorway: Nicolas'
voice. "What's going on here?"

Verdette's face blanched. She grabbed for the scroll and started to
clumsily roll it, tearing the ancient parchment further. Nicolas saw it
and bellowed furiously, starting to push past Perenelle toward the girl.
"No!" Perenelle roared back at him. As he glared at her, as Verdette
started to cry and Élise cowered against Perenelle's workbench, rattling
the retorts and jars there, Perenelle ducked her head. "Let me take it
from her, my husband," she said, more calmly. She stroked the sardonyx
cameo pendant around her neck, deliberately, knowing it would remind
him of the promise that he'd made to her five years ago, when she'd
been pregnant with Verdette. Sometimes that worked when Nicolas
was in a rage. Sometimes.

Nicolas was still scowling, his hands clenched at his sides as Perenelle backed away from him, crouching down beside the wailing
Verdette but never turning her back on Nicolas. "Give me the scroll,
Verdette. Let it go. Gently, gently, and stop crying. There's no need for
that." She took the scroll from the girl. Verdette clung to Perenelle's
skirt, hiding behind it. The child was no longer crying, but Perenelle
could hear her voice catching with silent sobs. "Now, apologize to your
Papa, and tell him you'll never, ever touch anything in his library again.
Go on, tell him."

Perenelle was watching Nicolas carefully, ready to stay between him
and Verdette if he threatened her. Verdette had been just beginning to

walk when Nicolas had first beaten her: the infant had stumbled into a table and knocked over a vial of ink on papers on which Nicolas had been working. Before Perenelle could reach her, Nicolas had plucked up the crying girl by one tiny arm, wrenching it so that Verdette screamed, and began swatting her with an open hand. Perenelle hated the look on his face, an expression almost of pleasure, the expression she'd sometimes glimpsed on his face when he'd tupped her angrily. She'd caught his arm as he brought it back to hit Verdette again, and the fury in his face then had frightened Perenelle more than ever. But, slowly, he'd released Verdette, then yanked his arm out of Perenelle's grasp. He'd stalked from the room without another word.

That was the first time. There'd been others: rarely, thankfully, but always brutal.

At such times, she thought of taking Verdette and fleeing, as she had before, but the resolution never stayed with her. She would hear the Nicolas of her early love in her head and the anger would leach away so much that the decision seemed unimportant. And Nicolas, as if to buttress her cooling temper, always reminded her of the law. *"The girl is my property,"* he told her more than once. *"If you leave, I can take her back and let the courts deal with you for taking her from me. She's mine."* *Then he would look at her and smile. He would reach out and lift the pendant.* *"You don't want to leave me, Perenelle. You know how much you mean to me."*

She would believe him, despite herself. It was as if her mind could hold no other truth.

She hugged Verdette, still hiding in her skirts with her arm while staring at Nicolas. "Go on," she said softly. "Apologize to Papa, then Élise will take you back to your own room."

"I'm sorry, Papa," Verdette said in a tiny, barely-audible voice muffled by cloth.

Nicolas said nothing. He still glared, his fists tight to his sides. "Go on, then," Perenelle said. "Élise, take her out . . ." Élise took Verdette's hand; together, they sidled out of the workshop past Nicolas, who stood aside to let them go. Perenelle felt relief surge through her, though she resolved to speak sternly to Élise later. She held out the scroll to Nicolas. "She tore the edges a little, that's all," she said. "Nothing critical was lost. If you wish, I'll make another translation and copy tomorrow for you . . ."

"I've already taken from it what I need," he grumbled, but his hands relaxed and he took the scroll without looking at it.

"You're upset by your meeting with the merchants?"

"Why do you say that?" Nicolas snapped. His eyes narrowed. "What did you hear of our talk?"

"Nothing," Perenelle told him. "I only heard raised voices as I passed by, and I know how the Provost aggravates you."

"The man's an idiot and should have stayed with his drapes," Nicolas spat. His hand tightened again around the scroll. "Marcel would hand us over to Charles of Navarre and the English, but King Jean will be ransomed from the blasted English soon enough and set back on the throne, and then where will we be?"

"You know this to be true?" Perenelle asked the question, but she knew the answer herself. She had seen the portents in the Tarot, and the cards had left little question in her mind when she had read them lately. She assumed that Nicolas, who also read the Tarot, if not as well or deeply as Perenelle, had seen the same in his arrays.

"I know it," he answered.

"Provost Marcel is a powerful force in the city. He's still not a man to offend, husband."

"He's not as powerful as he was, and he threatens all the *bourgeoisie* with his ambitions."

"Then we should pray to God that He brings down Marcel."

Nicolas laughed at that. "You may pray if you wish, wife," he told her, "but it is men who will need to act to answer those prayers."

The city broiled, the populace seared by a relentless July heat.

There was a dinner that night. Clouds had begun massing on the horizon during the late afternoon, and a strong breeze had begun to blow. Perenelle hoped it would rain, despite the muddy mess that it would make of the streets; she might at least not be sweltering in her surcoat and underdress—they were heavy linen, dyed with the expensive red dye Nicolas had procured from the clothier two streets over, and brocaded with stiff golden thread. The underdress was a pale blue, adorned with small jewels where the sides of the surcoat opened to reveal it. Her head was already beginning to sweat under the netted bowl of the newly-fashionable wig, though the style of her surcoat covered her shoulders, rather than leaving her neck and shoulders bare, as some in the court did now. Perenelle thought the new style fine for young women, but not for matrons like herself. The only jewelry she wore was the sardonyx pendant Nicolas had given her so long ago; she wore it because it was beautiful, but she also wore it because she couldn't bear to be parted from it, and so that Nicolas would see it.

The dinner was Provost Marcel's affair. That by itself was troubling. The rumors were that Charles of Navarre and his men were close to the city, that they would enter Paris at the Provost's invitation. From the Left Bank to the Right, and all over the Île de la Cité, the factions were stirring.

No one was in much of a mood for a gathering, but the Provost's invitation was not to be turned down. Nicolas, for his part, appeared almost jolly at the thought. "You are all to remain inside," Nicolas told the staff as they were preparing to leave. "Marianne, you and Telo are to bar the doors and don't let anyone in you don't know. We should return by midnight." He called to Telo, now a strapping lad of seventeen, and pointed to the door that Marianne was holding open. "You're to be the door guard tonight," he said. "You're to stay right here until we return. Do you understand?"

Telo nodded. "Nicolas," Perenelle asked, concerned, "are you expecting trouble tonight? Why these precautions?"

Beneath his best cloak, Nicolas shrugged. His face was impassive behind the hedge of his beard. "I expect nothing," he answered, "but it's good to be prepared for anything in these days."

Perenelle frowned. She crouched down to hug Verdette good-bye, and looked at Élise over the girl's head. "Make sure that Verdette stays out of trouble, and otherwise, do as Master Flamel has said. Let no one in that we don't know. We'll be back soon. Verdette, you'll behave, won't you? I want you to say your prayers especially well tonight, and go to bed early. I think it's going to storm. You'll do that, won't you?"

"Yes, Maman," Verdette said, her face so solemn as she nodded that Perenelle had to laugh.

Nicolas had already left the house. Perenelle stood, patted Verdette on the head. "Say a special prayer for me," she told the girl. She nodded to the servants, then followed Nicolas outside.

The July heat had also gifted the entire city with the overripe smell of a midden. Her surcoat was long, and Perenelle gathered up the train over one elbow so that it didn't become soiled during their walk. The central gutter of the rue Saint-Denis was clogged with offal and there had been no rain in over a week to wash away the effluvium—that would be another blessing if a storm came tonight. Overhead, the sky was already dark, the clouds masking the moon and stars. Perenelle found herself wishing that she'd read the cards earlier; there was a sense that something was to happen tonight. The street was strangely empty, only a few people venturing out. The closest shops were shuttered, their window ledges pulled in.

Nicolas waited for her at the gate of their house; he crooked his arm to her as she approached—in public, he was always careful that their marriage appear entirely proper and happy. He even managed a smile as she took his arm, and he noticed that she glanced at the sky. "If the storm breaks while we're at dinner," he said, "we'll borrow an oilcloth from the Provost. After all, he's a draper." His smile widened, as if he'd made a joke.

Nicolas set off down the rue. He carried a staff in his free hand, though it wasn't his formal cane, but an oak limb that she'd noticed in his laboratory a few days ago, the whorled knob of the top strangely dark, as if it had been in a fire.

The uncapped end of the staff *clunked* dully on the cobbles of the rue. "So, Madame," he asked, as if he were making conversation at the dinner, "how goes your work lately?"

She hesitated. Since Nicolas had given Perenelle her own laboratory, he'd rarely asked about her progress. Despite his gift of the space,
he seemed to believe that she could accomplish nothing and that her
puttering about was nothing more than a silly female dalliance, whereas
his own work was vital and all-important. He'd laughed when she'd declared, in the first days of her work, that she would seek to unlock the
Great Work: the Philosopher's Stone.

Nicolas had respect for Perenelle only for her ability to decipher and
translate the old texts, a task at which she was far better than he. That
was the payment she made for her laboratory—she had to translate and
copy all the many manuscripts he purchased. She had to give him the
knowledge they contained, even if she wasn't permitted to make copies
for her own research, nor did he ever acknowledge her help.

Sometimes she resented the labor, but she stroked the pendant and
those feelings would eventually recede. Nicolas loved her, despite his
gruffness, his temper, and his neglect. She could hear his voice as it had
been, kind and gentle, and her irritation would recede. He needed her;
that was enough.

She knew that what Nicolas sought in the old manuscripts was more
visceral and immediate than her quest for the Philosopher's Stone: the
spells and incantations of power. The only part of alchemy that interested him was the "Solve et Coagula" portion of the Great Work: dis-
solving the *prima materia* so it could be reconstituted in the coagula part
of the formula—mercury turned to solid silver, lead to gold; the white
and red stones. That way led to riches, after all.

For her part, Perenelle had no interest in that aspect. She had
turned her attention to the property of the Stone that was said to heal
and to give immortality: the liquid part of the stone, the elixir of life.

"It goes slow," she answered. "I fear that the answers I'm seeking
aren't in the manuscripts we've yet found, and I feel as if I'm groping
in a dark room while my hands are covered in thick mittens. I can
reproduce all the experiments my father started—as you know—but
what eluded him still eludes me. The mice to which I've fed my poor
attempts have all died a normal death, or they die early."

Nicolas laughed. The sound of his amusement bounced from the shop signs and buildings around them as they approached the bridge to the Île de la Cité, where the Provost's apartments were located. "And your work, husband?" she asked him.

"It goes better than yours," he answered. "I have begun to unlock the mystery. The manuscripts begin to talk to me." His lips tightened grimly. "And at an auspicious time."

"What's happening, Nicolas?" she asked him. "What are you expecting?"

He didn't answer at first. They stepped on the Ponte au Change, the Seine rolling underneath on its slow, wandering way to the sea. "The Provost oversteps himself," he said finally. "And it will cost him dearly."

"Something will happen *tonight?*"

"Perhaps," he answered. "But you will act as if you expect nothing. You will smile and be the perfect wife and companion, or you will regret your foolishness and Verdette will as well. You will show nothing. Do you understand me?" His arm tightened against her hand with the words. "Say it," he hissed.

Her eyes had widened, and she wanted to touch the pendant, though she couldn't with him restraining her. "I'll show nothing," she said.

"Good." The staff tapped on the cobbles again as they passed over the Seine. He released her hand. "That is all I require of you. Have the wits to follow that direction."

She nodded. She found the pendant with her now-free hand and she stroked it, letting the touch of it soothe her.

The dinner took place in the great hall of the Royal Palace, the very location an indication of how Provost Marcel now regarded his status within the city. The hall was lit with great sconces with the Valois sigils significantly missing below, and all the chandeliers were ablaze with candles. Liveried servants were on hand to usher them in, and Provost Marcel and his wife, Marguerite des Essars, greeted them at the hall's entrance. "Ah, Madame Flamel," the Provost said as he took her hand. "You look wonderful as always, and that necklace is gorgeous. You and Monsieur Flamel are a shining example of marriage for all of us. How is Verdette?"

"She's very well, Provost. Thank you for asking."

"She's a beautiful child. Beautiful," he said, still holding her hand and smiling, though his gaze slid across her face to Nicolas, speaking with Madame Marcel. "I smile every time I have the opportunity to see her. And she deserves to live in a world that values what you and your husband best represent. Let us look forward to that day, Madame Flamel."

"That is my one great wish, Provost," she answered. He inclined his head and she curtsied to him, passing into the hall as Nicolas made his own greetings to the man. Most of the diners were already there and seated: the bourgeoisie mostly—the wealthy merchants of the city. There was a heavy buzz of conversation in the hall, but few of the faces seemed to be smiling, and those few smiles were fleeting. She noticed that the minor nobles among the bourgeoisie were conspicuously absent, and none of those loyal to the Dauphin were in attendance at all. The air held a decided tension despite the brilliance of the hall and the festive draperies around the room—no doubt furnished by the Provost's own workshops. The hall might glitter and gleam, but those within were inhabited by a darker mood.

She felt Nicolas alongside her; she took his arm and they descended the few steps into the hall as servants pulled out the assigned chairs.

They were seated next to Benoît Picot and his wife Yvette, well down the table from the head where the Provost would be seated. Yvette was dressed in the latest fashion, her surcoat fully open at the sides to expose the lavishly embroidered underdress. She wore a pearl-laden choker and her shoulders were nearly bare, the low décolletage of the underdress and surcoat both frothing with lace.

It seemed to Perenelle that the others at the table kept glancing toward them—toward Nicolas. For his part, Nicolas seemed at ease, sitting back in his chair with the knob of his oak staff under his hand.

The long table was laden with fine china and silver; Perenelle wondered where the Provost had come by such rich settings. Yvette noticed her looking at the silver, and she leaned over to Perenelle, her sweeping headdress touching Perenelle's own. "Navarre silver," she whispered. "Or worse, English."

Perenelle nodded. She stroked the silver handle of the knife; it was cold under her fingertip.

The Provost had finished greeting the guests, and now he and his wife moved to their seats at the head of the table, two of the wait staff pulling back their chairs. One of the deacons from Notre Dame stood and intoned the blessing. As the diners crossed themselves and the priest sat again, there was a flurry of activity around the hall as the food was brought in. The fare was as lavish as the setting, which given the uncertain state of the city, was in itself another display of the Provost Marcel's influence. Steaming plates of grilled vegetables came out first, arranged so that the vegetables formed images of well-known Parisian buildings. Roasted swans and peacocks were set on the table, reconstructed with their feathers and beaks, and stuffed with an assortment of meats, which the wait staff proceeded to serve. Platters of breads and pastries were set close to hand. Wine was poured into crystalline goblets. For a time, the diners concerned themselves only with eating.

Some time later, a bell was rung, and Provost Marcel stood as a silence moved slowly down the table. "My friends, my compatriots, my allies," the Provost began, "the last few years have seen a great diminishment of our country and our city. The shameful performance of our army at Poitiers and the capture of King Jean were only the first signs. Since then, the dauphin has ignored the initiatives given him by the Estates General; he has tried to force upon us his Edict of Reform; he has devalued the very coins with which we buy bread and supplies. We here tonight—those whose sweat and energy are our city's greatest wealth, and who know best how to govern ourselves—are paying the price for the dauphin's incompetence."

With that, a murmur arose, with several of the men rising to their feet in protest. "Treason!" Perenelle heard one of them shout. "The dauphin—" but the Provost raised his hands and shouted louder.

"Hear me out!" he called. "It is time for us to choose a better ruler while we can." He clapped his hands, and four servants came in carefully handling a massive gingerbread-and-marzipan replica of the gates and towers of the Porte St. Michel. They set it down before the Provost. "King Charles of Navarre will be outside these gates tomorrow," he said. "I propose that we, the true leaders of the city, unlock the porte and welcome him in. I say, give me the keys and I will be the first to greet them."

The murmuring became an uproar, the uproar chaos. Everyone was shouting at once, gesticulating with fists and waving arms. A fight broke out mid-table, with a portly merchant pushed into the remains of a swan. Women shouted in alarm and moved back from the table. Perenelle rose with them, wondering which way she could flee. She looked at Nicolas.

And stopped. He was still seated, his head bowed over the oak staff, which he now clutched in both hands. His graying beard was moving, as if he was speaking, but she couldn't hear his words against the noise of the room. As she watched, curiously, she saw the knob of the staff seem to writhe under his hand, and a dark glow emerged from it, as if night oozed from the grain of the oak. No one else seemed to have noticed, but she heard a cry from the head of the table where Marcel had been standing, trying to shout down the crowd. The wail, high and shrill, turned everyone's head to the Provost. He was still standing, but now he clutched at his throat, his mouth working but no words emerging from his throat, only that unearthly, horrible keening. A terrible agony was written on the Provost's face: in the corded muscles of his neck; in the bulging, wide eyes; in the tongue that lolled from that open mouth, black as a lump of coal, black as the head of Nicolas' staff; in the heaving, desperate breaths he was trying to take; in the bloodless color of his face. Marguerite was shrieking alongside him, calling for someone, *anyone* to help as she grasped his arm.

The Provost's wail stopped suddenly, as if severed with a knife, and the silence was more horrifying than the sound. He seemed unable to take in a breath. He swayed in his wife's embrace. Perenelle glanced from the Provost to Nicolas; he was staring at the Provost's agony, no longer muttering, and there was an eager intensity to his gaze and a curve to his lips under the rampart of his beard. He was evidently taking great pleasure in the Provost's suffering, and that frightened Perenelle—she'd seen the ghost of this same expression in his face when he punished Verdette or one of the house staff.

In his hands, the knob of the oaken staff swelled and burst, a split running suddenly down the length of the wood, the staff shattering to splinters above his hand. At the same moment, the Provost collapsed, falling onto the marzipan replica of the gates and crushing it underneath him.

Nicolas' face had split into a grin. He released the broken staff, letting the pieces of it clatter to the floor. Perenelle saw Picot nod to Nicolas and clap him on the back. At the head of the table, Marguerite broke into sobs. ". . . Dead," someone proclaimed loudly. "The Provost is dead."

There were scattered cheers around the table at the news, mingled with shouts of alarm and anger.

Perenelle, frozen in shock, started when she felt Nicolas take her arm. "Come, Perenelle," he said. "We should leave."

She stared at him, at the placid satisfaction in his face. "You did this."

"I did," he answered calmly. "And so did you. After all, it's you who translated the scrolls from which I took the spell. I'm sure that in the eyes of the law, you'd be as guilty of this murder as I." His finger reached out toward her; it stroked the face on the cameo at her breast. "So you'll be silent about this, won't you, my dear wife? Be silent," he repeated, and his finger came up to lift her chin. His dark eyes held hers, unblinking, and his smile was chilling. "Or you'll pay far worse than the Provost. I promise you that."

Perenelle took in a shuddering breath. The pounding of her heart was louder in her ears than the shouting in the hall. The servants had fled the hall; the Provost's men had fled with them, leaving the bourgeoisie who had opposed the Provost triumphant. Only Marguerite was left, clutching at her husband's body.

"Come!" Nicolas commanded, and he pulled at her arm. Numb, she followed him from the hall.

~

Perenelle Flamel: 1370

"May your daughter's marriage be as perfect as your own."
"You're such a blessed couple; you must be so proud of all you've done."

"The Lord has rewarded you for all that you've done with this wonderful day. You and Nicolas are indeed high in His favor."

Perenelle smiled and nodded to all the remarks as she moved through the crowd at the chapel of the Saint-Germain-des-Auxerrois church. Nicolas, his beard now completely gray, his body beginning to stoop, was shaking hands with the invited guests on the other side of the central aisle, along with the Dubois family. Alaine Dubois, Verdette's soon-to-be-husband, was there with Nicolas, looking handsome and far too young to Perenelle's eyes. The Dubois family were bankers, with holdings in Auvergne and purse strings that led directly to the court of Charles V. It was Nicolas' rising influence in Parisian circles, and the amounts of money that he had donated to charitable works around the city, that had brought the Flamels and thus Verdette to the attention of the Dubois family. Alaine was the youngest of the four male children Madame Dubois had produced. The oldest son was married to the daughter of a courtier within the king's inner circle; the other two had been married into wealthy guild families. The Dubois were willing to gamble the least of their male offspring on the hope that a relationship with the Flamels might be a profitable match.

"He's a handsome one; Verdette must be pleased."

"You must be praying that Alaine is as good and gentle and kind a man as your Nicolas."

Verdette and her attendants were in a small room off the chapel; Perenelle, still nodding and smiling like a marionette responding to the strings of its handler, knocked on the door. "Verdette," she said softly. "It's your Maman."

The door opened to a cascade of giggles and whispers, and Perenelle was ushered inside. Verdette was standing in the center of the room as her attendants made last-minute adjustments to her dress. Perenelle smiled at the scene, her eyes filling unbidden with tears. "You look beautiful," she told Verdette, sniffing and wiping at her eyes. "A perfect angel."

"Maman . . ." Verdette opened her arms, and Perenelle went to her, hugging her hard, as if to keep the memory of her forever. Verdette's arms wrapped her, and she felt Verdette waving at the attendants.

"Would you leave us for a bit?" Verdette asked, and the attendants, chattering and laughing, left the room, closing the door behind them. Verdette held Perenelle at arm's length. "Maman, I can still smell that laboratory about you even when you scrub and wear perfume. You stay too much in there—who's going to stop you from working yourself to death once I'm gone?"

That brought the tears to Perenelle's eyes again, and she saw moisture gathering in Verdette's eyes as well. "You're happy, Verdette? I know how frightening it is, to marry a man you don't really know well . . ."

"It's what Father wants," Verdette answered. "I couldn't do better with anyone else here in Paris. He's told me that many times."

"Yes. He's said that to me, as well." *And he'd made it clear that Verdette would marry the Dubois boy, whether Perenelle or Verdette objected or not.* "But it should be what you want as well."

"Alaine is a good man, and the Dubois family is a good one. I like him, Maman. He's gentle with me, and kind."

Perenelle nodded. "Then I'll be happy with you," she said.

"And you, Maman? Will you be happy afterward, with Father?"

"I will be fine," she told Verdette, but her daughter shook her head. "That's not what I asked, Maman. I asked if you'll be happy."

"I'm happy with my work. It keeps me interested." She touched the pendant around her neck. "And Nicolas can be a good man."

Verdette nodded. "I always wondered if it was the work you liked so much, or the fact that when you were in the laboratory with your chemicals and those dusty manuscripts, *he* left you alone."

Perenelle shook her head. "No, that's not the only reason. I *do* enjoy the work—I have since I was younger than you and I was working with my own father. You and your father . . . well, whether he admits it or not, I help him with his work, and that also gives me pleasure. When I'm in the laboratory, I feel as if the entire universe is there before me, with all its secrets waiting to be discovered . . ." She laughed. "Listen to me, going on about this, when you're about to discover your own life. This is your day, Verdette. Let's not talk about me."

She kissed her daughter's forehead, her hands clasping her head under the lace of her ceremonial headdress. Perenelle's hands . . . sometimes it surprised her, seeing the wrinkles and the dry skin that were beginning to show her age. And Verdette—she was taller than Perenelle now. When had that happened?

Verdette's fingers had gone to Perenelle's breast, running down the gold chain she wore around her neck. Verdette fondled the sardonyx cameo there, her fingers caressing it lovingly. "I know that I'm one reason you stayed with him, Mamam, but I'll be gone now. Your reason to stay is gone after today. You can leave him now. You'll always have a place you can stay—in my new household."

"I know," Perenelle said. She smiled against the tears that threatened once more. "I know that, and I thank you for it. I'll never stop loving you, Verdette; you will always have my heart. Now—let's stop talking and get you married."

You can leave him now . . . The words touched emotions inside Perenelle, feelings she thought she'd forgotten over the years. She felt a yearning for that freedom, and she felt sudden disgust that she'd remained with Nicolas all these years. But her hand sought the pendant, and as she stroked the sculpted miniature of her own face, the thoughts receded like distant storm clouds, and she felt only the ancient pull toward Nicolas.

She smiled at Verdette and took her daughter's hand. "Come," she said. "It's time . . ."

2:
POLYHYMNIA

Camille Kenny

Today

THE *BENT CALLIOPE* BUSTLED on Friday nights. The Lower East Side was the current "hot" neighborhood for the arts in general, and live music beckoned from several venues every night: *C-Squat*, the *Bowery Ballroom*, or the *Mercury Lounge*. The music scene dragged in outsiders and hangers-on who filled the streets most nights; the bars on Rivington, Delancey, and the nearby streets took in the overflow and the regulars: those who lived here and who wanted a quieter refuge.

Not that the *Bent Calliope* was ever quiet. On Friday nights, the *Bent Calliope* brought in a DJ, who set up in the front corner of the bar. Dance music pounded through his PA system. Camille's crowd generally avoided that area, taking over the opposite rear corner of the bar, where the bass throbbed mostly through the floorboards and where people might still talk without straining their throats.

The group commandeered the large table there; usually a half dozen or more people would have shown up by 8:00, with the group fluctuating in size as the evening progressed. Camille arrived, as she usually did, around 8:30—wanting to be certain she was there before David arrived, if he *did* arrive. He hadn't called her to say otherwise, but she wasn't certain he would show, and she wasn't certain whether or not it would be better that way.

"Hey, Camille!" Morris spotted her as she made her way through the dance floor crowd after stopping at the bar to snag a Guinness. He waved to her over the intervening heads. "What happened the other day? I swear I saw you in the crowd, then all of a sudden you vanished and never showed up at all." He opened his arms, and she slid into his fierce hug. As he bent down, she kissed him.

"Sorry, I wasn't feeling well," she said when they broke apart.

"Feeling better now?" That was Mercedes, pulling out the empty chair next to her and gesturing to it. Camille nodded and sat; Mercedes' arm remained around the back of the chair, her fingers caressing Camille's shoulder. Kevin sat across from them, drumming on the table to the beat from the DJ's mix—he and Morris were laughing about something. Emily was talking energetically with Rashawn, her hands sweeping wide as if she were painting the air with invisible brushes. Joe and James were missing, but would probably turn up later, together. A few other members of the group might or might not stop in. All in all, a fairly typical Friday for the Bent Calliope Group, as they were already calling themselves. "After you were over the other night, I wrote the most incredible scene," Mercedes said, leaning close to Camille's ear. Her voice was tinged with a Puerto Rican accent, and her long, black hair frothed around her face. "I swear, it was just flowing out, but I'm so close to it that I can't really tell how good it is. Would you be willing to read it and give me your opinion? I know you'll give me an honest critique . . ."

The group of various creative artists had coalesced around Camille over the past few years, since she'd begun frequenting the Bent Calliope. It was the hope of her presence that brought them together, though none of them would have acknowledged the fact. Camille was their catalyst, the gravitational force around which each of them revolved. They pretended that each of them was the true center, but it was Camille who held them together, the dark sun to their glowing planets, each of them tethered by the green strands of their creativity.

For Camille, it was like being enveloped in a bath of energy, luxuriating in a vibrant spirit that flashed and sparked around them from the glowing emerald of their soul-hearts. She consumed it, taking the radiance into herself. She could already feel the tingling deep within her, as if she'd spent the last hour downing shots of espresso. But as much as this sustained her, the collective energy of the group still wasn't truly satisfying. She kept herself at a distance from them, spreading herself out among the group rather than choosing a single one of them. From each of them, she took what she could, but it wasn't the same as being *with* someone. They nourished her, but she was left with an eternal sense of hunger and not-quite-emptiness. It was enough to keep her from falling into depression and ill health, but the group couldn't give her all that she wanted.

They couldn't give her what she needed, but what she needed would also, inevitably, bring *him* back to destroy it.

She hugged Mercedes. She could nearly taste the pleasure in Mercedes' mind, the tendrils of her green heart embracing Camille. "I'm so happy to hear that," she said. "Of *course* I'll read it, dear. E-mail a PDF to me, why don't you, or send me an epub file, and I'll take a look at it over the next few days . . ."

She felt David's presence in the *Bent Calliope* as Mercedes gave her a hug and a soft kiss, and saw him a moment later. He altered the flow of energy around her, tugging at her even as his presence caused the other tendrils to slide away. David evidently saw her as well, hesitating at the edge of the crowd as if uncertain of his welcome. "David!" she said. "Come on, sit down. You wanted to meet the *Bent Calliope* Group? Well, let me introduce you around."

She went around the table, giving David their names. "Hey," David said to Morris. "I caught your show at the gallery over on Delancey last month. Nice stuff."

Morris grinned. "Thank you. Trust Camille to grab someone with excellent taste. A photographer, eh? Did you notice the litho prints I had mounted in the little room in the back—the subject look familiar?" He nodded his head toward Camille. "She's a lovely model."

David glanced at Camille, at Mercedes' arm still draped possessively around her. "That's something I'd like to know for myself," he said.

"Ah, so you've noticed too. A wonderful face, and her body's not half bad, either." Morris blew Camille a kiss across the table; Camille gave him the finger in return.

Camille saw David's eyes widen with the remark, and widen further with her response. Kevin laughed—whether at David's discomfiture or at her gesture, Camille couldn't tell. "Morris, you're hopeless," Kevin said. "Camille, tell him—you're actually a musician at heart."

"Nah," Rashawn interjected. "It's dance—now there's the perfect expression of all of the arts. In dance, you have everything: music, a moving sculpture with the dancers, an animated painting, and the beauty of the figure."

Then they were all talking at once, each defending their own medium: a laughing, furious babble. Camille glanced up at David and smiled. "Artists," she said, leaning close to him. "Once they start talking about their work, you can't shut them up."

She'd expected David to plead that he had to be elsewhere and leave early, but he remained deep into the night. He said very little during the evening—he answered when spoken to, laughed at the jokes, bought a round for the group, but otherwise mostly watched and listened. At one point in the evening, he pulled a small digital camera from his pocket and asked if they'd mind him taking a few candid shots; no one objected, and he would lift the camera at times to snap a shot: no flash, always using only the ambient light.

Camille felt him staring at her much of the time; whenever she glanced his way, their gazes seemed to meet and hold for a breath or two. She drank much more than usual: because she was nervous and uncertain; because she was, she would admit later, stupid.

She wondered if he could feel what she felt, if he noticed how—inside—she responded to his presence so much more than the others, if he saw how she was nearly always within an arm's reach of him. The others had realized the dynamic, she was afraid. She could see it in the group, in the way they chattered and their body language: they all wondered whether David was going to become another one of her confidants. Perhaps they worried he might become more—because each of them, to some degree, considered Camille to be their own special friend, who was interested more in them than in any of the others.

For some, a potential rival could color their soul-hearts with dark, bitter jealousy.

She drank because then she could pretend to be enjoying herself, could pretend that this was just another evening with the Calliope Group, could pretend not to be worried. And if this turned out to be a mistake, then she could blame it on the alcohol.

By one in the morning, most of the group was beginning to make excuses to leave. David watched as she embraced and kissed each one in turn as they left. Mercedes was the last to go—they talked for a long time with David between them, the two women's arms around the back of his chair and their fingers occasionally intertwined. Mercedes finally yawned dramatically and pushed herself away from the table. Camille could feel David's regard on her as they said good-bye, as Mercedes gave her a long and lingering kiss, as Camille—her arms around Mercedes— reminded her to send the chapter she'd written. Mercedes whispered in Camille's ear, her voice hot and breathy. "Have fun, *mi amor*." She glanced meaningfully at David's left hand. "Even if he *is* married."

Mercedes released Camille, then touched David's arm. "Good to meet you," she said. "Be nice to her."

David smiled as if he understood, though he said nothing.

Camille sat down next to David as Mercedes walked toward the door through the now-thin crowd. The movement made her a little dizzy. Their table was ringed with the ghosts of their drinks; too many of them had been Camille's. How many Guinnesses had she had? Four? And the shots of Jameson that Kevin had bought them . . . "So what did you think?" she asked him.

"Of the group? They're a talented bunch. But I already knew that."

"That's it?" She wondered if she slurred the words slightly. The room seemed to tilt; she caught herself swaying on her stool.

He shrugged.

"I think I know what you want to ask, David," she told him. Without the drinks, she probably would have stopped there or never said anything at all. But the words continued to bubble out from her. "I saw you watching. You're wondering if I'm Mercedes' lover. Or Morris'. Or maybe we're just terribly incestuous with everyone." She spread her arms wide, nearly hitting him.

"Are you?"

"That's my business," Camille said. She could hear her voice slurring the words: *Thass my biznuss . . .* She rubbed her head, trying to clear away the fumes. *This isn't the way you wanted it to go*, she thought. *Just shut up.* But she couldn't stop the words from continuing to tumble out. "Let me tell you about the Calliope Group, David. Their creativity, their energy: it's like *food* to me," she said. "Didn't you feel my hunger when we met? Couldn't you feel the pull?"

He gave a snort of laughter through his nose at that. Had he had too much to drink himself?—she couldn't remember. "Oh, so you're, what? An art vampire?" he asked. "Strange, you don't really have the faux-Goth look."

She leaned in toward him. "Would you like it if that were true?" She snapped her teeth together and put her lips next to his ear, whispering. "Would you enjoy it if I sucked the creative energy from you? I'd do it ever so slowly, so you could feel every drop oozing from your body . . ."

"Stop it, Camille," he told her, and for the first time she heard irritation in his voice. "You're drunk." The rebuke cut through the buzz of the alcohol, and she answered heatedly before she could think.

"Maybe. And you're married." She said the last word heavily, stretching out the syllables as if tasting them. Then contrition welled up inside her. "I'm sorry," she said. "I shouldn't have said that. I shouldn't have said *anything* that I just said. I didn't mean . . ." She sucked in a slow breath and let it out again. "David, I'm sorry. I didn't want to make a wreck of the night. I had a good time. I'm glad you came, glad you got to meet the group. I had a good time *because* you came." He was staring at her. "I should shut up now, I think." She closed her mouth dramatically.

He stared for several seconds before saying anything else. "I really have to be going." He stood up, his chair scraping against the wooden floor. "I'll get a cab. We can share it."

"I'll walk home. It's only a block and a half."

He shook his head. "No," he said firmly. "It's too late, and you've had too much. You stay here and I'll get that cab for us."

She was too tired to argue. In the cab, she leaned her head on his shoulder, and—cautiously—his arm went around her. Neither of them spoke. The closeness relaxed her. She snuggled against his side for the brief ride, luxuriating in the feel of his warmth. She felt his fingertips sliding down her arm, stroking her skin softly until the cab came to a stop at the curb in front of her apartment. David told the cabbie to wait, and walked her up to the door of the brownstone. She plucked the key from its pocket in her purse and turned it in the lock. With the door halfway open, she turned to him.

"I'm not going to ask you in," she said.

"I wouldn't come in if you did."

She nodded. He was very close to her. She could have reached up and pulled his face down to hers. She yearned to do exactly that. She shivered, as if the night had suddenly turned cold, but the heat of his soul-heart drew her, and made her want to lean into him. *You shouldn't. You can't.* "Your cab's waiting, David," she told him. "I'll call you?" At the last moment, the sentence lifted upward into a question.

He nodded. "Do that," he said.

She stepped inside and closed the door. It was very nearly the hardest thing she'd done in ages.

Her sleep that night was restless and disturbed. When she did fall asleep, her dreams were haunted by a man chasing her with a sword through a bewildering city landscape—both modern and ancient, all at once. Though she couldn't see the face of her attacker, she knew who it was, and the knowledge made her try to run faster, but in nightmare slowness, her legs refused to respond and he was nearly upon her as she fell, as she heard him laugh, as she heard the *snick* of the blade through the air and felt it pierce her neck.

She could see the blood spurting, felt her head separate from her body, and the world rolled crazily as her head went careening away.

She screamed and woke suddenly in her bed, the echo of the scream already fading in her ears, with her bed sheets wound around her and her head pounding. The sun was up, splashing light against the far wall; the clock by her bed said 7:32. The taste of old Guinness was in her mouth. "Christ, it's too early," she muttered. Her cat Verdette—a gray-furred French Chartreux—stared at her in annoyance from the bottom of the bed. Camille lay back, trying to find sleep again and knowing it was already hopeless. With a sigh, she swept aside the covers and sat on the side of the bed, stroking the cat, which began to purr.

"If only everyone were that easy to satisfy," she told her, "it'd be a much better world." She sat there a long time, with Verdette curled contentedly on her lap. Finally, she realized that she'd made a decision.

She called David later that morning, when she figured he might reasonably be awake. The sound of his low voice in her ear made her smile. "Camille? I didn't expect . . ." His voice trailed off.

"I'm really sorry about the end of last night," she said. "I hardly ever drink like that, not that I expect you to believe me. And judging by the way my head's pounding this morning, that's a damned good thing. I just wanted you to know that I appreciate, well, everything." She took a sip of the strong coffee she'd brewed—she was on her third mug now—and hurried into the words she'd prepared. "David, I never gave you the answer I intended to last night. I've been thinking about your offer. The answer's 'yes.' If you're still interested in photographing me, you can."

Over the phone, she heard the soft clatter of keys, as if he were typing on a laptop. "You're sure?" he asked

"I'm sure."

"Then . . . Do you want to come to my studio later this afternoon? I'm free today if you are. Maybe around 3:00?"

"I'll be there." The silence between them stretched too long. She could hear his breathing. Her gaze went around her apartment: the three paintings on their easels, unfinished and (to her mind) unsatisfactory; the equally unsatisfactory ones she'd actually put on the walls; the violin propped in one corner, the case pale with dust; the neatly-labeled jars at the rear of the kitchen table, with their brightly-colored powders and crystals; the Tarot deck wrapped in silk to one side.

Her life in a few quiet images.

You're sure you want to do this, so soon? After what happened the last time? Without having found Nicolas yet?

"I'll see you in a bit, then," she said finally. As she ended the call she looked at Verdette, and touched, softly, the pendant around her neck. "I know it's a mistake," she told the cat. "But it's mine to make, isn't it?"

David's studio was on the third floor of what had once been an industrial building now turned into residential apartments; he and his wife Helen lived on the second floor below the studio. Camille thought the lower floor of the apartment was more Helen than David. It smelled of her, a faint sharp perfume, and the interior decorating was too perfect, too mannered and too *Architectural Digest* to be David, she thought. Helen didn't appear to be home; at least she made no appearance as David let her wander around, and David didn't mention her.

But she was there, in spirit if not in fact.

None of David's prints were on the walls of the living area. There were, instead, framed reproductions of paintings—expensive prints on textured canvas. "Monet, Degas, Sisley, Renoir, Mary Cassatt," Camille said, glancing at them one by one. "Someone really likes the Impressionists." Camille stopped in front of another one set near the stairway leading to the upstairs. "Gustav Klimt," she said. "*Portrait of Emilie.*" She nearly whispered the name, then took a long breath. "Interesting. She was his true muse. The painting's out of period with the rest, though."

"That one's my choice, I'm afraid—the painting just really struck me when I saw it. You obviously know your art."

"I'm a bit of an art history buff," she said. "You know that Gustav slept with most of his models, don't you? He had children by some of them as well, but never with Emilie. Poor, dear Emilie." She stared at the Klimt for several seconds more before turning back to David with a smile. His eyes had widened, but he said nothing.

She'd worn a simple white tank top over her bra, an old, comfort-able pair of jeans, and the sardonyx pendant on its golden chain over the tank top: casual clothing that said she didn't consider this a spe-cial occasion. Minimal makeup. Just another day. She could sense him watching her as she peered around the apartment. "Nice place," she said. "I'm glad you didn't come in last night. My apartment's a complete wreck. This . . . It's very nice, David."

"I can't take credit for it," he told her. He pointed to the ceiling. "I'm only responsible for what's up there."

"And the Klimt."

"And the Klimt," he agreed.

They walked up the open metal staircase to the cluttered stu-dio above. Here, little had been touched. The walls were unpainted, gouged drywall, with exposed brick in the corners. The wooden floor was stained and scratched, the ceiling high with exposed beams and ancient fluorescent fixtures dangling from wires. Long black exten-sion cords writhed over the floor like motionless constrictors. There were two still life studies set up with flood lighting arranged around them, several stands with rolls of backdrop paper, tripods and studio lights with the black wings of shutters attached to them. She wandered around while David watched her. Barber's *Adagio for Strings* was playing on a stereo system attached to an iPod.

"Classical?" she asked. "Really?"

"My tastes are eclectic," he answered. "The next song could be any-thing from Celtic to metal. I like being surprised."

"Good," she told him.

David had several of his prints arrayed along one wall, the line of them uneven, some in frames, some matted but unframed, a few simply dry-mounted on poster board—yes, the artwork on the walls down-stairs was definitely Helen's, Camille decided. She walked slowly along the line of photos, looking carefully at each one. A few of them were nudes—not Helen, but other women. Camille could feel David watch-ing her, heard a camera lens snap onto a camera body.

Here, in his studio, in this place that was full of him, she felt David's pull intensely. His green heart swelled and the aura of it surrounded him.

"Like them?" he asked.

"Wonderful compositions, gorgeous lighting, and truly appalling presentation," she said. "But I see why your clients like you, anyway."

"I wish Helen felt that way," he said it quickly, then seemed to regret the statement. "Sorry," he said. "It's just . . ."

"Just what?"

She thought for a moment that he wasn't going to answer. He pointed the camera in Camille's direction and snapped a shot. "She thinks I should be looking at another career. Sometimes I can believe her. Those clients you mentioned have been scarce recently. I'm not that up-and-coming young guy anymore; I'm becoming the guy who almost made it and didn't." Camille nodded, ignoring the camera. "You know," he said, "I really should have you sign the release form."

"I told you I didn't need a release. I trust you."

"A release protects both of us, not just you." He sounded like he was reciting something he'd memorized.

"Do you think you need protection from me? Do I look that frightening?"

He chuckled at that. "Hardly. But I can't afford to be sued. This is all I have, right here."

Camille smiled. "Then don't do anything with the pictures without asking me first. And trust me."

His sigh was just louder than the outside traffic. "Helen checked with a law firm where she works, and they said—"

"There's nothing magical about forms," she told him. "My signature on a line isn't a talisman. It won't ward off bad things or lend you any real protection at all, and it won't stop me from doing whatever I want to do." He was already shaking his head. "Fine," she said. "Give me the damn release."

She signed the form without looking at the words there, handing it back to him. Their hands touched as he took the form, and she felt the warmth of his skin, the softness of his fingertips. She wondered what they might feel like on her face, or running along the length of her arm. "Thank you," he said. "I'll make you a copy before you leave."

She smiled at him. "Hope you and your lawyer feel better now. I don't need a copy, though. I trust you, David." She continued wandering around the studio, going to the large south-facing windows. She leaned against the wooden frame: chipped white paint, the window grimy and dusty. From the side, she heard the clicking of a motorized shutter.

"That's good," he said. "Stay there, Camille; the light's wonderful. Don't try to pose. Just be yourself."

She could visualize what he was seeing in the camera's viewfinder: a strong chiaroscuro with the sunlight streaming through the glass, the studio a darkness behind her. Her face would be almost a cameo, like the one around her neck. She cupped the pendant in her hand, the shutter continuing to click.

The air around her was charged and electric—it was David that she felt: his energy, his passion, his promise. She let the atmosphere envelop her, inhaling it as if it were sweet oxygen. She looked at him from under lowered eyelids—at him, at the lens of the camera. "Yes, that's right. Excellent," she heard him say. The shutter continued its relentless, imperative beat: a mechanical heart.

Click. Click. Click . . .

She could sense him, staring at her through the viewfinder, all of his focus there. She was his world, all that he saw right now. She reached down, her hands crossed at her waist, and took the hem of the tee, pulling it slowly up. She heard him inhale, but he said nothing. He didn't encourage her, but he also didn't stop her.

Click. Click. Click . . .

She pulled the tee over her head and off, let it drop to the floor. Her head down, her hair a red-highlighted waterfall over her shoulders, she opened the front clasp of her bra. She slipped the straps down her shoulders, let them fall. She could feel the cold stone and metal of the pendant between her breasts. The entire time she looked up at him, at the camera, her expression almost defiant, her chin lifted.

"Do you always leave that on?" David asked. She realized, almost belatedly, that he was talking about the pendant.

"Yes," she told him. "Always."

The single eye of the lens stared at her, hungrily. She had seen artists stare at her that way before. Before, she had nearly always also been their lovers.

Click. Click. Click . . .

She turned sideways to David again, looking through the window once more to the skyline outside. She could feel the sun, could feel the air moving across her breasts like the arousing caress of a ghost. *It's always like this, the first time. A frightened heat in your belly, a shivering anxiousness. He feels it, too. Listen to how his breath shivers . . .*

Click. Click. Click . . .

His hand touched her bare shoulder. He still held the camera to his eye with his other hand. "I want you to turn—" he began. His hand slid toward her neck; she caught it between head and shoulder, trapping it there, luxuriating in the feel of his caress. She smiled up to him, hearing the click of the camera's motor drive. She found his hand with hers, brought it down so it just touched the swell of her breast . . .

"What the hell!" The voice—a woman's voice—swept away the vitality and strength and heat in the room and stopped the heartbeat of the camera. David pulled his hand away. Camille's head craned around as her own hands, instinctively, started to move to cover her breasts. She forced them to stay down, to look as calm as if she were fully dressed. The woman was attired in a business pants suit, the bangs of her hair, cut in a conservative bob, dark with sweat as if she'd just walked several blocks.

"Helen? What are you doing here this early?" David lowered the camera as he took a step away from Camille. He looked from Helen to Camille and back.

"Interrupting your afternoon fun, it looks like," she answered. Helen glared at Camille her gaze dropping once to her exposed breasts and the sardonyx cameo there. "You—whoever you are—put your clothes on and get the hell out of here."

"David was photographing me, that's all," Camille said. "I'm just . . . just a model."

"I'm sure that's all you are," Helen answered, her voice low and angry. "Now, get out of here."

Camille put on her bra, slipped the tee over her head again. Helen stood in the doorway to the studio, watching her. "He's much more talented than you think he is," she said as she passed the woman. "You should open your eyes and see it. You should love him for his gift."

Helen sucked in her breath as if she were about to retort, but said nothing. Her blue eyes were searing, her hands were curled into fists with polished red fingernails digging into flesh. Camille kept walking.

"You're dragging street sluts in here behind my back?" she heard Helen shout at David as she descended the stairs and walked through the living area toward the door. Camille saw an expensive leather briefcase on the couch that hadn't been there earlier. "Again? Christ, David, that one has to be ten years younger than you . . ."

Camille opened the door. She shut away the rising argument and David's answer as she closed it again behind her.

David didn't call that day, nor the next. By the third day, she was certain that her decision had been made for her. She wasn't going to call him—any further contact with her had to be his decision; she'd already made her own choice when she'd gone to see him, when she'd let him photograph her, when she'd let him touch her.

The rest, she told herself, was up to him. It was fate telling her that going after him had been a mistake.

On Sunday, she laid out the Tarot, but it told her nothing about David; the array was definitely concerned with her other quest, with Nicolas. Every card howled at his presence nearby. Both the Four of Swords and the Four of Wands showed in the array, both cards linked to hospitals and medical issues. She went down to the corner store and bought the Sunday paper; in the obituaries, there were four deaths listed where the person had been a patient at Mount Sinai Hospital, and the local section was screaming about another body found in Manhattan that appeared to be the work of the Black Fire killer.

Camille went to the copies of the old manuscripts she kept in the closet; she read—as she had a hundred times before—the Finding spell, placing it within the sardonyx pendant as she always did. She went to the site of the latest Black Fire casualty: in Roosevelt Park. The crime tape was still up though the investigators had already left the scene. Standing outside the tape, Camille could see the outline of a blackened section of grass where the body had been. As she stared at it, the pendant throbbed on her chest—not as deeply as it would have had Nicolas been standing there, but the spell could feel the residue of his presence.

Nicolas was responsible. She had no doubt of that now, none at all. She looked around, almost guiltily, as if she might see him watching her from nearby. She would find him; she *had* to find him, or guilt would consume her: these murders were at least partially her fault.

Camille spent much of the rest of the afternoon walking around Mount Sinai, watching the doctors and nurses who were entering and leaving the hospital, searching for a familiar face, a familiar body shape.

None of them were Nicolas. The Finding spell slowly evaporated from the pendant, and though she thought she could feel a faint tug of his presence around the building, it was far fainter than it had been around the site of the Black Fire murder. He'd been here, but not recently.

Sunday evening, she went to the New York Aikikai, an aikido dojo she'd joined upon arriving in New York, and worked out. Over the last few decades, she'd become fascinated by the art and its concept of self-defense, and had studied it in several cities and under several instructors; she held the rank of Nidan, a second-degree black belt. The class left her breathless and gloriously sweating. She reveled in the throws and being thrown, letting the activity dissolve her tension and her uncertainty in the crystalline moment. A weapons class followed, and she stayed for that, letting the heft of the wooden bokken tire out her arms until there was only the thin *shfftt* of the blade through the humid air as she cut and cut and cut, imagining that it was *his* body that she was attacking.

But after folding her hakama and putting her dogi in the gym bag and walking back out onto the streets, reality soon came back to her. She found herself watching the shadows in the street, ready if someone emerged from them. She kept her purse open, prepared to pull out the Ladysmith if someone attempted to accost her. But no one did.

Monday morning, promptly at 9:00 AM, her cell phone rang. She looked at the screen, feeling a certain disappointment when she saw that it was, as promised, the detective Bob Walters calling. "Mr. Walters," she said, accepting the call. "Any news?"

She could hear his head shake before he spoke in that growling, too-early-in-the-morning voice. "I'm afraid not. Ms. Kenny, I can't in good conscience continue working on this case when I think you're most likely wasting your money. Without a name, without a current photograph . . ."

"Money actually isn't an issue for me."

He nearly laughed. "In this economy? You're a rare one, then. Are you certain? Your bill's already into five figures."

"I'll stop by your office later today and pay you for your work up to now, and give you an advance for another week. I really want to find this man, Mr. Walters. It's important to me, and I'm certain he's here somewhere in the city."

"And you know this how?"

"I can *feel* him." That pronouncement was greeted by nothing more than a breathy silence on the other end of the line. Camille hurried into the quiet. "Can you tell me that you never listened to your gut when you were on the force, Mr. Walters? Didn't you sometimes just *know* the truth?"

He sniffed, and she heard what might have been a sip of coffee. At this time of the morning, at least, she hoped it was coffee. "I listened, sure," he said. "Saved my butt a few times, too—and got it chewed on a few times as well, since my gut turned out to be wrong. Your gut might turn out to be a very expensive one."

Camille shrugged, even knowing he couldn't see the gesture. "Not finding this guy might turn out to be more expensive, as far as I'm concerned," she told him. "Please, keep working on this."

She heard a long inhalation rattle the earpiece. "It's your money, Ms. Kenny, and my checking account it's feeding. All right. I'll keep the file open. I'll e-mail you your bill right now, and I'll see you this afternoon—if I'm not in, you can just shove the envelope under the door. Have a good day."

He hung up before she could respond.

Monday evening, after dropping off Bob Walters' check, she listened to Kevin's new band. She thought their music interesting—a blend of funk and progressive, with odd time signatures. She could tell that the group was tight and well-rehearsed, and Kevin, on drum set, was displaying chops that she hadn't known he possessed, driving the band like a maniac. But after a set, she was ready to leave. She stayed for their last set, despite her edginess, and went back to Kevin's apartment afterward for a drink, but declined to spend the night when he asked.

Tuesday morning, she read Mercedes' chapter with Verdette sitting and purring on her lap. She called Mercedes, who invited her over for lunch. Camille left her apartment early, putting another Finding spell in the pendant, packing the Ladysmith, and spending another fruitless hour in front of Mount Sinai before going to Mercedes' apartment to discuss her book. She found that she needed the closeness and the comfort; they ended up in bed together. Later that evening, they went to the *Bent Calliope* and met with the group.

Their laughter and their energy did little for her; their company seemed flat. The taste of their green hearts was thin gruel for her hunger. She found herself struggling to smile at their jokes or to respond to their flirtations, and left early that evening.

On Wednesday morning, her cell phone buzzed on her nightstand. She looked at the display: David. She held her breath, the phone in her hand as it vibrated. Just before the call went to voicemail, she touched the button. "David," she said.

"Hey, Camille. I just wanted to say . . ." She heard his breath rasp in the speaker. "I'm really sorry about the other day. Helen shouldn't have gone off on you like that. That wasn't fair to you. What happened was entirely my fault."

Verdette hopped onto the bed, butting her head against Camille's hand. She massaged the cat's ear; purring, she curled into Camille's lap. "I don't blame Helen; I can understand her reaction," she told him. "I'm sorry, too. It wasn't just your wife; I shouldn't have . . . well, you know. I can sympathize with how she must have felt and what she was thinking."

"Either way," David answered, "it shouldn't have happened. I told you—she and I, well, we've had some issues recently. This is just part of it. I'm just sorry you got dragged into my relationship problems." Another pause; Camille wasn't certain what to say. "Listen," David continued just before the silence reached an uncomfortable length, "we're having a party here tomorrow: some of my friends and clients, some of Helen's. She understands now that nothing was going on between us, that I'd asked you to model for me, that's all, and she agrees that she overreacted. Why don't you come over tomorrow and let us both apologize in person."

Verdette gave an irritated cry, and Camille realized that she was pressing too hard on the cat's spine. She forced her fingers to relax. "That's really not necessary."

"Maybe not, but I'd appreciate the opportunity."

"Would Helen?"

"I told her I was going to invite you."

Camille tried to laugh. "That's not actually an answer, David."

"I promise you, Helen will be fine with you being here, and I'd like you to come. Say yes. Besides, I have a few pictures you might want to see."

"David, I really don't need the drama." Verdette arched her back in feline ecstasy, her paws kneading Camille's legs through the coverlet. She remembered the session before Helen's interruption, the connection with David, the feeling of being one with him. *You want this. You know you do.*

"There won't be any drama. I promise. Tell me you'll be here. Camille, I'm not going to accept 'no' as an answer."

She did laugh then. "All right," she told him. "No drama. I'll be there."

She dressed conservatively: a black, knee-length evening dress with a high neckline, her pendant sparkling outside it, conservative heels, a small leather purse, her hair pulled back and up. David had told her that the party would start around 8:00; she figured 9:00 was late enough— she didn't want to be the first to arrive, certainly didn't want to have to make awkward conversation with Helen and David until other guests arrived. She could hear several voices beyond their apartment door; she could sense the other people as well, the tendrils of their presences reaching out for her, several of them with green soul-hearts but none of them nearly as strong as David.

He was there as well; his soul-heart blazed.

She checked her lipstick in the small mirror of her compact and knocked on the door.

She didn't know the person who opened the door. She smiled at the man anyway and stepped inside when he gestured to her. The babble of several conversations battled with bland smooth jazz from a speaker system in the corner. There were at least a dozen people in the living room and more in the kitchen, judging by the sound. Neither David nor Helen was visible. Camille felt alone and vulnerable, a polite smile frozen on her lips, the energy of the room confusing and unsettling.

"You look familiar. Have we met?" One of the men had come up behind her, a glass of wine in his hand. He looked to be in his early forties, she guessed, his brown hair thinning on top and starting to gray at the temples, a middle-aged paunch bulging over the belt of his Dockers.

"No," Camille told him. "I'm a friend of David's."

"Ah, so am I," the man nodded, taking a sip of wine. He held out his hand. "I'm Jacob Prudhomme. I own Prudhomme Gallery over on Delancey. David exhibits there; I sell one or two prints a month for him."

Camille shook the proffered hand. "Camille Kenny."

"What is it that you do, Camille Kenny?"

"I dabble. Paint a little, play music a little, do a few other things you'd probably call terribly New Age-y."

He smiled; it reminded her of the expression Verdette had when she was about to pounce on an insect. "Yes, but what do you *do?*" he persisted.

"That *is* what I *do,*" she told him, with the same emphasis. "I have a small trust fund from my, uh, family for income."

"That must be nice, to have that kind of freedom to pursue your avocations, to allow yourself to be a true *amateur* in the correct sense of the word." He pronounced the word in the French manner. He sipped the wine again. He was staring at her. "Wait a minute. Now I know who you are. You're the new muse David's found, the one he's been raving about." His gaze drifted down from her face to her chest and back; he didn't appear to be looking at the pendant. "Yes, that's it. I recognize you from the new set of photos he was showing me."

"Interesting," she said. She managed to keep smiling. "I haven't seen those shots yet myself."

"You'll be impressed," he told her. "Best of his work yet. You obviously inspired him. I think they'll sell well."

Her smile tightened. She made her excuses and moved away from him, staying at the edge of the crowd. She caught a glimpse of David in the kitchen; she saw that Helen was there with him and decided against going to him. Camille moved along the wall to the staircase leading to the studio and walked up, glancing at the Klimt painting as she passed it.

The studio hadn't changed much. It, at least, was blessedly empty of partygoers. David had placed a new array of 11 x 14 black-and-white photos on the wall: just the bare prints, unmounted and placed on the wallboard with pushpins, curling around the edges. Her face gazed back at her from the photographs. She looked at them one by one, stopping for a long time at the last of them: her figure was half in shadow, the shot taking her in from almost waist up, her breasts bare. The field of focus was narrow but incredibly sharp, each pore on her face and her skin highlighted by the oblique lighting. The tones of the picture ran from nearly white to a rich black in the background. She was looking up at the camera with a solemn, almost longing expression on her face, her lips just slightly parted as if she were about to say something.

She could feel the hunger again that she'd been feeling at that moment—and the sense of having the hunger filled. *Yes, he pulls you to him, but you could still let him go. The others at the* Bent Calliope, *they can still satisfy you for a while and give you time to do the hunting you need to do. Let Walters help you find Nicolas and then deal with him once and for all; if that means you lose David, then you lose him. There will be others: you know that, as many of them as you want . . .* She nearly shook her head at the thought. As she gazed at the picture, she heard footsteps on the stairs and felt David's approach. She didn't look at him or say anything, but waited until she felt his warmth along her back.

"How'd you know I was here?" she asked.

"Jacob told me he'd talked to you, and that he'd mentioned the pictures. You weren't downstairs, so . . ."

"Jacob's not very subtle."

"He goes after what he likes, and he likes my work and gives me a place to display and sell it," David answered. He moved closer; she felt his side brush hers. "I saw you looking at that one. That's the most striking image, I think," he said. "The expression you have . . . It's perfect. Do you agree?"

"I'd agree that it's the best of the ones you have up," she answered. "I'd have to look at the others first. What does Helen think?"

If he noticed the deliberate insertion of his wife into the conversation, he ignored it. "I showed them to her. She really didn't say much." His arm went around her shoulders. She hesitated, simultaneously wanting to pull away and wanting to lean her head against him. He felt right; he felt comfortable. "Thanks for coming, Camille," David said, his voice soft. He leaned his head down; his lips brushed against her hair. "That means a lot to me. Since I've met you, there's . . ." He stopped. She felt the surging of his soul-heart, and she wanted to take in the emerald tendrils and taste them, to let them pass through her so she could give it back to him again, reinvigorated. His head lifted again. "I'd like to be able to keep working with you, Camille."

She took a step sideways so that his arm dropped away. "To keep 'working' with me? What exactly does that word mean to you, David?"

She didn't get an answer. They both heard Helen's voice calling for David, then her footsteps on the stairs. Camille moved another careful step away from him. Helen came partway up the steps, halting when she saw the two of them. "Oh," she said. The single word contained volumes.

"I was showing Camille some of the photos from our session," David said.

"So I see." Something that might have been a smile ghosted over Helen's lips but never quite reached her eyes as she looked at Camille. "You're very attractive, Camille." The name came an instant too late, as if she didn't want to say it, as if the taste of it was like dry dust in her mouth. "As David's pictures show. Quite amply, I might add." Her gaze went to David. "Jacob is looking for more wine; I told him you'd open the Cabernet. Would you mind?" David looked at Camille; both women noticed. "Don't worry. I'll entertain your guest while you're busy," Helen said.

David didn't move. "Go on," Camille told him. She forced a smile. "I'm fine."

"I'll be right back," David said. Camille wasn't certain who he was addressing. They listened to David descend the stairs. Helen stood at the top of the steps, staring at Camille's pictures, at her half-nudity.

"Did I overreact the other day?" Helen asked. Her gaze remained fixed at the photographs.

"No. In your position, I might have had the same reaction," Camille answered.

Helen nodded, her lips pursed. "That's honest, at least. Do you like him?"

"I think David's extremely talented."

"And that's all?" Helen did smile then. "You don't have to answer. It really doesn't matter; I know how David feels. I can tell; he's not very good at hiding things. Has he talked to you about us?"

"Not really," Camille answered, though she was certain that Helen wouldn't have believed her even if she'd actually been telling the truth.

"Well, you should know that it's not all my fault. David's still a child. He hasn't figured out yet that there's a real world out there and he needs to grow up. He still thinks that all he needs is his talent and that everyone will naturally beat a path to his door. He has more than enough artistic talent; what he *doesn't* have is the business and marketing sense he needs to go with it. And forgive me for my candor, but I doubt that it's your business acumen that makes him interested in you. He still believes he can have whatever he wants if he just wants it badly enough." She glanced back at the photos, standing between Camille and the steps. "Or whomever he wants," she added. "You wouldn't be the first one, dear. Or the last. I just thought I should warn you."

"I should leave," Camille said. "Excuse me . . ."

Helen didn't move. She cocked her head slightly. "Perhaps you should. But let me tell you something. I know more about you than you think."

Fear was a cold knife in her stomach. *No, that's not possible. He can't know, can't have found me first. Not this time.* But she had to admit that it was possible, however unlikely. Prudhomme had already seen the pictures David had taken of her, and presumably had them at his gallery for sale. Nicolas knew her preference for artists all too well, and might well have gone to the various galleries around town to see if he could find evidence of her. There she'd be, her face in stark black and white. Prudhomme would have told him who the photographer was, and it would have been like him to investigate David further, to find Helen.

It *was* possible. And if it was true, it changed the game. "What is it you know?" she asked. "And who told you?"

Helen gave a short laugh, but her gaze left Camille as she spoke. "No one has to tell me anything. I can see it for myself, and I think I've made myself clear." Helen stepped aside, smiling. "Sorry to see you go so soon, Camille. Really."

David was starting up the stairs as she came down. He saw her face and frowned. "Camille?"

"I have to go," she told him.

"Wait. What do you mean?" He reached out for her arm, but she shook him off. "Camille?"

She didn't answer him. The guests closest to the staircase were staring at them, the conversation quieting as they sensed the conflict. Ignoring them, she walked across the living room to the door. It wasn't until she was outside the building in the cool night air that she allowed herself to give in to the tears.

INTERLUDE TWO

Perenelle & Nicolas Flamel

1394 – 1418

Perenelle Flamel

1394

"YOU CAN LEAVE HIM NOW."

Verdette had suggested that to her, but Perenelle never had, despite the temptation. These many years later, she still wasn't certain why that was. One reason was simple habit; over Verdette's time with them, Perenelle had become used to her life with Nicolas. The years pressed more in on her with each passing season, making her brittle and afraid of change. By the time her daughter had married, she'd been nearly half a century old, already an elderly woman in the eyes of society. The paths of her life were already worn deep and escaping the ruts felt too difficult a task, and the thought of establishing a new life exhausting.

Now, another quarter of a century on, she was in her seventies: a crone and nearing the end of her road. Old, slow, stooped, her body sagging and wrinkled like a half-empty sack. There was no new start waiting for her. Not now.

Another reason was her work. Verdette had been right about that, at least—being in her laboratory was Perenelle's greatest and only pleasure. Her laboratory was comfortable and familiar, as was the library of reference material she'd cobbled together over the decades, intermixed with Nicolas' manuscripts. She feared that if she left, he would not let her take the manuscripts or her chemicals and equipment. This work was what consumed her now that Verdette was gone, living with her husband and children in Avignon. Perenelle had seen Verdette only twice in those twenty-four years, had held her grandchildren only those few times, though there was a painting of Verdette's family in the main hall of the house.

The work was what took the place of Verdette, and took the place of the affection she had once carried for Nicolas, so long ago that the very idea of it sometimes made her cackle with self-deprecating amusement.

Still another reason was because she knew, as Verdette had, that Nicolas also needed her, even if he was far too proud and arrogant to admit it. A few months after Verdette's marriage, she and Nicolas had undertaken a trip to Spain in search of additional manuscripts for their library—Perenelle suspected that Nicolas had insisted on Perenelle's going along only because of her prowess at translation: he was afraid that he'd miss something potentially valuable. They had come across an ancient, wandering Jew in Bilbao. He claimed to have a book he called the *Livre d'Abraham le Mage*—the book of Abraham the Mage, which the old man claimed contained ancient alchemical formulae, including (he insisted) the true recipe for the Philosopher's Stone, which could turn base metals into precious silver and gold and impart eternal life. Perenelle, with Nicolas breathing at her back, had looked over the book, but the scrawled letters were difficult to decipher, and seemed to be written in a code borrowed from several languages. The man himself said he hadn't been able to translate it.

At Perenelle's urging, Nicolas had purchased the book. On their return, Perenelle had begun to slowly break the cipher and begin translating the text; through the formulae in the book, she had been able—with great difficulty and much effort—to transform mercury into silver in small amounts, though the process was long and laborious and cost nearly as much as buying the silver outright. Still, her work brought the household a significant profit. Nicolas bought the houses to either side of them, connecting them to their house and creating their own small "estate" in Paris.

Nicolas, for his part, was less interested in the alchemical work.

Instead, he pushed her to translate the spells and incantations in the book: it was magic that interested Nicolas, not the mixing of chemicals and the purification of compounds. He also had more success than Perenelle in his pursuits: the spell which had killed Provost Marcel was a trifle compared to the spells he could now perform: spells that, had he ever shown them publicly, would have had him accused of witchcraft and devil worship. He had truly become an accomplished mage, and he laughed at the small, minor spells that Perenelle was able to work. Perenelle's alchemy had added to the household income, but it was Nicolas' spells that made them rich.

The greater goals, turning lead to gold and finding the elixir for immortality, were hinted at in the book, but there were missing pages and lacunae in the book, and those goals still eluded Perenelle.

However, their accomplishments had served the Flamels well; they were famous now, and with fame came increasing wealth and patronage as well—for Nicolas. He was hailed as an alchemical genius and scholar; his advice was sought after by the greatest minds on the continent. Perenelle was dismissed as simply the great man's wife, who assisted him but who added nothing of her own to his success.

In her prayers at night, she would admit to God that jealousy was not only a fault of Nicolas'.

And still another reason she had not left was because she felt she could not. When she was most haunted by the desire to leave, she would find herself wanting to take in her hand the pendant that she always wore, the pendant he had given her that night when she was still pregnant with Verdette. Though the feelings and memories the cameo always evoked had faded somewhat with time, the pendant still brought back the vestiges of love that she'd once felt for Nicolas. The emotion would fill her again, driving away all her doubts, her concerns, her fears, her distaste for the man. It was as if everything ill about Nicolas was erased, and she was given a new slate on which to inscribe her feelings.

She wondered at that, from time to time, but the thought was elusive and small, and never permitted Perenelle to catch it and examine it. The thought would dance away and be forgotten.

*　　*　　*

"Would Monsieur Flamel perhaps be interested in this?" the man asked. "I received this from my father, and he from his, and where it came from before that I don't know. I wouldn't part with it, but . . ."

The last statement was accompanied by a shrug that said more than words could. Nicolas still kept the manuscript store open, though he himself was never there anymore, and the store's income no longer mattered to them. Telo, who now managed the storefront, snorted derisively back in the shadows. Perenelle glared at him.

The man's clothing was fine, but was already beginning to show signs of wear and too many repairs; in a few months, Perenelle decided, it would be in tatters. His wife and three children—two boys and a girl, all of whom looked to be between seven and twelve years of age, watched from a respectful few steps away in the street. Cloth bags and trunks were at their feet; Perenelle could see the sleeve of a nightdress and the brass column of a candlestick protruding from one.

A Jewish family leaving Paris: it was an everyday sight since Charles VI had ordered the expulsion of all Jews from France. The Jewish population had been summarily commanded to sell their possessions and depart the kingdom. Nicolas had already purchased old books and manuscripts from several of the Jewish scholars in the city; evidently the word that the Flamels might buy old manuscripts had gone through the Jewish community.

She wondered whether they also knew that Nicolas was eagerly buying the houses of the Jews for a pittance and selling them for a huge profit later, or renting out the property if he thought it was well situated. He'd already made another small fortune; donating a tithe of it to the church justified the near theft to Nicolas. *"They have to leave the houses in any case,"* he'd said when she questioned the morality of his actions. *"I don't force them to sell to me. They're the ones who take the price I offer when I show them the gold francs that I can put in their pockets immediately. And afterward . . ."* He'd shrugged. *"What I do with the property afterward is between me and God, and I give Him His portion."*

"I'm afraid that Monsieur Flamel isn't here at the moment," Perenelle told the man, and she saw his shoulders sag. His face was already coated with dust from the streets; she wondered what the family would look like a few days from now, wearily passing through the countryside to Spain or perhaps to Aquitaine. "But let me look at what you have," she hurried to say. "The monsieur and I have the same interests . . ."

The man ventured a faint smile. He motioned with his head toward the eldest boy, who came hurrying forward with a small case that he handed to his father, who passed it to Perenelle in turn. Perenelle placed the case on the shop ledge, pushing aside the scrolls and books there set out for sale. She opened the case and looked in, the distinct scent of must and old paper rising to meet her. She glanced at the first sheet of yellowed, brittle paper, lying on top, taking in a breath. She looked first at the man, then at Telo, who had taken a few steps toward them as if he intended to examine the manuscripts with her. She suddenly didn't want that, for what Telo knew Nicolas would inevitably know as well. "Telo, why don't you take your lunch now?" she said. "I can deal with this; it's not worth your time. Go on."

Telo gave another snort. "As you wish, Madame." He shook his head in the direction of the Jewish family and went to the back of the store and into the house, calling out to the cook as he went. Perenelle opened the case again, and gently reached down to take out the sheets, manuscripts, and books there. They *were* indeed old, and not in the best of condition. She could see moth holes and damage from water and mold. But the manuscripts . . . They were an odd assortment: personal journals, fragments of the Kabbalah, portions of the Pentateuch, and a few pages that tugged immediately at Perenelle because the handwriting, the hodgepodge of languages, and the obvious cipher in which it was written was immediately familiar.

She was certain that those last pages were the missing portion of the book of Abraham the Mage. Those were alchemical formulae written there, she was sure. "These have been with your family for a long time?"

"Generations, Madame Flamel," he answered.

"Do you know what they are, or where they came from?"

He shook his head. "No, I'm afraid not. I kept them for their age, and because I thought that maybe they might be valuable. I know that they've suffered from their age, and that must have hurt their value. Still, I would keep them yet, but we already have more than we can carry." He looked back at his family, and Perenelle saw the pain and fear in his face. "But I couldn't accept less than five francs for them. Surely Monsieur Nicolas, with all his connections and rich patrons, could find someone who would be interested in them . . ."

"Five francs, then," Perenelle said, interrupting the man's spiel.

Shock and confusion showed on the man's face; no merchant ever bought anything without first haggling over the price and bemoaning the expense as if it would come from their very flesh. Perenelle knew that if he asked for five francs, he was hoping to get three. Perhaps only two, considering his desperate circumstances.

"Madame?" the man asked, as if he'd misheard her.

"I said five francs was a fair price," Perenelle told him. She untied her purse from her belt, grimacing at the protest of old, knobbed joints. She slowly counted out eight francs and laid them on the shelf next to the case. The man looked at the coins, evidently now more puzzled than before.

"Madame Flamel, you have put *eight* francs there."

"Strange," she told him. "I see only five. Perhaps it's my age." She looked past the man to his family. "I'd suggest you take the francs, Monsieur. You will certainly need them for your travels."

He stared at her, blinking once. Then his grizzled face creased in a wide, gap-toothed grin. "Madame Flamel is very generous," he said. "I won't forget this, and we will tell everyone that there are still good people in France."

He inclined his head to her, then swept the coins in his hand. They clinked brightly as he put them in his own purse. Then, hugging his son, he went back to his family. Perenelle watched them as they gathered up their luggage and began walking. She stood there until she could no longer see them before placing the manuscripts carefully back in the case. Telo would be gone for a while yet; even at her shuffling pace, that would give her time to take the case to her laboratory.

She never told Nicolas that she'd bought the manuscripts. She kept the pages hidden from him, stashed where she would work on them at night, slowly translating them word by painstaking word. They were the pages she needed to complete her quest; she could feel that for a certainty. They would help her create the elixir.

God had gifted her with the possibility, had made certain that she alone received the knowledge. This was nothing she would share with Nicolas. No. This would be her accomplishment alone.

~

Perenelle Flamel: 1402

PERENELLE COULD FEEL THE January chill all the way to her bones. The cold seeped into her joints, making them stiff and un-cooperative, though that was hardly unusual. She was in her eighth decade. What hair she still had was sparse and utterly white, her face was a savaged desert landscape of wrinkles and folds, her curving spine seemed to bend her over further with each passing month—she found herself staring at the floor at her feet when she walked unless she delib-erately lifted her head. She could manage little more than a shuffle, and required a cane to keep her upright. Most of those who had been born in her time were long dead.

Even her daughter, Verdette, was gone—four years ago now, of a flux. Perenelle had thought that the grief would kill her; when the let-ter came from Perenelle's grandson, the pain had been so intense that she thought her heart would burst inside her chest. Parents were not supposed to outlive their children—that wasn't right. Verdette had left behind six grandchildren and several great-grandchildren, all living far away from Paris. Perenelle still wrote them letters; occasionally, they would write back—usually when they wished to borrow money.

"Wife, have you seen the ground unicorn horn?" Nicolas interrupted her reverie. "I've looked everywhere and I can't find it."

The years had treated Nicolas just as meanly, even if he was the younger of them, in the last years of his seventh decade. His beard was now long and white though his head was bare, his flesh spotted. His hands shook with an eternal palsy, and though he didn't yet use a cane as she did, his steps were now slow and careful. He glared at her, his mouth half open to reveal the gaps of his missing teeth.

She quickly covered up the manuscript on her desk, placing a piece of blank parchment over it. "In the cabinet to the right of the table," she told him. "On the middle shelf in the small brown jar."

Nicolas grunted and left her. She heard him shuffling down the hall back to his laboratory. "Old bastard," she muttered, grimacing. "I should have left you long ago, as Verdette told me I should." Her hand started to go to the sardonyx cameo under her tunic and housecoat, as if by habit, but her arm ached and she never completed the motion.

The two of them were bound together. She knew neither she nor Nicolas would have been as successful without the other, despite the fact that their relationship was so often loveless, rancorous, and bitter. Worse, she was far the better of the two at alchemical work, and that made Nicolas jealous. It wasn't enough that Nicolas surpassed her with incantation and spells; no, he made certain that everyone thought he was the alchemical genius as well. He told the customers for the expensive curative potions the Flamels sold that he had made them himself, when that was *her* skill.

Perenelle would have been comfortable with simply being known as Nicolas' companion and assistant, if she had felt that he appreciated her presence at all, if he—even privately—had acknowledged how important she was to the mutual research they were doing and the accomplishments they'd achieved. After all, Perenelle had been satisfied when she saw how her pushing of Marlon, her first husband, had made him a far better musician. As her father had said, she'd been Marlon's genius, his muse; she would have been content to fill the same role with Nicolas. But he never allowed that; all the credit had to go to Nicolas alone, and he treated her as a possession, a tool he could use and discard as he pleased.

They remained together, bound in long habit, enmity, and spite as well as their conjoined magical and alchemical quests.

When she could no longer hear him, she slid the blank parchment aside, staring down with rheumy eyes at the faint lettering on the ancient paper—one of the pages from the Book of Abraham that she'd purchased from the Jewish man. Nicolas no longer kept his manuscript shop; Telo had died the year after Verdette, and Nicolas had sold off most of the shop's inventory. Perenelle still maintained her own small laboratory in their estate—they lived on the rue des Saints Innocents now, close to the Île de la Cité. The Flamel compound consisted of what had once been four houses but were now interconnected, set on an intersection with a courtyard behind, enclosed by the houses and a stone wall across the back of the property. The courtyard was a garden, private and cool. They had an entire corps of servants, and a household manager—Marianne, who had remained with the Flamels over the years—to watch after them.

Perenelle's laboratory was in the smallest of the houses, as far from the bustle of the estate as she could manage, where Nicolas rarely went himself. She rolled up the manuscript, and grimaced as her knees protested her rising from her seat. Her ivory-handled cane was within easy reach; she tapped her way to the door, where a maidservant looked surprised at her appearance and curtsied. "Are you hungry, Madame? I was just coming to summon you. Cook is ready to put luncheon on the table."

Perenelle waved away the servant. "I'll be working this afternoon," she said. Her voice quavered now; she hated the sound of it. "Tell Cook to have one of the kitchen servants bring me something; she can leave it outside the door of the laboratory."

"Oui, Madame." The maid curtsied again and fled. Perenelle continued on her slow way. Everything seemed to take three times as long as it had when she'd been young. When she'd purchased the papers from the Jewish family, she'd thought that she would quickly solve the riddle of the Philosopher's Stone, that she would soon discover the elixir of immortality. Almost a decade later, she was closer, but the secret still eluded her. She often wondered whether she would be permitted to live long enough to see her experiments through, but thus far God seemed to want her to continue working. Sometimes, on the worst days, she thought that might actually be God's punishment for her arrogance; that, and the fact that Nicolas, in his 70s, seemed destined to remain with her as well.

Nicolas had a half dozen apprentices and helpers working with him. Because of her increasing lack of mobility, Perenelle had in the last few years taken on a single apprentice, a young girl named Musetta. She was a scrawny, homely child, an orphan who had been taken in by one of the charity houses that Flamel money had established. The girl could follow directions—usually with a rather frightened intensity—but otherwise showed little native talent for alchemy and no imagination at all. That was fine with Perenelle; the less Musetta knew, the less she could tell anyone. Perenelle had given her a little room in the same wing as the laboratory; she tapped on the door with her cane as she passed, and the girl emerged in a fluster. "Bonjour, Madame," she said, ducking her head and curtsying as she tucked stray strands of dry, light brown hair under her cap. Her plain, wide country face attempted a smile. "I hope you're feeling well today."

"I'm no worse than usual," Perenelle grumbled. "Here . . ." She fumbled in the pocket of her robe, pulling out a large, ornate key and handing it to Musetta. "Open the doors for me, girl." As Perenelle shuffled down the corridor, Musetta ran ahead a few steps to the stout oaken doors at the end and thrust the key into the keyhole set there. She turned the key; they heard the *snick* of the lock and Musetta pushed the doors open, stepping aside to allow Perenelle to enter before scurrying quickly to light the candles in the room.

The smell always struck Perenelle first: a rich mixture of scents that was nearly overwhelming, everything from the stench of sulfur to the flowery odor of citrus to the metallic tang of the various powders arrayed in their stands near the workbenches. She remembered Verdette remarking on the smell that clung to Perenelle from her hours in the laboratory, and the memory made her smile. Musetta opened the shutters to the two small and high windows in the room, allowing cold winter sunlight to bathe the wooden tables and glisten on the glass jars. A sunbeam pinned two cages, each of which held perhaps a half dozen mice. Perenelle placed the manuscript down at the desk in the corner of the room while Musetta poked at the coals in the hearth. As Musetta coaxed the fire back into grudging life, Perenelle went to the cages, peering in myopically at the animals. The mice in the first cage were gray-haired and elderly, moving slowly and with difficulty as she looked in on them.

The second cage was different. There, the mice peered back at her with eyes like polished black buttons, their snouts wriggling as if they found her aroma as strange as that of the lab. They all looked active, young, and sleek except one: that one appeared to be nearly dead, thin and emaciated, its body trembling, the rib cage visible under patchy skin. The mouse panted as it lay on its side; even as Perenelle watched, its breathing stopped and it went still.

Yesterday, it had appeared no different than any of the others. Perenelle frowned—she would need to make a note of this. "So close . . ." she muttered. So close, but the formula was still flawed, the secret still hidden from her.

"Madame?"

"Nothing," she told Musetta. Musetta shrugged and began straightening up the workbenches. Perenelle wondered how much the girl actually understood. The elderly mice in the first cage were actually younger than any of the "young" ones in the second cage. The mice in the second cage had once been near death from old age, yet now they seemed to be young and vital. In that second cage, Perenelle had taken the most recent version of the elixir she had deciphered from the secret Book of Abraham and dribbled it over their food. The mice had regressed in age as the elixir worked on them, returning to their vital youth—except that, one by one over the next few days, they would age dramatically in the course of a few hours and die, as if their longevity had finally caught up to them and run its course in a matter of moments. She could make them young again, but they would die even sooner than the untouched ones, as if their lifespan suddenly accelerated, with months passing by in moments. Their sudden collapse puzzled Perenelle; nothing in any of the manuscripts suggested what might be the cause, and nothing she added to the mixture seemed to stop it.

So near to success, yet . . .

"Musetta, dispose of the dead one and bring one of the others over to the bench," Perenelle said, tapping the cage. She hobbled over to the bench, settling herself in the chair there, and unwrapping a towel that held a barber-surgeon's tools. Musetta, looking uncomfortable, carried one of the mice over to Perenelle. Perenelle looked at the girl's hands as Musetta handed her the creature: young hands, the skin smooth and elastic. Her own hands, by contrast, were stiff-jointed and wrinkled, the skin liver-spotted, rough, slack, and dry. It was difficult to remember her own hands once being like the girl's.

The mouse wriggled in Perenelle's grasp, and she caught its neck in her fingers, twisting hard. The *crack* was audible; Musetta gasped, her hands going to her mouth as the mouse went still and limp. "Gracious, girl," Perenelle said, "it's no different than what Cook does with the chickens. Really, you must get over this squeamishness." Perenelle flipped the mouse on its back, using pins to tack it down spread-eagled to the surface of the table. She slid a board over to her; there, another mouse was pinned, one from the first cage that she had dissected yesterday, its skin sliced down the belly and pulled back to reveal the internal organs. "I want to see if this one differs inside. Is that so difficult for you to understand? Bring me the *Canon Medicinae*; place it there, on the reading stand . . ."

The candles had burned well down before Perenelle rubbed at her eyes and pushed away the lens through which she'd been peering. There was no significant difference that she could discern between the two dissected mice. She sighed and pushed away from the table. "Musetta," she said. "Clean up the mess here. Unpin the bodies and burn them before they begin to stink. I need to write up my notes." Groaning as she forced stiff joints into motion, Perenelle went to her desk. She took down the large journal bound in red Moroccan leather and unlocked it, opening the stiff parchment leaves to the bookmark where she'd left off. She sharpened a quill with the small penknife in the drawer, uncapped the inkwell at the top of the desk, and began writing, blotting when the pen spattered. She'd been writing for some time, enough to fill the page, when she heard Musetta scream.

"Madame!"

"What *now*, child?" Perenelle asked querulously. Setting down the pen, she blotted and sanded the paper, turning in her chair. "Did you—"

Perenelle stopped. Her breath caught in her throat. Grasping her cane, she pushed herself up and went over to the workbench. She stared down to where Musetta's finger was pointing. The apprentice had taken out the pins from the mouse from the experimental cage, and the creature was writhing and twisting on the table. Even more strangely, the great, bloody cut that Perenelle had opened from throat to tail was beginning to close and heal, as if she were watching the work of weeks in a few breaths. The neck, lying at its strange angle, was moving as well. As they watched, the cut closed completely and the head straightened. The mouse's chest heaved, as if it were gulping air, and it flipped over. Its eyes were open; it panted, and the tail wriggled as it took a step. "Madame, it's a miracle," Musetta breathed. She made the sign of the cross. "Or the devil's work."

"It's neither," Perenelle snapped. She put her hand palm up on the table; the mouse climbed into it, sniffing. She stroked the soft fur, feeling the animal's heartbeat under her fingertips. "Here, put him back in the cage," she said to Musetta, but the girl only shook her head, her eyes wide, refusing to touch the animal. Perenelle gave a huff of exasperation and put the mouse back in the cage herself.

"Finish your cleaning," she told Musetta, "then lock the laboratory and bring the key to me in my rooms. And speak of this to no one, do you understand. No one." *Especially not to Nicolas* . . . She glared at the girl, who nodded furiously.

With a sniff, Perenelle looked again at the mouse, happily nuzzling its fellows in the cage, and left the laboratory.

*   *   *

Two days later, the mouse she had killed remained stubbornly alive, though one of its companions had undergone the sudden rapid aging and died. Then, a fortnight later, that mouse also followed the path of the others, becoming ancient in a matter of minutes and expiring. Another failure.

Perenelle pored over the manuscript, checking her laborious translations and the notes in her book. Perhaps the essential oils she'd distilled hadn't been pure enough? But no, she'd been careful and was certain that there'd been no contamination. Yes, she'd needed to make an educated guess toward what some of the ingredients were, and there were the annoying lacunae in the manuscript—she could have missed something vital there. She had consulted astrology to be certain that she was performing her experiments during the most propitious times; she had crafted intricate spells from the most ancient texts and performed them to speed her work; she had read the Tarot to see if the cards could hint at her mistake.

But . . . if the elixir had ever worked, why weren't there immortals walking the earth now? The logic of that seemed inescapable. Wasn't it more likely the author of the manuscript, whether it had been Abraham the Mage or not, had failed in his quest, or the manuscript would have remained in his possession forever. It had taken years of experimentation and further study for Perenelle to fill in the gaps, to create the current version of the elixir. Years, and her experiments had shown that the elixir wasn't entirely myth. She could give her mice back their youth for a time, but were they immortal? No.

So close, so close . . .

There was something missing yet, something critical. She knew that. She could *feel* it. She spread out the cards of the Tarot again; they mocked her. There was the Magus, but the card was reversed, and flanked by the Seven of Swords, representing futility, and the Five of Swords, defeat. There was no solace to be found there.

She went to their shared library, sneezing in the musty air as she examined the *Mappe Clavicula*, the *Turba Philosphorum*, the fragments of the works of Jabir and Albertus Magnus that they'd managed to collect over the decades. She searched them for additional clues.

"What are you doing, wife?" Nicolas asked her one morning not long after, finding her at the reading desk in the library. He limped into the library—gout had bothered Nicolas for the last several years, making it difficult for him to walk when it flared. He shuffled close enough to peer over her shoulder. "The *Turba?*" he sniffed. "Why?" His eyes, already heavily overshadowed by the white wings of his eyebrows and the ledge of bone above them, narrowed even more, suspiciously. There was only the bare glint of brown pupils in the shadows, coaxed out by the candles on the desk. The nostrils of his wide nose flared. The flames wavered in the breeze of his movement as a knobbed fingertip stabbed at the text. Perenelle longed to tell him that it was none of his concern, that her research was for her own work alone.

But instead she looked away from him, staring at the finger that impaled the parchment. "I've been looking at Abraham the Mage again," she told him. "I had a dream that I mistranslated some of the lines, one I couldn't get out of my mind, and was using the *Turba* to check."

He sniffed again. "If you *have* mistranslated," he said, "you've set back my work, woman. I'll use your miserable hide for a shawl for the precious time you've wasted. A stupid *dream*, she says . . ." He huffed. His hand slapped the desk hard close to her hand and she jumped, her body protesting the sudden movement.

He left her. She stroked the pendant around her neck, but it took her long minutes to calm herself again enough to continue reading.

That evening she went to the laboratory. She took the small vial of her elixir and held it up to a candle, staring at the amber liquid. She shook her head. "We're starting over," she told Musetta. "From the beginning. Maybe this time . . ."

The work took nearly the rest of the year. Perenelle consulted the astrological charts for the timing of each step; she found the purest ingredients she could scavenge in Paris; she had Musetta boil and scrub and scour each of the beakers and retorts so that no contaminants could enter; she oversaw the distillation of the essential oils herself. She measured and remeasured each component.

The mice in the second cage died, one by one, as she worked, all falling to the same rapid and sudden aging. The untouched mice in the first cage gave birth to a new generation, following the usual pattern of life and dying in their normal time.

The work was tedious and long, and she entered each painstaking step of it into her leather-bound notebook: as the winter of 1402 gave way grudgingly to spring, and spring to the sweltering heat of the Paris summer, summer to the colors and slow death of autumn, and autumn to winter once again.

Once more, she had the elixir in a small vial. Once more, she took old mice from the first cage and dribbled drops of the precious elixir into their food. Together, she and Musetta watched the transformation she'd witnessed once before: their fur losing their gray, the bodies becoming young and muscular once again, their energy returning— and this time, the change was more rapid and decisive than before. "You've done it, Madame," Musetta breathed, staring down into the cage.

"We'll see," Perenelle grumbled. "This much I've done before."

Perenelle went to the writing desk to jot down her observations. Musetta cleaned the workbench, then asked permission to leave the laboratory. She seemed strangely eager; shaking her head, Perenelle told her to go. She thought nothing more about it, though her dreams that night were strangely troubled. She woke well before the sun rose, lying there for a time before deciding that sleep wasn't going to come to her, and that she might as well work.

She went to the laboratory, wanting to see if there was any change in the mice, a strange feeling of foreboding enveloping her. She found the door open. Nicolas was inside, her notebook open on the reading desk before him, along with the pages of the missing portion of Abraham the Mage's book, the pages she'd never allowed him to see.

"What are you doing here, husband?" she asked, though she already knew: Musetta. The girl had betrayed her. She wondered how long she'd been whispering to Nicolas about her experiments. Her hand trembled on her cane; her voice did the same.

Nicolas straightened, his wizened face set in a furious scowl. "*You!*" She saw spittle fly from his lips. "You've kept this from me! Devil! *Deceiver!*" He pushed away from the writing desk and the chair went tumbling onto the floor. He went to the workbench and his hand swept angrily across the beakers, retorts, and jars there, sending them crashing down in a thundering spray of glass and pottery.

"No!" Perenelle screamed, hurrying toward him before he could do more damage. The vial of the precious elixir was still there, shivering in its stand. Perenelle struck at Nicolas with her cane; with a laugh, he spoke a word of Arabic: the cane was wrenched from her hand by an invisible fist as she cried out in pain and frustration.

"You miserable, treacherous old hag!" he shouted at her. His hand described an arc in the air as he spoke spell words again. The cane whipped through the air by itself; her hand came up too late. The ivory and silver head slammed into her skull. For a moment, the world went white, as if the snow outside blinded her, and the pain . . . She found herself sprawled on the floor amongst the shattered glass, her head and jaw throbbing, a red stream spilling over her left eye, her body cut in a dozen places, her mouth full of the metallic tang of her own blood. She tried to push to her feet again, glass shards digging into her palms, but the cane came down again, on her ribs this time, and she had to gasp for air. "You did this and you didn't tell me!" Nicolas was raving, his hands still moving. "Well, I don't need you now, wife. I have your notes. I can replicate everything you've done, and do it better."

She managed to get to her knees. She grasped the edge of the workbench to pull herself up, her entire body protesting. She didn't know where Nicolas was, didn't know if the cane would come down again in the next moment. She blinked away blood from her eyes, tried to suck in a breath.

His arms swept across the workbench once more, more glass cascading down. The vial of the elixir shivered in its stand but didn't fall. She heard Nicolas begin another chant, his hands moving in the pattern of a spell, and she knew he intended to kill her, kill her as he had

Provost Marcel, so many decades ago. In desperation, she snatched at the vial; he saw her at the same moment, and the chant stopped. "So that's it!" he exclaimed. "Give it to me!" His hand reached out.

She felt she had no choice. A quick spell, and he could snatch it from her. She wrenched out the cork that plugged the glass. Blood from her mouth dripped down into the mixture, but she tipped it over her mouth despite that. She gagged, feeling the bittersweet, oily stuff mixing with the blood there, and forced herself to swallow. She couldn't drink it all. It burned like fire in her throat so that she couldn't breathe. She told herself that she didn't care if it killed her: she would go to God gladly and plead her case.

Nicolas plucked the vial and the remaining elixir from her nerveless hands as her cane struck at her again; she flailed back, blindly. Her throat, her stomach, were being consumed by fire, the ferocious heat spreading through her body. She felt as if her ligaments and muscles were being ripped apart and knit back together once more. She wiped at the blood in her eyes; she could see clearly again, more clearly, she realized, than she had in many years. Nicolas, his face a rictus of fury, was moving his hands directing another blow of the cane, and she reached out for it—she snared it easily in mid-strike, and she marveled at the hand she saw attached to her arm: the swollen knuckles gone, the skin smoothed and supple: young hands. She heard Nicolas gasp; felt the spell dissolve with his shock. As the cane clattered on the floor, Perenelle doubled over again, her body heaving, the large muscles in her back spasming. She screamed, and the pain released her.

She felt something else as well: the sardonyx cameo that she'd worn for so long also burned on her chest, and she felt something inside it break with the heat of the change being wrought upon her by the elixir: a spell, an old, old spell—and with its death, she knew how Nicolas had held her here for so long. *A Binding, placed within the pendant . . . He forced you to stay . . .*

Nicolas was staring at her, one hand up to his mouth. "What have you done, woman?" he gasped. He took a step toward her, the anger still in his eyes, and she . . .

Still in pain, confused, afraid that he'd use another spell to kill her, she *ran*. She ran, marveling at the feeling of it, at the ease, and at her ability to make the decision she had wanted to make for so many decades. Her clothes were huge around her and she had to clutch at the folds to keep her dress from falling from her body. The sardonyx pendant, empty now of its spell, swayed underneath. She could hear Nicolas shouting behind her, shuffling after her with his old man steps, and she *ran*. She didn't stop running until she was in the street, until she found herself out of breath before Notre Dame on the Île.

There, she sank down to her knees, and she prayed, not caring about the stares of the passers-by around her.

She didn't attempt to go back, though she felt regret at her decision to immediately flee: with her new youth, she could have fought him, could have at least taken her precious notebooks when she fled. She might have had time before he could throw another spell at her.

But the decision had been made in the moment, right or wrong, and could not be undone. She knew that Nicolas would have alerted the house staff. Those among the staff that she might trust, such as Marianne, would undoubtedly no longer recognize her. Her notes—the work that had consumed her life until now—were gone. He would have taken them, locked them away for his own use.

Her long decades of labor were lost to her.

Perenelle was living in rented rooms on the Left Bank, on rue de Feurre near the university. She was still amazed by the glimpses of herself that she caught in windows or bits of polished metal, in what she saw when she undressed at night. She was a young woman again, shed of the weight and wrinkles she had acquired over the years. Her breasts were small and firm, as they had once been; her stomach flat as if she'd never borne Verdette. Her hair was long and lustrous, its dark plaits sparkling with the red highlights that she'd thought gone forever. She was younger in appearance than when she'd married Nicolas; she was, perhaps, the age of the Perenelle who had fallen in lust with and married Marlon, the poor musician.

She marveled. But Perenelle also remembered her mice, and she wondered when the same fate would come for her, to age decades in a matter of hours and die in agony.

The elixir had gifted her with a renewed youth, but she had no idea for how long. The gift had not been without pain and without cost: she was nearly penniless now, the few francs she'd found in the purse tied to her dress's belt had dwindled to bare sols and deniers. Waves of the continuing transformation had racked her body during the first few days; pain that had doubled her over and made her cry out aloud. To the landlady, a middle-aged grandmother named Elita Pelletier, Perenelle had pleaded that her monthly visitor inflicted terrible cramps on her. The woman was sympathetic and brought her a tea that she said would ease the pain—it didn't, but the kindness helped.

Worst, the transformation had touched her mind. The fire that had burned in her body had burned there as well. Her final confrontation with Nicolas was a haze, a memory seemingly overlaid with the mists of years rather than mere hours. And the knowledge she'd spent so long learning. . . . Where was it? She could recall snatches of what she'd once known so well, but those remnants were fleeting and incomplete. She could remember them one moment and they would have vanished in the next. She couldn't hold any of it, couldn't concentrate, and that bothered her most of all.

The languages she'd learned while translating the Book of Abraham and her skill of writing: they remained with her, though. Perhaps she could make a living as a scribe for some of the scholars who lived in the area. Right now she needed time: time to decide what to do, time to figure out what had happened to her, time to plan how to get her notebooks back from Nicolas so she could begin her work again.

Time. She didn't know how much of that she had.

There was also a nagging sense of absence inside her. Something was missing; she felt a need akin to physical hunger inside herself. She thought at first it was the spell that Nicolas had placed in the pendant. Perenelle had taken off the pendant quickly after leaving Nicolas, afraid that some remnant of the Binding would cause her to go shambling back to him. But she borrowed Madame Pelletier's Tarot cards, and the reading told her that the pendant was now merely that: a cameo of herself. She put it back on and held it—it was like holding any piece of jewelry, so she kept it on.

It would remind her to never let anyone deceive her that way again.

The sense of something missing inside remained, however, and was stronger in the presence of certain people—mostly the scholars in the area—as if they could draw her to them, but she wasn't certain why that was or how it manifested or what it was that she could do with it. She felt . . . incomplete. Hollow.

The third morning after her escape, she went from her rooms down to the ground floor of the house. The landlady's husband, Tremeur Pelletier, was a seller of manuscripts as Nicolas had once been, his clientele largely drawn from the professors and students of the university, and the bottom floor was given over to his shop. Perenelle found the shop ledge already open and down, the morning light streaming into the shop, his assistants scurrying about to move the least valuable manuscripts outside for the passers-by to browse through. There were already three or four customers in the shop.

"Ah. Bonjour, M'mselle Cantrell," Tremeur said as Perenelle descended the stairs: he was a stout man, his hair still brown though it had long ago retreated to a thin fringe around his ears, the top of his head so polished it glistened in the sunlight. She had given the Pelletiers her name from when she had been married to Marlon; it had seemed easiest. She doubted that, even if Nicolas tried to find her, he would remember Marlon's surname.

"Bonjour, Monsieur Pelletier," she answered. "It appears that it will be a profitable day for you."

The man laughed—a genuine laugh that boomed loudly enough that those in the shop glanced over to him. "A busy day, but probably not all that profitable," he answered. "Academics are quick to tell me how lamentably poor they are, and students . . . *Phah!* They're beyond poor." He laughed again at his own joke. "Oh—seeing you has made me remember. I heard news yesterday that I thought you might find interesting. Perenelle isn't a common name and so I wondered if perhaps your parents hadn't named you for Madame Flamel, the wife of the alchemist. Well, the news around the city is that Madame Flamel has died. Not surprising, I suppose, given how old she was. I suppose that means she and old Nicolas haven't yet managed to create the Philosopher's Stone, eh?" He loosed another barrage of laughter, but it died quickly. "M'mselle?"

His announcement had caused the world to spin around her once, as clumsily as a dancing bear. Perenelle gripped the railing of the staircase hard with both hands to steady herself. Her heart pounded against her rib cage and for a moment she couldn't breathe. "M'mselle," she heard Pelletier ask, "are you ill?"

She forced a pale smile, and straightened, taking a slow breath. "Thank you, Monsieur," she said, "but no. It was just a momentary dizziness. It has passed now."

"Good," the man said. "Why don't you go to the kitchen? Madame Pelletier is preparing breakfast; I'm sure some of her tea and croissants would help. I confess I'm rather hungry myself."

"Then I'll bring you tea and croissants myself, Monsieur," Perenelle told him, and the man beamed.

As she made her way past the bins of manuscripts to the kitchen at the rear of the house, the musty scent of old paper brought back memories. *Nicolas has declared me dead.* She could do nothing to deny it; certainly no one would believe that she was Perenelle Flamel, looking as she did now. If Nicolas said she was dead, she was dead—he had the money and the influence to silence any questions. He could have an empty coffin placed in the tomb he'd had commissioned for himself a few years before, in the small cubby reserved for her underneath his own lavish final resting place.

She was afflicted with a sudden loathing for the city, with the desire to be somewhere new, somewhere fresh. How could she remain in Paris, knowing that he was also there, knowing that she might come across him, that she might have to deal with him? He was nothing without her; let him *be* without her, then.

She could feel the cool stone of the pendant under her clothing. She clutched at it through the cloth: the only beautiful thing that Nicolas had given her other than Verdette—and like Verdette, a reason she had stayed with him.

So Perenelle Flamel was dead. *Très bien.* She would be someone else.

~

Perenelle Flamel: 1418

IN NEARLY EVERY WAY that the statement could be interpreted, she was no longer Perenelle Flamel. The woman who'd been Nicolas' wife for half a century was a phantom glimpsed through a fog.

She called herself Isabelle Leveque now, the model and lover of Jean Petit, a miniaturist who had once studied with the master Jacquemart de Hesdin and who was now trying to establish his own studio in Chartres near the great cathedral. Jean was one of those Isabelle thought of as "*les personnes vertes,*" the people with the green hearts.

The first years immediately following her departure from Nicolas and Paris in 1402 had been miserable ones. She had thought several times that the fate of the mice on which she'd experimented was about to fall on her. She was both ill and lethargic; she had no energy and found the one thing she'd always been able to do—to concentrate and focus on a creative task—stripped from her. She expected that she would wake each day to find herself suddenly ancient and dying. Instead, the illness and weakness only persisted and became more acute.

She began to think that the elixir had been only a curse: a long, youthful life, yes, but one that was a miserable, muted, and sick existence. A black mood wrapped around her. She prayed to God to take her, to end this. It would be better to die than to live this way.

And God gave her a sign.

She had noticed the green-hearted people even as she prepared to leave Paris, though they were rare creatures. A few of the customers who came to Tremeur Pelletier's manuscript shop near the university were the first she noticed, but even on the street, she might pass one of them. It was as if she could see inside them, into the very core of their soul, and there deep inside would be that pulsing, throbbing verdancy like a second heart: a *soul-heart* is how she thought of it, sometimes very small, and a few of them—a very few—so large that the light of it seemed to threaten to overwhelm the person who contained it. The *les personnes vertes* were usually, she came to realize, people with occupations that required both creativity and inventiveness: writers, poets, artists, musicians, the occasional scientist or thinker, male and female both.

She found, also, that *les personnes vertes* drew her, as if she were a dusty iron filing attracted to a lodestone. When she was near one of them, the weariness and sense of illness seemed to briefly lift in that emerald radiance, to return like a veil of rain afterward.

It took her another miserable year and more to realize that she was able to attach herself to the green soul, that she could touch the radiance with her mind and coax it from the person, that the energy of their soul-hearts could feed her and give her back at least some of the vitality she thought she'd lost forever. It took yet longer to understand that when she did that, the green heart inside the person would also grow in response to her touch, slowly but certainly, and that the growth of their soul-heart led to a corresponding increase in their creativity.

She could exist in a symbiotic relationship with the soul-heart where each fed the other.

Her first experience with that phenomenon was with a musician in Troyes, one of the many towns to which Perenelle traveled on leaving Paris. His name was Philippe, a composer of chansons and motets, who possessed a heart of the most beautiful emerald that Perenelle had yet seen. She heard him playing a lute in the town square and singing. He was perhaps thirty-five, his temples already touched with gray, and he seemed pleased that this handsome, if tired-looking and poor young woman appeared to be entranced by him even while the townspeople passed him by with a few glances and occasionally tossed a denier in his lute case. Perenelle, for her part, was held in the pull of him, and as he played, she could see in her mind the tendrils from the soul-heart, snaking out from him and wrapping about her. It was like nothing she had experienced before.

This was true magic, this was a mage's spell, and she gasped at its touch. Instinctively, she drew the power in with her breath, released it redoubled with her exhalation so that it returned to him. The malaise that had afflicted her for a year now fell away in that instant, as if she were a starving person presented with a feast.

She wanted nothing more than to be with him, this Philippe, forever. Yet it wasn't love—at least not love as she'd thought of it before. There was no romance, no lust, no stirring within the loins. This was another type of communion altogether.

As she stood there, entranced, his voice became stronger, his fingers loosening and nearly flying on the strings of the lute; those passing by stayed a moment longer to hear him, and by the end of the day, there were silver sou mixed in with the deniers. He asked her name; she told him that she was Giselle Boulanger. They talked as he counted his coins—"You were good luck for me, Giselle; I've never made so much before"—and he bought her dinner that evening and shared his bed with her that night. She listened to the compositions that he said he had in his head but never played, and his green soul-heart held them both.

"Giselle" stayed with Philippe a year. He taught her to play, and she found she had a small talent for music herself; he taught her the chansons and told her she had a strong and lovely singing voice. She remained with him until a passing noble heard Philippe and invited him to play for the court in Paris. She had shaken her head sadly when he told her he was going to Paris, when he asked her to accompany him.

"I won't go back there," she told him. "I can't. But you . . . You should go, Philippe. Play for the king. You belong there." Allowing him to leave had devastated her inside, though she tried not to let him see it. His excitement, his pride, and his new ambitions were too obvious, pulsing in the soul-heart of his. She had smiled bravely, had allowed him to give her a pouch of sols he had saved. He had told her that he would return for her, and she knew it to be a comforting lie.

She remembered her father's words: ". . . *that's your gift, daughter . . .*" Her gift—and, it would seem, the payment she must make for the gift the elixir had given her. She realized it as he left her, when she felt the dull malaise slip over her again with the absence of his green heart.

Her gift. Her curse. This would be a bitter payment, which she would make far too many times.

After Philippe, there had been a parade of others, and a parade of false names for her as well. She had been living with Jean Petit in Chartres for two years, since 1416, watching his skill painting miniatures strengthening with each passing month. Already, he'd been commissioned to illustrate a Book of Hours for the Archbishop of the cathedral. His star was ascending fast.

She learned with him and assisted him: she now knew how to mix pigments so the colors would be vibrant and long-lasting; how to trim a brush; how to mix the colors to create new shades and hues. She practiced alongside him, and he helped her find her own skills with painting.

And for two years, and longer, Perenelle/Giselle/Isabelle also tried to rediscover the secret of the Philosopher's Stone, the elixir that had given her this extended youth—for now, sixteen years gone from Nicolas, she still appeared to be in the mid-20s, her joints blessedly loose, her hair luxuriant, her skin flexible and soft, her eyes unglazed by the film of cataracts. She still feared that each day might be her last, that her age would spew suddenly through her in a matter of seconds or minutes, leaving her an ancient, withered, and dead husk, but each day eventually passed and she was still the same. Often, as Jean painted, she would work in a small laboratory in the back, mixing potions and chemicals, poring over manuscripts she had managed to buy, attempting the spells that she half-remembered, reading the Tarot for guidance.

It was a laborious climb back. The indefinable, ineffable spark was still there in her efforts—at least while in the company of another's green soul-heart. But there was a cloud over her mind of the last years with Nicolas. She had to begin again at the beginning, with the experiments she'd started with her father. She began to think that this, too, was a payment for her youth: the elixir had not only made her dependent on the talent of others for her health, but she was little better than a rank apprentice, struggling to comprehend everything set before her.

If she had the notebook, where she'd written it all down: all the formulae, all the processes, all the observations . . . But that was gone. That was in Nicolas' hands. But she persevered, taking in the radiance from Jean's talent and using it for herself while at the same time she strengthened him.

As for Jean himself, he was a good person, a devout Christian who treated her well, though she told herself that she wasn't in love with him, that she wouldn't *allow* herself to be in love with him. He had asked her to marry him several times; she had refused each time even though she knew her obstinacy both puzzled and hurt him. But she could not, knowing that she would either age suddenly and die, or that she would stay eternally the same as he aged. Either way, at some point she would be forced to leave him, because it would be obvious that she was something other than mortal. That was a dangerous thing, for accusations of sorcery or of pacts with Satan could lead to arrest, torture, and a painful, public death.

She would enjoy Jean while she could. And when she no longer could stay with him, she would leave him and Chartres behind and change her name yet again.

Jean came in from his studio, his tunic dotted with paint specks where he'd absently wiped his brushes. "It's too pleasant a day to stay inside," he told her. "Why not take the air with me, Isabelle?" His long nose wrinkled at the smells in the room; he was already looking older to her, the wrinkles deepening around his eyes and on his forehead. *We change so quickly—was it that way for me, too?* "It would do you good."

She sighed and put a cover over the bubbling retort with its smell of sulfur—a walk might indeed be good for her, clearing the fumes from her head so she could think better. "Give me a moment," she told him. "I'll meet you at the door; we could walk to the boulangerie for some croissants . . ."

Outside, the air was more pleasant than in her laboratory, she had to agree. They walked with arms linked along the rue Saint-Julien, nodding to the passers-by who knew them, passing the street musicians, the jongleurs, the puppeteers, and the simply indigent who all vied for the loose change of the townspeople and the devout. With the political uproar in the wake of the horrific, costly defeat of Charles VI's army against the English king Henry V at Agincourt; with the Duke of Burgundy's capture of Paris last month (though the dauphin had escaped the city); with the king being called *le Fou*, the Mad, more than *le Bien-Aimé*, the Beloved; with English troops holding many of the northern cities; with all that, Chartres was uneasy and its mood solemn. The troubles had increased the numbers who came to worship at the great cathedral, the white steeples of which could be seen for miles and which held the *Sancta Camisia*, the tunic of the Blessed Virgin.

"I don't know why you lock yourself inside with the terrible smells," Jean said to her. "I could teach you to paint portraits of ladies for their lockets—pieces they would wear proudly, like the pendant of your mother's that you wear: beautiful work, that. But this alchemy . . ." He shook his head. "It's not good for your health, Isabelle, and it's dangerous as well. I'd hate for you to die before your time."

She nearly laughed at that. "That's not something you should worry about," she told him.

"Ah, but I do," he answered. His hand patted hers possessively. "Though that reminds me of something I wanted to tell you. Speaking of alchemy, the news from Paris is that Nicolas Flamel has died."

Nicolas dead . . .

She couldn't breathe. She staggered, and Jean's arm tightened around hers to steady her, stopping in the middle of the narrow, cobbled street. "Isabelle?"

"I'm sorry," she told him. "I . . . I knew Monsieur Flamel once. He's dead? You're certain?"

"That's what I'm told," Jean answered. "You look pale, Isabelle. You see, it's the fumes; they affect you."

"I'll be fine in a moment," she told him. "Just let me catch my breath . . ."

Nicolas dead . . . If that were true, then she needed to return to Paris to see if she could recover her notebook, and with it, the formula for the elixir. This might be her only chance before it was lost, if it wasn't already too late.

She was first told on entering the city that Nicolas Flamel had last lived in the parish of Saint-Nicolas-des-Champs, but that turned out to be a house for the indigent set over a tavern, an edifice that Nicolas had built a few years after she'd left: another one of his charitable efforts to mask from the public the ugliness that she knew was the true Nicolas.

After establishing that the house was the wrong one, she went back to their estate on the rue des Saints Innocents; she knocked on the door and asked the servant who answered—not Marianne, whom she doubted was still alive—if this was the residence of Monsieur Flamel. Indeed it had been, the maid told her, but the Monsieur had recently died. Perenelle gave her name as M'mselle Jacqueline Fournier, and said that she had unfinished negotiations with Nicolas Flamel and wished to speak to whomever might be in charge of his estate.

The maid brought her into the front parlor. The room had barely changed from the time she'd left, other than being a decade and a half older and shabbier. Not long afterward, a man entered the room. He was in his mid-to-late 40's, portly with red-veined cheeks. His clothing was aristocratic and well-made; his hands were fat and looked unused to any labor. He looked at her with eyes half-lost in folds as he inclined his head to her. "M'mselle Fournier," he said. "I'm Didier Dubois. I am the grandson of Nicolas Flamel and the executor of his estate. I'm told you have been in negotiations with my late grandfather?"

She nearly could not speak. She stared at Didier, whose name she well remembered: Verdette's first son, who she'd last seen when he was ten. She marveled that her grandson could appear to be so much older

than she, that he had no recognition of her at all, that she could
see traces of Nicolas and herself in his face. She wanted to pummel
him with questions: *how are your children, my great-grandchildren? Why,
your firstborn Verdette, who you named after your mother, must be old
enough to have children of her own already. What of your brothers and
sisters? Are they well? Do you ever talk about your grand-mère Perenelle
and remember her?*

But she sat in silence until he cocked his head at her. "M'mselle?"

"I represent my father, who's unfortunately too ill to travel," she
told him finally. "Like your *grand-père*, he is an alchemist. We were
negotiating with Monsieur Flamel for some alchemical manuscripts—
particularly those that had once belonged to your *grand-mère* Perenelle
Flamel." Saying her own name again sounded strange in her ears. She
described the notebook to Didier as she remembered it: the red leather,
the shape, the size. "He had agreed to sell the notebook to us, but then
we heard the news of his unfortunate death. I've come to see if we can
complete the negotiations and take possession of the notebook, which
would mean so much to my father's work."

Didier was shaking his head before she finished. "I regret that I'm
aware of no such negotiations. I've gone through my *grand-père's* corre-
spondence and I saw nothing from your father concerning such a notebook." He raised his hand as Perenelle started to speak. "In any case, I
regret to tell you, M'mselle, that the very day that my grandfather died,
a young man was seen leaving the house with most of the valuable notebooks and manuscripts that were in the laboratory and library. There's
nothing left of any significant value in his library, and certainly no notebook as you describe. I assure you that I would know of it."

A young man, taking with him all the notebooks and manuscripts. . . .
A fist of suspicion clenched her heart, squeezing hard. "How is it that a
thief could enter the house so easily, and at so auspicious a time?" she
asked.

"Indeed, M'mselle," he answered, scowling. "I have asked the
household staff that very question, and none of them can give me a
satisfactory answer. Unfortunately, I live in Reims and so I wasn't pres-

ent at the time. The funeral arrangements were handled by two of my grandfather's assistants—who are also now suspiciously missing, though neither of them matches the description of the thief. I arrived in Paris after my grandfather's body was interred. I understand that there are rumors that some of his manuscripts were buried with him in his tomb, but . . ." His shoulders lifted in a shrug. "You'll understand that I'm not willing to disturb my *grand-père's* grave for rumors. I'm afraid, M'mselle, that your journey here was wasted. If you would like, I can accompany you to the library and his old laboratory, and you may see for yourself . . ."

She was certain that there was no hope, though she allowed Didier to show her the library and laboratory, if only to walk again in her old house. The library had been stripped bare of the important papers: the Book of Abraham was prominently missing, and none of the books on the shelves were her notebook.

All of it was gone. Vanished.

She was terribly afraid that she knew where the notebook might be.

Perenelle spent three days watching the Flamel tomb and noting the flow of people around the *Cimetière des Innocents*, owned by Saint-Germain-des-Auxerrois—a church to which she and Nicolas had heavily contributed. She made especially certain to pass by the cemetery at various times of the night: to see how it was secured; to determine if there were guards or keepers who patrolled the grounds when the sun fled. If any did, they seemed to stay inside the small church attached to the north end.

She couldn't blame them. The stench of the cemetery was nearly unbearable. The *Cimetière des Innocents* had a fabled reputation, for to be buried in the consecrated soil here, it was said, would release the interred soul immediately into heaven. As a result, the cemetery's popularity had led first to the establishment of mass graves for the common people, then to the creation of *charniers*: galleries and arcades built along the cemetery's walls where the dead were placed on display after the flesh had rotted away from their bones, all so that the ground they'd formerly occupied could be used to bury fresh (and freshly-paying) bodies. During the day, merchants hawked their wares from stands set among the charniers, selling religious trinkets. The stench of decaying flesh was as eternal as the sleep of the dead; Perenelle, like most of the visitors, wore a perfumed scarf during her excursions to the cemetery.

The Flamel tomb—where she was supposedly interred as well— was near the entrance to the church. A polished granite sarcophagus mounded over the grave with a newly-carved tombstone set on top of it, the marks of the mason's chisel still fresh on the letters. Three figures dominated the top of the stone, with alchemical signs between them. She stood before the tombstone for some time, trying to imagine Nicolas' body under the sarcophagus.

She could not. But she had to be certain, and there was only one way to prove her suspicions.

On the third evening, she hired two men after some discreet inquiries around the Left Bank. The pair were burly laborers, men for whom a gold tournois would buy silence and obedience. In their grim company, with the moon masked behind thick, brooding clouds, she made her way back to the cemetery in a hired carriage, with shovels and picks hidden under her companions' cloaks.

She had prepared a few alchemical formulae as well, small ones she remembered from the old books and her time with her father, or had gleaned from the manuscripts she'd acquired since leaving Nicolas. As the carriage driver careened away, as if pleased to leave the cemetery and its foul air in his wake, they approached the wrought iron gates to find them secured with a chain and padlock. One of the men raised his pick, but she shook her head at him. She handed the shuttered lantern to one of the men and went to the padlock, sprinkling a compound of rust and bituminous earth into the keyhole of the padlock, and dripping into the lock opening a thick liquid from a vial. There was a hissing and fuming from the keyhole, causing her two companions to step back muttering as the lock shuddered and fell open. She pulled it free of the chain, unlooped the heavy iron links, and swung open the closest of the gates. She held up the vial to her companions before putting it back in the pocket of her cloak. "Remember, Messieurs, I could do far worse to you if you disobey me," she whispered to them. That wasn't true, but the effect was what Perenelle was after. The two men looked at each other, handed her back the lantern, then followed her into the cemetery.

They made their way quickly among the graves to Nicolas' tomb. She pointed silently to it, but shook her head when—again—one of them lifted his pick. She set the lantern on the ground and approached the sarcophagus. Perenelle dusted a pale white powder over it that seemed to glow in the darkness; she took a taper from her cloak, lit it in the lantern's flame, and touched the fire to the powder, stepping back quickly. A flash like summer lightning illuminated the graveyard as a following thunder growled warning. Her cloak was battered by bits of stone as she brought her hand up to cover her face in its folds. When they could see again, the granite of the sarcophagus had been shattered into a hundred pieces.

She hoped that her companions attributed her actions to sorcery and assumed she could cast spells at them that would do similar damage. She nodded to the men, keeping her face stern. They moved quickly forward with their tools, shoveling aside the broken rock. She watched them and watched for the lanterns of any guards, but either no one had noticed or none wished to approach. The *t-chunk* of the shovels, the grunts of the men as they worked, and the sound of stone hitting ground seemed impossibly loud in the night.

After a time, she gestured the men aside and she examined the grave. Under the sarcophagus, she could see Nicolas' coffin, but only that. No boxes which might hold manuscripts, no sign of anything else. She gestured again, and one of the men inserted the flat head of his pick under the coffin lid. He pried up the lid with a grunt as nails and screws protested and wood splintered. The other man grabbed the edge of the lid and opened it up further until it fell aside

The man with the pick dropped the tool. "*Putain de merde,*" he muttered. Both men moved a step back from the grave, crossing themselves. Perenelle took a step forward, opening the shutters of her lantern to shine light into the darkness of the casket.

It was empty, as she had half-expected it would be. Nicolas wasn't here, because Nicolas wasn't dead.

But the coffin wasn't *quite* empty, for she saw a flash of white in the lantern's glow: a roll of parchment, sealed with wax. "Go!" she told the two men. She threw them a pouch holding the money she'd promised them. The coins clinked as the pouch was caught. "You've been paid for your work. Now leave me."

They did so, grabbing their tools and running from the cemetery, their boots crunching on the gravel of the walks. Perenelle reached into the coffin and plucked out the scroll. The red wax seal had been impressed with Nicolas' signet ring. She broke the seal and unrolled the stiff parchment. The words were few, written on three separate lines:

I've taken your knowledge and used it for myself.

In time, I'll take the rest.

I promise you a long and miserable life.

She crumpled the parchment in her hand, her heart pounding. From the nearby church's entrance, she heard the creak of hinges and saw the wavering light of a lantern in the crack of the door. She thrust the parchment into a pocket of her cloak, and she fled.

As she left, she imagined she could hear Nicolas' low, sardonic laughter pursuing her.

3:

EUTERPE

Camille Kenny

Today

"CAMILLE, I need to talk to you. Please call me."
There were at least a half dozen variations of David's plea in her voicemail. "I want to see you, but I'm not going to do that unless I know it's what you want." An equal number sat in her text message inbox. "Call me. Please. Call me."

She deleted them all unanswered.

Emotion warred with logic inside her. Desire fought caution, need battled reserve. *He's one of the few shining ones. If you pass him by, who knows how long it might be until you find another. You already want him. You like him. You need this. You deserve another chance.*

Yes, she answered that internal voice, *but Nicolas may already know, and if he doesn't, he will soon enough. I want to stay the hunter and not the hunted. If I let him glimpse my presence, that all changes, like it did in Vienna. He'll come after me again and maybe this time* . . . She didn't allow herself to finish the thought.

She laid out the Tarot on her kitchen table, she consulted the astrological charts; neither gave her any comfort. She burned incense and chanted a spell of comfort, but she still had trouble sleeping, her fears bleeding off into restless nightmares. A dozen times or more she found herself reaching for her cell phone, holding it and imagining herself dialing David's number, playing over the possible conversational gambits in her head. Each time she put the phone back in her purse.

She tried to find what comfort she could in the group from the *Bent Calliope*. She needed their energy; if she had stayed alone in her apartment without the nourishment of any soul-hearts, she would become sick and lethargic: at least Morris, Mercedes, and the others could keep her going. She went to the bar every night, remaining there as long as she could, soaking in their vivacity, basking in the warmth of their conversations. She had gone home with one of them each night, not wanting to spend the night alone with her own thoughts, talking to Morris or John or Rashawn about their work and taking in their fervor, trying to fill herself with momentary passion to keep her going for another day.

Tonight, she had left with Mercedes.

"Who is it?" Mercedes asked. She spoke in her Puerto-Rican Spanish. Her hand stroked the length of Camille's side from hip to shoulder, warm and soft. Her fingers traced the slope of Camille's breast and tangled in the chain of the pendant, lifting it, stroking the carved face as if she were reading braille. With the touch, Camille felt the connection between the two of them strengthen, felt the surge of energy into and between them strongly enough that she sucked in her breath in pleasure.

"What do you mean?" Camille asked. She also spoke Spanish, but hers was a lisping, proper Castilian. Camille remembered how Mercedes had laughed at her accent the first time she'd heard it. "*You sound like you're from Madrid,*" she'd joked.

In the dimness, Camille glimpsed a smile. Mercedes was lying on her side, facing Camille on the bed, one arm propping up her head. "I mean, *mi amor*, that all of a sudden you're paying so much attention to us that there has to be something else going on. Mind you, I'm not complaining; it's been too long since we've had a chance to be together this often. The others might not see it, but I do—since I've been around you, my writing. . . . Well, you've made me see everything differently, and better. I've sold the last three stories I've written; I've managed to snag an agent for the novel. You've done the same for the others. They were talented before, but now . . ."

"I didn't do any of that. You all did it yourself." The lie came easily. Camille knew the truth: Mercedes had been a mediocre writer, someone with far more ambition than talent. But there had been enough, simmering there deep inside, that Camille had been able to coax it out, to draw it into herself and return it to Mercedes enhanced and blooming, a feedback cycle that benefitted them both. In Camille's mind, Mercedes' creative talent was an emerald well in the core of her body—the soul-heart, the source from which she could draw the sustenance that she needed. Like the rest of those in the group, Mercedes could only be taken so far. Her well was not as deep or as expansive as Camille needed, not alone, but the creative energy of her in combination with Morris and Joe and the others could sustain Camille for a time.

The well: lying there with Mercedes, Camille could dip into those green waters and taste them. She sipped at the energy, her eyes closing. "You did it yourself," Camille repeated into the flow.

Mercedes let the pendant fall from her fingers. She slid her free hand under the fall of Camille's hair, gently cupping the side of her face. She leaned in, her kiss wafting over Camille's lips like a moist zephyr. "Bullshit," Mercedes whispered in English as she drew back, and Camille saw the smile return. "So who is it?" she asked again, back in Spanish. "That Danny guy you brought by the other night, the photographer who hardly said two words?"

"His name was David, not Danny."

"Danny, David, whatever. Tom the bartender told me the two of you left in a cab together. Did you have fun?"

"He's married. You reminded me of that, remember?"

Camille felt Mercedes' shrug, the mattress springs protesting. "All right then, did you have adulterous fun?"

"No."

"Did you want to? Uh-uh-uh, don't answer"—her forefinger pressed against Camille's lips—"I can already tell. So why didn't you go ahead and do it?"

Camille didn't answer. She couldn't answer, since the answer was far too complicated, and she wasn't certain herself of where the truth lay. Mercedes chuckled alongside her. "For an enigma, you can be awfully transparent sometimes, *chilla*. What happened? Come on, you have to tell me."

"You're a writer. I'll just end up reading about it in one of your stories."

"And you claim you don't help me. See? Go on, spill."

She did, as much as she felt she could, as much as she thought Mercedes would actually understand. She told Mercedes about their photography session, about Helen finding them, about the party, about the messages afterward.

"All that is why I'm never going to be in a monogamous relationship," Mercedes said afterward. "I hate to say it, but I really can't blame this Helen; it sounds like she's only trying to protect what she has, but she also sounds like she's entirely the wrong person for David. Of course I'm sorry for you, darling, stuck in the middle. Relationships suck. Too much drama. Great stuff for writing about, though." Her fingers stroked the damp fleece between Camille's legs. "That's why I stick to casual sex. It's much easier. Usually."

"You don't really believe any of that. If you found the right person . . ."

Mercedes laughed again. "If I say it enough times, maybe I *will* believe it, eh? Maybe I already know that right person, and if she were willing, maybe I wouldn't believe it at all." They both knew who she meant, but Camille remained silent, and Mercedes took in a deep breath before letting it out again. "All right, then. You need to talk to him, Camille. Call him back. Go see him. E-mail him. Something. Anything. You should find out where things stand. You know you want to. Just admit it."

With the words, Camille felt the knot in her stomach loosen and she realized that Mercedes was telling her to do exactly what she longed to do. *You need him, and he needs you . . .* "Thank you. You're right."

"I am a Puerto Rican woman, and thus I am wise beyond my years,"

Mercedes answered, laughing. "And now that we have that settled, I'm not going to let this chance to seduce you pass by. Lay back, woman, and let me show you why you shouldn't settle for a man . . ."

"So have you decided to drop this?" Bob Walters asked Camille as she entered his office. He rubbed his thinning hair and leaned back in his chair, sipping at a hopelessly stained mug of coffee. Walters appeared to be badly in need of either a secretary or a shredder. His desk was overloaded with stacks of manila files, arranged in dangerous towers that threatened to avalanche into each other. The desk's top could have been wooden, metal, or veneer—there was no way to tell, since every available inch of it was covered by paper. It had looked the same when Camille had first hired the man. She wondered whether the file cabinets lined up behind him held anything at all, or if they were as impossibly stuffed as his desk. "If you're looking for progress, I don't have any to report. No one seems to have seen your mysterious friend, if he's in the city at all."

Camille laid a check on the papers in front of Walters. He glanced at it and shook his head. "Good money after bad," he said. "Unless you've some better lead to give me."

"I might have," she told him. "Helen Treadway. Currently married to David Treadway. Here's their address." She handed him a slip of paper. "I don't know what her maiden name might have been, but I figure you can find out. It's possible she may be in contact with my guy. I want you to follow her and see." She didn't tell him that she wanted him to do this because, if it were true, then Nicolas would be less likely to notice a professional like Walters tailing Helen than an amateur like herself, and because she thought the possibility rather unlikely anyway. *Nicolas can't have found me already. Helen's little comment was just meant to intimidate me, to keep me away from David.*

"It's 'possible,'" Walters repeated. "And how likely is that possibility, or am I going to be sitting in my car all day and night for nothing?"

"I don't know," Camille answered. "I figured that's what I pay you to tell me. Hire someone else to do it if you want—just make sure he or she's good at it."

Walters let out an aggrieved sigh. A forefinger prodded the check, then his hand covered it and he swept it into the middle drawer of the desk as he opened it, shutting it again emphatically. "You bought yourself another week. I'll check out this Helen Treadway, see where she goes. I'll call you if anything breaks. Anything else?"

Camille lifted her shoulders. "One small thing. I know David Treadway, the husband. If you're watching their place, you might see me."

Walters' eyebrows climbed the craggy ledges of his forehead. "You know him that well, eh?"

"I know him," she said. "And that's all *you* need to know. Call me if you find my guy; if not, then maybe you're right and I'm wasting my money. But you could use it to hire someone to clean up this place."

"What for?" Walters asked. "I know where everything is. Somebody else'd just make a mess of things."

She waited two more days before she found herself on the street outside David's apartment, staring up at the windows that she knew were his studio. She waited as if expecting a sign, perhaps a glimpse of him behind the glass, or perhaps Helen, striding confidently and possessively through the street door. She glanced up and down the street; Walters' car was nowhere visible; that could mean that Helen wasn't there, or it could mean that Walters was hiding himself better than she realized.

The universe remained stubbornly noncommittal. People slid past her on the sidewalks; cabs crawled by in the street, honking their horns at slow traffic; an airplane painted twin contrails in the sky. The city bustled around her, ignoring her and stubbornly refusing to give her anything that might resemble an omen or sign.

She grasped the pendant in her left hand, clutching it so tightly that she could feel the edges of the carved stone pressing into her palm. She recited an incantation. As she closed her eyes and the last words of the charm left her lips, she nodded. David was there; she could almost see him in the darkness behind her closed eyelids: a pulse of emerald light.

She released the pendant. She hurried across the street and up the steps to the street door, and pressed the buzzer for his apartment. "Hey," she said when she heard the intercom click on and David's voice ask who was there. "It's Camille."

The buzzer sounded, and she pushed the door open. Down the hallway, she saw his door open. David stepped into the hallway. Camille couldn't decide if he was irritated or delighted. "Camille. Come in, come in. I had the strangest feeling just a moment ago, like I knew you were outside, then the buzzer rang . . ." He stepped aside as she approached, though she stopped short of the door.

"Helen?"

David seemed to laugh, a nasal snort. "Just come in," he repeated. She did, and stopped almost immediately. The room had changed. The Impressionist prints were gone, though the Klimt was still on the wall near the stairs to the studio loft. The bulk of the furniture was gone. The few scattered chairs and the scarred coffee table all alone in the center left made the room look forlorn.

Camille heard the door shut behind her as she surveyed the room. "Helen's gone," she heard David say. "We've separated—we had a big argument and discussion the day after the party and decided we needed the time apart. That's what I wanted to tell you. It just didn't seem something to say in a lousy message, especially when I didn't know if you were listening. I thought . . . I thought I'd lost both of you."

She turned to him. His gaze was on the bare room more than on her, with the same expression on his face, snagged somewhere between frown and smile. "I'm sorry," she told him, though part of her felt nothing but relief. "I feel responsible."

"Don't." He spat out the word, then lifted a shoulder as if to soften the sound. "This was coming whether you were around or not. You just forced us both to see what we already knew but wouldn't admit." He laughed again; a shattered and uncertain amusement, the sound echoing against the empty walls. "She's living with some friends. Left me this place since my studio's here." Another bitter laugh. "Not that I'm going to be able to afford to keep it—which I think was her plan. It was her salary that usually paid our rent."

Camille said nothing. She could feel the resentment and anger and uncertainty inside him, dark as smoke. His eyes glittered with moisture, but he blinked it away, sniffing hard once. He looked again at her. "I was going to the *Bent Calliope* tonight to find you, if I hadn't heard from you. I was going to try your apartment again if you weren't there. You can believe that or not, but it's the truth."

"I believe you."

He nodded. "I'm glad you came by."

He was standing close to her. He lifted his hand as if he were about to touch her, then let it drop back to his side. He was staring at her, and as she brought her hand up to the pendant, hanging outside her blouse, he followed her hand's movement. He took a step toward Camille, looking down at her. She wanted nothing more than to give in to the impulse to sink into the embrace she knew was waiting, to lift her face up to his for a kiss . . .

"David . . ." His hands were on her shoulders. She felt him pull her toward him, but she resisted. "David, you—we—need to think about this. You don't know how dangerous this is. The other times . . . Being with me hasn't always been good for my lovers."

"I'm not them," he said, the words a husky whisper. "Besides, how many 'other times' can there have been for you?"

More than you would believe . . . She couldn't say that to him. Not now. Probably not ever. "You don't know me," she told David. "Not yet, and not well enough."

"I've at least met your friends. They seemed fine."

"I don't think you and I usually have the same kind of relationship with our friends."

She watched David's eyes narrow at that, the same suspicion she'd seen in his eyes when he'd first met the others at the *Bent Calliope*, when he'd seen her hugging and kissing each of them, when he'd seen the casual touches, the looks. "You mean . . . ?"

She took a long, slow breath, watching his face. She nodded. "Yes."

His eyebrows arched higher. "*All* of them?"

"Yes. All of them. At one time or another."

"Oh." The word came out strangely flat and emotionless. "That's not the answer I expected."

"Helen told me that you had affairs with your models."

His face colored in embarrassment, which almost made her laugh. "I'm not going to deny that, but I'm not proud of it, either," he said.

"And you really shouldn't be, but none of that matters to me," Camille told him. "I don't care if it was love or lust or just sex. Do you understand? I don't care what you did in the past, David. All that matters is what happens going forward and what we can be together. I want you to feel the same way about me."

"These 'relationships' with your friends . . . Will *they* be going forward? I'm not saying I can't handle that; I just . . . I just want to know." She didn't believe him. She rose up on her toes and kissed him quickly for the effort, though.

"I won't promise to be monogamous, David. We can start that way, if it's what you need, and maybe we'll end up that way, but I can't promise that it will *always* be that way—and I won't expect it of you, either. I'm fine with whatever happens as long as you don't lie to me, and I won't lie to you. If that changes things for you, then at least you know up front. So *does* it change things?"

She could see him mulling that over, staring somewhere past her. Finally, he shook his head. "No, I don't think it does." His hand stroked her shoulder. "The other day, when I was taking those shots of you . . . Would you have let it go further, if Helen hadn't interrupted us . . ."

She shook her head. "No. At least I wasn't intending for that to happen. I was your model, nothing more—just like I told Helen. Did I want it to go further? Yes, I did, very much. But it wouldn't have been fair to her, and it wouldn't have been fair to you, either."

He cocked his head toward her. "Not fair to *me*? I don't understand."

"No, you don't. You don't understand what being with me would mean. You can't."

"Camille, that's true of every new relationship. They're all steps into the unknown. Let me make up my own mind, unless it's *you* who aren't certain. Is that it, Camille? Then tell me this is all one-sided. Tell me you don't feel what I'm feeling."

Camille opened her mouth, but there were no words. She could sense him, could caress the deep well that existed inside him, so full of potential—not just for him but for her also. She could see the rich energy pulsing around him, a verdant aura that beckoned her, that pulled her hunger to the front of her consciousness and made her realize just how much she'd missed this type of closeness, this linkage, this union. "I . . ." She heard herself say. "David . . ."

His arms came around her, and this time she didn't resist. His lips sought hers, and she responded to his heat with her own fierce hunger. Her mouth opened to him. When they broke apart, gasping, his eyes were open, staring at her. His taste remained in her mouth, sweet. "*On n'aime que ce qu'on ne possède pas tout entier*," Camille whispered.

"What?"

She smiled at him. "Nothing," she said. "Come here."

She curled her arm around his neck and brought him down toward her.

"What's that you're singing?" David called out from the little dining nook in Camille's apartment. Camille, in her robe, was stirring scrambled eggs and mushrooms over the stove. She hadn't realized she was singing anything at all.

"*Si, si luci adorate*," she told him. "It's Vivaldi."

"Classical, eh? You have a nice voice."

"Thanks."

"Got another question for you. Do you really believe in this crap?"

Camille craned her head over her shoulder to see him—dressed only in his boxers, his hair sleep-tousled—holding up a Tarot card: the Two of Discs, she noted. *Change and fluidity*. It seemed an appropriate card for him to have plucked from the deck.

She'd spent the first two nights at his place, but she never felt entirely comfortable there. Helen still lurked in strange places in the apartment: in the scent of the bathroom, in the arrangement of the kitchen, in the very absence of her. David's wife was a ghost haunting the place, though David didn't seem to notice her. Camille had finally told him that she needed to get back to her apartment and to her life—and if he wanted to, he could spend the night there.

He had. She wasn't certain yet that she was any more comfortable here; David was a new factor. But he fit her perfectly. His soul-heart fed her well, and she was already feeding him in return, even if he didn't know that yet.

"You call this 'crap'?" she asked him. "Didn't your mother teach you that it's terrifically impolite to make fun of other people's beliefs?" The eggs had firmed up; she slid a serving into each of the two plates to the side of the stove. She sprinkled shredded cheddar cheese over the eggs, added the toast she'd already buttered, and a fork. A plate in each hand, she went to the table where he was sitting and slid the plate in front of him. She kissed him and sat down. Verdette padded between her feet, leaning hard against her legs and purring—the cat entirely ignored David, and Camille hoped he'd already learned that he should do the same with her: a line of dried blood down his forearm was a reminder of when he'd tried to pet her, that first night. "Put the card back on the deck and eat," she told David.

"You didn't answer my question," he said as he put the card back on top.

"Answer my question first. What makes you think that the Tarot is crap?" she asked.

He glanced at her cautiously and took a forkful of eggs. Swallowed. "Tastes really good."

"Uh-uh," she told him. "You're not getting out of this that easily. Why is the Tarot crap?"

David frowned and tapped the deck of cards. "Come on, Camille. Magic, the occult? Seances and fortune-telling and stuff like that? Isn't it all crap and fakery?" He took another bite. "Aren't you going to tell me how wrong I am?"

She shook her head. "No, you can believe whatever you want, as long as you're bright enough to admit it when you find out you're wrong. I was just curious."

"Am I going to find out I'm wrong on this? Are you going to prove it to me?"

"Maybe," she told him. "Or someone else might show you." She hated saying that—it was as if she might conjure up the very scenario she most hoped to avoid. Her fears rose inside again: *This has been a mistake. A mistake . . .* "Right now, I'm going to eat my breakfast. Then I'm going to take a shower."

"Want company?"

"Why do you think I mentioned it? You can scrub my back."

He grinned.

They finished eating quickly. The hot water ran out before the shower was finished.

After drying her hair, Camille put her robe back on. She found David looking at the paintings propped on the easels and along the walls of the spare bedroom she used as a studio, and she sat on the bed to watch him. He moved from one to the next, then scanned the supplies on the desk in the middle of the room. She could feel the emerald sea inside him pulsing as he looked at them; the feeling made her want to take up a brush and begin working. "Oils," he said, leaning close to one painting and sniffing the surface. "I thought everyone was using acrylics these days."

"I'm just an old-fashioned girl. Do you paint?"

"I used to. I started out painting; took a lot of studio classes in college, and studied Art History. Then I fell in love with photography and haven't touched a brush in years. Your paintings remind me of the one in my apartment: the way you elongate the figures, the colors, the way you place them on the canvas."

"The Klimt," she said. "Yes, Gustav was . . ." She stopped, finding her breath caught in her throat. ". . . a big influence. Maybe too much of one. I've had a couple gallery owners tell me the paintings are interesting, but too derivative."

"You don't agree." His tone made it a statement, not a question.

"Doesn't matter if I do or if I don't. That's their opinion. I don't let it upset me."

"Klimt's paintings were flatter and more decorative than yours, and your anatomy is more realistic. Not only that, but you're using washes and building up the color in transparent layers like a Renaissance painter. Klimt never did that. Look how your shades almost glow in the finished ones." He grinned at her. "Art history," he said. "Sorry. Still, that technique's pretty much a lost art. Now everyone just slaps on the paint in big opaque splashes."

"I told you I'm old-fashioned."

"You're good, too."

She smiled at the compliment. *I'm good, but I can also hear what you're not saying, that there's still something missing: the flair that would make the work exceptional. Good, but not great. Competent, but not quite a master. I can bring out in others what I can't find myself.*

"Glad you like them," she said.

He continued to pace the room as she watched him, leaning against the doorway. *Three days now with him, and already the energy has come back. I feel like picking up the brushes that I haven't touched in too long. I feel like working with the chemicals and doing the experiments I've given up for too long. I feel like I can find myself again. I feel like I've been dozing for decades and am finally waking up once more.*

A motion caught both their eyes: Verdette, emerging from the half-open closet door. David crouched down, his hand stretched out toward the cat. Verdette hissed even as Camille said "I wouldn't. Really."

David shook his head, but he straightened up. "Cats usually love me. Honestly."

"Not Verdette. I'm afraid she's very much a one-person cat. Sorry."

"Ah, she'll give in one day. She'll have to."

"I admire your confidence," Camille told him. Verdette leaped onto Camille's lap, leaning into her possessively as David glanced at the closet, opening the door fully. Glass jars gleamed in the sudden light, the chemicals bright inside them. Retorts and burners huddled on the top shelf, and in one corner, notebooks were crammed onto the shelf. "Jesus," he said. "What have you got here? A meth lab? Or do you make your own pigments, too?"

"I *do* make my own pigments, but I've an interest in chemistry beyond that. You said you used to paint? I dabble in chemistry, too."

He eyed the closetful of jars. "Isn't this a tad dangerous?"

"Not if you know what you're doing. And I do."

"Uh-huh." He closed the closet door gingerly. "You can sing. You're interested in the occult. You paint. You stockpile chemicals in your closet. You own the most un-cat-like cat I've ever known. What other secrets are you hiding from me?"

Camille stood—Verdette growling in annoyance and slinking away—and took a step toward David. She dropped the robe from her shoulders, standing naked except for the sardonyx pendant between her breasts. "Do you see any secrets?" she asked him.

He shrugged. She could see him struggling to keep a stern face. "I don't know," he said. "But I do think this requires a thorough examination . . ."

Later, she was standing at the window in the breakfast nook of her apartment, leaning against the wall and looking out the window down to the street, two floors below. It had rained that morning, but the clouds had been shredded by a strong wind out of the west, and the sun had returned just in time to create a stunning, blood-hued sunset.

"Take off your clothes," David said.

She looked at him, standing at the opening between the nook and the kitchen, dressed as she was in jeans and a T-shirt, and laughed. "Again?"

He hefted a camera in his hand—the Hasselblad, its single glassy eye staring at her. With the motion, Camille felt the surging of the green heart inside David, and she understood. "It's the light," he told her. "I love the way it's streaming through the colored bottles on the windowsill, and I love the way it's caressing your face. The colors on your body would be gorgeous." As he spoke, she felt the embrace of the talent he held, spreading out and wrapping about her, making her a part of him. She inhaled as if he had touched her with his own hands, the warmth of the sun suddenly very insistent. The feeling was sexual, yet even more intimate than that. *Yes, I remember this . . .* This was her gift and also the curse: she *needed* this connection as much as he did.

Camille wasn't simply sharing David's body; she was sharing all of him, breathing him in and exhaling him, the two of them briefly one. She could *see* the colors now: not just the core emerald but the rest of the spectrum as well, brightening where his soul-heart touched her, and streaming back to him enhanced. His green heart contained the rare tints and hues she'd seen so few times before.

She wondered at how he couldn't see it also: it was all so vivid, so real in her mind.

Silently, she removed her clothes, stepping out of them and kicking them aside. She left on the pendant; if he noticed or cared, he said nothing.

"What do you want me to do?" Camille found it hard to speak. The electric snarling of the aura surrounding them filled her ears.

"Stay close to the window—yes, right there, so the sunlight is just touching the side of your face. Now look at me . . ." The shutter was already chattering, running through exposures as he held down the button with one hand and adjusted the lens with the other. He didn't speak again, just let her move as she wished: gazing at him, at the camera, feeling herself filled with his energy. It burned in her, made her want to go to the other room and take out paints and brushes; to sing; to take down the notebooks and delve again into the intricate alchemical world.

This is how Nicolas finds you. This is what he can sense and what draws him. You were hunting him; now he'll also be hunting you in return. Are you ready for him? Are you prepared to lose David in order to take him out? You're going to bring Nicolas to you, and he'll attempt to destroy everything you have, and he'll destroy you too if he can . . .

The thought pierced the euphoria of the sharing, dimming the brilliance, and she heard the Hasselblad resume its motorized chattering. "Yes, keep that expression, Camille—you look so melancholy all of the sudden. No, no, no, don't change anything . . ."

He continued to shoot pictures for another few minutes, then set down the camera. Camille sat in one of the chairs around the nook's small table. Her fingers toyed with the pendant. Her hands were shaking slightly, as if she'd consumed an entire pot of coffee, a shivering high running through her body. The immaterial glow about David had paled, but the connection was still there, tenuous, and she sipped at it while she could: a dessert after the feast.

"You know, I've never seen you without that," David said. It took her a breath to realize what he meant.

"Oh," she said, lifting the pendant. "No. I told you that on the first day; I never take it off."

"Whoever gave it to you must have meant a lot to you."

"He could have," she answered. "But he fucked it all up, and I was stupid enough to let him. Now it's mostly a reminder to myself. A talisman, perhaps."

His lifted eyebrow asked the question.

"It reminds me to be careful about who I trust and how far I trust them," she answered.

"Ah. More magic." He nodded, but he didn't press her further. He seemed to be waiting for her to say more if she wanted to do so, and yet he was comfortable with the silence. That sensitivity made her smile. She put her hand on his, still cupped around the motor drive of the camera. Underneath the table, Verdette rubbed up against her bare legs, her tail curling around Camille's ankles.

"Y'know," she told David, "here I am all naked and you're still in all those clothes. It hardly seems fair . . ."

Camille's cell phone rang about nine in the morning. She threw the covers aside and slid from the bed, trying not to disturb David. Verdette, curled up against her legs on top of the covers, mewled in irritation, yawned, stretched, and padded after Camille as she went into the hallway to pull the cell phone from her purse. She glanced at the screen: Bob Walters. She hit the "Accept Call" button with her finger and put the phone up to her ear.

"Hey," she said. "You're up early."

"Yeah, and now you are, too. Sorry." He didn't sound particularly apologetic. "But you said to call if I found your guy. I'm not sure, but I think I might have."

The news made her stomach clench, caused her fingers to tighten around the phone's gel case. "You might have?" she repeated.

"Yeah. I was following up on this Helen Treadway—and thanks, by the way, for not telling me she'd left your friend, and I hope you're having fun with him. It took me two days to track down her new place— and I saw someone yesterday coming from her apartment who matched your description: short guy, but his hair's more blond than dark and cut really short. About the right age, and his features are close enough. I followed him, but he managed to lose me—which, let me tell you, isn't easy to do. He just kinda vanished." She could hear the annoyance in his voice. "So far, he hasn't come back. I've set up a 24/7 surveillance on Ms. Treadway's new apartment if he does, and my people have instructions to follow Helen whenever she leaves. We'll track him down eventually. It all depends on how fast you want it to go."

Verdette jumped up on the hall table, trilling anxiously. Camille reached out with a hand to stroke her. "What do you mean?"

"I mean there are things I'm allowed to do, legally, and things that I'm not. Those things that I'm not allowed to do are a lot more expensive, but they might save time."

"Things like . . . ?"

"Things that you're not going to know about," Walters answered, "because I won't tell you."

"Fair enough. How expensive?"

"Ten large, upfront, with no guarantees. And none of that's going to me, incidentally."

Camille sucked in a breath. She heard a cough from the bedroom, then a naked David appeared in the hallway, leaning against the wall and rubbing sleep-tousled hair. She watched him as she spoke to Walters. "All right. I can get that to you," Camille said. "Go ahead."

"Yeah. I'll go ahead when your check clears or you hand me the cash. You've seen my office; I don't have that kind of money just sitting around gathering dust."

"It'll take a couple days. I'll have to liquidate a few assets." She saw David's eyebrows rise quizzically.

"It takes as long as it takes. In the meantime, I'll keep doing what you've paid me to do. Maybe we'll get lucky and we won't need the other methods. I'll keep in touch, okay?"

She heard the abrupt click of the receiver on the other end. She brought the phone from her ear and touched "End Call." "Who was that?" David asked. He yawned and crouched down, holding his hand out toward Verdette, who pointedly ignored him.

You told him there wouldn't be any lies. "My financial adviser," she answered. "He thinks that everyone keeps the same schedule he does."

"You should tell him that artists aren't usually the 9 to 5 types."

"I'll do that. Next time." She put the phone back in the purse, then smiled at him. "You really have one of the worst cases of bed-head I've ever seen. I think we should take a shower and get rid of it, and then we'll fix some breakfast. Sound good?"

"Sounds delicious," he said. "Both options."

INTERLUDE THREE

Costanza Bonarelli & Gianlorenzo Bernini

1635-1640

Costanza Bonarelli

1635 – 1636

S HE HAD NEVER GLIMPSED a soul-heart that was quite the match of Gianlorenzo Bernini's. Fortunately, or perhaps unfortunately, Costanza (she rarely thought of herself as Perenelle anymore) was at that time married to Matteo Bonarelli.

Matteo Bonarelli was another in a succession of minor relationships. His green soul-heart was small and shallow, but he was also a gentle man and kind to her, and if she occasionally strayed from him to be with another person whose soul-heart beckoned more to her, he would always take her back. She did not love Matteo, though she liked him well enough. She often felt guilty for her use of him, but he complained rarely and accepted her as she was—that was enough.

Matteo could sustain her and he was understanding, so she remained with him as he moved from Arezzo, where he was making a meager living with his sculpting and painting, to Rome.

To Rome: where the already famous Gianlorenzo Bernini—knighted by Pope Gregory XV with the title of Cavaliere—had his studio.

Matteo, on their arrival in Rome, had taken her to view the *Apollo and Daphne* that Bernini had created for the recently departed Cardinal Scipione Borghese. Costanza had been, quite honestly, stunned. She knew Ovid's story, of course: how Apollo had been smitten by the nymph Daphne, pursuing her, and how as he was about to capture her she transformed herself into a laurel tree. Here, somehow captured in a single, massive piece of white Carrara marble, were the two mythological figures: a heroic Apollo reaching to touch the side of Daphne, who was captured in the midst of her metamorphosis. The figures were life-sized and nearly seemed to breathe. The artist's chisel had managed to coax an incredible range of textures from the stone: polished skin, granular earth, rippling cloth, fluttering leaves, and windswept hair.

"*Possiede la mano del dio,*" she heard Matteo whisper in awe as they gazed at the work—*He possesses the hand of God*—and she could only echo his sentiment.

Cavaliere Bernini, under the weight of more commissions than he could easily fulfill, was gathering around himself a cadre of skilled studio assistants to help. Matteo, with Costanza at his side, presented himself, his references, and his master piece—a small "Daniel and the Lion" in bronze—at the artist's studio.

After seeing the man's work, she expected to see a similarly heroic figure approach them. Instead, Bernini was a gaunt man in his 30s, wearing a filthy sculptor's smock well-dusted with marble fragments, a mallet still clutched in one hand. His brown hair was lightened with marble dust; he had a mustache upturned at either end and a wedge of straggling hair down the center of his chin; his restless but intense eyes were the color of old polished oak.

Early on, in the wake of her discovery of Nicolas' empty grave, there were many she found with soul-hearts that were fiery and huge, in which she could have easily lost herself. Yet she always held back, settling for someone with lesser talent and lesser visibility. *Nicolas might find you if you're too obvious*—that was her thinking. In the intervening two centuries, Costanza—under far too many names for her to remember—had lived with a long succession of minor artists: painters, sculptors, musicians, singers, writers, philosophers. She'd sought out groups of them at times, using their collective energy to keep her healthy, active, and anonymous. She'd done so with one eye always looking behind her, half-expecting that Nicolas would appear and make good on the threat of the note he'd left in his empty grave. In truth, she wasn't certain she would recognize Nicolas: if he had, like her, returned to his youth after taking the elixir, well, she remembered him mostly as he had been in old age. He could have passed her on the streets many times, and she might never have noticed him.

After two centuries, it was easy to nearly forget him entirely. The only thing she kept of his was the sardonyx cameo. That, she wore every day; she wasn't certain why—it had become her talisman, her charm. It was as much a part of her as her breath.

She continued to search for those with the green soul-hearts, *les personnes vertes*. She had no choice in that; without their nourishment, she became sick and lethargic. She wondered if Nicolas had the same compulsion.

The creative energy on which she was destined to feed was more than mere sustenance. While she remained in the presence of their green hearts, she could also pursue her own talents: painting; learning an instrument; discovering that she had a singing voice that could be trained; pursuing scholarly studies. And, of course, trying to rediscover the knowledge that Nicolas had stolen from her, the secrets she'd once written down in the notebook.

She made progress, though slow and laborious. She bought old scrolls and tried to translate them; she purchased chemicals and powdered minerals and solvents, and played with them. But thus far she had found little success, though she uncovered the occasional small spell she could work, and she'd reproduced several of her father's old experiments. But there were months and even years where she couldn't set up a proper laboratory or couldn't obtain the materials she needed, because she had to move on—as she inevitably did.

If those to whom she had become muse became abusive or jealous or suspicious of her, she would leave them and her current identity; for those special ones who became companions, friends, or lovers, she would wait until her lack of aging became painfully obvious, and she would vanish one day from their lives, never to be seen again.

The soul-heart before her now, in whose glow she stood like a frozen woman before a great fire . . . this soul-heart wouldn't be one of the quiet ones, one of the hidden ones. If she stayed here, if she bound herself to this one, there would be no hiding—not from a soul-heart this large.

Is this really what you want?

There was no answer inside her to that question. Not yet.

Costanza barely dared to breathe as she felt Bernini's green heart. His radiance filled the entire studio and enveloped her. She had never experienced a soul-heart like this before, already seething and full, yet with still-untapped potential she could bring out. She could feel the glow beating and pulsing as Bernini walked around the table on which Matteo's sculpture had been placed, fingers prowling his chin hair as he examined Matteo's work closely. Twice, as he paced, his gaze flicked suddenly from the piece to Costanza. He seemed to regard her with the same appraising intensity that he did Matteo's sculpture.

She knew then that he felt her presence as she felt his.

"You've a decent resume and come with good recommendations," Bernini said to Matteo at last. His voice was a low growl, vibrating with the same intensity as his gaze. "Competent enough work, this. I can pay you seven silver scudi a month. When you finish your work for the day, you may use your studio space for working on any commissions of your own. I also have a man who will rent you lodgings close by for a reasonable rate. You can start this Martedì, if you wish."

"Pardon me, Cavaliere Bernini," Costanza interrupted. She knew Matteo; he would take the offer, thinking it was the best he could do. "My husband is worth more than seven scudi when he will be crafting angels and cherubs for you that no one will doubt come from the hands of the master himself."

Bernini's piercing gaze found her again, and he laughed, a long and low chortle. Matteo looked down at the floor. "And pray, Signora Bonarelli, what do you think I should pay your husband?"

"I should think an artist with his undoubted skill deserves no less than twelve scudi a month."

Bernini's mouth seemed to tighten in amusement. "I can offer eight. No more."

"Eleven," Costanza answered, "and the Cavaliere should be grateful for the bargain. Rome is an expensive city."

Bernini gazed again at Matteo's sculpture. His long fingers slid over the bronze figures as if willing them to move. "Ten," he said finally, "and your husband should be grateful that his wife's beauty makes it difficult for a man to argue with her."

"Agreed," Matteo interjected quickly, his head coming up as Bernini nodded and gestured to one of the workers in the studio to come over.

"This is my brother Luigi. He'll show you the studio and your working space, and put you in touch with the man for your housing." He turned to Costanza and gave a slight nod of his head. "Signora," he said, his gaze holding hers for a breath.

"Cavaliere," she answered with a curtsy. She smiled at him, and his lips turned upward under his mustache.

And with that, he was gone.

She already knew that they would be lovers. She already knew that she had to feed on his great talent. She could make it blossom so it might shake the very world.

Every day, Costanza would bring Matteo his noon luncheon. She would eat with him, sitting at his bench and gazing at the work on which he was engaged: a portion of the coat of arms that would go over the tomb of Pope Urban VIII. The marble angel rested on the bench, rough-cut with the marks of the chisel still apparent and—two weeks into Matteo's employment in Bernini's studio—now half-freed from the marble block in which it had been trapped.

After their lunch, Costanza would wrap up the plates and cups and place them back in the basket, and take her leave of Matteo. On her way from the studio, she would stop in the well-lit main room, where Bernini himself was working on the allegory of Charity for the tomb. The massive group—a mother clasping her child, with the weeping child alongside her, the mother gazing down sympathetically toward the crying infant—was only half finished, yet the face of the mother was already captivating in its expressiveness. Costanza could feel the artist's soul-heart throbbing as he worked, tapping at the chisel with a wooden mallet, flakes of marble falling away in a slow snow.

And each day, like a lover furtively stealing a kiss when she thought no one was looking, she would open her mind to that green heart and take it into herself, letting its fire course through her, breathing his energy in and breathing it back to him increased and enhanced. He never looked at her, but she knew that he felt her behind him, knew that he must feel her touch.

Today was no different; she left Matteo and paused at the open archway that opened into Bernini's personal studio. She leaned against the arch; sunlight poured in from the southward-facing windows, making each marble dust-mote sparkle and gleam against the emerging figures from the Carrara marble block. Bernini was sculpting the folds of the robe the mother wore, tapping each wrinkle carefully and glancing occasionally at a small-scale clay model resting on his workbench. She closed her eyes momentarily, letting herself open to the soul-heart, tasting it as it moved through and around her, nearly fondling it, her fingers moving involuntarily as if to touch.

He'd never spoken to her before, never indicated that he knew she was watching him. But today, he spoke, without turning around. "Have you ever sculpted, Signora Bonarelli?"

"No, Cavaliere Bernini. I've painted a little. That's all."

"Then you must try. Come here." He turned to her finally, gesturing with the hand holding the chisel. She set down the basket and approached him. He gave her chisel and mallet, turning her to face the sculpture. Up close, the mother's face peered down at her, smiling. Bernini moved behind her, his body a heat along her back. He took her hands in his own, closing his fingers over hers. His breath lifted the hairs on the back of her neck. "You have to let the stone talk to you," he said. "Let it tell you what's caught inside. You must be careful, because what you take away, you can never put back. So it's best to go slow. Gently. Now, go on, place the chisel there, in the groove I just made. Angle it a little more . . ." His hand guided hers. "Now, tap the end with the mallet; firmly, but also softly. You want to coax and tease the stone, not tear at it. You want to dance with it, like a lover."

She struck the chisel, feeling his guidance of her stroke. A flake of stone fell away, continuing the groove along the line he'd started. His voice was a low, hungry growl in her ear. "There. You see how it feels? The power of creation in your very hands—can you feel it, like you're caressing the marble? She wants you to release her. Again—once more."

Another tap, another small flake of stone. She felt his lips touch the back of her neck in the same instant, and she breathed in sharply at the touch, her body leaning back against his fully. "I've felt you watching me, Signora." His breath was warm; his lips brushed her skin again and she gasped. "Every day you've watched, and while you did, I could see her more clearly—the mother inside the marble. She's you."

His green heart wrapped her like a cloak, warm and safe and comforting. She inhaled the power with every breath and gave it back to him, redoubled. The radiance swelled around them like an ocean tide, and there was a hue to it that she'd never seen before: a thread of brilliant lapis lazuli that wound about the two of them.

"What now, Signora?" Bernini asked behind her, his muscular arms enclosing the two of them, the statue forgotten. "You must tell me. You must make the choice."

She turned in his arms, looking up at him. She handed him the chisel and mallet so that his arms relaxed around her, but she didn't step back. She remained there, her body against his. "I'm going home," she said. "You know where that is."

His gaze held hers, his lips slightly parted. She touched them with a finger, letting it slide slowly down his face to his chin, then away. "And your husband?" he asked.

"He'll be here for hours yet—and he has a small commission of his own to work on as well."

"And what of afterward?"

"Matteo is pleased to be associated with Cavaliere Bernini's studio.

Neither of us would wish to jeopardize that relationship. What Matteo doesn't want to see, he won't see."

"Ah, so that's how it is." He set mallet and chisel down on the workbench, bending away quickly and moving back in almost the same motion. His hand stretched toward her; his forefinger curled under the silver chain around her neck and lifted the cameo from where it nestled between her breasts. "That's a beautiful piece," he said. "Is it Roman?"

"French," she told him. "And very old. It's been in my family for a long time."

"It looks much like you." He slowly allowed the cameo to slip back to its resting place. His forefinger brushed the slope of her breast, the barest touch.

She thought he might bend down to kiss her, but she saw a shadow on the archway and took a quick step back. Bernini's brother Luigi appeared a moment later. He stopped when he saw Costanza, and a knowing smirk appeared and vanished on his face. "Gia," he said to Bernini, "Cardinal Barberini is here and asks to speak with you."

"Ah." Bernini took another step back from Costanza. "Tell him that I'll be right with him, as soon as I change my smock. Give him some wine and refreshments while he waits."

Luigi gave a short bow of his head, then smiled at Costanza. "I'll inform His Eminence that you'll be there directly, then. Sorry to . . . interrupt." The pause before the last word was tangible. Luigi bowed again and departed.

"I'll leave you to your business, Cavaliere Bernini," Costanza said. She picked up her basket again and moved toward the archway.

Bernini called after her. "After I speak with His Eminence, I will probably take a walk to clear my head," he said. "Perhaps if I walk toward your apartment, I might find a glass of wine waiting for me there?"

Costanza stopped. She turned and smiled toward him. "You might," she said. "If you walk that way."

Costanza Bonarelli: 1638

"YOU ARE FANTASTIC, *il mio amore*. I am so fortunate that you came to me."

Gia—as she called Bernini in their private moments—stroked her face with his hand: not her face of flesh, but one wrought in polished marble. They'd been making love on the couch in his private chambers. The afternoon was chilly for early September; Costanza pulled her chemise around her shoulders though Gia was padding naked around the room.

She'd sat for the marble portrait bust over several weeks a year ago, not long after they'd become lovers. Gia had first sketched her from several angles, then created a model from clay to use as a rough guide for the finished work. The clay model, now dry, cracked, and fragile, still resided in her and Matteo's house near the studio. She sometimes wondered if the physical reminder bothered Matteo, but he said nothing to her, as he said nothing when she took out her chemicals and worked with them, or when she painted the miniatures that she sometimes sold in the market, or when she sang as she walked to the market for bread and vegetables. Matteo, she knew, loved her even if she did not love him, and he wore Bernini's horns as gracefully as a man could. She suspected that Matteo somehow understood what she had done for him and his soul-heart, how it was her gift that had made him worthy of being in Bernini's studio at all.

The radiance of Gia's green heart enveloped them both, shot through with that deep and saturated blue, the hue she'd never glimpsed before, and which she was certain signified the true bond between them. *Per-*

haps this time it is love, she sometimes told herself. *Perhaps this time that's what I'm feeling.*

The thought nearly frightened her. She'd thought she'd been in love with Marlon back when she was Perenelle, but even before he'd died, she'd realized that she'd fallen in love with an idealization of him, not the man himself. She'd thought she'd found love with Nicolas, also, in those first days. She'd believed he was a kindred spirit who would treat her as a peer and an equal, but that, too, had been a cruel chimera. Since taking the elixir, she'd been with men—and a few women as well—who she liked and admired, but had that been love, or was she mistaking that emotion for the need to feed on their soul-hearts? The soul-hearts kept her healthy and active; without them, she quickly became frail, ill, and lethargic. Without them, her existence was a living purgatory.

It was easy to call something "love" when it was the nourishment that she must have.

She wondered if it was the same for Nicolas. She wondered if the elixir had demanded the same of him. She wondered where he was, if perhaps he regretted having left the threatening note in his coffin for her to find, if his anger and bitterness had been quenched in the intervening centuries.

Now, she breathed in Gia's glow as if it were the purest of air, and she gave it back to him replenished and strengthened. She imaged that they were two beings combined into a joyous, unified one during those long hours that she was sitting for him, even more than when they lay together afterward, her legs wrapped around Gia's hips and her arms clutching his head to her breast as they found release together.

"The world will look on you this way and fall in love with you as I have." Gia smiled and came over to her. He took her hands and leaned down to kiss her. "You are happy?"

"*Sì,* I am very happy," she told him.

Costanza and Bernini had been lovers for almost three years now. Matteo's cuckoldry was a quiet joke throughout the studio though no one dared mention it aloud in case Cavaliere Bernini might overhear and be angry enough to fire them—the master's temper was nearly as legendary as his skill. The marble bust he'd created of Costanza fairly shouted to the world that the two of them were lovers.

In the piece, her face stared boldly at the viewer, her chin lifted almost in defiance, her hair swept back as if in a soft wind, her lips slightly parted. Her chemise was open, a blatant invitation, with one side falling back to show a hint of her cleavage just above the base. She was depicted not as a saint or an angel, but as a sensual and erotic woman. Gia kept the bust in his own rooms; he had turned down, he claimed, a dozen offers to sell it. "I want you only for myself," he told her. "No one else can have you."

She laughed at that, pleased, and hugged Gia, kissing him deeply. She felt satisfaction in knowing that her image was so well received, that Gia had placed so much of his love and talent into crafting it. The two of them reveled in their love, in Costanza's role as Bernini's true muse. It was difficult to hide their affection, and they did so poorly.

There were artists in the studio who whispered that this was Bernini's finest portrait bust, the epitome of the craft. The gossip around the studio was that the latest patron to inquire about purchasing it was Abramo Maroncelli, who was said to be a distant nephew of Cardinal Antonio Marcello Barberini, Pope Urban VIII's younger brother. *"Luigi says that Signor Maroncelli offered the Cavaliere more than the Holy Father paid for his own portrait bust."* That was the whisper that Costanza had heard; whether it was true or not, she didn't know, but the bust remained on Gia's mantel.

"I would like you to come with me in two days to Cardinal Barberini's *palazzo*," Gia said. He was still looking at the bust, as if trying to see any flaws in the finish.

"Gia?"

He turned to her, smiling. "Oh, I know. Propriety. Matteo will also accompany us—the cardinal wishes to talk to me about designing a fountain for his gardens, and Matteo will be my chief assistant for the project; that will be reason enough for him to be there. I'll tell him later today after you've left."

"He'll be pleased to hear that," Costanza said. "But why am I to come?"

"His Eminence's nephew will be there as well." He gestured back to the portrait bust. "He has said to me many times that he wishes to see if the face that I've sculpted truly matches the reality. Since I've refused to sell him the bust despite his entreaties, it would seem that's the least I can do for the poor young man."

"I don't know, Gia . . ." She started to tie the neck strings of her chemise, but Gia came over to her and stopped her. He slid the sleeves down her shoulders once again, letting the chemise pool around her waist. He kissed her, his fingers sliding through her thick hair. "I'll give Matteo a few extra scudi for the two of you to buy some proper clothes. Can't have my assistant looking as if I can't afford to pay him, can I?— and especially not the woman who has given me such inspiration."

The blue hue in his green heart deepened as he spoke the words. She could taste it, as sweet as a summer orange.

Yes, she thought as she opened her lips to his. *This must be love. This time, it must be.*

One thing she could never get used to was the rapid change in fashions. Fancy dress for women just a decade before had required wearing a hooped and stiffened farthingale under the dress, with the high bumroll in back that, to Perenelle, made an exaggerated mockery of the female form. Men wore embroidered *justaucorps*, knee-length coats with ruffled, turn-back collars, worn over tight breeches and hose. Both men and women had worn huge ruffs, so that their heads seemed to be offered on a platter of stiff and intricate lacework, which forced the wearers to keep their chins lifted. Coiffures were high, with a woman's long hair drawn up through a wire cage on top of her head, and the wealthy adorned themselves with ostentatious jewels and pearls.

The wealthy still retained the ostentation, the jewels, and the pearls, but at least the fashions had relaxed somewhat. The manteau dress Costanza wore was looser and made of silk, with several petticoats underneath, the lacy ruff now lay over her shoulders rather than tight around her neck, and she could wear her hair down once more. Both Gia and Matteo wore large, plumed hats, shirts with laced cuffs under slashed and puffed coats, colorful breeches rather than hose, and boots of soft, supple leather, but the resemblance ended there. Matteo's outfit was plainer and more workmanlike, as befitted his status, but Gia shone and gleamed like a true noble. Gia's hat was especially large and ornate, and adorned with a golden brooch that lifted one rim, and the lace around his neck was pinned with a large pearl. He appeared comfortable here, as if he were used to the luxury that surrounded his patrons.

Costanza clung to Matteo's arm as they were ushered into one of the waiting rooms of the *palazzo*. Servants stood in their uniforms at either side of large double doors at the other end of the room. The molding around the walls and framing the door was gilded and intricately carved, the ceiling was arched and painted with a scene of the muses of arts and sciences gazing down from the clouds, done in a false perspective that made Costanza dizzy, glancing upward. "Orazio Gentileschi," Gia said, following her gaze. "Competent enough, if a bit old-fashioned, but everyone says his daughter's actually the better painter."

There was a quick rap on the doors, and the door-wards quickly pulled them open; Cardinal Barberini entered, accompanied by a secretary. The cardinal's robes were black, but he wore the red hat of his office. The goatee that hung from his chin was white and his face was thin, and he walked carefully with a slight stoop; Costanza imagined that he'd been a tall man in his youth. He walked up to Gia and extended his hand; Gia bent to kiss his sigil ring. "Your Eminence," he said, "this is Matteo Bonarelli, who will be assisting me with your fountain, and his wife Costanza."

"I'm pleased to meet all of you," the cardinal said, as both Costanza and Matteo also kissed the ring. His voice was a pleasant baritone. "My secretary has prepared the plans and the contract, and I'd like to go over the sketches that you so kindly sent me the other day, Cavaliere Bernini. Perhaps Signora Bonarelli would like to wait on the portico overlooking the garden while we discuss my expectations? It's pleasant there, and I'll have someone bring refreshments."

Gia gave her a surreptitious nod, and Costanza curtsied to the cardinal. "Thank you, Your Eminence. That's very kind."

"Then let's get to work. Gentlemen?" Cardinal Barberini and his secretary left, and one of the door-wards bowed to Costanza.

"Signora, if you'll follow me . . ."

The portico was indeed, as the cardinal had said, pleasant and warm in the afternoon sunlight, and servants quickly brought out a pitcher of cold water and plates of fruits and vegetables, setting them on the small table next to her seat. The gardens the portico overlooked were splendid, bright with squares of flowers, predominantly in reds and purples, all arranged in a hexagonal pattern around a central court with geometrically-trimmed hedges and stone benches. Costanza wondered if that was where the fountain was to be placed.

A hedge-maze lay just beyond the court, and Costanza could see several workers in the garden: pruning and trimming, pulling weeds, watering the plants. She found herself wondering at the cost of maintaining such an extravagance. It was a raw display of power and wealth, to have this much land and be using it not for growing food but simply for pleasing the visual sense.

"It's beautiful, is it not?" The voice spoke *Romano*, but with a decided French accent. Costanza turned, rising from her chair, to see a man standing at the entrance to the portico: dark-haired, clean-shaven, perhaps in his early twenties, and dressed in expensive clothing, a ruff of gleaming, intricate lace draped over a black jacket with wide, slashed sleeves, embroidered with gold and silver thread; through the slashes, Costanza could see bright red satin.

His gaze traveled down her body and back to her face. His face cocked slightly to the right as he studied her.

"I'm sorry," the man said. "I didn't mean to startle you, Signora. I am Abramo Maroncelli, the cardinal's nephew, and you—well, I must say that Cavaliere Bernini's work, despite his mastery, pales in comparison to the flesh." He smiled and bowed low as Costanza flushed and smiled. "It's obvious that God himself is still the master sculptor, and all of our artists' attempts to reproduce such beauty are futile."

"Signor Maroncelli, your uncle would undoubtedly think you blasphemous, nor would I think he'd approve of such obvious flattery."

"Ah," Maroncelli answered, "but it was he who told me that I would find a flower fairer than any in his garden in this very spot."

"His Eminence may be forgiven for his aged eyes, and for being overly polite in front of my husband and Cavaliere Bernini. You should be more careful, Signor; isn't your uncle also the Cardinal-Protector, in charge of the Inquisition?"

Maroncelli's smile broadened, and he bowed again. "He is, and I agree that I wouldn't care to be put to his tests. My uncle is utterly relentless in his pursuit of purity and truth." For a moment, Maroncelli's face took on an expression that seemed almost familiar to Costanza, his gaze unfocused and internal, as if he were contemplating something that pleased him. "Relentless," he repeated, then seemed to shake himself from reverie. "But that's hardly a subject for a lady such as yourself."

"Indeed," Costanza agreed. She wondered if she had somehow met Maroncelli before, though she thought she would have remembered such a meeting. He was staring at her as intently as she watched him. A suspicion came to her suddenly, paired with a feeling of dread in her stomach. *No. That can't be . . .* "Your accent, Signor," she said to him hesitantly. "Are you from France?"

"I am," he answered. "From Cagnes-sur-Mer, near Nice. My mother was French, my father was from Genoa. I was educated in Paris for a time; I'm afraid that still colors my speech." The ease with which he gave her the tale eased her suspicions somewhat. "Your own Romano is very good," Maroncelli continued, "but do I detect the barest hint of an accent? Perhaps also French?"

"You've an excellent ear then, Signor," she told him. "Most people don't notice. You're right; I have spent a little time in France myself and can speak the language, so perhaps I've a bit of that in my speech."

"You've a Parisian lilt, I should think," Maroncelli added, and Costanza struggled to maintain the smile.

"I was in Paris, yes," she told him. "Very impressive, Signor. I applaud you."

"I'd guess that we're close to the same age. Why, it's likely we were in the city at the same time. We should have known each other then."

"Indeed, Signor. But fate obviously had different plans for us."

"Ah, but I don't believe in fate," Maroncelli answered. "I believe that we create our own fates—even though it sometimes takes us far longer than we'd like to accomplish our goals. But if one persists, and if one lives long enough . . ." He lifted his hands and let them drop again. Again, the gesture seemed oddly familiar to her. "And if one could live forever, why, just think of what you could accomplish," he said as she stared at him. "It was a pleasure to meet you, Signora. I won't take any more of your time. I can see why Cavaliere Bernini chose to immortalize your face. I'm certain that with your beauty and charm, Cavaliere Bernini's work isn't the only time your likeness has been crafted in stone."

He smiled then, and his gaze drifted down to her décolletage. Costanza had to force herself not to reach for the cameo hidden under the cloth there. She felt a sudden coldness.

"Signora," Maroncelli said, bowing again to her. "Enjoy your day. Perhaps I'll yet convince Cavaliere Bernini to allow me to possess you." He let that statement linger for a breath. The corners of his mouth twitched. "In your marble form, of course," he added finally.

With that, he bowed quickly and left her. She realized that she'd been holding her breath, and let the air rush from her in a gasp. She pressed her fingers against the sardonyx pendant under its blanketing of linen and satin.

Those eyes . . . It could be Nicolas, but I don't know . . .

She stared out at the garden, but she found no solace in its manicured beauty.

∼

Costanza Bonarelli: 1639

WHEN NOTHING HAPPENED FOR a few months, as winter gave way to a new year and advanced toward the awakening of spring, Costanza nearly forgot her meeting with Abramo Maroncelli. The worry and the burning in her stomach slowly ebbed away, and she went days without thinking of him and wondering.

"Stanz," Matteo said. "I'm glad you've come home." She'd come back that afternoon from a liaison with Bernini to find him already sitting at the table in their small kitchen. He looked tired, the skin under his eyes dark, his black hair matted and beginning to thin, his chin stubbled with gray now. Even the glow of his soul-heart—never anywhere near as fiery as Gia's—was paler than usual. For the first time, she saw his age—*I can't stay with him for many more years, not without pretending to become old myself—and that would be another, bigger lie between us.* She straightened her cloak and tucked her hair back under her cap. She wondered if he could smell Gia on her, though she knew he'd say nothing.

"Did Cavaliere Bernini release the assistants early?" she asked, though she knew he hadn't, for he'd been with her. The pretense mattered; it allowed them both to pretend that neither of them knew of her affair with Bernini. If such things were spoken aloud, if the affair were acknowledged, then Matteo would have to act, for his honor's sake. Neither of them wanted that.

"No," he answered. "I asked to be released early today."

"You're not feeling well?" She felt a sudden rush of concern, and went to him, touching his forehead. He leaned back in his chair, shaking his head and tapping a packet on the table that she hadn't noticed that morning when she'd left.

"I'm fine," he told her. His voice was tired also. "But I've received a letter, one that concerns you."

"A letter? From whom?" She felt the tightening in her stomach again. She was afraid that she knew.

"From my sister in Arezzo," he told her, and her fear receded for a moment. He unfolded the letter, his forefinger prowling the letters. "She tells me that a priest came from Rome to talk to her two weeks ago—he came under the sigil of Cardinal-Protector Barberini, wanting to know about *you*, Stanz: when and how I met you, who your family was, where they were from."

The burning in her gut returned. "What did she tell them?"

"She was frightened—as no doubt the priest intended. She told them what she knew; that your family name was Nesci, that your parents were from Florence. The priest told her that he would go on to Florence, and he would talk to your family there. He is probably there now." Matteo lifted his head from the letter. "Why is the Cardinal-Protector asking about you and your family, Stanz? I don't understand."

"I don't know," Costanza said, but she knew. She knew.

"Well, I'm sure your family will answer whatever questions the Cardinal-Protector might have. Your mother's still alive, isn't she?"

She nodded, mutely. She wondered whether the Cardinal-Protector—or more likely, Abramo Maroncelli—already knew that there was no Nesci family in Florence, or if there was, they wouldn't know of her. And as for Maroncelli, she was just as certain that if she investigated his background, she'd find that he was no more a nephew of the Cardinal-Protector than she was his niece.

She'd find that his identity was as false as her own. But what would Maroncelli do with that information?—that was the question she needed to answer.

"I thought you'd want to know," Matteo told her. His sympathy, his empathy, his obvious concern tugged at her, making her feel guilty. *Here's true love,* she thought. *It's sitting right here in front of me. But it's not enough. I need more than mere love.* She felt tears welling in her eyes, and she willed herself not to show them. "If there's something wrong," he continued, "if you can tell me, maybe I can help, or we could talk with Cavaliere Bernini together and ask him to use his influence . . ."

She was shaking her head before he finished. "It's Signor Maroncelli," she told him, "the man who wanted to purchase the bust Cavaliere Bernini made of me. Perhaps he thought that he could get my family to intercede on his behalf. I'm sure it's nothing more than that."

Matteo glanced at the letter again. He folded it, pressing the creases with his thumb. She went to him, bending over him to kiss the bald spot on the back of his head. "You're so very sweet to have been concerned," she said to him. She took his hand, pulling him up from the chair. "Come with me. You're home early; why don't you let me reward you for your concern, eh?" She kissed him; he didn't respond at first, but she kissed him again, harder and more urgently, and finally she felt his lips relax under hers.

She led him to their small bedroom, hoping he could not glimpse the worry and guilt beneath the false smile she gave him.

She'd seen Signor Maroncelli slip into Gia's office clad in a sumptuous, expensive, fur-trimmed robe. The sight had frightened her.

Over the last few weeks, not long after Matteo had received the letter from his sister, Gia had become increasingly withdrawn from Costanza. Gia always worked harder than any of his assistants. He would labor with mallet and chisel from dawn to evening, his arms still strong when his assistants, Matteo among them, had stopped with arms aching and trembling from the constant impact of steel on marble. But recently, he no longer made time during the heat of the afternoon or at dusk to come to her, and when she went to the studio with Matteo's lunch, he would avoid her. The few times he had come to her since, during the day in her own rooms, he'd been rough and quick, almost angry in his lovemaking, and the lapis hue that had invaded his green heart had gone pale, receding like a moon tide.

"What is wrong, Gia?" she asked him the last time as he was dressing, rushing as if in a hurry to be away from her.

"Nothing." The word was a snarl, nearly spat out.

As she so often did, in distress she found herself reaching for the pendant around her neck, under the nightdress bunched over her waist. "Gia, you can't say 'nothing' when I see the pain in your eyes and when you won't even look at me after we've been together. Have I done something to offend you?"

"If you don't know, then I certainly can't tell you," he answered gruffly.

"What do you mean?"

But he gave her no clear answer. He left her, weeping, in Matteo's bed.

That was the difficulty with love, she knew now. With love, there was the possibility of pain and grief. When there was only affection, as she had for Matteo, she could not be hurt. Not this way. Not this deeply.

She would remember that.

She'd gone to the studio today hoping to talk with him, but the door to his room shut behind Maroncelli, and if Gia had seen her there, standing amidst the bustle and dust of the studio, he'd given no sign—and with Maroncelli inside, she didn't want to knock.

"Perhaps I can make it better with Gia, Signora," a soft voice said from behind her: Gia's younger brother Luigi. He had no green heart at all. Costanza had come to detest the man over the years; his voice was smooth as oil, and his hands seemed to constantly find her arms, shoulders, and sides. More than once, he'd given her conspiratorial winks as she and Gia engaged in conversation, or he'd find excuses to stand behind Gia when he was sketching her, her chemise unbuttoned, and she'd feel him staring at her. The models that Gia employed were all hired through Luigi, and Costanza knew from Matteo that those who modeled for Gia himself were those willing to grant Luigi extra favors for the privilege. A few months before, she'd even spoken to Gia about Luigi's unwanted attentions, but he had only laughed at the time.

"Better?" she asked Luigi now, almost angrily. "What do you know, Luigi?"

His lips twitched with an imitation of a smile. He smelled of garlic and onions from his lunch. "My brother, he's a jealous man, Signora. He doesn't like to share."

"I have a husband, Signor. Your brother knows that."

Luigi's smile flickered like a windblown candle. "Indeed, and perhaps he wonders how many besides him you've entertained in your husband's bed?"

She felt her face going hot. "Then your brother worries about nothing."

"Nothing?" Luigi's hand rose, slid down her arm, and Costanza took a step back from him. He followed, still too close to her. He leaned in to her, his voice soft. "Is that what you say? With a young woman as attractive as you, Costanza, how could he not be suspicious? If your husband allows one person, even one as famous as Gia, to soil his bed, why not another, or three, or many? If someone were whispering that poison in Gia's ear, why shouldn't my brother listen?"

"Who?" Costanza demanded. "Do you mean Signor Maroncelli? What is he whispering?"

"Why, that you were willing to open your legs for whomever comes to your door," Luigi answer. "And I am thinking, if that's true, why wouldn't she do that for *me*, who has wanted her no less than my brother for so many months?" His chuckle was low and sinister. He licked his lips.

Anger flared in Costanza. Almost without volition, her right hand drew back and slapped Luigi hard across the cheek. The crack of her hand against his flesh was loud in the studio; his cry of pain louder. "*Merda!*" Everyone was suddenly looking at the two of them: Costanza standing with a scowl, Luigi bent over with a hand to his cheek. Back in the studio, she heard someone laugh. She also heard the door to Gia's office open. He was standing at the door, staring at her; she caught a glimpse of Maroncelli behind him; the man was smiling and chuckling also. They both quickly turned away. She tried to imagine Maroncelli's face as that of a much younger Nicolas than the one in her head.

Yes, it could be him . . .

"Cavaliere Bernini," she called to Bernini. "A moment . . ." Bernini had to hear her plea, but he gave no sign. He had already closed the door. Again, out in the studio, one of the assistants laughed. She whirled about to face Luigi once more, and he took a step back as if he thought she was going to strike.

"*Vaffanculo!*" Luigi said vulgarly, with a wave of his hand.

She spat at his feet and left the studio.

Matteo had been given a small commission from one of Cardinal Barberini's priests: a Communion chalice. He'd told Costanza that he would be working on it late, so she was surprised when she heard the door to their two-room apartment open not long after she'd retired for the evening. "Matteo?" she called. There was no answer, but she heard footsteps in the outer room and a throaty belch. Someone bumped into the table there: she heard pottery rattle and a muffled curse.

"Matteo?" she called again, tossing aside the covers. In the night, she could barely see. She grabbed the candle from the stand beside the bed and spoke a single spell word in Arabic, one of the first spells she'd re-learned: yellow flame flickered to life on the wick. At the door to the bedroom, a man leaned against the jamb: Luigi.

He was drunk; she could see that immediately from his disheveled look and the half-lidded expression. "*Buona sera*, Costanza," he said, slurring the words and wiping the back of his arm across his mouth. "I saw your husband at the studio, and so . . ."

"Get out!" Costanza shouted at him. "You're drunk; get yourself home!"

"Costanza . . ." Luigi leered at her in the candlelight. "You look so lovely. Let me stay with you."

"That won't happen," she told him. "I'm telling you that you must leave."

His lips curled in a sneer. "That's not what Signor Maroncelli told me. I talked to him. He said that you've had dozens mount you, that even he had shared your bed. He said that you'd welcome me."

"Signor Maroncelli?" Costanza gasped. She saw the candle shiver with emotion. "He doesn't know me at all. I swear on the Virgin's mantle."

Luigi scoffed. "I told you—it was Signor Maroncelli who told Gia about your whoring," he said. "He said he'd thought he recognized you from the bust; that's why he'd wanted to buy it, and once he saw you, he knew for certain. He knew you very well, he said. He told Gia that he could tell him what he hadn't sculpted." Luigi's gaze was on her breast, and she realized that he was looking at the sardonyx carving on its chain. She remembered that Gia had asked her to take it off when she'd sat for the carving, but she'd refused. Bernini had shrugged, and gone on to simply leave out the pendant in the sculpture.

Maroncelli knew that . . .

Her suspicions hardened into certainty, a knife in her gut.

Luigi took a step toward her, his arms open as if he expected her to step into his embrace. Instead, she made as if to throw candlestick and holder at his head. Luigi ducked and stepped back. "Costanza, *il mio amore . . .*"

"I'm not your love. And if you take another step, I'll guarantee you'll never make love to a woman ever again. I promise you that."

He ducked his head, like a scolded child. "Costanza, why can't you love me as you do Gia? Besides, Gia is away; he told me he has business elsewhere tonight . . ."

"Luigi, the wine fumes have addled your head. I tell you again, you must leave."

"Not even a single kiss?" He pouted dramatically.

"Not even that."

He slumped down against the doorjamb, sliding down to a sitting position. "The wine exhausts me," he said. "Let me at least sleep here."

Costanza sighed. "No, you can't sleep here," she told him. She set the candle down on the bed stand again and went to him. "Give me your hands, Luigi," she told him, and when he responded sleepily, she pulled. He tried to grab her as she brought him to his feet; she beat his hands away easily, then put his arm around her. He staggered with her toward the door of the small house. She opened the door, gratefully letting in the cool night air, which helped to dispel the fumes emanating from Luigi. After the dimness of the house, the moonlight seemed nearly as bright as day. "Now," she told him, "go home or go back to the tavern. I don't care which."

"Costanza," he slurred, "you are so beautiful and kind . . ." He bent his head down and planted a sloppy kiss awkwardly on her cheek.

"Get yourself home," she told him, pushing him away.

"I could make you happy," he told her. "More than Gia. I don't care how may men have already had you." He looked at her so piteously that she chuckled.

"I'm sure you will make some other woman happy one day," she told him. "Go *home*, Luigi."

He tried to kiss her again and missed, then waved to her and started to walk off. As he took a few awkward steps from her, Costanza felt an emerald presence even as she heard Gia's voice shout angrily into the night: "Luigi!"

Bernini strode from the shadows, half running as Luigi turned. The artist was carrying a metal bar, and as he approached his younger brother, as Costanza screamed at the two of them, he swung it so hard that she could hear the sound of it in the air. Luigi's arm came up to shield himself, and the first blow knocked him down to the cobbles. "*Bastardo!*" Bernini shouted at his brother. "*Testa di cazzo!*" The bar swung again, hard, and Luigi howled in pain as it struck him in the chest. He pushed himself up, half-crawling, half-limping away. Costanza ran to Bernini as the artist lifted the bar yet again, grabbing at his hand. He pushed hard and she collapsed to the ground. His green heart pumped, but she could not touch its anger. She reached out to him, unable to speak. "*Puttana!*" he shouted at her: *whore!* "To come out on the street half-dressed, and with *him* . . ."

He spat in her direction, then turned back to Luigi, who was limping away. "Gia, no!" Costanza shouted. "This is a mistake!" She spoke another spell word as Bernini lifted the iron bar again. A flash of light filled the street, and a crack of deep thunder rolled away. For a moment, even expecting the flash, Costanza was blinded. Around them, she could hear doors and windows opening, and people calling out. Blinking, she saw Luigi turn the corner, saw Gia rubbing at his eyes, the iron bar rattling on the stones of the street. He picked it up and staggered away in pursuit of Luigi.

She started to follow, then stopped, sobbing. She could feel the stares from her neighbors, could hear the amused comments. She gathered up her nightdress around her, and went back into her house. She pulled the door shut behind her, and collapsed to the floor, weeping.

Matteo came home not long afterward, as she was sitting at the table in the front room, head in hands, her face streaked and her eyes red with weeping. "Matteo?" He would not look at her. He walked past her toward the bedroom. "Matteo, it wasn't my fault. Luigi came into the house; I threw him out. That's all. But Gia . . . Cavaliere Bernini. He was waiting . . . He thought . . ."

"I know what he thought," Matteo said. "Luigi came back to the studio, and the Cavaliere not long after. He took a sword from his office and threatened Luigi with it until his brother ran. Luigi's taken sanctuary at the church of Santa Maria Maggiore."

"May God have mercy on us," Costanza breathed.

"Indeed," Matteo said.

"I have to talk to Gia," she said desperately. "Luigi said that it was Signore Maroncelli who has caused this. I need to explain to him about Maroncelli . . ."

"The Cavaliere won't see you," Matteo interrupted before she could finish the thought. "He told me to tell you that. And I've been released from his employ. I'm to go in tomorrow morning and clear away all my work and tools."

Her chest hurt; she could not breathe. "Oh, Matteo . . . This is all my fault."

"Sì," he answered dully. "It is." He said nothing else. He went into the bedroom and closed the door. She followed him. He was standing there, silent and stricken, his shoulders slumped. He seemed to be star-ing at Bernini's clay version of Costanza's bust, placed on a high chest on the far side of the room. She came up behind him, putting her arms around him, so hard that she felt the pendant pressing into her skin between them. His green heart, so pale alongside the glory of Bernini's, flickered with the blue that bound him to her, the blue that she had always ignored and never returned, the blue that was there even now, after all this.

"Matteo," she husked, "can you ever forgive me?"

"You are what you are," he answered. "I knew that when we married."

"But even knowing, I have still hurt you."

"Sì." The admission burned. It flamed in her breast.

She released him, going to the clay bust. She picked it up, and with a cry, threw the sculpture hard against the wall. It shattered, going to dust and fragments.

They slept together that night, back to back without touching. In the morning, when he went to Bernini's studio to collect his things, she accompanied him. Bernini wasn't there. Silently, she helped Mat-teo pack away his tools and the works of his own on which he'd been working. The other assistants watched silently, pretending not to notice either of them, talking to each other about nothing. After they hired a quartet of apprentices to help carry everything back to the house, Cos-tanza saw a carriage arrive at the studio's entrance. Signore Maroncelli stepped down from the coach as a footman opened the door.

He saw her at the same time, and his lips curled into a familiar, sardonic smile. He nodded to her.

A lance of fear impaled her, rooting her to the spot. Her mouth opened, and she could only whisper a name: "Nicolas . . ." Matteo was staring at her. Maroncelli—a young Nicolas, the Nicolas she'd never really known—strode by her in a miasma of perfume and a hush of ermine.

"So nice to see you again, my dear," he said as he passed them. He spoke in French, not Romano. "Such a lovely young face you have . . ."

*   *   *

Costanza slept uneasily that night. Her dreams were dominated by images of Nicolas—his face as it had been so long ago, aged and bearded; now morphing into that of a leering, laughing, youthful Maroncelli. She was in bed with Gia, holding him as he thrust into her, and his face above her shifted suddenly, and it was Nicolas mounting her, the bed frame pounding against the wall, thudding loudly, *boom* and again *boom* . . .

She woke with a start, the thudding still echoing, and there were footsteps and forms rushing into the bedroom, lanterns swinging their beams wildly around and hands grabbing at her and Matteo. She heard Matteo shout in alarm, then groan as she heard the sound of a blow. In the erratic light, he crumpled to the floor. In the confusion, in the panic, she couldn't think. She struggled against the hands holding her, and someone opened his lantern fully into her face. "Such a pretty face," she heard someone say. Metal flashed in the yellow light. She felt the slice of a razor across her face at the same moment: a quick slash, then another, and another and another as she screamed and tried to writhe away and turn her head, hot blood flying away with each movement, the horrible bright pain searing her, her vision smeared with red.

Men laughed. She felt someone tug at the collar of her nightdress, ripping it down so that she was exposed to him. She was pushed down on the bed, and she realized that they weren't going to be content with having ruined her face. She kicked at the hands that were grabbing at her legs and trying to pry them apart, rolling and trying to summon spell words from her memory. She managed to find her feet, to run to the stand where her chemicals were stored. She grabbed at a large vial, throwing it down on the floor so that the glass shattered between her and the attackers, and she lifted her hands, palms forward toward the attackers, feeling the blood pouring down her face and neck, hot rivulets running down between her exposed breasts. She spoke the spell word of flame, directing it at the wreckage of the vial. A fury of white-hot sparks erupted from the floor, hissing and fuming, alighting on the men and igniting their clothing. She heard the men scream in terror and fright and pain, beating at the flames as they ran from the house. She recognized at least one of them: they were Bernini's house servants.

So Gia had sent them.

She took the blanket from the bed and beat out the remaining flames, then sank to her knees, in exhaustion from the attack and from the loss of blood. She heard Matteo groaning and pushing himself up. "Stanz—" he started to speak, then he must have looked at her. "*Il mio dio*," he breathed. "What have they done to you?"

She reached up to touch her face with shaking fingertips, feeling the gaping, long edges of the cuts, feeling the ribbons of flesh that had been sliced open and now dangled down. Her vision went dark and she almost fainted from the shock.

Costanza sobbed, her tears mixing with the blood.

She heard Matteo stagger up, then run out of the house, shouting in the night that they'd been attacked, calling for help. She didn't know how long she sat on the floor, leaning against the bed. She heard Matteo come back in, felt him press soft cloth against her face and pull the tatters of her nightdress around her. Lanterns again swung their light through the two rooms, and Costanza saw the uniform cloaks of *vigilanza*, the constabulary.

"Here she is," Matteo was saying. "They broke into our house, they assaulted me and they slashed my wife's face and tried to rape her . . ."

She looked up at the vigilante officer's face, saw him grimace at the sight of her bloody disfigurement. "Costanza Bonarelli?" he asked, and she nodded weakly. "I have orders to arrest you for adultery and fornication," he continued. "You will come with me."

As Matteo protested, as Costanza's mind reeled, he gestured to the men with him. "Pick her up and bring her along," he said. Matteo tried to stop them, but the *vigilanza* pushed him back. "Don't make this worse, Signor," the officer said. "I've no orders to arrest you, but I will if you force the issue."

Matteo started toward him again, but Costanza called out. "Matteo! No!" He stopped, looking at her, stricken. She shook her head, which sent stabbing waves of agony through her skull. "Go to Gia. Tell him he's done enough."

With that, exhausted and fighting unconsciousness and pain, she allowed them to pull her along with them: out into the night air, out into the eager crowd that had assembled around their house, out to the waiting prison carriage.

The Castel Sant'Angelo was a dreary, shabby building, once a mausoleum for the Emperor Hadrian and now serving Rome as a prison. Costanza was in a large cell with several other women imprisoned for the same offense, some of them prostitutes and some married women who'd been caught with their lovers. Her two days in their rough company, with the rats, the human waste, the filthy straw and floors, were among the worst of her life as she tried to regain her strength, cut off from the green hearts that had sustained her. She gave one of the guards a message to pass to Matteo; she was shamed by the payment the guard demanded of her, not certain that he would even pass on the message afterward.

But Matteo came on the third day, and she was permitted to walk with him in one of the prison courtyards. She could hear the guards laughing at him and making rude jokes; she knew Matteo heard them as well. "This isn't fair, Costanza," he said to her as they walked, her arm linked in his. She sipped at the energy of him, though his soul-heart was closed in and feeble. "I've learned that Luigi has been tried and exiled to Bologna. I've petitioned to have you released, but the magistrate refuses to see me. He's another of Cardinal Barberini's relatives, I'm afraid." He shrugged. "I have a meeting with the magistrate's secretary tomorrow. Perhaps by now Cavaliere Bernini will have relented." He stopped, looking at her. "I'm so sorry, Costanza. Your poor face, and I don't have the money to buy your release."

Costanza touched her cheek softly. The *vigilanza* had called for a doctor to treat her, and the man had clumsily sewn up the cuts on her face. They looked worse now than they had that night: angry red lines crisscrossed with black thread. The doctor had told her in a flat, unsympathetic voice that she might not die from infection since the blade had been sharp and the wounds relatively clean, but that the scars would be thick and terrible, that her face would always be a horror. He gave her the news with almost a satisfaction, implying that it was no less than she deserved.

"It's not your fault, Matteo," Costanza said. "Thank you for trying. Did you bring what I asked you to bring?"

He glanced around to be certain no one was watching. "The yellow powder, the black granules, and the white? Yes, here they are." As he pretended to embrace her, he passed her three paper packets. "Why did you want this?"

"They'll keep the vermin away," she told him. It was as good a lie as any other.

"Ah. It's not healthy for you to stay here," he answered. "This place . . ."

"I won't be staying here long," she told him, and Matteo looked at her strangely.

"Stanz, I told you . . . all the bribes I will have to pay, well, I don't have the funds yet, not until I'm paid for my last work, and even then it might not be enough. You'll need to be patient, but I'll have you released."

She hugged his arm. "Don't worry," she told him. "Worry about yourself. I will be fine." She smiled up at him. "Matteo, you deserved far better than me. You did."

"Hush, don't say that. Before I met you, I was nothing. After we were together, I started to truly find my craft. You helped to make me a decent artist, one worthy of Cavaliere Bernini's studio." He opened his hands, showing them to her: the calluses from holding the chisel and hammer. "I have done more than I ever thought I would, with you. I will always love you, Costanza. No matter what."

His words brought stinging tears to her eyes. She knew that he wanted her to repeat the words. But she could not; instead, she buried her head in his sleeve. "Then I hope you'll forgive me," she told him.

He didn't understand her; she knew that he wouldn't. "For being with Cavaliere Bernini? I already have."

She managed a wan smile. "I wish you happiness, Matteo. I truly do."

"We'll have that," he told her. "Together. As soon as you're out of this terrible place."

He patted her hand as if that ended the discussion. But she knew that his wish would never be fulfilled.

~

Costanza Bonarelli: 1640

SHE SHOULD HAVE STAYED away from Rome, but she returned a few months later.

Witchcraft, it was whispered: witchcraft was how Costanza Bonarelli had vanished from her Castel Sant'Angelo cell the same night that Matteo had come to visit, and she was now wanted by the Cardinal-Protector for questioning. She knew that she must leave Matteo and Bernini and Rome, that Costanza Bonarelli must die, as all of her pervious incarnations had. It was especially vital for that to happen since Nicolas had found her, and she knew he was still here in the city.

She heard the rumors about Maroncelli/Nicolas in the Castel, how when the Cardinal-Protector interviewed and tortured heretics, that his nephew was always there with him, that it was he who actually wielded the instruments, that he enjoyed the work far too much.

She slunk away from Rome in darkness and humiliation and fear. She departed in tears at the pain she was causing Matteo for her abandonment of him. She found a goldsmith in Tivoli who had a subdued green heart and a willingness to ignore the face of a scarred young woman if the rest of her was comely enough, and she stayed with him long enough to recover and recuperate.

But she came back to Rome because she wanted to see Gia one last time. Bernini had been charged in the assault on Luigi; the hearing with the magistrate was public and well attended. Costanza remained at the rear of the room, her face well cloaked. Her fingers, involuntarily, stroked her cheeks, where her face had healed quickly and well. Despite what the doctor had told her, the scars were already barely visible, faint white tracks on otherwise unblemished skin: whatever the elixir had taken from her, it had also gifted her with the power of rapid and complete healing.

Bernini stood before the magistrate with his usual fiery demeanor, answering the judge's questions curtly and forcefully. The massive glow of his green heart surrounded him and Costanza felt the pull again, though she didn't dare touch it for fear that he might sense her presence. Costanza, peering about the courtroom, glimpsed Maroncelli standing near the bench where Bernini was giving his testimony. Seeing him, she slid back into the shadows of an alcove.

Her hand touched the pendant around her neck, then went to the pouch on her belt, heavy with vials of chemicals. If she could get close enough to Nicolas before he saw her, if she could throw them and speak the flame spell . . .

The court officer hammered his staff on the tiles for attention.

"Cavaliere Gianlorenzo Bernini," the magistrate intoned, cutting off Bernini's protestations of innocence, "this court finds you guilty of an unlawful assault with intent to murder your brother Luigi and fines you 3,000 silver scudi. You will pay the fine within thirty days or face arrest."

Whispers erupted around the room. "So high a fine," someone said close to Costanza. "Why, the attack was perfectly justified; they say his brother was laying with the Cavaliere's own mistress. The whore should be the one to pay."

Bernini leaned forward over the witnesses' bar, his mouth open as if he were about to protest the decision, but Maroncelli went quickly to him. He placed his arm around Bernini and whispered something to the artist. They conversed for a minute, then Bernini bowed to the magistrate and signed the document the court officer placed before him without a murmur. They started down the aisle as the next case was called before the magistrate.

Costanza moved with them, sliding in close behind them, her fingers on the vials in her pouch, picturing Nicolas alight in flames or writhing with the touch of acid on his skin. Nicolas was still speaking to Bernini. ". . . already talked with my uncle. His Eminence has interceded directly with His Holiness on your behalf, Gia. His Holiness will cancel your fine, though not without demanding an alternate payment of you, one I think you won't find too onerous. You've heard of Caterina Tezio . . . ?"

She cupped the first vial, started to lift it from the pouch and throw it toward him.

She let the vial fall back into its bed of cotton.

Did she hate Nicolas that much? Yes, he had been the one who whispered the poison gossip in Bernini's ears; it was undoubtedly Nicolas who had goaded Luigi until the man gave in to his temptations. It had been Nicolas' orchestrations that had torn her from Gia's green heart.

She could attack him now, when he wasn't prepared for her, when he wasn't expecting her revenge. She could do to him what he'd done to her.

Yet . . . Nicolas hadn't been the one who attacked Luigi. Nicolas hadn't held the razor that had sliced her face and nearly killed her. And surely the elixir had also taken as much from Nicolas as it had taken from her. He must suffer as she did. Surely it had bound him as it had bound her, perhaps in some other, even more terrible way.

Worse, she doubted that she *could* kill him. Not this way. He would recover and heal, as she had.

Do this, and you're no better than him.

She hesitated: as Bernini and Nicolas walked out into the Roman sunlight, as the crowds pressed between her and her quarry, and the hesitation meant that the moment was lost.

She let them go, wondering if this was a mistake she would come to regret.

4:
ERATO

Camille Kenny

Today

S HE NOTICED FIRST THAT she didn't feel the pull of the group as she usually did. It was still there, but fainter and no longer quite so compelling. They might have been anyone she passed on the street, those with the faint touch of a green aura to them, those she might have ignored.

David, alongside her, was most of what she felt.

"Hey, the prodigal returns!"

Morris was the first to see them as they entered the *Bent Calliope*. He waved to the others, pointing into the crowd to where the two of them stood. Camille smiled at him, and clutched her hand more tightly around David's as she approached the group. "And," Morris added, "it looks like we know the reason for her recent absence, too." He appeared less happy at that, staring appraisingly at David. The smile underneath his hard eyes seemed almost a mockery; of the members of the Calliope Group, it had been Morris and Mercedes who had been her most frequent lovers, and it had been to their soul-hearts that she had most closely bound herself. Rashawn, Joe, James, Kevin: they all glanced up from their drinks without saying anything.

It was Mercedes who came up to Camille, took her other hand, and kissed her, leaning in to whisper as she looked sidewise at David: "I see you took my advice. Good for you."

Camille squeezed her hand and released it. "Hey, everyone," she said. "You all remember David Treadway, I hope?"

There were muttered greetings from around the table. Deliberately, Camille circled the table, hugging and kissing each of them in turn before returning to sit next to David. Morris watched her most intently of all of them. He took a long sip of his beer as she sat. "It's been what, ten days and you've finally surfaced. He must be impressive. So is David here willing to share?"

"Shut the fuck up, Morris," Mercedes told him before Camille could respond. "This isn't your business. Camille doesn't have to answer to you or to any of us for who she spends time with."

Morris spread his hands wide as if protesting innocence and surprise. "What's wrong? The man deserves to know what kind of incestuous group he's gotten involved with, doesn't he?"

"I already know," David said, and Camille glanced over to him. He was staring directly at Morris, and she could see the challenge in his eyes. "And Mercedes is right. It's Camille's business. Not anyone else's."

"Including yours, I assume?" Morris asked. There was too much edge to the question, and too much mockery in his smile. "So you certainly won't mind if. . . ."

"David's already told you what you wanted to know," Camille interjected before Morris could finish the statement. "Right now, so everyone here knows, I'm with David. Period. End of story." Morris' smile went tight and fixed at that. Camille pretended not to notice. "And now, the next round's on me, as my apology for being away so long. So everyone order up before I change my mind."

She ended up buying the round after that as well. It seemed to take the group's mind away from David's presence, and they fell into their usual patterns. Later that night, as Camille was returning from a trip to the restroom, Morris intercepted her near the bar. "So what's really up with this?" he asked, speaking loudly to be heard over the bar's music and the hundred conversations around them. "All of a sudden you're not interested in us?"

"You mean 'us' or 'me,' Morris?" she answered.

To his credit, he managed to look embarrassed. "Look, Camille, you gotta know you really mean a lot to me. Since you've been around, well, things have been different. Better. I can see that more than any of the others, and I don't want to lose that. I know I'm not the only one you sleep with, but we've been together a lot, and . . ." He lifted one shoulder. "I miss that. I miss you."

"I'm here now, aren't I?"

"Yeah. But it's not the same. Not with *him* here, too." His lips twitched, as if he were tasting something sour. "I checked into the guy since the first time you brought here. He's got some prints here and there, but not that much of a reputation among the gallery owners except Prudhomme. Hell, I've had half a dozen more shows than he has, and he's gotta have ten years on me. And he's *married*."

"He's separated."

"Yeah, since *you've* shown up he's separated," Morris scoffed.

"Look, I don't want to talk about this," Camille said. "And I don't want you to be upset with me, either, Morris. You're my friend; I want to stay your friend."

"That's exactly what I want, too."

She gave him a smile. "Then we're good, aren't we?"

She started to brush past him to return to the table. His hand reached out and grabbed at her arm. "I'm worrying that you've made a mistake, Camille," Morris told her. "You gotta know that."

"Then it's my mistake to make, isn't it?" she answered. "Isn't that part of the artistic process—learning from your mistakes?" She looked down at his hand. Slowly, he released his grip. He nodded, and at least he tried to match her smile.

But she felt his gaze on her and David the rest of the evening, and she asked David to leave long before the bar closed.

She went to the bank that morning as soon as they opened; David left the apartment at the same time, saying he was heading back to his own place to catch up on neglected work. On the way to Walter's office, she stopped to visit Morris at his studio.

Morris rented third-floor studio space at an ancient warehouse near the East River that had been taken over by an artists' cooperative. Most of the artists there created crafty, easily accessible work that sold at various festivals throughout the east coast. Camille could sense their presences in the building: faint green sparks glimmering in the darkness behind her eyes, most of them barely perceptible. As she climbed the worn, bowed wooden steps of the warehouse toward Morris' studio, she felt him easily overpowering the others, an emerald glow that seemed strangely darkened to her, with an unusual feel that made her tilt her head in puzzlement. He was working, all his attention on whatever he was doing. At other times, she would have let herself be absorbed into the warm sauna of his creativity, would have allowed herself to absorb it and return it to him enhanced. Had she done that, he might have felt her in that disturbance, might have turned to see her as she approached the open door.

Not this time.

His studio was a large, high open space, dotted with several of his sculpture pieces: spindly figures twisting around each other, as if captured in the midst of a dance or an erotic encounter. His prints were on an unpainted wallboard back wall: lithographs whose style echoed the sculptures. She recognized her face and figure among them; she had posed as a model for Morris several times in the last few years.

He was standing before an armature a few feet taller than him, welded from wrought iron in the vague shape of two figures who looked to be locked in a struggle. A large tub of green-brown clay was placed next to the armature, in front of Morris. The lower portion of the sculpture was already slathered with clay with the marks of shaping tools on it, the feet and lower legs already recognizable. As Camille, watched, Morris reached down and took a double handful of the clay, slapping it around the skeletons of the armature, pressing it into position.

She watched the throbbing of his green heart within him: strong, but not as vital and nowhere near as brilliant as David's. It could never be like David's. It could never feed her the same way.

"A new commission?" she asked from the doorway.

She couldn't quite decipher the look he gave her; somewhere between pleasure and irritation. "Hey, Camille," he said. "Where's David?"

"At his studio," she told him. "Working, like you. What's this piece?"

"It's called 'Vengeance.'"

The title and his slow, pleased pronunciation raised the hairs on her arms. "A dish best served cold?" she asked, and he smiled momentarily.

"You'd never make it in a trivia contest. That's 'revenge,' not vengeance," he told her. "Besides, the title's not my idea. The man who commissioned it wanted that to be the title, though he said he was leaving the conception up to me; all he wanted was a piece that fit the theme."

"So you've a new patron—congratulations. Who is he?"

He nodded. "Name's Timothy Pierce. Lives uptown, and has more money than he knows what to do with, so he's dabbling in the arts. Actually, Prudhomme put me in touch with him; said that the guy had decent taste—he likes me, after all—is thinking he might start collecting, and was looking for a modern sculpture for his condo: somebody up-and-coming, but not too terrifically expensive yet. Somebody whose work is likely to increase in value. Prudhomme sent him my way." She could hear the pride in his voice. "What brings you here, Camille?"

Guilt, mostly. But she wasn't going to admit that to him. "We didn't leave things in a good place between us the other night," she said. "I wanted to talk to you about it, just to make sure we're fine."

He shrugged, wiping his hands on his jeans but not stepping away from the sculpture. "Not much to talk about, the way I see it. You've made your preferences plain enough. You know how I feel about you, Camille. I think I've made that clear. But if that's not what you want, well, as you said, it's your life and your choice."

"Being with David doesn't change how I feel about you, Morris. I wish you could understand that."

He shook his head with a wry smile. "C'mon, Camille. That's bullshit, and you know it. Things *have* changed. They've changed a lot." He reached down and picked up a double handful of the clay. *Slap! Slap!* He slammed the clay onto the armature hard enough that the whole structure shuddered. His long fingers pressed the clay into shape.

"You never cared before that I slept with the other people in the group."

"No, I didn't. I'm not a jealous or possessive guy; I was willing to share if what you wanted was an open relationship. That worked for me. It just doesn't seem that David feels the same way."

But you are possessive, she wanted to tell him. *That's what all this is really about.* "It's not David who's making that decision," she told him.

"Ah." He stepped back and looked at the clay-draped armature, not at her. "Then I guess none of what I think really matters, does it?"

"Morris . . ." She sighed. "I care a lot for you. I don't want this to pull us apart so we can't stay friends."

Morris exhaled loudly. His hands fell to his side like stones, the clay on his fingers staining his jeans. "Friends," he said. "Yeah. And if I still want more than that?"

"I'm sorry, then," she told him. "Right now, friendship is all I have to offer. Who knows—that might change again later on. I'm just playing this by ear. You can understand that, can't you?" She lifted her hands.

"Yeah. I guess I can. I'll grant that you've done a lot for me and I've enjoyed you being around." He glanced at the prints, at the lithos for which she'd posed. "My new patron? He liked the lithos I did of you, too. In fact, he bought one of them from me—supposedly your face reminded him of his ex-wife. He told me, 'You really captured the self-absorption in her face. It makes you hate her and love her at the same time.' "

Camille drew in her breath with that, the words stinging her so that her cheeks flushed. "Are those his words or yours, Morris?"

"His." Morris glanced back at the armature. The heavy clay thickened his fingers. He gave a second shrug and bent down to the clay bin once more. "I just drew what I saw," he answered. "I wasn't making any judgments about you. But I can see what he was saying. Look, I don't want to sound mean or petty, but you asked. You always do what most pleases you, Camille. Isn't that the definition of someone who's self-absorbed?"

She didn't know how to answer that. The silence stretched on for too long. She could hear Morris' hands working the wet clay in the bin. "Look, we're as okay we're going to be right now," he said finally. "I don't hate you, but I'll admit that I'm hurting a little. Give me a little time, and I'll get over it. I promise. Is that fair enough?"

"Yeah," she said. It came out breathy and uncertain. He still hadn't looked at her. He lifted a double handful of clay. "Good," he said. "And now, I got work to do. So if you'll forgive me . . ."

"Sure," she said. "I have another appointment anyway." She walked toward the studio doors, the sound of clay being slapped onto the armature following her.

"Here it is," she told Walters. "Ten thousand. A cashier's check, so you don't have to wait for it to clear my account."

The investigator pressed his lips together. He picked up the check and stared at it contemplatively, then let it drop back to the papers that littered his desk like bleached autumn leaves. "You know, I think we'd figure out exactly who Helen Treadway's seeing without this. It'll just take a little longer."

"I'm in a hurry," she told him. She was still feeling irritation from the conversation with Morris. "Deposit it today, and tell your friend to do whatever it is he does."

She didn't tell Walters that the Tarot array that she'd set out for herself the night before had shown the Magus—the card she had associated with Nicolas since she called herself Perenelle—close to her, with threatening swords close by. The Princess of Pentacles, who she thought might be Helen, was beset and hemmed in by them, and the cards of the Major Arcana that entered the array colored the reading with ominous warnings. Yes, Camille was hunting Nicolas, but now he was hunting her at the same time, and he had his own resources—none of which cared much for legalities, and many of which were beyond her own capabilities.

She had to hurry, or he would find her first. If that happened . . .
No, you won't think about that now.

Walters folded his hands on top of the check. His craggy face looked up at her. "You know, you're about my granddaughter Beth's age. Maybe that makes me sentimental."

"Mr. Walters, y'know, I've already had about as much condescension this morning as I can take . . ."

His slab of a hand lifted; he shook his gray-fringed head and leaned back in his chair, which creaked dangerously and threatened to over-balance. "No. Hear me out. This is a lot of money for someone your age. I don't care where or how you got it, but . . ." Gray-blue eyes regarded her. She could imagine those eyes on the other side of an interrogation table, cold and unblinking. "Camille Kenny. That's an unusual name," he said. "Y'know, I get curious about my clients, especially the ones who give me interesting jobs or interesting requests. Sometimes I check them out a bit, just to know them better. What's strange is that Camille Kenny doesn't have much of a paper trail prior to five years ago. None at all, as a matter of fact. No schools attended, no jobs, no residences, no licenses, no nothing. In fact, I found a birth certificate for Camille Kenny, born in Cincinnati—you were born in Cincinnati, right, to Ted and Elizabeth Kenny?—born the same day you were born and with the same social security number. Only trouble is that according to a death certificate I ran across, *that* Camille Kenny died two years after she was born."

Camille flushed. A slow panic began to build in her stomach. She started to turn, to leave. "Wait, young lady," Walters said loudly. He hadn't moved from his reclined position. "I ain't a cop. Not anymore. I don't give a damn if you're who you say you are or not. Camille Kenny, at least for as long as I can find out anything about her, seems to be a decent enough person. Maybe better than most I run into or have worked for. I'm just pointing out that there's a lot that's strange about this quest of yours—and it's not just this mysterious guy you're trying to track down. I don't need the whole story; I'll do the job you paid me for and shut up. However, I think you got a wild hare up your ass with the Treadway woman. For all you know, the guy she's seeing ain't your guy. In fact, from what you've told me, that would be a huge coincidence. It's probably some poor schmuck who works where she works: a rebound lover. Why toss all this green at a wild card?"

"If I tell you that I have my reasons, will that be enough?" she asked him.

It was hard to tell whether he shrugged or not; the chair creaked, but he might have just been adjusting his position. "This guy—he's a danger to you?"

"To me, and to *anyone* he's around. Trust me on that."

"You said a while ago that he goes through a lot of aliases. Same reason as you?"

She hesitated before answering, then decided there was no reason to try to pretend. "Yes. And no." She hesitated a moment. "And I have another name for you to check: Timothy Pierce. Supposedly lives uptown somewhere. Likes to collect art."

"You think he's your guy?"

"Don't know. Maybe. Why don't you find out?"

After a moment, Walters leaned forward again, the chair's springs protesting against the abuse. "Fair enough," he said. "You're my client; I'll trust you know what you're doing. I'll cash the check and get my guy started on things, and I'll check out Pierce. Should only take a couple days. In the meantime, if this guy's such a danger to you, if you're worried about him getting too close, you got anything to protect yourself?"

She nodded. The purse, with the Ladysmith and a few vials of chemicals snuggled inside, lay heavy at her side, and there were the spells she memorized each morning burning in her head. "I can take care of myself. And, Mr. Walters, if you do find him, please don't let him see you or think that you're on to him. I'm telling you, if he believes you represent a threat to him, he'll do something drastic about it. I know him; you don't. He's capable of anything. Anything. I want you to be very careful."

He grunted. That was all the answer she received.

From Walters' office, she went back to her own apartment. David was still gone. She fed Verdette, stroking the cat absently as she pondered the meeting with Morris and her conversation with Walters. "I don't know," she said to Verdette. "Maybe I'm making a mistake staying around here. Maybe I should just pack up and leave the city before David gets back, just drop everything. I could start the hunt again later, when I *know* he's not expecting me. Maybe we could go back to Europe for a bit. To Paris. Would you like that?—though you know it would mean a few months in a cage for you again."

Verdette only purred mysteriously in answer.

She opened her laptop on the small kitchen table and googled *Timothy Pierce Manhattan*, then checked the various images that came up. None of them looked to be Nicolas. She frowned and closed the laptop again.

She went to her bedroom. The katana she used for iado and aikido practice stood on its stand on top of her dresser, but she ignored that—one couldn't walk around the streets of the city carrying a sword. Instead, she opened the drawer of her nightstand, burrowing through her panties until her hand touched a box at the back. She pulled out the wooden case and opened it: the velvet nest for the Smith & Wesson Ladysmith .38 was there. She took the Ladysmith from her purse and plucked the cleaning rag from the box to wipe the burnished and blued steel and polished wood. She'd bought the revolver several years ago, before she'd taken the name she now used.

She hefted the weapon in her hand and put it back in her purse. *Yes, Nicolas is somewhere here in the city, but he hasn't found you again. You're misreading the cards and the signs. You're still the hunter, not the prey . . .*

But inside, the doubts were growing louder. *Helen's boyfriend, Morris' patron—they could be the same. That could be Nicolas. And if that's true, then he knows who you are. He knows to look for artists, to look for those whose talent is suddenly blossoming. And you know that the longer you let him live, the more people will suffer and die for his pleasure . . .*

She gave Verdette a final rub around the ears and left the apartment; she didn't expect David back until evening, and the refrigerator was looking exceedingly forlorn. If nothing else, grocery shopping might take her mind away from the paranoia.

She found David back at her apartment when she returned, watching television. She put the canvas grocery bags down at the door, set her purse on the couch and went to him, straddling him in the chair. She hugged David fiercely, kissing him with an urgency and passion that surprised even her. "Hey," he said, pushing her away from him slightly. In this light, his eyes were nearly blue, and quizzical. "It's only been half a day. Did you miss me that much?"

"Yes," she told him, her arms still firmly around his shoulders. "Do you mind?"

He laughed. "Do I look stupid?"

"Good. You can help me put groceries away, and then we can go do whatever you'd like."

She led him toward the door and the bags there. As they passed the couch, she felt David's hand pull against hers. "What's that?" She glanced back to see him staring at her purse; it had sagged open and the handle of the Ladysmith was visible, nestled between her wallet and cell phone, the handle displaying the polish of having been handled many times. "You carry a *gun?*"

"Yes," she told him, "and I also have a permit. I have a sword, too, remember?"

"You study a martial art—that explains the sword. Why do you have a gun?" He was still staring at the handle.

She knew he wouldn't believe the truth. Couldn't believe it. *I have the gun because it would stop Nicolas. For a little bit. But not forever. Shooting him will never stop him forever, no matter how many bullets I put in him. But I do know a way, and I'll use that after I shoot the bastard.* "There's this guy . . . a stalker," she said.

"You have a stalker?" he repeated. "Why haven't you called the cops? Who is he? Do you have a restraining order on him? And why am I just hearing about this?"

"It's not a subject that comes up in many conversations. 'Hi, I'm Camille and I have a stalker' is not exactly a great way to start out a relationship. But, yes, I have a stalker." She looked at him, still holding his hand. "David, is this a problem?"

"Well, no," he answered. He didn't sound entirely certain. "It's just . . . Who is this guy? How long has this been going on?"

It was easy enough to make up a believable mixture of truth and lies that made him subside into concerned empathy: she told David it had been going on for a few years, that he used various names and moved around a lot, that the police were aware of it but weren't able to do much about it and didn't consider it a priority. Yes, he'd threatened violence. No, she hadn't had contact with him in a long time, and maybe, maybe he'd given up stalking her. "Then why this?" he asked, pointing at the bag.

"Because I don't *know*," she told him. "Because if he is out there, I want to have a defense."

"Ever had to use it?"

Have I shot Nicolas? Yes. More than once. But never with this gun. Could she use the weapon? She had no doubt of that. But it seemed best to leave that unsaid. "No," she said, "but I wouldn't want to *not* have it if I did need it. Can you understand that?"

"I suppose. You're scared. I get that."

"But . . . ?"

He shook his head. "I'm sorry, Camille," he told her. "I gotta be honest. Having a gun around . . . I'm bothered by that. I'm not a gun person. I've never owned a gun, never fired one, don't intend to ever own one. I really don't like the idea of having one in the apartment or in your purse."

She could feel the certainty in his voice. The green hue that had connected her to him was drawn tight inside him, closed off. *You could lose him over this.* The realization was a cold fist in her chest, but she hesitated. Losing David would free her and protect David at the same time—she could go somewhere else, take on a new name, lose herself again. She could do what she'd been tempted to do a few hours ago. She'd allowed her desire for someone and her obsessions and needs to overrule her judgment in the past. Yet having found another possibility like David and feeling again what he could give her made her want to hold it even more tightly.

You're still hunting Nicolas. That's the most important task right now. He hasn't found you. If you find him or if Walters does, then you have to be able to do whatever you need to do. As long as Nicolas is around, David is in danger. You know that.

If she wanted David, if she still believed that the decision to bond with him was the right one, she had to make a decision. "I understand the way you feel," she said. "But I made the decision to carry the gun for my own safety, and I did the work necessary to do that. It wasn't a decision I made lightly, and I'm very careful about it. Is it a deal breaker, David? Because I have to be honest here: I'm keeping the gun."

She watched his face, watched the emotions that flitted past his eyes and touched the muscles of his jawline that pressed his mouth into a thin line.

"Okay," he said finally, and she began to breathe again. "I don't like it. I'll never like it. But . . . okay, if that's the way it has to be, then I'll trust you."

She smiled. "That's all I ask," she told him. "That's all I'll ever ask of you. Thank you, David. You have no idea how much that means." She went to him, embracing him tightly. "You have no idea," she repeated.

She encouraged David to return to his studio the next day. After the confrontation over the handgun, she wanted—no, she *needed*—the connection with his green heart. Being with David while he worked on his photography would provide that. "I'll cook up the salmon I bought and we can eat there. I just have to feed Verdette before we go. You can work; besides, I'd like to see those prints of me you took the other day on something other than my laptop, all cleaned up and photoshopped."

He shrugged, though without the enthusiasm she might have wanted. "Sounds okay. I don't know how much longer I can keep the place, anyway."

"Don't worry about that," she answered. "I told you; I have a trust fund. I can pull money from it if you're short. The studio's yours; it'll stay yours."

"You don't need to do that."

"You don't want to be a kept man?" The joke fell flat; she saw the flash of embarrassment in his face. "David, if we're going to be together, then part of the deal is that you have to let me help you. There's not really room in my place for you to set up your cameras, lights, and backdrops, or to arrange your computers, monitors, printers, and all the framing stuff. You need to keep your studio."

He paused, and she felt the wall within him open, the lush radiance tentatively embracing her again. "That logic works both ways, Camille. In my studio, there's more than enough room for *your* stuff—your paintings and easels, your keyboard and amp, your computer. Even that damn chemistry set of yours. I'll bet Verdette would love the extra space to roam around in. That'd exorcise Helen's ghost, if nothing else—she absolutely hates cats."

"Are you asking me to move in with you?"

He shrugged. "One place would be cheaper than two, especially in this city. And I like cats—even if the cat doesn't seem to like me."

"I'd have to think about it," she told him, and wasn't certain whether it was disappointment or relief that crossed his face. "We've known each other, what, a few weeks now? We don't have to make a decision this quickly. In fact, we shouldn't. We can take our time. For right now, let's keep both places—until we're sure."

We have all the time in the world. But that wasn't true. Not for David, at least.

He seemed satisfied with that answer.

They spent the rest of the afternoon and the evening at the studio. She watched David work, satisfied to sit behind him as he brought up images on his display and manipulated them, content to bask in the radiance that emanated from him as he worked, to enhance it even as she revived herself with the energy, to open the soul-heart within him even more so that he could pull deeper from the pool. "Yes," she heard him say to himself more than once with satisfaction: as he cropped a picture or adjusted the levels so that the image seemed to pop and sizzle on the screen. "That's nice . . ."

He printed out the best of the photos to mount and mat later; she made dinner. After they ate, they made leisurely love on his bed—not, Camille was happy to notice, the bed that he and Helen had shared; Helen had taken that. Afterward, he sat up and stretched. "How about the *Bent Calliope?*" he asked. "It's still early."

"You're sure?" she asked. Morris seemed to swim up before her, the lines of his face as hard as if he'd carved them into himself. *"You always do what most pleases you, Camille. Isn't that the definition of someone who's self-absorbed?"* "If you're suggesting that for my sake, you don't have to."

"No," he said. "Let's do it. Throw on your clothes. I had a good day of work; let's go celebrate."

They walked to the *Bent Calliope*, six blocks from David's apartment. For the last block, the street was nearly empty of other pedestrians, and Camille found herself suddenly apprehensive, the half-sinister conversation with Walters returning to her again. *Nicolas is out there somewhere. He's here in this city, here close by* . . . She remembered other times, walking through dangerous and dark urban streets, and she shivered. David must have felt the apprehension, or perhaps he only thought she was cold; he put an arm around her.

As they passed an alleyway half a block from the *Bent Calliope*, she heard running footsteps in the darkness and glimpsed a darker shape moving toward them in the twilight.

"*Arrêt!*" she shouted, spinning away from David and plunging a hand into her purse. The Ladysmith was buried; instead, she pulled out a vial of dark, metallic powder, holding it back and high and ready to throw. Latin and Arabic words roiled in her head, as if inked on a mental scroll.

"Jesus, Camille," someone in the darkness laughed, the voice familiar: Rashawn. "A little jumpy tonight, are we?"

Adrenaline still buzzed in her head, but she brought her hand down and put the vial back in the purse. David was looking at her, eyebrows high on his forehead. "Damn it, Rashawn, you gave me a start," Camille said. "What are you doing sneaking up on us like that?"

"I saw you two and thought I'd catch up. Never saw you move quite so fast before. You'd think you'd been watching the movie with us." She laughed again.

"What movie?" David asked.

"*Nosferatu*. The Regal had their silent movie night tonight and we all went—everyone but Morris and you two, anyway. The others are already inside; I had to go back to the apartment for a few minutes." She grinned at Camille. "Did you just shout at me in French?"

Rashawn didn't wait for an answer. She stepped between them and linked arms with David and Camille; in the shaft of streetlight, Camille could see strands of bright color splashed on her dark skin as Rashawn pulled them toward the glow of the *Bent Calliope*, with Ink already craning his balding head curiously in their direction from his usual stool. Ink waved them in as they approached, and a few minutes later, they were sitting around their usual table in the rear.

As they had the last few times, the group seemed strangely lethargic to Camille. The shared light within their soul-hearts seemed dim and pale and tasteless; she wondered how she had kept herself healthy and active with the thin gruel it offered. She knew that feeling was because of David; even with Morris' contribution, the sustenance they offered her now seemed unpalatable and insufficient in comparison.

She tried to ignore the guilt the thought stirred, along with the memory of her conversation with Morris. Maybe she *was* self-absorbed, but she also had a right to be happy. None of them could understand what she'd experienced in her life. None of them understood everything that had shaped her. She had the right to do whatever she needed to do to survive and thrive. That's what all of them were doing, after all. She'd given the Calliope Group more than they'd given her, all of them.

The justifications didn't quite convince her or assuage the sense of unease.

The conversation at the table centered mostly on the film they'd just seen. "It's better than most of the crap that's out now," James was contending. "There's a genuine atmosphere to *Nosferatu*, and genuine horror, stuff that comes from the mind and not from blood and gore. Nowadays vampires are too goddamn cool and sexualized—they're nothing but romanticized wet dreams. A real vampire would be raw and visceral and violent, not handsome and sanitized."

"I don't know," Mercedes said. "I kinda like the sexy vampire genre. And you gotta admit it sells. Heck, I've thought of writing one of those myself, if I could find the right angle on it."

"I don't know what it is about vampires," James responded. "What's with you women swooning over them? To a vampire, we're just meat on the hoof. Cheeseburgers with legs. How romantic is that?"

"It's the bad boy syndrome," Rashawn answered. "Y'know, like 'Beauty and the Beast.' We think that gorgeous, troubled, edgy guy is going to fall totally and completely in love with us and we'll be able to tame him. We'll change everything in his life to make him our ideal mate. Not to mention that having a vampire lover would make for some fine protection. It'd be a hell of a lot better than a gun."

Camille felt David glance at her with the comment. She wondered if he remembered the vial she'd nearly tossed at Rashawn. He certainly would have been surprised if she'd actually done that; it might have made him forget the Ladysmith.

"Bullshit," James answered. "Look, if there really were vampires and not just a bunch of Goth wannabes play-acting like them, you'd just end up as lunch. A dead lunch. Or worse, you'd become a vampire just like them. Vampires feed on you; that's all they want."

"Now who's spouting bullshit?" Rashawn said. "You can't understand. You're a guy."

"Hey, I *like* guys." He put his arm around Joe. "I just know which ones are worth having, and it ain't the bad boys. Bad boys just stay bad boys; you can't change them, and they only cause you pain and heartache, or worse."

"Sounds like experience talking," Mercedes interjected, and the group laughed as James held his hands up in surrender. "Personally, I don't think becoming a vampire would be such a bad tradeoff. You gotta give up daylight, and you have to feed on people and drink their blood, but in return you get to live forever. That's not a bad bargain, to me. I could deal with that."

Joe, leaning into James with his arm around him, shook his head. "You're kidding, right?"

Mercedes laughed. "Not at all. I'm serious. If a vampire showed up and offered to turn me, I'd have to seriously consider it. What about you, David? Would you accept the offer? Eternal life for a few minor quirks like needing to drink blood and really slather on the sunscreen? Would you make the trade?"

David's shoulders lifted. "Maybe. Depends on which vampire rules you're playing by. If I could just keep plasma in my fridge and not have to go hunting for victims every night and killing people, and not have the peasants storming my castle with pitchforks and torches, well, then I can see the temptation. I guess I could give up seeing the sun."

"Ah, so as long you can treat us poor humans like traveling milk bars you can tap when you need a fix, you'd think about it." Mercedes glanced over at Camille. "Girl, what's with that face? You look like you found a fly doing the backstroke in your Guinness."

Camille had found the conversation more irritating as it went on. She tried to smile and failed. "Why is living forever such a wonderful idea to you people?" she asked.

"C'mon," Rashawn answered before Mercedes could speak. "Are you saying that you'd turn down eternal life if you could have it? All that time to read all the books you wanted to read, to experience everything you want to experience, travel every country in the world, see everything you wanted to see . . ."

"Do everyone you wanted to do," Joe interjected to laughter.

"Watch every last one of the people you love grow old and die while you live on," Camille retorted. Her hand sought the pendant under her T-shirt, caressing the unseen edges of the woman's face. "Feeling miserable for a century at a time, or frustrated or threatened most of the time. Experiencing every bit of the horrible nastiness the human race can inflict on itself, up close and personal. Eternally hiding what you are because you're different and they'd tear you apart if they found out. Having to change identities every few decades just so you're not found out. Yeah, sounds perfectly wonderful, doesn't it?"

"No one said that there wouldn't be a downside," Mercedes said. "If you live forever, at least you can have hope that, if you just wait long enough, you'll be able to find your way out of any misery you experience. When you get old and frail, there isn't much hope for the future. When you only get one shot at life, it has to be a good one or a lucky one."

"Humans aren't *designed* to live forever," Camille persisted. "Not up here." She tapped her forehead.

"The only one who would actually *know* that is someone who *has* lived forever," Mercedes answered. "Good luck finding someone like that. You might think all that, Camille, but you can't say it's absolutely the case. Unless, of course, you're a vampire. David, let us see your neck."

David, chuckling, dragged down the collar of his shirt. Mercedes made a show of examining the skin closely. "Nothing. No marks at all, not even a good hickey. Shame on you, Camille. You got this big juicy guy and you haven't taken advantage of him." She pretended to bite him herself, snapping white teeth together just under his chin, then giving him a large, showy kiss. The others laughed; Camille smiled wanly.

She sipped at her Guinness, listening as the conversation continued around the table but not really joining in. She leaned against David, enjoying the feel of his body. Mercedes, on her other side, leaned over and whispered into Camille's ear. "You two look comfortable," Mercedes commented. "Is it going to last forever?"

"Forever's a damn long time," Camille answered.

But it might be possible, she wanted to answer. Maybe this time, it could happen, if she dared to risk it. Maybe this time, she might.

Camille could feel David watching her as they walked back to his apartment. She kept her hand close to her purse, with the vials and the Ladysmith. "You're watching every shadow," he said to her. "Your stalker?"

Camille shrugged. "No," she told him. She wondered if he could hear the lie. "I'm just a little jumpy, I guess."

"What's his name? You haven't told me."

"He's had a dozen names or more. I don't know which one's the real one anymore, or which one he might be using right now."

"Then what does he look like, in case I see someone like that hanging around?"

"He's short," she began, then had to chuckle. "I'm sorry, David, but he's also had as many looks as names. Short hair, long hair; bearded, clean-shaven; dark hair, light hair; thin, stocky . . ." *He's used all the dodges I've used myself, and I've been just as efficient at keeping Nicolas from finding me.* "I'll know him if I see him. I'll know the face, no matter how much he's tried to disguise it."

"If you do see him, I want you to tell me," he insisted. "Promise?"

"Promise," she told him. "But maybe I've managed to lose him. I haven't seen him in a long time."

One lie, one piece of half-truth. She hugged David closer. She wished she felt as confident as she sounded.

Lies. All my relationships begin in lies and evasions. But there's no other way . . .

The night was warm, and David suggested they go up to the roof of his building to enjoy the moon and the few stars that could break through the sky glow of the city. They brought up a bottle of wine, a baguette, cheese, and two folding chairs. David had carried along a camera as well, and Camille could feel him gazing at her through the lens. The verdant warmth of his soul-heart mingled with the warmth of the wine in her stomach.

"You didn't seem to care much for the conversation at the *Bent Calliope* tonight," David commented. She heard the shutter click as he spoke.

"It was just silly," she answered. "All that garbage about vampires . . . I guess I wasn't in the mood for it."

"It's interesting to think about, though. Death is the one thing that all we humans share, the one thing we all have to face. Even those vampires who could live forever have to worry about someone coming along and putting a stake in their heart, don't they? Heck, for someone who could potentially live forever, I could see life becoming so precious to them that they became paralyzed by it, living in total fear about accidents or murder, the paranoia so bad that they can't even step outside of their house. Maybe I should write that novel—what do you think?"

It was probably the wine. That's what she told herself afterward. Camille sprang up from her chair as David was talking. Before she could allow herself to think about it, she bounded from the roof to the brick ledge of the building, teetering there with her arms outstretched fifty feet above the street.

"Chris'sake, Camille!" David jumped up from his chair. He started to run toward her, then evidently thought better of it. He stopped two paces from her, his hands outstretched imploringly. "Camille, please come down from there."

"What if you really *couldn't* die?" she half-shouted to David as she walked along the narrow, rounded concrete top of the ledge. "What if no matter how badly hurt you were, no matter what agony you endured, your body simply wouldn't *allow* you to die? Then eventually you might not feel anything. There'd be nothing to be afraid of: not for yourself, only for everyone else you knew . . . And *that's* the real problem: having to worry about those you love because they're so damned fucking *fragile*."

She let her hands drop. She looked down. The pavement seemed to beckon her, spinning about with the fumes of the wine. *Maybe this time it would really be the end. Coda and finale. It would be so easy to let go, to find out . . .*

But she could feel David's concern and his affection and his energy. The tendrils of his soul-heart held her, and for the first time with him she could see rivulets of lapis invading the green, and she knew that she could no longer leave him. She was bound to him now.

She had found *that* kind of love again, all unlooked for, and just as compelling. Now he was her responsibility, and she had to protect him.

The realization did not make her happy. She knew the consequences of love. Nicolas had taught them to her. Now she *had* to find him, and find him quickly. Tomorrow: she would call Walters tomorrow and push him; she would redouble her own efforts, go and check out all the hospitals, maybe even send an anonymous tip to the cops about the Black Fire murders . . .

The world spun about her, wine-flavored.

"Camille . . . Please . . ." David stretched his hands out to her. His skin glowed emerald and aquamarine in the dark.

She took his hand and let him guide her down.

"Christ, you just scared the shit out of me."

"There was nothing to be afraid of," she told him. "I'm not going to die from a fall. That's not my fate."

After they made love, she couldn't manage to find sleep. Her body was shaking as if she had a fever, while David lay snoring softly alongside her. After a time, she rolled quietly from the bed so as not to disturb him, and padded barefoot in her nightgown up the stairs to David's studio. He had a haphazard collection of watercolor tubes and half a block of 14x20 Aquarelles Arches paper. She managed to find a clean brush that would serve; she borrowed an old plastic dinner plate from the kitchen to use as a palette for mixing the colors, and brought up a cup of clean water and a roll of paper towels.

She began to work, without any plan, without sketching on the paper first, laying down washes of color that grew more intense and dark as she worked. A face emerged from the paper: male, scowling, furious, mouth open in a shout of rage, spittle flying from engorged lips, nostrils flared with emotion. She slid a palette knife under the opening in the pad, slicing away the top sheet to expose a fresh one, and she began again: another face, this time with furrowed eyebrows over dark eyes that nearly filled the paper, stark and staring, all reds and purples.

Again she sliced off the paper and began painting: an elongated figure, half-emerging from bloody shadows, ominous in stance, a single hand in the light holding a sword that glimmered menacingly, the white of the paper shining through.

"If those are your dreams, then no wonder you didn't want to sleep."

The voice, from immediately behind her, broke her from the half-trance. She started and tried to rise from the stool on which she was sitting, the brush dropping from her hand onto the plate with its dabs of pigment. Hands went around her, and she stiffened momentarily before relaxing.

"David!"

"Of course," he said. His stubbled face rubbed against her neck as she leaned back against him. "Who else were you expecting?" He kissed the top of her head. He let go of her with one hand, picking up the first sketch she'd done. "You're frightened of someone," he told her. "I can see it right here." He shook the paper; it rustled in his fingers. "Is this the man who's stalking you?"

She shrugged in his embrace. "I don't know," she told him. *Yes, it is. That's Nicolas' eyes, his face . . .* "They're just what I felt like painting. They're not very good."

He echoed her shrug. "I wouldn't say that. A little crude, maybe, but I'd say there's an honest darkness here. Tell me about him, Camille. Tell me what you're trying to say with your brush."

"I don't know that I can," she answered, knowing it was another lie, knowing that she wasn't going to tell him because she didn't trust that he'd believe or understand the tale, and that if he did, he might leave her to protect himself. "I wish I could, I really do. But . . ." She shrugged.

He nodded at that and kissed her head again. "Then I'll just let you work it out this way. I understand." His warmth left her and she turned and caught his hand before he could move away.

"I think I'm done for the time being," she said. "Let me clean up this mess, and I'll come back to bed."

He smiled at her and started to walk toward the stairs and the bedroom below. "David," she called out to him as he put his hand on the railing. "Thank you for not pressing. I . . ." *Love you.* The words were there, hanging in the night air, and she almost said them. Almost. ". . . appreciate that," she finished.

He yawned. He waved a hand. "Come back to bed," he said.

She stared at the paintings for several minutes, half-tempted to rip them up and destroy them. Instead, she picked up the plate, her brush, the cup of now-dirty water, and the paper towels.

She went downstairs.

INTERLUDE FOUR

Anna Giraud &
Antonio Lucio Vivaldi

1737

Anna Giraud

1737

S HE WASN'T SUPPOSED TO hear the comments, but she did.
The stone-and-brick tiles of Venice were puddled, washed tem-
porarily clean as rags of dirty gray clouds scudded like sooty gondolas
across the sky. Those people caught out walking in the Piazza San Marco
kept the hoods of their cloaks pulled up, crouching near the shelter of
the Doge's Palace or the Basilica. The figures of the four tetrarchs at
the corner of the Basilica seemed to be huddling together in misery as
the rain pelted them, the dark porphyry stone from which they'd been
carved black with moisture. The awnings of the market stands sagged
under the tempest, drooling streams of water as the merchants scowled
at the largely vacant square in front of their stalls. Even the flocks of
pigeons searching for food on the piazza appeared to be forlorn.

Anna paused in the shelter of the arches, waiting for the rain to
abate. She had visited one of the minor functionary's offices within the
Doge's Palace with Paolina, making sure that their travel papers were
in order. Carlo Goldoni, the Venetian playwright whose tragicomedies
Belisario and *Rinaldo di Montalbano* had recently played to rapturous
reviews, was speaking to a knot of his sycophants under a nearby archway, his voice carrying faintly but audibly across the space between
them.

"Ah, that lady there, you mean?" he said, obviously in response to a comment one of his companions had made. His heavy-lidded gaze slid in Anna's direction as he spoke: Goldoni reminded Anna of an overgrown frog. "Well, there's a story there. That is Anna Giraud. You know the red priest, the one who writes music for the orphans' choir at the Ospedale della Pietà? Antonio Vivaldi? The man is an excellent violinist but a mediocre composer—if you remember, I did the libretto for his *Griselda* a few years ago, and his melodies hardly did justice to the words I gave them." The sycophants chuckled agreeably at that.

"In any case," Goldoni continued, "Vivaldi's taken on Signorina Giraud as his favorite singer; she's been given the lead in all his operas since *Farnace*. Look at her; she must be three decades younger than him, and common-born as well: the daughter of a French periwig maker, I'm told. She's hardly beautiful, though I must admit she is elegant. She has a small voice," and here he put his thumb and forefinger so closely together that they nearly touched, then spread his arms wide, "but many languages in which to harangue."

His sycophants burst out into more laughter at that. "She and her half-sister—that's the older woman accompanying Signorina Giraud—they both stay with the red priest as his housekeepers, and Signorina Giraud travels with Padre Vivaldi wherever he goes," Goldoni continued. "All entirely innocently, no doubt."

He snorted his amusement, and the others guffawed with him. Then, as if Goldoni were entirely unaware that she had overheard the entire commentary, he faced Anna directly, gave her a small wave, and bowed ostentatiously in her direction, smiling at her as if they were old friends coming across one another in the great square.

"Pay no attention to the man, Anna," Paolina huffed, sniffing in irritation and taking Anna's arm to pull her along, away from the cluster of men. "He's a boor, and has no real talent at all."

That wasn't true; Anna knew. She was aware of Goldoni only by reputation, but she could sense the man's soul-heart even from this distance. While the energy there wasn't towering and overflowing, the pool of talent within him was substantial with as yet untapped potential. But the internal glow was riddled with a sickly yellow from the man's enormous ego—he *knew* he possessed talent, and probably believed he was destined to be remembered forever for his work.

Anna hoped he was wrong. He would hardly be the first great talent lost to history.

Unfortunately, she had to admit, Goldoni's assessment of her own talent was all too accurate, and that rankled most of all. She had always been able to sing, but in her bonding with Lucio—as she called Vivaldi in private—she had found that while she fed his green heart, he was also feeding hers, enough that she had become passable, if barely so, as a professional singer.

Passable, but no virtuoso. Certainly not as polished and radiant as many of the singers who had accompanied her in Lucio's operas. She had some talent in that direction, but unlike other creative endeavors where the talent resided in the mind, the intellect, and the imagination, the *body* was also involved in singing, for it gave the voice's basic qualities. She knew that it was simple nepotism that gained her the starring roles: the fact that she was Lucio's lover, that she was his companion. Like too much of her life, her status as a singer was a charade.

She'd attempted to convince Lucio that his performances would be even more stunning should he choose someone else, someone with a more powerful voice who could do proper justice to his music, but he would never listen to her. He would shake his head—that shocking mane of bright orange-red hair that had given him his nickname as *il Prete Rosso*, the "red priest"—and fling his arms about in animation. "No," he'd wheeze, with a breathy, almost panting voice; Lucio suffered from *strettezza di petto*, a "lightness of the chest" and could not exert himself physically. "*You* are my singer. No one else. You. No one else understands my work as you do."

So Anna glared at Goldoni but said nothing. The ranks of his sycophants shifted slightly as she and Paolina continued on their separate ways, and Anna's own breath caught, as if Lucio's ailment had suddenly afflicted her.

That one, the one whispering in Goldoni's ear: his stature, his features, the way he stares at me . . .

She touched her face, as if feeling invisible scars from a century ago. "Please don't let him have found me again."

"Anna?" Paolina asked. "What did you say?"

Anna shivered in the rain, realizing she'd spoken aloud. She stared at the men around Goldoni as they were walking away, uncertain. *No, it couldn't be him. It can't be him.* She pulled her cloak closer around her face. Her clothing hung heavily on her with the rain, and the hem of her dress and overcloak were soaked through. "We should get out of this weather," she said. "We need to make sure Signor Vivaldi has had the servants pack everything. I'll be glad to leave Venice behind. The damp isn't good for his health. Come, sister . . ."

Paolina had been three when Anna had taken her from her father in Corsica. Anna had come there after leaving London, where she was involved with a minor English musician, Edward Braddock, the Master of the Choristers of Westminster Abbey. Braddock had been her lover for years, and she was looking far too young. Braddock was not one of those with a green heart of incredible depth, so it had been easy to walk away from him, to take on yet another identity elsewhere, and traveling south against the English winter had been a pleasant thought.

There were few in the little village outside Bastia in Corsica who had even a hint of the green heart about them, but Paolina's mother Maria was one. Anna—who was not yet Anna—lived next door, and she encouraged Maria to follow her passion for art and become a painter, even though her husband had expressly forbidden it. Anna had paid for Maria's surreptitious lessons with an artist in Bastia, had brokered the sale of a few of her sketches. But, in the end, Anna's encouragement had ended up costing Maria her life: the husband had discovered the deception, becoming enraged and jealous, and he had beaten Maria to death in a drunken stupor one night. Anna had been the first to discover the body, with the frightened and wailing Paolina clutching at her dead mother while her father snored, his clothing smeared with Maria's blood, in their bed. Anna had taken the child and left the village and Corsica altogether, sick at heart and racked with guilt over Maria's death.

She couldn't blame Nicolas for that. She had done that terrible damage all by herself.

Paolina, like her father, had no green heart at all. But Anna had declared that Paolina was her relative to anyone who asked: first masquerading as Paolina's aunt, then as her much older sister and, more recently, as her younger sister. She made up a plausible story of how she had come to be the girl's caretaker. She sometimes wondered whether Paolina remembered anything of her old life or her mother's tragic death. Paolina never mentioned her old life, nor commented when people assumed she was the elder of the two of them. With the lines growing more prominent on Paolina's forehead, Anna knew that one day, all too soon, the charade would fall apart as Paolina continued to age and she did not. One day, if they remained together, people would see Paolina as Anna's mother, then her grandmother.

Like the rest of her affairs and lovers and marriages, her relationship with Paolina, and thus with Vivaldi, could only be temporary. That would be true with or without Nicolas' presence—but if Nicolas was here, it might be a short time indeed.

She shook her head at the thought. *It's not Nicolas. It can't be.*

She glanced back once again at Goldoni and his people as she and Paolina made a dash across the piazza, scattering pigeons. She looked for the shorter man, whose face averted from her so she could not see it again, and she worried as she pressed her fingers against the sardonyx pendant under the front of her dress.

In her dream that night, she saw Nicolas' face. When she laid out the Tarot the next morning, she felt his presence in the cards. His mocking laughter was held in the sound of the vials in her alchemical lab striking together as she packed them for their journey. The Vivaldi household in Vienna was preparing to move to Ferrara for several months, where Lucio had been asked to stage an opera season, including at least one new work of his own which would, of course, feature Anna.

She stared from the windows of their house looking for Nicolas' features, searched the faces of those crossing the bridges or gliding by in the hired boats.

"Signor Vivaldi is asking for you," Paolina said as she entered Anna's bedroom on the third floor. "The servants have moved all the furniture from the ground floor up to the next in case of flood, and sheeted most of it already. I'll make certain that the house will be ready for your return next August."

"Thank you," Anna told the young woman, embracing her. "I don't know what we'd do without you running the household." She kissed her forehead. "I'll go see Lucio," she told her. "If you'd finish packing my dresses, I would be so grateful, dear."

Vivaldi was in the first-floor drawing room, sitting on one of the cloth-draped chairs as servants bustled about around him. The score for a new opera was laid on a table in front of him, and he tapped his chin with a forefinger as he looked at it. His powdered white periwig was askew, with curls of red hair now fading with age escaping from underneath. Anna clucked. "Lucio, really," she said. "This will never do. What will they say if you go out this way?" She knelt alongside him, adjusting the wig and tucking his hair underneath again. His frock coat was stained with ink from the score, as were his fingertips. She *tsked* again. "Look at you. You're a complete mess."

"Anna, you fret too much. I was just resting here waiting for you." He rose from his chair with a groan, reaching for the walking stick that rested against it. The effort made him lean hard on the stick for a moment, bent over as he regained his breath. His face flushed a blotched pink, then regained its normal color.

"The air here's bad for you, Lucio," she told him. "It's good we're leaving Venice again. I know it's your home, but the dampness gets into your chest."

"Bah," he said, waving one hand in dismissal. "It's nothing. We'll go to the performance at Teatro San Salvatore this evening before we leave; the music will make us feel better. The program is Pergolesi's *Il prigioniero superbo*, with a *buffa* intermezzo, *La serva padrona*. They played in Naples last season to a good response, I'm told. That sounds interesting, doesn't it?" She could hear the whistling in his chest as he drew in a breath.

The memory of the afternoon's encounter made her shake her head. "Perhaps we should remain at home tonight, Lucio," she told him. "That way you can rest before we set off to Ferrara. We could ask a few of our friends to come over and dine with us. We could create our own musical evening. There's still time—the servants could uncover the pianoforte and the furniture in the drawing room . . ."

He shook his head. "No, no. I've already accepted the invitation for us. What's the matter, Anna? You usually look forward to these evenings."

He was right in that. The last several years had been kind to Antonio Lucio Vivaldi, and through him, to Anna as well. The "red priest"—Vivaldi was nominally still a priest, though he hadn't had official functions within the church or celebrated the mass in decades—had met Anna in 1721; she had become his lover soon after, and she and Paolina had lived with him since 1723, the longest time she'd lived with anyone since Nicolas himself. In 1730, she had accompanied him to Prague along with his father, where two new Vivaldi operas had premiered. They returned to Venice, but also had resided briefly in both Mantua and Verona, where *Semimmide* and *La Fida Ninda* were performed. The Ospedale della Pietà paid Vivaldi a fixed honorarium of 100 ducats a year to produce concerti for the musical students there; recently, the English librettist Charles Jennens had purchased a few of his compositions, and there were commissions for Vivaldi from both the Austrian and French courts. Anna's life with him was easy and peaceful, and his capacious soul-heart surrounded and nourished her as few before had.

As Bernini had, in his time.

She was happy with Lucio, though it was becoming more and more difficult to hide her lack of advancing age. Already, people were calling her "surprisingly well-preserved" despite her attempts via cosmetics to appear older.

Maybe it's time to think of leaving him. Maybe that's why I think I keep seeing Nicolas. After all, the last time was a century ago . . .

She patted Lucio's cheek as he gave her an exaggerated pout. She tried to remember the face she'd seen in the piazza; perhaps it *hadn't* been Nicolas with Goldoni. Perhaps she'd been mistaken. Yes, such a mistake would have been easily made through the rain and mist, and perhaps her mood had clouded the Tarot cards when she laid them out.

"Then we'll go," she told him. "Let me go find Paolina, and have her help me get ready."

But she would also prepare something else, just in case her fears and the Tarot were right, and Nicolas walked the bridges and courtyards of Venice.

Applause filled the Teatro San Salvatore after the performance, arising mostly from relief rather than appreciation. Even the players seemed to sense it, giving perfunctory bows and not bothering to return for an encore. "Well, what did you think, my dear?" Lucio asked, leaning over toward her in their box.

She shook her head. "The intermezzo was entertaining."

"But the rest?"

"The rest was utterly forgettable," she answered succinctly. "Tedious and long."

Lucio grunted at that, but she saw the amused glimmer in his eyes. "I thought the soprano was too shrill. You would have sung the part far better."

She patted his hand, resting atop his cane. "You say that because you always hear me with your heart and not your head," she told him.

"I do not," he said, his chest puffing out as if he were offended, his lips pressed together.

"You do, and I love you for it," she told him. She wanted to lean over and kiss away the scowl from that tight-pressed and familiar mouth, but she could not, here in public. She consoled herself by patting his hand again: a sisterly touch, the touch a housekeeper might give to her long-time master, or a singer to her patron. It wasn't fair: she told herself that she loved Lucio, perhaps more than she'd loved anyone before, yet she could never show that in public. Never, for a priest could not marry.

They must always pretend chastity and innocence, even when the gossip and whispers about them were nearly ubiquitous. "Let's go home, Lucio. We have a long day of travel tomorrow."

They made their slow way from the box through the throngs clogging the hallways and stairs, stopping occasionally to speak to those they knew: the musicians, the regulars, the patrons of the arts. "Signor Vivaldi, Signorina Giraud," she heard someone call out, and she glanced over to see Carlo Goldoni waving at them from the head of the grand staircase to the ground floor.

"Ah, Signor Goldoni, a pleasure as always to see you," Lucio called out as Anna sighed. Goldoni bowed to the two of them as they approached. He seemed to have lost his sycophants, or rather, those around him were a different set than those following him in the piazza. Anna recognized none of the faces from the afternoon's encounter, nor did any of them resemble Nicolas in the slightest.

"And you as well, my friends," Goldoni responded. "I was just telling my companions that Pergolesi's work is that of an errant child compared to your own stellar compositions, Signor Vivaldi. It would be like comparing a single olive seed to an entire grove of fine, mature trees, a grove that has consistently produced the finest oil."

Lucio beamed at the extravagant compliment. "Signorina Giraud might agree with you," Vivaldi said, and Goldoni's bulbous eyes swung toward her. "She said she enjoyed the intermezzo, but found the *opera seria* tedious."

"Ah, yes," Goldoni purred. "The Signorina has a fine and cultured ear, as we know. Why, I was remembering the wondrous performance she gave in your *Griselda*. A pity the maestro didn't see fit to utilize her talents tonight."

"You're so gracious, Signor Goldoni," Anna told him, curtsying slightly. "But I fear I have only a *small* voice." She placed thumb and forefinger close together, imitating Goldoni's earlier gesture. The man's eyes widened slightly, and she smiled at him. His gaze quickly left her to return to Vivaldi.

"I thought the first act was poorly paced, Signor," he said, "and I must blame the libretto. Why, if I'd had the opportunity to tell the story myself, I would have severely trimmed the prisoner's lament . . ."

As Goldoni continued to expound on how he could have improved the libretto, they made their way down to the main hall. The bulk of the audience had already departed, as Lucio took the stairs exceedingly slowly to preserve his breath, and Goldoni had decided that he'd found a sympathetic ear. Anna followed alongside Vivaldi as he conversed with Goldoni, making their way outside to the series of arches that opened out onto a small courtyard in front of the hall. The rain from earlier in the day had ended. The cooler evening air was a relief after the stuffy atmosphere inside the theater, and Anna longed to return home and divest herself of hair extensions, dress, petticoats, and shoes. Lucio was already breathing heavily, just from the exertion of the stairs. The bulk of the crowd was moving toward the Grand Canal and their waiting private boats and *vaporetti*, or strolling along the Calle del Forno toward the Ponte di Rialto.

"Come, Signor," she said to him, taking Lucio's arm and nodding to Goldoni, who was still prattling on about the libretto. "We should not bother Signor Goldoni any longer. Our boatman is waiting."

They had just started walking in the direction of the canal when Anna saw movement in the courtyard: someone rushing from the shadows toward them, and in his hand, a glittering line of steel. She heard someone in the crowds shout in alarm as the man passed, the call echoing from the buildings around them. The attacker's gaze, she noticed, was fixed on her, not on Lucio or Goldoni.

Tall. Not Nicolas . . .

She had only a moment to respond, not enough time to reach for the vials in the pocket sewn into her dress. She flicked her hand toward the man, as if trying to ward him off and spoke a single word in Arabic. The flagstone immediately in front of the attacker tilted up a hand's breath, and the attacker's booted foot caught its edge. The man went down hard, arms splayed out to break his fall, and the thin saber he was carrying pinwheeled away from him, the steel ringing against stone. It landed near Anna's foot, and she snatched up the blade, placing it hard against the stunned man's neck. "Don't move," she told him. "If you lift your head, we'll see how sharp this point is."

Goldoni and Lucio were already calling out for help, and attendants from the theater came running out to the courtyard to take the man. As Anna pulled away the weapon, they lifted him up. No, he was definitely not Nicolas. The man's face was bloodied and scraped, as were his hands and arms, his breeches torn at the knees. He stared at them sullenly. Blood drooled from a cut lip and one nostril. She saw him glance back at the stone flag, still tilted strangely in the air.

"We should thank God, Signorina Giraud," Goldoni said, "that the flag on the courtyard was loose, and that this assassin was clumsy. Venice might have lost the great Vivaldi otherwise." Anna understood Goldoni's interpretation—to him, standing to one side, it might have appeared that the attacker was after Vivaldi, who was certainly the most well-known of the trio, but she had seen the man's eyes. He hadn't been intending to thrust at Lucio, but to his right, where Anna had been standing.

Lucio stood before the attacker, frowning at him. "I don't know you." He glared at the man; his breath whistled in the night air, harsh and fast. "Who are you?" he demanded. "Why did you attack me?" The man spat at Vivaldi's feet, the bloody mess landing near his shoe. Lucio drew his hand back and slapped the man hard across the cheek. "You'll tell us soon enough," he said. He took the saber from Anna's hand and gave it to one of the men holding the attacker. "Send for the authorities and have them hold this man. Tell the Council that I expect him to be charged and will send them my testimony against him." He looked at the would-be assassin again. "You'll be punished severely for this outrage."

The man only scowled. Anna thought that strangest of all—he didn't seem to fear the dungeons of Venice and his likely execution at all.

Lucio turned to Anna as the man was dragged away. She watched the attacker: she didn't know the face. He could have been a random thug, working on his own or perhaps someone had hired him. Had

Nicolas hired him?—that was the question she desperately wanted answered.

"You were indeed brave, Signorina," Lucio was saying. "You show us again your mettle and talents." He bowed to Goldoni. "Signor Goldoni, it was good talking to you. Signorina, let us walk . . ." He extended his arm to Anna; with a final nod to Goldoni, she took it.

They would leave tomorrow and this would be over, she told herself as Lucio huffed and labored alongside her, his breath gone from the exertion of the moment.

At home, she would be safe.

The house was in an uproar when they returned. The head servant of the first floor, a stick-thin and elderly man named Calorgero who had been in Vivaldi's employ for decades, met them at the door. He looked as if he'd been visited by ghosts. "Signor, Signorina, it's terrible . . . Awful . . ."

"What's terrible?" Vivaldi asked, and the servant shot a glance at Anna that made her shiver.

"The Signorina's sister," Calorgero stuttered. "It's so horrible . . ." Anna was already pushing past the man, who tried to hold her back. "Signorina," he cried. "No! You shouldn't—"

Anna rushed into the house; the ground floor was empty for the move, but she heard people talking above on the first floor, and she ran up the staircase, calling for Paolina. No one answered, but another of the servants appeared at the head of the stairs, his face pale and drawn. "Signorina," he said as she reached the landing. The rest of the staff was huddled there, all of them looking terrified and lost. "It was witchcraft. The Devil's work."

"Where is my sister?" she demanded. She could hear the head servant and Vivaldi entering the house on the floor below.

"In your bedroom, Signorina," the man said, and she moved down the hall, pushing through the knot of servants as he called out after her. "Please, Signorina. There's nothing you can do, and this is nothing you should see."

The door to her bedroom was open, and Anna hesitated for a moment before stepping in. The silence in the room was unnerving, and there was a strong smell that seemed strangely familiar. She stepped inside. Stopped.

Blood splattered the walls of the room. The curtain of her bed had been torn down and lay in red-streaked folds on the floor. On the bed Paolina was sprawled naked. Her eyes were open; her body had been gutted from throat to pubis like a market fish, the entrails spilling out on the sheets. Anna stopped a few steps from the bed. She sank to her knees, sobbing.

She knew. She knew who had done this.

"Signorina?" Calorgero's soft voice was reverential and hushed.

Anna sucked in a breath. "What happened here?" she asked the servant, her voice quavering. She tried not to look at the body on her bed, but couldn't help herself. She tried to look only at the face, the face that brought memories flooding back to her:

Holding and comforting Paolina the night her mother was murdered, letting the girl sob against her shoulder in the darkness, crooning soft words of meaningless comfort. "Shh, it will be all right, la mia piccola allòdola. You'll see. I'll take care of you and no one will ever hurt you. I promise . . ."

Paolina had laughed at Anna the first time they'd met Signor Vivaldi. "Look at you," she'd said. "You're positively shivering. When he was playing the harpsichord, you sat there entranced, like you were seeing something that none of the rest of us could see. And that shameless flirting afterward . . ." She laughed again. "What is it about you and artists?" she asked. "You're like a moth circling a torch . . ."

They were with Lucio in Vienna, just two years ago, alone in their rooms in the hotel as Lucio attended some fête Anna had declined to attend with him. The two of them cuddled together as they had decades ago, and Paolina stroked Anna's red-tinged hair, comparing it with her own locks. "Look at the gray strands," she said. "You haven't changed, Anna, not in the twenty years and more I've known you. You still look the same as you did when you and my mother were friends. Tell me—what magic keeps you this way? Is it some potion that you've concocted with those chemicals you keep in your room? If so, I want you to give it to me, also."

Anna had laughed with Paolina, but the laughter had been tinged with sadness. *I would give it to you, if I could,* she wanted to tell her. *But the secret she'd once had still eluded her; when she'd last tried to replicate the experiment with mice, it had been the same old tale: the elixir gave them a brief return to youth, but they still always died: quickly and suddenly.*

Then there was the price. *Even if you had the elixir, would you give it to her, knowing that there is a payment she must make for immortality, as you have, as Nicolas has?*

That was a question she could never answer. Now, for Paolina, she would never have to.

Anna's head was pounding and she felt as if she couldn't breathe. "Tell me," she told Calorgero once more. She thought she heard Lucio struggling up the stairs, and she closed the door. She wasn't certain why, but she wanted to hear Calorgero's tale before Lucio was present. "What happened here?"

"It was not long after you and the Signor went to the opera," Calorgero told her. "We noticed a choking, dark vapor filling the house, as if there were fires in all the hearths and every flue in every chimney had been closed. I could barely see through the clouds filling every room. It sent all of us coughing and gasping for breath." He glanced at the bed, then looked away again quickly. Anna saw the muscles of his jaw bunch and relax, and his throat pulse as he swallowed. He looked at the stained walls, at the ceiling, at the floor between them. "I tried to find your sister," he continued. "I called for her and I thought I could hear her screaming, but then the vapors overcame me and I fell. I don't know how long I remained asleep, but when I woke up, I saw the rest of the staff just beginning to wake also. I called for your sister again, but she didn't answer. We began searching for her, and I . . ." He gulped once more. "I found her here, as you see her. I sent one of the kitchen staff to get help, but then you and the Signor arrived, and . . ." He waved a hand at the room. ". . . you see what has happened. I am so sorry, Signorina, but there was nothing we could have done. This was sorcery. A terrible black sorcery. It must have been."

The door opened and Vivaldi stepped into the room. He stopped a bare stride from the door. Anna heard the wheeze of his breath. "*Porca l'oca!*" he spat, then made the sign of the cross. "May God have mercy on her poor soul. Anna, who has done this horror?"

"I don't know," she told him. Her voice shook against the lie, her gorge rising in her throat so that she had to swallow the bitterness. She forced herself to go toward the bed, pulling a sheet over Paolina's body to the neck to cover her, then reaching down with trembling fingers to close her eyes. Somewhere outside, on the canal, a couple laughed incongruously. Near the door, Lucio huffed and gasped, his breath fast and labored.

"See that Signor Vivaldi is given cognac and something to eat," she told Calorgero. "There was some excitement at the theater also, then this. Tell him what you've told me, but Signor Vivaldi should rest before the authorities arrive."

"I'm perfectly . . ." Lucio started to protest, then broke into a fit of coughing. ". . . fine," he finished, dragging his sleeve over his mouth.

"Hush," Anna told him. "You *will* be fine, once you've rested. But for right now, recover your strength; you'll need it."

"Then come with me, Anna," Lucio said. "You shouldn't stay here, in this—" He stopped; she wondered what word he intended to use.

Anna shook her head. "Let me stay here for a bit. I wish to pray for my sister, and clean her face before people see her. She'd want that. Please . . ."

"As you wish, Anna. Should I send up one of the maids to help you?" She shook her head in mute answer. "I'll have them wait just outside if you need them," he continued. "Anna, I'm so sorry. I don't know what to say."

She managed to favor him with a wan, uncertain smile, and Lucio and Calorgero left her. When the door shut behind them, Anna finally let herself give in to the grief and terror, to the great racking sobs that welled from deep inside her. "I'm sorry," she told Paolina. "This is my fault. My fault. I never thought he would do this . . ." She let the sorrow take her again.

Nicolas. Everything said it was him: the magic, the spell that put everyone to sleep. Her command of magic had always been mere conjurer's tricks compared to his. She'd *seen* him kill with a spell, and had watched the pleasure he took in his power.

Nicolas.

She glanced around the room. On her dresser, in a space that seemed to have been deliberately cleared, sat an envelope of stiff, ivory paper with Anna's name scrawled across the face in an ornate hand. She went to the dresser, picked up the envelope, and turned it in her hands. The flap had been sealed with red wax, but there was no insignia pressed into surface. She felt her heart flutter once against her ribs. She broke open the seal and pulled out the single folded sheet inside; the words there had been penned in a thick red-brown ink; Anna was terribly afraid that she knew exactly what that "ink" had been.

P—

If you're reading this, then you've survived the little message that I sent you earlier this evening, as I'm entirely confident you will. Don't worry, that was only a simple, friendly reminder of my feelings toward you—we both know now that we don't die easily and heal altogether too quickly and well. I'd really hoped to scar you for the rest of eternity. I might have been satisfied with that. Now I understand that the best way to hurt you is to hurt those nearest you.

By now you're aware of the gift I've left you. I can assure you that her death was slow and painful and agonizing, and that she was awake to experience most of it. An exquisite death; one that gave me great pleasure. It will sustain me for some time, so you needn't worry that you'll see me in the immediate future. But you will see me.

The old priest-musician of yours is your lover. I know that. And so I'll make certain that both he and you suffer for that love—slowly, in small steps. I urge you to stay with him and try to protect him,

because I'll make it my duty to see that he's brought down with you,
down to the level you deserve. You can't imagine the pleasure that will
bring me, or perhaps you can understand that better than anyone.

I am your eternal companion. No one else.

N

Anna crumpled the paper in her fist, as if she could obliterate the words with the pressure of her fingers. "I won't let you do this," she told the air, told Nicolas. Her voice was a dead thing; it had no energy, no life. She looked again at Paolina's face, at peace now in a place where Nicolas could no longer hurt her. She felt the need to check on Lucio, but before she left the room, she went to the trunk at the foot of the bed and re-trieved the traveling pistol in the bottom compartment. She placed it in her belt—she would make certain that it was cleaned and oiled, and that she kept it nearby. When she and Lucio eventually went to Ferrara, after they buried Paolina, she would be taking that with her also.

Ferrara was still a walled city, as it had been for over two centuries: mas-sive fortifications surrounded the town on all sides. The Po di Volano, a branch of the greater Po River to the north, formed an additional defense: the stream had been diverted to become a moat between the outer walls and inner walls. During the reigns of Ercole d'Este and his son Alfonso (who had married Lucrezia Borgia, about whose predi-lections there were terrified whispers), those walls served the city de-fensively, as Ferrara warred with both Venice and the Papal armies. In recent decades, the city had begun to spill beyond the ancient fortifica-tions, though they were still fitfully manned, and the gates of the city remained open.

Anne and Lucio's carriage jounced through the northern gates and into an opulent, vibrant city with wide boulevards and impressive *pala-zzi* for the rich. Ahead, they glimpsed the massive, high brick walls and bastions of the Castello Estense at the center of the town, and the squat towers of the Cathedral of St. George. Ferrara was still Venice's rival, but it was now in the arts and music that they warred with each other.

"We'll have a wonderful stay here," Vivaldi said to Anna as the carriage lurched over the cobblestones of the street, the hooves of the horses punctuating his speech. "You deserve it, after what you've been through." Since Paolina's death, Lucio had been especially solicitous toward Anna, which had only made her more alert to watch for Nicolas. She hoped that their leaving Venice so soon after Paolina's burial would keep Nicolas from them.

If not—she had her own preparations and her own small magical skills.

They heard the driver calling out warnings to pedestrians. The sights, sounds, and smells of the city swelled around them through the open windows of the carriage: the hammering (and inventive curses) of a smithy as they passed; the animated and varied conversations of the people on the street; the yeasty fullness of bread baking; the impudent, bright colors of flowers in the window boxes of the houses. "Cardinal Ruffo was most complimentary in his letters, Anna," Lucio continued. "He said that an opera season under my direction will be a crowning achievement for Ferrara, and that my own opera will undoubtedly be the chief jewel in that crown. He was also most generous in the salary he offered. I'm very much looking forward to meeting him. We'll have much success here; I'm certain of it. We'll begin rehearsals within the week—it will be good for you to be singing again."

The carriage swayed as they turned at an intersection, moving toward the cathedral and Ruffo's offices as both Cardinal and Archbishop of Ferrara. The driver finally reined the horses to a halt in front of a brick edifice. Valets hurried to the carriage to place a step at the door and open it for them, hands extended to help them down. Anna emerged first into the sunlight, taking the proffered hand and stepping onto the flags of the courtyard. The cathedral loomed just across the street, the towers throwing long shadows toward them. Anna dusted the worst of the road dirt from her clothing as Vivaldi was helped from the carriage, breathing heavily. He glanced around the entranceway of the building, looking visibly disappointed at their reception.

"I thought they knew to expect us this morning," he said to Anna.

A young priest was hurrying toward them from the entrance stairs, his robes billowing behind him. She nodded toward him.

"Perhaps they've just realized that," she said as the priest nearly skidded to a halt before them. The man did not look pleased. He glanced from Vivaldi to Anna, and his glance was sour and appraising.

"Signor Vivaldi, Signorina," he said. "Cardinal Ruffo has asked me to escort you to his offices immediately."

"Very good," Lucio told the young man. "Perhaps we can have our driver take our trunks to the house that he has arranged for us in the meantime."

"Actually," the priest said with a twitch of his mouth; he was looking more at the ground than either of them, "Cardinal Ruffo would like your driver to remain here for the moment." He didn't give them time to question the statement. He gestured toward the building. "If you'll follow me . . ." he said, and began walking quickly toward the stairs up to the entrance.

"I don't understand," Lucio said, frowning and not moving.

The priest stopped, grimacing as he turned back to them. "The cardinal will explain, Signor. Please. . . ." He gestured again, and Lucio sniffed in irritation, but began following the man. Anna took his arm, so she could help support him on the marble steps. Lucio was huffing by the time they ascended the dozen or so steps, and the priest continued into a cool atrium, from which double staircases led up to the next floor. There were several people moving about the atrium, both priests and others, and Anna could feel their stares as they entered.

Their escort started up the left-hand stair and Vivaldi groaned.

"A moment, Monsignor," Anna called out. Her voice echoed coldly on the polished marble walls. "Signor Vivaldi must rest before he can attempt those stairs."

The priest paused, though without good grace. When Lucio finally began to move, he hurried up the staircase, the two of them following far more slowly. Lucio was out of breath when they arrived at the top, with the priest now waiting for them down a hall before a set of carved, oaken double doors. The room beyond was richly appointed, with heavy brocaded curtains, and large paintings set on all the walls. The faces in the portraits—most of them in ecclesiastical robes—seemed to regard them as the priest gestured toward chairs set around a heavy table. "The cardinal will be with you shortly," he said, closing the doors to the hallway and then vanishing through another door on the far wall. He shut that one as well.

Lucio sat heavily in one of the chairs, scowling. "This is an outrage, to be treated this way," he fumed. "Made to wait like beggars, with no refreshment after a long ride." He wheezed and coughed into a perfumed handkerchief. "If this is the hospitality of Ferrara, we should have stayed in Venice."

"I know, Lucio," Anna told him in a whisper, patting his hand. "Perhaps there's been some mistake." She didn't dare do or say more; she had a strong sense that they were being observed, though that may have derived from the dour, stern faces in the portraits staring at them. "Surely the cardinal will realize this and apologize."

The inner door opened again perhaps a quarter of an hour later, with the same priest intoning, "His Eminence, the Cardinal and Archbishop Tommaso Ruffo." Both Anna and Lucio rose to their feet, then each bent a knee as the cardinal swept into the room. He was white-haired and moved with the ponderous care of the elderly.

He moved first to Vivaldi, holding out his hand with the ring of his office. Lucio took the proffered hand and kissed the ring. "Your Eminence," he said.

Cardinal Ruffo then offered his hand and ring to Anna. The man's skin was clammy and mottled with age, furrowed with ridges and wrinkles. His eyes were dark and rheumy, with white wings of eyebrows set on the bony ledge above them. She touched her lips to the ring; the gold strangely warm. "Your Eminence."

"Please, both of you, sit," Ruffo said, the first words he'd spoken. Anna noted that the cardinal himself did not sit with them, but remained standing. "Signor Vivaldi," he began without niceties, "some troubling information has come to my attention which has caused me to reconsider my offer to you. I've been told that, as a priest, you refuse to celebrate the sacred Mass."

"Your Eminence," Lucio answered heatedly, "that is not true. I have not refused. I fear that I'm *unable* to lead the Mass. The fumes of the incense, the kneeling and rising, the walking . . ." Anna could hear the wheeze in his breath. He thumped his chest. "I have not the breath for it. I was forced to most reluctantly give up that service to the church. I regret that loss every day and pray to our God that He sees fit to restore my health so I can once again perform those duties."

Ruffo scowled. His fingers prowled the purple sash around his scarlet robes. "Certainly a *priest* . . ." He paused, emphasizing the word. ". . . would offer up his suffering to the Lord in return for the miracle He grants us during the Mass." He waved away the protest that Lucio started to make, and Anna saw the cardinal glance quickly to her, the scowl deepening on his face, before returning his attention to Lucio. "But that is a small thing compared to the vile rumors that are circulating regarding Signorina Giraud, her sister, and you, Signor."

"Your Eminence—" Vivaldi began, but the cardinal again waved his hand in dismissal.

"I cannot, in good conscience and with my duty to the church, allow you to work in Ferrara, especially under my patronage. I am therefore rescinding the offer made to you, and must insist that you and your . . ." He seemed to consider the word he wished to use. ". . . *companion* depart Ferrara immediately. The monsignor here will give you twenty ducats for the expense of your journey, and we have made arrangements for you and the Signorina tonight in a palazzo outside the city walls." He took a long breath. "I am genuinely sorry for this, Signor Vivaldi, but this behavior of yours . . ." He shook his head. "I cannot condone it."

"Your Eminence," Lucio began, but the cardinal held up his hand, stopping any protest Vivaldi might have made.

"I have nothing more to say." Ruffo inclined his head to Lucio, who appeared numb and stricken, and—perfunctorily—to Anna. He turned to leave as the priest opened the inner door for him.

"Your Eminence," Anna spoke, and the man looked back at her over his shoulder. "Who told you these poisonous lies?"

"Lies?" he asked, with seeming amusement. "I assure you that I trust my source, Signorina."

"Who told you?" she persisted. "I ask you to name our accuser so that we might defend ourselves."

Ruffo's scowl deepened with her blunt insistence. "I trust my source, Signorina," the cardinal repeated. "That should be sufficient for you. I will pray for a safe return journey for the both of you." And with that, he was gone.

The priest closed the door after the cardinal. "Your carriage is waiting," he said to them. "I'll give the driver directions to the palazzo."

"Signorina," the house valet said as Lucio started up the stairs toward his bedroom, following a quartet of servants with his trunks. Her own servants, with her two trunks, waited as she paused. "I was asked to give you this when you arrived . . ."

The valet handed her an envelope with her name inked across it in a familiar, ornate hand. She peered at it, her stomach suddenly knotted. "Who gave this letter to you?" she asked.

"Monsignor Lorenzo Ceribelli," the man answered. "He arrived here yesterday from Rome, on business with Cardinal Ruffo."

Anna could feel her hands sweating as she held the envelope. She thanked the valet and went to her own rooms, pointedly well down the hall from those of Lucio. There, she opened the envelope. The missive inside was brief, but unmistakably in Nicolas' hand, and written in French: *Cour. Une heure après dîner.* Courtyard. One hour after dinner.

She sent a note to Lucio that she was not feeling well and would dine privately in her room. She made certain that the traveling pistol was serviceable, that the flint was secure and the powder in the pan dry, the ball in place in the barrel. She nestled the pistol in the pocket of her cloak, its weight a reassurance. She thought of her chemicals, still packed away in one of the trunks, but there was no time for that, even if one of the servants could bring them to her. The vials she had sewn into the padded satin belt of her dress would have to suffice.

She waited, eating almost nothing from the tray the kitchen servants brought to her. From the balcony of her room, she could see the small courtyard; she watched the shadows lengthen and evening spread its purple veil over the olive trees there. No one entered the courtyard, no one walked there—the family who owned the palazzo was away. Once, she thought she heard Lucio's voice from an open window, but otherwise the palazzo was quiet and serene. She heard one of the pages escort Lucio down to his dinner, and return with him an hour and half later. Finally, she left her room and went down the stairs, passing through open arches into the court.

The smell of jasmine, growing on trellises around the court, was strong in the still evening, the petals now opened and full. The courtyard was shielded on three sides by the house and its two wings, but was open to the field and pastures beyond at the far end. There were benches set at intervals along the path that wandered through the garden, and Anna sat on the bench nearest the main house, where she could see much of the courtyard. The moon was rising, bathing the landscape in its silvered glow but making the shadowed corners seem darker yet.

She heard him before she saw him, a rustling at the open end of the courtyard, then the sound of boots on the flagstones of the path. She rose, and he stopped a few strides from her. He bowed, then smiled when she didn't respond. Like her, he appeared to be in his twenties, and he was dressed (as he had been when she'd last seen him) in a monsignor's robe and sash, with a crucifix around his neck. She remembered the features now: Maroncelli's face, Nicolas' face. "Perenelle," he said. He spoke in French, not in *Veneziano*. "A lovely pendant you're wearing. And your face is as smooth and untouched as ever. What a shame; I'd hoped to rob you of your beauty forever, but alas. We both know now that the elixir had more than one gift to give us."

The fingers of her left hand started to lift toward her cheeks but she stopped them; they went instead to the cameo on her breast, the pendant he'd given her so long ago. Her right hand she kept in the pocket of her cloak, curled around the wooden stock of the pistol. A knife would not kill him, any more than it would kill her, but a lead musket ball, ripping and tearing through his body, perhaps even into his heart—it was possible that might. She put her hope on that. "You were the one who went to Cardinal Ruffo."

A grin. "*Oui*, I did. He's a very old-fashioned man, the cardinal, and very firm in his faith. He was most terribly distressed to learn about the sinful behavior of the composer he'd hired." He shook his head in mock sadness. "A priest who won't celebrate mass, and who plows the field between the legs of his favorite singer and housekeeper, and probably that of her sister as well."

"Bastard!" she hissed. "Murderer!"

He spread his hands wide. "Did I lie to the cardinal? Did I tell an untruth? I think not." His smile collapsed and his eyes narrowed. "We will live forever, Perenelle, and the one thing that will make my long life a pleasant one will be if yours is a misery. You can't believe how sweet your torment tastes to me. You're like a fine dinner: not something I want every night, but for those special occasions."

"Why? Why can't you simply leave me alone? Go live your life, and let me live mine."

He shrugged. "We both have to pay for what's been given us," he answered. "I know what your payment has been: I know that you *need* these artists that you find. And me . . . Well, I have my own needs, my own requirements for the gift of life. Should I tell you what your elixir has given me as my need, or have you already guessed? Being in the church for many of my lives has allowed me to fill my own hunger most excellently. Ah, the Inquisition . . ." He paused, then his lips curled momentarily. "It's *your* fault, Perenelle, *your* fault. Your fault for having created the elixir, for tempting me after I saw you run from me as a young woman again. If I'm a monster, then I am of your own creation." He took a breath.

"What do you want, Nicolas?"

"Why, I've already told you," he said. "Why don't you sit? I've a rather long tale to tell, one I think you'll find interesting." When she didn't move, he shrugged. "As you wish. Stand, then. Do you miss your old notebook, Perenelle? I know you've been trying to recreate the potion, and I know that so far you've not been able to do so. You were always the best of us with alchemy, as I was the better with magic." He lifted his hands as if he were about to cast a spell, and she stiffened, ready to fire the pistol. But his hands dropped again. "Yet I have something you don't. *I* have your notes, all nicely written down and detailed. Every step of the process. Not that it's done me much good. Those mice you kept: they all died, didn't they? Age caught up to them, in a single moment, and they died in agony. I know, because I replicated your experiment after you left: first with mice, then . . ." He paused. ". . . with people. You should know, by the way, that it's a truly horrible death for a person. I can't imagine the pain they must experience, but I can hear it in their shrieks and see it in the terror fixed on their faces after they die." He smiled. "And I can *taste* their pain, also. It's wonderful. Still, your elixir is a failure, Perenelle."

"But it *does* work," she protested. "Look at me. Look at you."

He shook his head. "There was something different with that version of the formula, some change you made but didn't write down, or perhaps it was only an accident—something introduced to the potion that you didn't notice. When I finally decided that if I didn't take the elixir I was going to die myself, it was *your* potion I took—what was left in the vial from that day that you took it and changed before my eyes. *That* one worked for me as it did for you."

She was already shaking her head. "That one was the same as all the rest. I did nothing differently."

Nicolas shook his head. "You're wrong. It was different. I've followed your notes *exactly*."

"Then give *me* the notebook," she told him. "Let me try. You've missed something. As you've noted, you were always best at spells, Nicolas; I was your superior in the laboratory. I can find what's wrong with the formula."

He laughed. "Handing you the notebooks would give you what

you want, and I've no intention of allowing you that much satisfaction. You'd give the potion to this red priest of yours, wouldn't you? You'd keep him with you forever. No, no, no. I intend to keep the notebook— your misery at watching everyone you love inevitably age and die is part of my pleasure."

He took a step toward her; she retreated the same distance, removing the pistol from her cloak and showing him the weapon. He chuckled dryly. "Is this a jest? You can't kill me with that."

The barrel trembled with his words. "You can't know that."

"Ah, but I do. Remember your face, my dear wife? We both heal very well. I know: three times now I've sustained wounds that would have killed a normal person, including being shot by a firearm. That won't kill me. I *do* know that much."

"We're alchemists, Nicolas. We believe in what we learn. Maybe you're right, but it's an experiment I'm willing to try. After all, you sent a man with a sword after me."

He scoffed. "My little friend at the opera? He was just a reminder, as I said. I told him that if he didn't kill you, then I'd kill his lovely wife— she was already dead, of course; he just didn't know that. He couldn't have killed you. I haven't figured out quite how to do that yet, though I will, I will. In the meantime, I've taken that woman you called a sister as the first step. For the second—well, you actually are fond of that fool of a musician Vivaldi, aren't you?"

"You leave him alone, Nicolas," she grunted. The pistol quivered in her hand as her finger tightened on the trigger. "You've done enough damage already to him."

He was watching her intently, studying her. "Ah, you *are* in love with him. That's so delicious. Well, let me make a deal with you then. I'll leave him alone—if you do the same."

"No."

"So quick an answer; it says so much. I warn you, Perenelle, if you don't do as I tell you, I'll make you regret it. I might not be able to permanently hurt you, but your Signor Vivaldi isn't immune, is he? And there's *so* much gossip I can spread, too. I wonder which would be the most painful for him and you: to destroy his career, or destroy him physically as I did to Paolina—that was her name, wasn't it? Or maybe I should do both, and have the pleasure of his death and of tasting your grief."

"I'm warning you, Nicolas."

He shook his head. "You've nothing with which to bargain, Perenelle. I've told you what I want—and I'll have it, one way or another."

"No!" The word was a shout; with it, her finger convulsed on the trigger. There was a click, the flint struck metal and sparked, and the powder in the pan flashed. The pistol bucked in her hand and with a cry, Nicolas spun around, blood blooming from a sudden hole in his chest, his priestly robes going dark and wet as he collapsed to the ground, sprawled awkwardly on the courtyard's path. His breath gurgled in his throat, and a line of blood flowed from his mouth.

She dropped the pistol. Nicolas still didn't move, lying on the flagstones of the courtyard.

"What's this commotion!" She heard the cry from the palazzo. She saw Lucio at his balcony, staring down at her. "Anna! What's happened?" She heard footsteps from the house as Lucio disappeared from his balcony. She ran toward the house, meeting the house valet on the way out.

"I was attacked," she told them. "There's a man in the courtyard. I had to shoot him . . ."

The servant stared, then moved past her, waving at the other servants gathering, gape-mouthed, in the area. She could hear Lucio lumbering down the stairs, puffing like a great bear and shouting for her. She went to him, embracing him hard. "Oh, Lucio! It's so dreadful. I had to kill him, I had to. He's the one who killed poor Paolina . . ."

He hugged her tightly. She could feel his chest moving, could hear his breath rattling in his lungs as he stroked her hair and shoulder, could feel him pressing the pendant she wore into her skin. She sobbed helplessly, closing her eyes as if she could shut out the sight of Nicolas falling, of the blood flowing from him and pooling underneath. "I thank God you're safe," Lucio whispered. "He hasn't hurt you, then?"

She shook her head, unable to speak. She clung to him, as if she were afraid he was about to be snatched away from her.

It seemed minutes before the house valet came hurrying back to them. "Signorina," he said. "You wounded the man, but no more. There is blood on the stones, and I glimpsed Monsignor Ceribelli fleeing toward the rear vineyard. He wouldn't stop when I called after him; though he was moving only with great difficulty. I've sent two of the servants in pursuit, and they should catch him easily; I've sent another man to the cardinal to inform him."

"He's not dead?" Anna asked. "You're certain?" She remembered Nicolas falling, remembered the blood spilling from him.

"Not unless the dead can walk, Signorina," the valet told her.

"There, you see," Lucio told her. "You haven't killed him. They'll catch the man and he'll pay for what he did. It's not as bad as you feared."

No, it's worse. He was right, then, and he's still out there. But she didn't say that. Instead, she hugged Lucio more tightly, knowing what she must do now.

The servants didn't find the monsignor, nor did they return to the palazzo that night; instead, they were found dead not far from the low rear wall of the grounds the next morning. Both had strange burn marks on their chests, as if a black and silent lightning had descended from the clouds to spear them even while Anna, Lucio, and the rest of the servants were standing nearby.

A vile sorcery was suspected, especially when it was discovered that there was no Monsignor Ceribelli on the papal staff, despite the letters of reference from the Vatican office he had presented to Cardinal Ruffo. For two weeks, Lucio and Anna remained in the palazzo while the incident was investigated, while urgent messages flew back and forth between Cardinal Ruffo and Rome, while the false Monsignor Ceribelli was hunted but not found.

For those two weeks, Anna refused to come to Lucio's room at night: even though he asked, even though she longed to do exactly that. A slow realization burned inside her, more painful than anything Nicolas could have done.

"This is for the better, Lucio," she told him at breakfast that day, when he saw that her trunks were packed and stacked near the door of the palazzo. "I'll be leaving this morning."

"I don't understand," he said. "What have I done?"

She smiled at him and dared to touch his cheek, though she knew the servants were watching them closely and reporting back to Cardinal Ruffo. "You've done absolutely nothing," she told him. "It's a beautiful morning, Signor; come, walk with me, would you?"

She glanced pointedly at the servants along the wall. Lucio grunted and rose from his chair. Together, they walked out into the courtyard. The day was warm and sunny, and the smell of jasmine was gone, the flowers closed tightly in the sunlight. They walked slowly, with Anna making certain that she remained a careful hand's breadth from him. "Lucio," she said softly. "I love you, but you can't be Vivaldi, the famous red priest and composer, while I stay with you. Not anymore."

"Without you, I won't be Vivaldi either," he answered, and she wondered if he understood just what she'd done for him over the years, coaxing that great viridescent soul-heart into full flower. She could feel its glow even now, and it made her yearn to stay, to tell him that she'd changed her mind.

But she could not. Out there somewhere was Nicolas, and she knew he would fulfill his threat. He would heal, too quickly, and he would find another identity, and he would come after them, angrier now than before.

"You will always be the famous Vivaldi," she reassured him. "Your talent remains, whether I'm with you or not. Don't you see? This Ceribelli has given us an opportunity to undo the damage he's done. All you need to do is write a letter to Cardinal Ruffo, repudiating everything Ceribelli said about you and me, and swearing to him that everything you related about the lightness in your chest is true, asserting that your illness is the reason that you don't celebrate Mass. But for that letter to work, it requires a small sacrifice." She stopped. At her feet were the faint stains of blood on the flagstones, still visible in the cracks of the stone despite the servants' scrubbing. "It requires, Lucio, that I leave you so there can be no question that there's nothing between us," she finished.

"No," he said, shaking his head—the same denial she'd given Nicolas on this very spot.

"Yes," she told him. "It's the only way this can work."

"Never to see you again? No. That I can't bear."

"Perhaps it won't be forever," she told him. "I'll go to Vienna, or perhaps one of the towns nearby. When you come to the court there, we can be together for a few stolen nights if we're very careful. I'll write to you, and you will write me. We won't lose touch with each other. But . . ." She began walking again. "To convince Cardinal Ruffo and for you to continue to work as you have, I can't be with you. I'd only be a constant reminder of all the vile gossip. If I stay, the accusations will become truth in everyone's mind—all the more so because they *are* true."

"No," he said again, but the protest was fainter and less emphatic this time, and she knew that it was over.

"We must be apart at least for a time, Lucio. Perhaps we can be together again, later," she told him.

But she knew they could not. She might be with him now and again, but except for those times, she would take another name in some other place, and she would find another soul-heart to nourish and from which to take her own nourishment, and then another, and another . . .

Because if she didn't, Nicolas would come after Lucio in order to hurt her. She must keep moving so that Nicolas couldn't find her and the ones who nourished her.

Despite the eyes of the servants, she allowed herself to touch Lucio's arm. "Remember this, Lucio," she told him. "I love you. I always will. Forever."

5:
CLIO

Camille Kenny

Today

"WE'VE FOUND HIM." Walters' voice overloaded the receiver, and Camille quickly thumbed down the volume.

"What's his name? Is it Pierce? Where is he?" she responded, feeling a surge of adrenaline at Walters' words. *Now I can make plans. I can take him out of my life and make him pay for all he's done.* She could feel her hands trembling with the surge of emotion, and she clutched at the pendant around her neck to settle them. *This time, it'll be over. Forever.*

"Now hold on, young woman," Walters said on the other end of the connection. "I said we've found him, but I don't know much more past that. The person I hired managed to track the IP address of a man Helen Treadway was exchanging regular e-mails with. You were dead on about hospitals—the address is from Beth Israel. But I need to go there and talk to the hospital IT, so I know that the person at that address is actually the person you're looking for—I need to actually *see* him for that. But it feels good—your name and David's come up in a couple of the e-mails. I'm going there today; if it all pans out, I'll have a name for you and an address. Come by the office tomorrow morning and I'll give you everything I have on him. Meanwhile, you hang tight. And listen, if you want me to come with you when you confront him, I can do that, too."

"Okay," Camille said, though she knew she wouldn't take him up on that last offer. When she met Nicolas again, she intended to kill him. "Walters . . ."

"What?"

"Be really careful about this. I mean it. He's a dangerous man."

She could hear the laugh he suppressed. "Don't worry," he said. "I'm always careful."

She had lunch with Mercedes that day at *Annie's*; David was out making the rounds of galleries with his new portfolio; Mercedes worked for an ad agency nearby, writing copy and doing layout for commercial clients.

"You look happy," Mercedes stated flatly after they'd placed their orders. A smile ghosted over her lips. "That's good. *Bueno*."

Her tone made Camille tilt her head. "You don't sound as if you entirely mean it."

Mercedes fiddled with her water glass. "I do, dear. Honestly. It's just . . ."

"Just?"

She brushed back the ebon strands that had escaped from the ponytail into which she'd pulled her hair. "It's not the same for the rest of us anymore. I don't think you know what you meant to me. To *all* of us." The corner of her mouth lifted again, her lipstick, as always, a fiery red. "Okay," she said, "let me back up. I don't think you know what you meant to *me*, anyway. I'll let the others speak for themselves, even though I suspect they feel the same way. I miss having the part of you that I had, Camille. I really do. And so does everyone else."

"You sound like Morris."

Mercedes nodded, her eyebrows lifting slightly. "Morris *especially* misses you. He still hasn't shown up at the *Bent Calliope*, so I went over to his studio a few days ago to see him. He's bitter about you and David, Camille. Almost angry. Says he hasn't been able to work much at all since the last time the two of you talked. He feels betrayed. He heard that Prudhomme's really hot on David's work and is talking him up like he's the next Steiglitz. He insists that it's all because of you— your influence. Said that kind of stuff always happens around you, and that you've abandoned us and now David's the only one who's going to benefit."

"Is that what you think?"

Mercedes looked away, not at Camille, as she answered. "I don't know what I think." Her gaze returned. "But that's the way Morris thinks, and that's all that matters to him."

Camille shook her head; it would do no good to talk about Morris. Not anymore. Even if she somehow lost David, there were a hundred people with soul-hearts as glowing as Morris' or Mercedes' here in New York City alone, and there were still the others in the group she had collected around herself. If Morris was angry, then let him be angry. She had liked him but had never loved him; they had only used each other. *Self-absorbed, again* . . . "What about you?" Camille asked, trying to shift the topic. "How's the novel going?"

A shrug. "Ay, *puñeta!* Slow. I'm in the middle, and there's always a point there where I think I've totally lost my way, and everything I write just seems to suck." She spread her arms wide. "Guess I'll be keeping the day job for now."

"Would you like me to read the new material you have? I'd be happy to do that. Why don't you e-mail me the section you're working on? Maybe a set of fresh eyes on it could give you an idea of what you need to do. It's the least I can do."

"Sure." There was little enthusiasm in her voice.

"Mercedes, you have the talent to sell your novel," Camille told her. It was the truth; Mercedes's green heart was limited; it wasn't a massive radiance like David's or like others that she'd known in her life. Yet she possessed talent, and more important than that, she had the dedication and necessary passion for her art. Camille knew all too well that someone who plumbed the depth of her talent to its final essence might be more important to her discipline than someone with greater potential who never utilized that talent to full extent. Camille had helped Mercedes find all the pathways within that green heart, but the woman had done the rest herself, and the drive that Mercedes possessed was something no muse could provide. "You need to keep believing in yourself."

Mercedes favored her with a dim smile again. "Thanks," she said. "I try. And I am happy for you. David's a lucky guy. I hope he knows it."

"I'll try to remind him."

Their conversation trailed off into small talk about the group and about the small triumphs and failures they'd all seen: the jazz band Kevin had put together to play his original work; Rashawn selling a painting; Joe's play closing after a disappointing week and bad reviews; James finishing the book based on his dissertation. As Mercedes was checking her cell phone to see if it was time to get back to the office, Camille asked the waitress to bring their check.

"Oh," the woman said. "There's no check. A gentleman paid it for you."

"Who?" Camille asked. She could feel the pendant around her neck as if it were made of lead. She glanced at Mercedes, who shrugged.

"He's already left," the waitress said. "But he said to give you this." She placed a napkin on the table. On it, in smeared ink, was drawn a crude image of a guillotine. Seeing it, Camille's breath was snared in her throat.

"What did he look like?" Camille persisted. "Was he short?"

The waitress nodded. "Yeah. Shorter than average, anyway. Light brown hair, kinda long. A nice smile. About your age. Not bad looking; had a little bit of an accent, maybe. You know him?"

"Yes," Camille said. She found that she could barely breathe. "I think I might."

"Camille?" she heard Mercedes saying as she stared at the napkin. "What's the matter? Does that mean something to you?"

Camille finally drew in a long, shuddering breath. "I'm sorry," she told Mercedes. "It's really nothing." She crumpled the napkin in her hand, crushing it tightly as if she could somehow squeeze the life from the hand that had drawn it. "It's a poor attempt at a joke from a former lover. It just . . ." She forced a smile to her lips. "It startled me. I didn't know he lived around here. And, hey, at least we get a free lunch from the bastard, right?"

The laugh she gave was mirthless. The sound hung in the air, weighted and unconvincing.

Outside, she looked around carefully, searching for Nicolas, for anyone whose features were somewhat familiar, anyone who appeared to be
watching her. She saw no one; the crowds on the sidewalk passed by
without a second glance, and she noticed nobody loitering or pretending
to be looking into a shop window while really watching her. She hugged
Mercedes and walked with her to the corner where they separated.

She stood there, turning slowly. No, no one appeared to be ob-
serving her or taking notice. The napkin was still balled in her hand.
*Nicolas. It has to be Nicolas. He wants me to know that he's found me first.
That he's hunting me, too.*

"You bastard!" she shouted suddenly against the clamor of traffic.
"You coward! Show yourself! C'mon, you sadistic son of a bitch! Let's
have it out between us right now, right here! Let's finish it!"

A taxicab honked as it changed lanes; the person the driver had cut
off laid on his own horn. The people nearest glanced at her strangely,
then—in proper New York fashion—ignored the crazy person's out-
burst entirely. Otherwise, there was no answer.

There was a trash can on the corner. Camille tossed the napkin
toward it. It bounced once on the rim and fell back onto the street.
Sighing, Camille picked it up again.

She put it in her pocket.

"Hello?" Camille called into Walters' office. There was, as usual, no
one in the small reception room, but the door to his office was closed—
which was unusual, and through the speckled, translucent glass of
the door, she could see a figure moving around, though she heard no
conversation.

The figure in the office moved toward the door: a splash of blue
pants and a yellow shirt, far too thin to be Walters. The doorknob
turned and Camille saw a woman standing there. She looked to be in
her early-to-mid-twenties, with curly, dirty blonde hair cut short. It was
her eyes that caught Camille the most: her mascara was smudged and
ruined, and there were tracks on her cheeks from tears. The woman ran
a hand over her face as she glanced at Camille. "Can I help you?"

"I'm looking for Mr. Walters. I'm one of his clients, and we had an appointment to talk this morning." The woman looked as if she were about to cry once more. She pressed her lips tightly together. Camille remembered Walters mentioning a granddaughter—*about your age*—and she felt a sudden quick stab of fear. "Are you Beth? His grand-daughter?" she asked. "Is everything all right?"

The young woman shook her head wordlessly. "Grandpa . . ." the word came out choked and solitary. "He's . . ." She couldn't say more. The tears came then, unbidden and full. Camille went to her, taking her hands and leading her to the receptionist's chair. Beth's shoulders shook with her sobs as Camille crouched down in front of her, still holding her hands and feeling tears well up in her own eyes in sympathy.

"I'm sorry," Beth said after a few moments, taking in a long shud-dering breath. Her fingers pressed Camille's fingers. "This is hard . . . We got the news late last night. Grandpa's dead." It was all she could say. She bit at her lower lip, closing her eyes.

Camille felt the shock hit her: a fist of cold air. She gasped, a hand going involuntarily to her mouth. *Be really careful about this* . . . Those had been nearly her last words to Walters. And now . . . "What hap-pened?" she asked Beth.

A sniff. Beth plucked a Kleenex from the box on the table and dabbed at her eyes. "No one's really sure. They found him in an alley. He'd been . . ." She stopped. Took a breath. ". . . burned really badly," she continued, "but they told me it wasn't like he'd been set on fire, more like he'd been struck by bolts of lightning—but there wasn't a storm or any clouds last night." Camille shuddered at that. *Nicolas. This has to be Nicolas.* "They're thinking it may be the same person that killed all the other people, the Black Fire murders, but . . ." Her eyes found Camille's, stricken. "The detectives all remember Grandpa. They said they won't stop until they find the person who did this. Gina Palento—she was one of Grandpa's friends in the department, and was his partner just before he retired—anyway, she's coming over this morning to look into Grandpa's case files. I thought I'd try to straighten some things up . . . thought maybe it would help . . ."

The tears came again, and Camille waited them out, holding Beth's hands. "Can I get you something," she asked. "I could make some coffee, or get you a glass of water?"

"I'm fine," Beth said. "Gina, I mean Detective Palento, should be here in a few minutes, though. She might want to talk to you since Grandpa was working on something for you."

The thought caused the coffee she'd had that morning to rise to her throat, burning. Camille swallowed hard. "Sure," she told Beth. "If you think that might help. Look, why don't I make some coffee? Detectives always drink coffee, don't they?" She laughed shakily at the poor attempt at a joke, which garnered the barest of smiles from Beth but allowed Camille to rise and walk over to the cheap Mr. Coffee machine on the side table. She busied herself finding what she needed, putting in the filter, measuring the coffee, getting water, all the time thinking about how she might answer the questions this Palento might ask. What she didn't need was the NYPD looking into this case and her background—Walters might not have cared that she was using a dead child's name and social security number; the cops definitely would.

"I think I may have dropped something outside," she told Beth. "I'll be right back. The coffee should be ready in a few minutes."

Camille opened the office door, closing it again behind her as she stepped out on the little porch. She went down the battered concrete steps to the sidewalk. She stood there, caught in uncertainty. *If you leave, that detective's going to be even more suspicious, and then you may never find out what Walters discovered. If you leave, you're also leaving David, because you'll have to change your identity once more, have to leave the city, have to run. You'll lose this chance to take care of Nicolas, too.*

She took a deep breath, glancing up and down the street. People moved past her on the sidewalk on their way to errands or appointments; taxicabs, cars, and small trucks moved slowly down the one-way street toward the skyscraper canyons of mid-town. The city breathed all around her: loud, odoriferous, and relentlessly, defiantly alive. Somewhere out there, a small darkness lurked—a darkness that was attached to her, that was her responsibility.

"Fuck," Camille sighed, the obscenity tasting harsh in her mouth. She turned and trudged back up the steps. She hesitated there for a moment with her hand on the doorknob.

She turned it and pushed the door open. "Found it," she said to Beth. "Is the coffee ready yet?"

"Thanks for taking the time to chat with me, Ms. Kenny."

Gina Palento looked to be in her late thirties. A wedding ring glistened on her left hand, and her navy pantsuit was pressed, new, and fashionable. Her glossy, dark hair was clipped very short, the kind of cut with which one could step out of the shower, towel dry, and not worry about having to fuss with the hair. She wore minimal makeup; just a touch of eye shadow and foundation. She certainly didn't have the stereotypical rumpled and tired look that Walters had possessed. Her eyes were an icy and startling blue that verged on gray, set deep in a thin face with sharp cheekbones. She also had a green soul-heart; Camille could feel it, the radiance shining around her, though Camille didn't dare to touch it. She wondered what sparked that creativity in the woman.

"So . . ." Palento said, "just what had you hired Bob—Mr. Walters—to do for you?" Her voice was a gravely alto, and she cocked her head slightly with the question. She'd set a small recorder between the now-neatly stacked papers on Walters' desk; Camille could see an LED blinking on the device.

"He was trying to track down someone for me. A stalker. All I had to give him were a couple of photographs. No name. I . . . I know I hadn't given him much to go on." Camille looked at Walters' desk. She wanted nothing more than to dig into the papers there and see if she could find some clue to what Walters had found—what had caused him to be killed. But she doubted that Palento would let her look, and she didn't want the detective prying into her life. She shrugged. "I was going to tell him today to stop looking, that it was a waste of his time and my money."

Palento nodded. "Then you don't think your investigation had anything to do with his death?"

Camille shook her head. "I don't possibly see how."

"Uh-huh." Palento was nodding her head. Her finger hovered over the button of the recorder, then withdrew. "Stalkers can be violent. Was yours? Did he ever threaten you or hurt you?"

"Not really," Camille told the woman. The lie was bitter ash on her tongue. "He was just some guy I kept noticing following me. I didn't talk to him or confront him."

Another nod. "And you never reported this to the police?"

"I didn't think anyone would pay attention. After all, I didn't know who this was and hadn't had any contact with him. I figured you had more important things to worry about."

"So you were willing pay Bob a nice little fee to find out? Let Bob follow you and hopefully come across this character?"

"I thought if he could get me a name and maybe more information, then I could go to the police. But maybe the guy gave up on me, or maybe he saw Mr. Walters, or maybe I was just wrong." She thought she lied well; she had long practice at it. Palento was nodding again. This time, her finger did press the button and the LED flicked off.

"Well, thanks for talking to me, Ms. Kenny. If I have further questions, I'll be in touch. In the meantime, here's my card. You see that guy following you again, call me, okay? I hate jerks like that." Camille took the card from her, rubbing the cheap stock between her fingers. "You can tell Beth to come in now. I'm ready to talk to her."

Palento pocketed her recorder in her suit jacket. She picked up one of the numerous manila folders on Walters' desk and opened it. Her gaze flicked up to Camille as she rose from the chair across the desk, then back to the folder. It was obvious the detective was dismissing her.

"Beth," Camille persisted, "mentioned that you think it might be one of the Black Fire murders."

Palento stared at her. "It's possible," she said. An eyebrow lifted.

"Well, I hope you find him. The guy who did this to Mr. Walters and those others."

"We will," Palento said. "Thanks again, Ms. Kenny."

Camille nodded, and left the office.

*   *   *

She said nothing to David, mostly because she wasn't certain how to explain it or to tell him just how frightened she was—how frightened she was for both of them. He'd insist that they go to the police about her "stalker," and that would be a disaster: it would expose the fact that she'd never filed any report in the first place, as she'd told David she had; worse, it would arouse Palento's suspicions and she'd end up with her own false identity exposed.

In her older lives, having to change identities hadn't mattered as much, but in recent decades, that was becoming increasingly difficult, and it wasn't something she was willing to undertake lightly.

Camille consulted her Tarot, and laid out a reading so dismally bleak that she gathered up the cards before even attempting an interpretation. The second layout was nearly as foreboding; she put the cards away, shivering at the implications.

So she said nothing, and tried to make it appear that her mood hadn't changed, that she wasn't constantly looking over her shoulder whenever they were out together, that she wasn't scanning the street outside David's apartment to see if she recognized a figure watching in the darkness, that she wasn't afraid to return again to her own apartment because—if Nicolas had been in contact with Helen—he now knew the name she was using and probably her address; that she made sure she kept the Ladysmith with her.

From the scrolls she'd acquired in her current collection, she prepared the ingredients for the few spells she'd managed to master, and made certain they were cemented in her mind. She went to the sword on her dresser, went over and pulled the katana partially from the black, lacquered *saya*, looking at the glossy, oiled steel. She sighed and put the weapon back on the stand.

When David mentioned that Jacob Prudhomme had invited them to his annual birthday party a few days later, she agreed to accompany him, though without great enthusiasm. Still, after days of hearing nothing from Palento nor glimpsing Nicolas, her initial panic had calmed somewhat. "What are his parties like?" she asked him. "What should I wear?"

He grinned at her. "Anything you like. Jacob will have everyone there: from rich customers in formal dress to desperate artists wearing ripped jeans and grimy T-shirts. He likes to have what he calls 'a shocking mixture.' Says the result is more like actual art, then. The stranger and more outrageous you can dress, the happier he'll be. Pick out whatever you think makes you look good, or whatever you're comfortable in. It honestly doesn't matter."

"You *do* know that's absolutely no help to me, don't you?" she told him. "In fact, that just makes it worse."

He laughed. "Then wear nothing at all. He'd *love* that. Jacob'd probably claim you were a living sculpture. A vision of the Muse."

She scoffed nasally. "Yeah. That's *so* not going to happen," she said.

"He'll be disappointed."

"Him, or you?"

"Both of us."

"Then you'll both need to get used to disappointment." She managed a smile, then another thought struck her. "Helen won't be there, will she?"

David shook his head. "No. I seriously doubt it. Jacob knows that we've broken up, and I'm his client. I don't think he'd invite her."

That eased her mind. In the end, she decided on the classic little black dress and heels, with the sardonyx pendant dangling openly over the neckline. Into her small clutch purse, frowning as she did so, she placed a few vials and managed to cram in the Ladysmith as well. "What's the matter?" David asked, as she kept glancing out the rear window of their cab, trying to determine if the black Mercedes two cars back was following them.

"I keep thinking I've forgotten something," she told him. "Sorry."

Jacob Prudhomme had rented the penthouse suite in the Hotel on Rivington for the party. David flashed their invitation card to the security guard at the elevator, and they rode up in silence with two other couples, one in formal attire, the other dressed in what Camille assumed was an attempt at *haute couture*: matching silver jackets in metallic threads, bright red capri pants, she in purple stiletto heels and he in scuffed Chuck Taylors, both with spiked and product-laden hair, both of them wearing too much eye makeup for Camille's taste. She could see both couples trying to gauge her and David, trying to determine if one of them was someone whose name they should know, but saying nothing as the elevator made its long climb to the 20th floor.

David had told her that the penthouse suite was a triplex, taking up the top two floors of the hotel as well as a roof deck. The party was already well underway when they arrived, the bottom floor of the penthouse swirling with people, while wait staff in dress whites circulated among them. "David!" Jacob, his paunch well disguised in an expensive, fitted tuxedo, came forward out of the crowd as they stepped off the elevator (causing the two couples who arrived with them to narrow their eyes speculatively). He clasped David's hands. "So glad you've finally arrived. I have a dozen people here who are anxious to meet you. I have a temporary display with a few of your pictures up on the next floor, and they just *love* the shots. Charm them, and I think someone just might buy the entire set."

He patted David on the cheek and glanced at Camille, smiling. "In fact, introduce them to the subject of your photos, and I'm *sure* they will. Camille, my dear, you look fetching tonight. Is that sardonyx? It's a lovely piece; you must let me look at it more closely later—the style's very old. In the meantime, you two enjoy yourselves. If nothing else, it's a fabulous view." With that, he was off to greet someone else.

It *was* a fabulous view, Camille had to admit. Floor-to-ceiling windows on all sides revealed a glittering view of the nighttime Manhattan skyline, though few in the crowd were gazing at it. A glass-encased stair led up to the next level, from which they could hear the sound of a salsa band and people dancing. Everywhere, people had clustered in small groups, wineglasses in hand. Occasional loud chuckles or high laughter punctuated the general white noise.

Not surprisingly, Camille could sense several people with green soul-hearts in the throng: artists, musicians, intellectuals—their presence lent a faint glow in her mind. She opened herself to them and took in a long breath. She could nearly drown in the creative energy here, and it made her feel half-drunk already.

Camille snagged a glass of Merlot from a passing waiter. "Is that the mayor over there?" she asked David, tipping her glass in the direction of one of the groups.

"Yep," David answered. "Along with Senator Evans. There's at least a dozen other faces you should recognize scattered around: politicians, actors, society people, the whole gamut."

"Jacob runs in high circles."

"He says everyone has walls that need art, and the richer they are, the bigger their walls."

Camille laughed. "A wise man," she said. "Should we go up and see your exhibit on the second floor? I want to know just how embarrassed I should be."

"Didn't I tell you that you should have come naked? Then they *would* recognize you."

She bumped him with her hip and drifted through the crowd toward the stairs.

The salsa band was loud and exuberant, and the insistent beat made her sway helplessly in time as she and David walked between the portable walls of the exhibit. Jacob's tastes were wide and varied. There were paintings: oils, acrylics, and watercolors, both realistic and abstract; lithographs, etchings, ink and pencil drawings; a few small sculptures on stands—and, pinned in the light of small Fresnels, David's photographs of her in black and white.

Her face stared back at her. Her body filled the frames, sensuous and languid, light painting the curves and valleys. "You certainly do have a lovely body," a woman commented from behind them, and Camille and David turned to see Helen. Camille found herself protectively clutching her purse with its vials of carefully mixed chemicals and gun, the delight she'd felt at being here at the party vanishing in that instant.

The smile on Helen's face appeared to have been applied with her lipstick, and she was looking more at David than Camille. "You always had a great eye for models." Then, with a moue of disgust, she waved her hand. "I'm sorry," she said to both of them. "I told myself I wasn't going to be catty or mean, and . . ." Her gaze went to Camille, and for the first time, Camille felt sympathy for the woman. "I'm truly sorry, Camille. You didn't deserve that."

"You don't need to apologize," Camille told her. *Is he with her? Is he here?* She ached to cast a Finding spell, but couldn't, not with both of them watching. "I understand. Let's forget it and start over."

Helen gave her a small smile. "I'd like that."

"Helen," David said. He didn't move to hug or embrace her. "Good to see you. I didn't expect Jacob to invite you, actually."

"Actually, he didn't," Helen said. "You were always his star, not me. I'm here because Timothy's bought some pieces from Jacob."

Timothy. The name was a blow that nearly staggered Camille. *Him . . .* She could feel her face going pale, and sweat beading at her hairline. *Not here. I'm not ready for him here.*

"Oh," David said. He glanced at Camille, his eyes narrowing as he looked at her face. "I didn't tell you about that. Helen has a . . . friend she's been seeing." He turned back to Helen. "So that's still going well?"

"Yes," Helen said, and her smile was genuine and enthusiastic. "It is. Come on, I'll introduce the two of you. He's up on the roof terrace."

David looked at Camille again. "Sure," he said. "We'd like to meet him."

He started to follow Helen up the staircase to the roof level. Camille stopped at the foot of the stair. "He works at Beth Israel," Camille heard Helen say to David.

"Beth Israel?" David answered. "So he's a doctor?"

Helen laughed. "I told you that the other day. Weren't you listening?"

Camille clutched at the handrail. David glanced back, his face quizzical. "Camille? You okay?"

"Yeah," she said. "I'm coming." She opened the snap of her purse as they emerged onto the roof. The cedar hot tub was filled with a half-dozen guests who appeared to be wearing nothing at all. Others, mostly couples, were standing around the terrace or sitting at the tables. Camille approached a man standing near the railing.

He was short, with longish brown hair, and Camille was feeling the beginning of panic even before he turned, before Helen spoke. "Dr. Timothy Pierce. Timothy, this is David Treadway, my soon-to-be former husband. And Camille Kenny, his . . . current muse."

The eyes, the mouth, the way he stood . . . The shock hit Camille so hard that she took a step backward, the instinct to flight almost too strong. But she resisted. Her hand slipped into her purse, her fingers searching out the handle of the Ladysmith and flicking off the safety. She didn't believe he'd be blatant enough to attack her here. Not in public; it wasn't his way. But if he did, she'd respond. *You can shoot through the purse. If you see him start to cast one of his spells . . .*

If he was equally startled at seeing her, he gave no sign. "Hello," Pierce/Nicolas said, holding out his hand to David. "Good to meet you, and to finally see your work. Jacob knows that I was looking for good pieces for my office; now I've found some." He extended his hand to Camille. "And you've found a most beautiful model," he said. "Worthy of Bernini, I have to say. Such a lovely, exquisite face and body."

His hand hung in the air between them. With a twitch of her lips, Camille removed her hand from her purse and took it. He pressed slightly too hard and slightly too long. "Dr. Pierce," she said, as if tasting the name. Her hand went back into the purse, her fingers sliding around the wooden handle of the Ladysmith, her index finger curling around the trigger. "Cosmetic surgeon? Fixing those faces you find so attractive?"

His returning smile was cold. "I'm afraid not. Research Oncologist. I'm studying experimental ingredients for chemotherapy." His eyes held Camille's "Chemistry is my passion. That, and amateur magic."

"You know my friend Morris Johnson, I believe. The sculptor."

He chuckled. "Ah, yes. Him. Now I remember where I've heard your name before. Morris is a talented fellow, though he seemed distraught that you'd abandon him for David here. I've commissioned a work from him."

"I'm sure you'll like it," Camille told him. " 'Vengeance.' That's a sinister title, I have to say."

"Yet that particular emotion drives many people through hard times when they might otherwise give up, don't you think? Vengeance is a passion with incredible power, as I'm sure you realize."

"And you do as well, Dr. Piece."

"I believe many of us have something they desire to achieve more than anything else," he answered. "In fact, I'm willing to bet you're one of those people yourself. What is it that drives you, Ms. Kenny? Is it also vengeance?"

"Well, you two are certainly the conversationalists," Helen interjected quickly before Camille could answer. She laced her arm protectively with Pierce's, smiling tightly; she stood half a head taller than the man, just as David towered over Camille. "Isn't this a perfectly gorgeous view? David, wouldn't this make a lovely photograph?"

David glanced at the landscape before them: the dancing swirl of red taillights and blue-white headlights, the sound of the streets muted and distant, the buildings defined by fluorescent-illuminated office windows and the city-glow behind them through which a few stars managed to glitter. "Not really, just a postcard like a thousand others," he commented, then glanced down toward the deep canyon of the street. "That'd be a hell of a nasty fall, though."

"Oh, you'd be surprised what kind of a fall someone can survive," Pierce said, glancing down the flank of the building, then over to Camille. "I've seen people manage to live when I was convinced they'd die." He smiled. "When they *should* have died," he added. "Some people are stubborn that way. They think they're supposed to live forever."

David and Helen laughed. "Yeah, I was afraid I was going to see something like that myself recently," David said, and Camille knew that he was remembering her dancing on the ledge of his studio rooftop.

"Well," Pierce said, "it's a genuine pleasure to meet the two of you. I should go downstairs and talk to Jacob about buying a few of your photographs. Helen, shall we?" He nodded to them as he and Helen walked off, his gaze lingering on Camille.

Shoot him. Shoot him now. But that wouldn't kill him and she had nothing with which she could finish the job. It would only end with her arrested and in jail for assault, and Nicolas would slip away from her once more.

Or worse. Much worse.

David put his arm around Camille. "Well, that wasn't so bad, I guess . . ." he started to say, then stopped. "You're trembling. What's wrong?"

She took a long, slow breath. She slid the safety of the Ladysmith back on. "Nothing," she told him. "It's just a little chilly up here."

"What are you doing here?"

Helen was holding the door open only a crack, with the chain still significantly attached to the frame. She peered at Camille through the opening. It was not a friendly stare.

Now that she was here, Camille wasn't quite certain how to proceed. She'd played the scenario over and over in her head in the last few days. She'd watched Helen's apartment from the park across the street, hoping to see Nicolas: the Ladysmith in her purse, her katana in its nylon bag strapped to her back, her dogi bag as camouflage at her side as if she were going to aikido class. Girded for war, she thought.

But Nicolas had never appeared. That didn't surprise her; he'd know that she might try to find him through Helen, so it made sense he'd make excuses to stay away. She'd watched Beth Israel as well; Nicolas never showed himself there, either.

He'd gone to ground somewhere.

And now she was here to warn Helen, to try to save her.

Camille had consulted her Tarot for guidance in contacting Helen, but none of the readings helped against the reality of the woman's glare over the chain. Yet she couldn't in good conscience say nothing to Helen about Nicolas—she knew him far too well. Helen was an innocent in this and deserved a chance.

"I need to talk to you, Helen," Camille told her. "It's important."

She waited, watching Helen's face, twisted in a moue of mingled irritation and uncertainty. Finally, Helen pressed her lips together and closed the door. Camille heard the rattle of the chain, and the door opened again. "I have to leave in a few minutes for an appointment," Helen said, her arm still blocking the door.

"That's fine. I won't be long."

Helen's arm dropped and she stepped back into the room. Camille entered.

The room—unsurprisingly after seeing how Camille and David's apartment had looked—was uncluttered and modern, with glossy hardwood floors covered here and there with expensive-looking area rugs. The Impressionist prints were up on the walls. There were magazines arranged tastefully on the coffee table in front of the couch; none of the titles looked particularly like something a male might have chosen to read. This was distinctly *Helen's* place. Not Pierce's. There was nothing of him in any of this. He wasn't staying here.

That didn't surprise Camille. She didn't expect that Pierce intended Helen to be a long relationship. He undoubtedly already had obtained most, if not all, of what he wanted from her.

Helen didn't sit. She stood, hands crossed protectively across her stomach, in the foyer without moving into the living room area, forcing Camille to also stand. "Well?" she asked. "What is it that's so important?"

"Pierce," Camille said without preamble.

Helen's eyes narrowed with the name. "What about Timothy?"

"You heard us talking at Prudhomme's party. I saw the look of suspicion you gave us, and the way you interrupted us as we were talking to hurry him off. Did we sound to you like two people who had just met? Did you ask him about that after we parted? Did you ask him if he knew me?"

"Yes," she admitted. Her arms tightened around her. "He said he knew *about* you through Prudhomme because he's been interested in David's photos of you, and that he'd bought a litho portrait of you from some other artist without knowing it was you, but that the artist had also told him a little about you." Helen scowled. "Nothing the artist had to say about you was particularly complimentary, either, from what Timothy suggested."

"That last bit might be the truth," Camille told her, "given the source. But not the rest of his story. The truth is that your Timothy and I have known each other for a long time. That's why I came here, Helen."

"I don't believe you," she said defiantly, though she wouldn't meet Camille's eyes.

"I know you don't. But it's the truth, nonetheless."

Helen looked away into the living room, as if searching for something there. "Are you saying you've slept with him?"

"We were married once," Camille told her. "He probably left that out when he was talking about me."

That garnered Camille another bark of disbelief. Helen's eyes were shimmering with tears. "I think you need to leave."

"What I'm telling you is true," Camille said desperately. "I'm sorry, Helen, but it's true. Pierce . . . he's a danger to you. I mean it. He'll hurt you, or worse. He can pretend to be charming, but he's a psychopath."

She wouldn't look at Camille. Her hands unfolded from her waist and wiped at her eyes, almost as if she were angry with them for betraying her. "Get out," she said. "Get out of here or I'll call the police."

"Helen, you have to listen to me. Pierce isn't who he says he is. He wants me, and now that he's found me . . ."

"My God!" Helen exclaimed. Her hands fluttered in the air. "You think he wants *you*? It's not enough that you took David away from me; now you have to destroy my relationship with Tim just as it's starting? Get out! Now!" This time she pushed at Camille, who had to take a step backward to regain her balance.

"Helen, I'm serious. You're in terrible danger, you really are . . ."

"Out!" She pushed again, and Camille felt the back of the doorframe hit her spine. Helen reached past her and yanked the door open. "If you *ever* bother me again, I swear I'll call the police. Out!"

Camille was still shaking her head, but she slid through the doorway into the hall. The door slammed shut almost before she was through. From the other side, she heard a sob, then the sound of the chain being set again.

"Well, that went well," she muttered to herself. "You tried." The excuse did nothing to settle the sour burning in her stomach and the atmosphere of dread that surrounded her as she stared at the door.

She did what little she could, driven partially by her own fear, partially by guilt at what this might mean for Helen. She went to Beth Israel after talking to Helen. The Ladysmith was heavy in her purse and the katana dragged at her back; Nicolas' magical skills might be impressive, but for her, a modern gun was far more effective. Nicolas would talk to her first before attacking, mocking her: that was his way. She should be able to get off the first shot and disable him, take him down for long enough to do more. He was pretending to be a surgeon; even without the katana, there might be medical instruments within easy grasp. In the right situation, in the right place, she might be able to do what she needed to do before someone stopped her. If she could kill Nicolas—finally, completely this time—then she'd accept whatever happened to her afterward.

It would be worth it.

But she wouldn't do anything unless she was confident of success. Just disabling him, letting him escape, being captured herself before she could finish the execution: none of that was acceptable.

The front desk gave his office location as in the building next to the hospital itself. She went to the office and stood outside for several minutes, looking in at a harried-looking female receptionist at the front desk. There were no patients in the waiting room, no indication that Nicolas might be there. After waiting ten minutes in the corridor, she opened the door and went in. The receptionist glanced up at her, looking suspiciously at the katana bag.

"I'm sorry," she began even before Camille could speak, "Dr. Pierce isn't in. Did you have an appointment today? I can reschedule you . . ." Keys rattled on the keyboard in front of her as she looked at the monitor. The young woman had long, curving artificial nails extending well past the fingertips; Camille wondered how she was able to type at all. The receptionist looked to be no older than twenty; she brushed long strands of hair from her eyes as she leaned toward the monitor.

"I didn't have an appointment. I'm an old acquaintance of Dr. Pierce's, and I was hoping to get a chance to talk to him for a few minutes."

The receptionist sniffed at that, and Camille saw a flash of irritation narrow the woman's eyes. "I'm afraid not. I don't know when he'll be in."

"Do you have his cell number? I could call . . ."

"You'll just be leaving messages like me," the receptionist said, then shook her head. "I'm sorry; I shouldn't have said that. It's been a lousy day."

"I'm so sorry to hear that," Camille said, with as much false sympathy as she could muster. Suspicion hardened in her chest. "It's Timothy's fault, isn't it?" she said. "He can be like that."

The receptionist gave a shrug accompanied by the faintest of nods. Lacquered fingernails tapped the keys. "I can't give you his cell number. He wouldn't like that."

"He didn't show up today, I take it?" Camille asked. The tightening of the receptionist's glossy orange lips answered her. *He knows. He knows I'm coming after him.* Camille gave the receptionist what she hoped was a sympathetic sigh. "That's so like him. He didn't give you any idea when he'll be back?"

"I'm afraid he didn't. And I have this afternoon's schedule of appointments to call and cancel yet, so . . ." She evidently thought that was too abrupt, for she smiled awkwardly at Camille and reached for a pen. "I'll tell him you stopped by. What's your name?"

"Don't bother," Camille told her. "I'll see him later. I hope the rest of your calls go easy."

"They won't," the woman said, "but I appreciate the thought."

Camille smiled at the woman. She left the hospital and went back to her own apartment.

"Where have you been?" David asked her. "You look worried."

She tossed her dojo bag and the katana bag into the corner next to the door and hugged him, harder than she intended. "It's nothing," she said. "I'm just feeling a little down." She stood on her toes to kiss him.

She could tell David that Pierce was her stalker, but then David really *would* insist that they go to the authorities, and once the police were involved, her fabric of lies would unravel: she would lose David as a result, and possibly have to leave her identity behind once again.

She could tell David the full truth, but he wouldn't believe her and there was very little in the way of evidence she could present. She hardly believed it herself.

So she could do nothing except to continue her search for Nicolas. At least she knew the name Nicolas was using now, even if she suspected he'd never return to Helen's apartment or his office at Beth Israel—if he didn't decide to entirely change his identity now that they'd found each other. All that was in her favor.

Still, Helen might call David and complain about her warning, and she had no good explanation to give him. Or Nicolas might do something on his own. The dread sat inside her, a dark, festering worry. She jumped at every unknown sound.

She made love to David that evening, trying to find some solace in his closeness and the intimate wrapping of his soul-heart around her. For two more days, despite her trepidation, nothing at all happened.

David's cell phone rang while she and David were in the studio: he was setting up a product shot for a commercial client while she was painting, with Verdette curled up at her ankles. David answered, and when he sat abruptly on a stool, she knew there was something terribly wrong. All the color drained from his face. Verdette mewled in irritation as Camille sat up. "You're certain?" David asked, twice, and each time his shoulders slumped further with the answer. "Oh, my God," he said several times. He was looking at Camille, his eyes stricken. "I can't . . . can't believe this. No, no; I'm okay. Just stunned. Do they know who did this? No? Let me know about arrangements, would you? Give your mom my sympathy, would you, and take care of yourself."

David closed the phone and stood there holding it in his hand, staring at nothing. She could see his eyes glittering in the light. Twin tears tracked the lines of his cheeks. Camille set down her brush. She knew, before he told her. "David?"

"That was Helen's sister Sally. It's Helen," he said. He blinked and another single tear rolled down. "Helen's been murdered."

"Oh, David . . ." Camille breathed. Her head was crowded with a thousand speculations. "How? When?"

"A day or more ago. Evidently Timothy called the cops when Helen wouldn't answer her phone; she'd been dead for at least a day when they broke in. She'd been tied to her bed, tortured, and beaten, maybe raped; they aren't sure yet. There were at least two people involved, according to the police. But it was really brutal. They had to identify her body by the teeth. The apartment was trashed; whoever it was that did this took everything valuable they could carry. The cops are thinking that it was probably a robbery gone bad, that maybe she surprised these people in the middle of things, that she tried to interfere and so they . . ." David took a shuddering breath. "I feel sick. I can't believe this."

Camille could. Camille was already certain of one fact: Nicolas had killed her—this had his stink all over it. He may not have done it himself, but he had been there or close by when it happened, relishing all the pain and torment. He'd taken everything he really wanted from Helen already, and now he was done with her.

"The visitation's on Wednesday," David was saying. "You'll come with me?"

She was shaking her head. *He* might be there, too, and she didn't want to see him again. "It wouldn't look right," she said.

"No one would be thinking that, or if they do, fuck 'em. Camille, I'd really appreciate it. I don't . . . I don't want to go there alone."

Which is probably exactly what Nicolas wants. She sighed. She stood up went to David and hugged him, cradling his head against her shoulder. "I'm so sorry for you," she whispered into his ear. "Of course I'll go."

She wondered, for a day, whether she had told David a lie. As she saw it, she had two choices: accept the gauntlet that Nicolas had cast down and kill him before he came after her or, worse, David. Or . . .

She could abandon "Camille Kenny" entirely and leave New York. She could go elsewhere and start her search all over again—

sometime in the future when Nicolas had taken on, like her, yet another identity.

Yet . . . she knew that if she did that, Nicolas might just kill David as he had Helen, if only because he would know the guilt that would rack her for that. He would feed on David's pain and anguish as she fed on his creativity, and that was a thought she couldn't bear.

No. This was war, and she could not afford to lose another battle. And, she had to admit, she didn't *want* to tear herself away from David's soul-heart and the nourishment it gave her.

She stayed.

The visitation room at the funeral home was crowded and too hot. The oversweet smell of flowers was cloying, and there was a scent of disinfectant lingering underneath. A rumble of hushed conversation surrounded them as they entered, with an occasional sob or sniff. Shorter than most, Camille couldn't see far into the room. She held onto David's hand, a tight-lipped and hopefully sympathetic half-smile on her face.

She hated visitations and funerals. They were symbols of death, which she had abandoned and which she feared.

"David!" A woman who looked like an older version of Helen came up to them. David released Camille's hand and hugged her. The woman's eyes were red-rimmed and bloodshot, her mascara smeared. She held David tightly, possessively, releasing him only after a long moment. "I'm so sorry," she heard David say to her, then he inclined his head toward Camille. "Sally," he said, "this is my friend Camille. Camille, this is Helen's sister."

Sally's lips tightened and her eyes narrowed. Then she nodded. "I've heard of you," she said.

Camille kept her face carefully neutral. "I'm terribly sorry for your loss," she said. "I can't imagine how devastated you must feel."

"Thank you," Sally answered, though the words were only a polite emptiness. "That means so much." She put her arm around David's. "Come with me," she said. "Mom's been just a wreck, and she always liked you so much . . ."

David glanced at Camille, who smiled at him. "Go on," she said, but Sally was already tugging him into the crowd, obviously not intending for her to follow.

She wandered the edges of the mourners, listening to some of the conversations.

". . . tragic, just tragic. Someone so young . . ."

". . . she seemed to be so happy recently . . ."

". . . God works in mysterious ways . . ."

"Camille," she heard someone call softly, and saw a man in a dark, expensive-looking suit detach himself from a group near the door: Jacob Prudhomme. They embraced quickly. "David's here?"

"Yes," she told him. "Helen's sister took him to see their mother. I decided to stay back here."

"Ah." Jacob nodded. "Probably wise of you. This was startling news for all of us. From what I've heard, she was dead for some time before she was discovered. Timothy Pierce evidently called her workplace when she wasn't answering her cell; they hadn't seen her and she hadn't called them. He went to her apartment and knocked on her door trying to rouse her, and finally called the cops and the landlord. It's all so horrible." He shivered.

Yes, she wanted to say. *Nicolas was making certain that his alibi was sound and playing the distraught boyfriend perfectly.* "Horrible," she agreed. "I'm sorry, Jacob; will you excuse me? The smell of the flowers is getting to me, I'm afraid."

"Certainly," he told her. "I should go see Helen's mother myself. David could use the support." He hugged her again and moved away into the crowd. Camille stepped out into the hallway toward a lounge area with coffee and a water fountain. She thought she was alone at first, then noticed someone stirring sugar into a Styrofoam cup of coffee. She stopped, startled, as he turned. The Ladysmith sat like an accusation in her purse; it would take several seconds to reach it, to turn off the safety, to use it. She turned over the spells in her mind, wondering if she should cast them now, before he was ready, even though they would be weaker than any he could cast himself, and he would be faster.

Her hesitation had already been too long.

"*Bonjour, Perenelle,*" he said. "*Est-ce que tout va bien?*"

"I'm not Perenelle," she said to him, also in the same archaic French, "anymore than you're still Nicolas. And I've not been very well—not with you alive. Why did you do it? There was no reason to kill Helen. There was no reason to kill Walters, either."

"No?" he asked with a smile. He stirred the coffee with the red plastic stick. He took the stirrer from the cup and held it up to her. "I suppose I could keep this, too. But now that it's served its only purpose in life . . ." Lifting his hand dramatically, he let the stick fall into the trash can alongside the table.

"People aren't disposable."

"Oh, I don't think either one of us really believes that. They all die anyway, so what's the harm in accelerating the process a little? Besides, with Helen *I* didn't do the killing; I just . . . watched. There are a few people I know who believe that they're now immortal, and in gratitude, they do whatever I ask them to do."

The sick feeling in Camille's stomach increased. "Again, Nicolas?"

"Why not?" he answered. "Their gratitude is so amusing and so useful, and their deaths are always so anguished and tasty. You're no different, for all your posturing. How many lovers have you had and left, discarded? You just don't want to admit that we're both the same. Both the same, Perenelle—as we always were."

"I was *never* the same as you. I've never been vicious or cruel. I never beat you the way you beat me when we were married. I don't kill those I've loved. Nicolas, we need to end this insanity. Let's go outside, right now, just the two of us, and do that."

"End it? In public?" He shook his head, clucking his tongue. "Isn't that a bit overdramatic, not to mention stupid? Mind you, I do intend to finally and completely end this." He smiled at her again. "But not tonight. Eventually. In my own time. When you don't expect it, when it's safe for me. But soon. I've told you this before, Perenelle: *you're* my passion. Besides, you still have something I want—and I *will* have it from you first."

She started to retort, to plead with him again, but a woman entered the lounge, going to the coffee machine and taking two Styrofoam cups from the stack alongside. Nicolas took a sip of his coffee. "You'll excuse me," he said, abandoning French for English. "I should get back to the family. Such a shameful, needless tragedy. Thanks for coming, Camille. I'm sure Helen would have appreciated the gesture, especially after your last conversation with her. Give my best to David, would you? He's such a talent." He nodded to her, then to the other person. He left, leaving Camille shaking and anxious.

The new entrant was looking at her, putting sugar in one of the two coffees in front of her on the table, and Camille realized that she felt the touch of a soul-heart within the woman, and that her features were familiar: Gina Palento, the detective she'd met at Walters' office, her short hair brushed, dressed as neatly as she had been there. She was staring at Camille as she put lids on the cups. "Ms. Kenny," she said. "I didn't expect to see you here." She cocked her head. "You knew the deceased?"

Camille thought for a moment about lying, but the detective would discover that far too easily. She struggled to smile. "I'm with David, Helen's husband." She saw her eyebrows climb with that statement. "They're separated," Camille added. "He was getting a divorce."

"Ah. Now that's quite a coincidence—I managed to catch both poor Bob's case and now this one, and here you are involved in both. Peripherally, I'm sure. Now . . . David Treadway; he was someone I wanted to talk to about this. Do you happen to know where he was three nights ago around 10:00 to midnight?"

"Saturday? He was with me that night. We had dinner in his apartment, then went out to the *Bent Calliope* around 9:00 and met with friends. We were there well past midnight. They can verify that."

"I'm sure they can," Palento said. "I had to ask—after all, he's the husband . . . separated or not. Do *you* know anyone who would have wanted to hurt Ms. Treadway?"

Camille hesitated, long enough to take a breath. Long enough to consider. "Have you talked to her current lover?" Camille said. "Dr.

Timothy Pierce. He's the guy who was just here. He's a surgeon at Beth Israel. If I were you, I'd ask where he was that night, and I'd look into his background, just to see if he's really who he says he is."

"I've already spoken to him, since he found the body. You were just talking to him—in French, was it?"

"We were talking," she admitted. "I don't like the man, though. I don't trust him."

"You know him that well?"

"Well enough to know that he's dangerous."

"That doesn't necessarily make him a murderer," Palento said. "I talked to him when we found the body. He seemed concerned enough then. Are you saying he's lying?"

"I'm saying that I think you might find him interesting, if you check him out thoroughly."

"Strange. He's told me the same about you. Though it seems you have an alibi." Palento stared at her for a moment longer, then lifted the two coffee cups. "I've left my partner in the other room. I should get back to him. The two of us have a lot to sort out on this case—and Bob's case as well. Good talking to you again, Ms. Kenny."

Carrying the coffees, she left Camille, who felt trapped: Nicolas was in the other room, so was Gina Palento and another detective, probably talking to everyone who ever knew Helen. Camille wondered what Helen might have said to some of them about her. She stayed in the lounge until she saw David emerge from the other room.

"I'd really like to go now, if it's okay with you," she told him. She could hear the trembling in her voice. She was pleased when he said nothing, but only embraced her.

She pretended that, for a moment, she was safe in his arms.

The trouble was that no one could keep her safe from Nicolas. She could only do that herself.

INTERLUDE FIVE

Marie-Anne Paulze & Antoine-Laurent de Lavoisier

1789 – 1794

Marie-Anne Paulze Lavoisier

1789

"I DON'T UNDERSTAND, Jacques-Louis. Now you *don't* wish to show our portrait in the Salon exhibition? I thought you were pleased with it; I know that we certainly were."

Jacques-Louis David managed to look sheepish. David was hardly handsome. As a young man, the left side of his face had been sliced open during a fencing incident, and the wound had left him with a distinct asymmetry when he smiled. The scars also held a tumor that swelled that side of his face and affected his ability to both eat and speak well. Jacques-Louis slurred his consonants. In a society that valued wit and discourse, that was a severe social disadvantage; it was only his skill as a painter that allowed him to survive.

As Marie-Anne waited for an answer, David glanced over at the portrait in question leaning against the wall, one of several of David's works gathered in his Paris studio in preparation for this year's Salon exhibition. There, caught in an ornate and gilded frame, Antoine-Laurent Lavoisier, Marie-Anne's husband, sat writing at his desk, dressed in black with a white periwig and looking up at Marie-Anne. She stood at his side, her own white wig covering her auburn hair, a white dress with a lace collar and a blue fabric belt, leaning on his shoulder while gazing serenely out at the viewer. Many of the devices of their shared passion for chemistry were also on exhibit in the painting: a bell jar, a barometer, a gasometer, and a water still sat on the desk in front of them, while a flask and a tap were on the floor nearby.

David had painted the portrait only the year before; the Lavoisiers had paid him 7,000 livres for the work. Marie-Anne had also been taking drawing lessons from him. Doing so also allowed her access to his great soul-heart, another of the vast ones; she doubted that he even felt her touch on him.

Most of the other paintings in the warehouse were older works, and safely free of controversy, but not all. The huge ink-and-pen sketch of *The Oath of the Tennis Court*, David's unfinished large-scale painting, was pinned to the wall across from Marie-Anne's portrait, along with *The Lictors Bring to Brutus the Bodies of His Sons*.

"I know I told you that I wanted to borrow the portrait, but—" David pressed his lips together tightly, sucking in his breath with an audible wet sound. "Marie-Anne, I must ask you to forgive me for what I'm about to say, and understand that I have no choice in the matter. You know that my sympathies are with the Jacobins and Robespierre, as I suspect are yours and Antoine's . . ." He shrugged. "I will just say it baldly. I've been told that if I display your portrait it might incite public agitation, since Antoine has been outspoken about tax reform and social issues." David shook his head. "This wasn't my choice, but the Academy's— forced upon them by the royals. I can't show my *Brutus*, either; they say it's nothing but a Republican symbol. They want no paintings in this Salon that have any possible political interpretation at all."

"Then why *are* you placing your paintings there, since so many of them lately are intended to have exactly that effect?" Marie-Anne interjected, and David shrugged. She knew why; she could feel it in the shifting patterns of his green heart: the Salon was still the premier event for French painters; it was still a showcase where careers were enhanced, and David was nothing if not passionate about his career. Politically, he might be an anti-royalist, but he also wanted to make certain that his career continued to advance, no matter who was in charge. "Jacques-Louis, Antoine and I aren't Jacobins *or* Royalists," she continued as David looked down at the floor. "*Oui*, Antoine has his position in the Ferme-Générale, but he's a lowly gunpowder administrator. Neither Antoine nor I care who runs the government as long as that government is good, and as long as we're allowed to pursue our studies—all we want is fairness for everyone. Look at me, Jacques-Louis—I have neither an abiding interest in tax collecting nor in taking down the king. We're not advocates for either side—so neither should be our portrait painting."

"This wasn't my decision," David repeated. "I'll have the painting returned to your house. And again, my apologies both to you and to Antoine."

Marie-Anne gave a sigh. There was no use arguing—or rather, it seemed there was nothing *but* arguing when it came to politics these days. "You needn't apologize for what isn't your fault," she told him. "It's the times we live in. I'm sorry for you, since it means that your newest paintings won't be in the Salon." She embraced him; he returned the gesture half-heartedly—she could feel him still staring at the paintings around the room. "My carriage is waiting," she told him. "You should come to dinner at our house next week. Antoine is concerned about you."

"I will," he told her, the words slurred more than usual. "You're right. It's just the times we live in . . ."

Marie-Anne reflected on that as she left the studio. Returning to Paris had felt so right, like coming home after a long time spent away. And being with Antoine had also felt right. His soul-heart was different from most she'd experienced: the visual artists, musicians, and writers. His passion was also hers; he loved the exploration of chemistry, and so she nurtured his energy and bound it to herself, allowing him to fall in love with her.

And theirs was a *true* partnership and exploration. Oh, certainly society credited Antoine with all the breakthroughs and discoveries, but he always insisted that she deserved just as much credit even if the world would not give it to her. She could be his Muse and allow his green heart to grow, and she learned as he learned.

She had already nearly gained back all the skills and knowledge she'd lost so long ago.

Antoine also allowed her to continue to pursue her other interests and abilities. As Marie-Anne Lavoisier, she translated the Irishman Richard Kirwan's "Essay on Phlogiston" from English to French, which allowed Antoine and others to dispute Kirwan's ideas on the respiratory process. One of the reasons she was taking lessons from David was so that she could create the sketches and engravings of her and Antoine's laboratory equipment for their joint treatises. As the spouse of the famous Monsieur Lavoisier, she hosted gatherings where the great minds of the day could discuss this new "chemistry" and her and Antoine's ideas.

She felt fulfilled; she felt creatively satisfied herself as she rarely had in her long life. She was happy; she was content.

They spent most of their time together working in the laboratory conducting research. Marie-Anne and Antoine had the relationship that she'd wished she could have had with Nicolas: a true collaboration, a genuine partnership. With him, with his unknowing aid, she was as close to the secret of the elixir as she had been in her last years with Nicolas. The aged mice to which she gave the current version of the potion regressed immediately in age, and would remain that way for weeks before the sudden, aggressive aging took them.

So close. So very close. She'd made certain to write down the process and ingredients, and to place those notes in more than one place. She was determined not to lose the notes again, not after the long centuries it had taken her to come back to this place in her research.

She loved Antoine as she had Vivaldi and as she had Bernini. And there was more with him as well. She was his friend; she was his peer and equal. It made their relationship very easy.

Or it had until the last few years, with the establishment of an Estates-General; with the Réveillon Riots in Paris, caused by low wages and food shortages; when the dismissed members of the Estates-General swore their oath in the Tennis Court; when the Bastille was stormed and taken by the citizens.

The world had turned uncertain and dangerous around her. Her precious Paris had become a place she sometimes didn't understand.

It was raining outside—a cold, teeming October rain. Pulling up her skirts, she ran from the studio to the carriage, glad for her cloak and wig, which kept her head mostly dry even if it itched her scalp. The carriage jounced as she stepped into it, the driver looking soaked and sullen as he held the door for her. Distantly, she could hear church bells ringing, which seemed strange. "What's going on?" she asked the driver, who shrugged silently. "The house, *s'il vous plaît*," she told him as he climbed onto the seat and slapped the reins at the placid horse. The carriage's ironclad wheels rang against the cobblestones as Marie-Anne leaned back against the cushions, closing her eyes and wondering how she wanted to tell Antoine that their portrait wasn't going to be permitted in the Salon.

She wasn't sure how long it was when she became aware of the sound of drums and many voices, chanting in unison and shouting. She glanced out through the rain-spattered window to her right, seeing the Hôtel de Ville besieged by what appeared to be thousands of people—nearly all of them women. It appeared that the mob had successfully breached the door of the hôtel, as she could see figures running from the doors with arms full of provisions, the few uniformed guards helpless in the face of the thousands. Nearby, several women were pushing a small cannon toward the street. The drums were loud and beating a cadence. "*À Versailles!*" she heard the crowd roar in unison. "*Apportez la maison de roi!*"

To Versailles! Bring the king home!

Before Marie-Anne could react or tell the driver to move on, she felt the carriage start to rock violently, the springs protesting madly as the mob pushed at it. Before Marie-Anne could react, the doors were yanked open and grubby hands were pulling her out. She glimpsed the faces—women, all of them, poor and dirt-streaked, many gaunt, drawn, and gap-toothed, their clothing soaked in the persistent rain. "Join us!" one of them shouted to her as she was pulled from the carriage. Her wig and bonnet were knocked from her head in the tussle, lost beneath the crowd. The rain soaked her bare head, darkening her red-hued, matted hair. Somebody pulled her to her feet, just as she was afraid that they would trample her as well. "We go to Versailles to tell our king we need bread and that he must come home to the people! Come with us!" The woman grabbed her arm and pulled her away from the carriage.

Marie-Anne had little choice but to go with the woman. The crowd was pressing all around, and she was forced to move with it. The rain beat down on them as they moved eastward on the boulevard from the hôtel, with Marie-Anne stumbling along helplessly with them. When the woman holding her arm released her, Marie-Anne began inching slowly to the side of boulevard away from the mob's center, taking her time. She saw the women at the edges of the crowd grabbing other women who were watching, pulling them into the group as Marie-Anne herself had been drawn in. People were waving banners and flags from the houses as the group passed with drums hammering, voices raised in chants and political slogans, and torches hissing and fuming in the rain. The crowd was growing ever larger and more boisterous—not just women now but also some men. Marie-Anne saw more cannon—taken from the hôtel's defenses, she assumed—being pulled along by women.

They were approaching the Place de Grève as Marie-Anne continued to seek the edge of the marchers. Over their heads, she could see the colorful uniforms of the National Guardsmen. The marchers began to call out to the soldiers: "Join us! We are the people! Join us!" Marie-Anne could see the Marquis de Lafayette, their commander and one of France's war heroes, on his horse; he was talking urgently to his lieutenants as the mob began to bunch up in the face of the soldiers. The noise level rose, and Marie-Anne was afraid that the confrontation would soon turn brutal. She pushed her way to the far edge of the crowd, toward the nearest cross street. Fists and elbows flew as she fought her way through, one smashing into her mouth so hard that she tasted blood.

Then, staggering, she was free of the worst of the mob and was lurching out among the onlookers on a side street. Exhausted from the struggle, Marie-Anne leaned in the lee of an alleyway between buildings. She was disheveled, her skirts torn, her hair a mess, and she could feel blood trickling down the side of her face and taste it in her mouth. She wiped at her mouth, drawing in a hiss as she touched puffed and split lips. That brought back a brief memory of Nicolas, when he'd attacked her just before she'd taken the elixir. *She'd tasted blood in her mouth then . . .*

Marie-Anne's eyes widened, her breath held.

Nicolas had scoffed at her in the garden of the palazzo. "*There was something different with that version of the formula, some change you made but didn't write down, or perhaps it was some accident—something introduced to the potion that you didn't notice . . .*"

Nicolas had been right. There had been one change that was never written in her notebook. She stared at the red stain on her fingertips.

Energy flooded back into her. She pushed herself away from the stones of the building. As quickly as she could, she left behind the cries of the mob and made her way toward home.

"Marie-Anne! *Mon dieu,* what happened to you! I was frantic with worry." Antoine ran down the stairs to hug Marie-Anne, his wig askew on his head as the servants fretted and fussed over her. After a moment, he held her at arm's length, his face registering distress. "You've been hurt, and you're soaked entirely through. Etienne, fetch some blankets; Josette, get a cloth to clean your mistress' face . . ."

"I'm fine," Marie-Anne protested. Antoine looked so worried that she hugged him again. "Truthfully, my dear. I'm fine, especially now that I'm home."

"What happened? The carriage driver came back saying that you'd been attacked and taken."

As they moved to the reception room off the foyer so that she could sit and be comfortable, as the servants brought wine, bread, and cheese for her and built up the fire in the hearth nearest her, Marie-Anne slowly gave Antoine the tale from the time she left David's studio, leaving out her epiphany regarding the elixir—she had never told him the truth about her private experiments; he thought she was working on a solution to help those with lung difficulties to breathe easier, as an adjunct to Antoine's own research disproving the myth of phlogiston. As she talked, Verdette, their ancient gray Chartreux cat, wove her way between Marie-Anne's legs, rubbing against her and purring content-edly when Marie-Anne finally reached down to pet her.

When she finished the story, now with Verdette curled in her lap, Antoine was shaking his head. "I didn't know what the Guardsmen were going to do," Marie-Anne told him. "So I pushed my way out of the mob. That's when this happened." Marie-Anne touched her now-scabbed and swollen lip. "Have you heard any news since?"

Antoine sighed. "Only that they have gone on to Versailles, with Lafayette's Guardsmen escorting them. None of this will come to any good. I'm afraid for our country, and afraid for us. Women marching to beg the king for bread, and a simple portrait considered too controver-sial . . ." His voice trailed off. "You must be exhausted, dear," he said, stroking her face. "Why don't you take a rest?"

She shook her head, the motion causing Verdette to look up at her. "No, there's too much I need to do. Don't worry about me, Antoine. I'm not that fragile." She smiled at him, feeling the gesture tug at her abused lips. "Why, I might just stay with you forever."

~

Marie-Anne Paulze Lavoisier: 1791

NEARLY TWO YEARS. That was how long it took her to find the perfect balance of ingredients for the elixir. Too little blood, and the elixir worked as it had before, granting the mice an extended youth and lifetime, but still forcing the sudden and rapid aging to eventu-ally kill them. Too much blood, and the elixir seemed to rage through them like a fire, regressing them to embryonic stages far too early to be viable, or simply killing them outright in a few moments. In her cages there were mice trapped in an eternal infancy—they were the most pitiful of all.

Nearly two years. Sometimes she thought that France itself was replicating her experiments, and—like her—eternally failing to find the right mixture. In the wake of what had come to be called the Women's Bread March, King Louis and the royal family had been forcibly returned to Paris from Versailles, but that had not ended the crisis. The next year brought the suppression of monastic vows and religious orders, saw the nobility abolished by the National Assembly, and in February of this year, there had been the "Day of Daggers," as Lafayette ordered the arrest of over 400 aristocrats at the Tuileries Palace. The royal family, in June, had tried to flee to Varennes, but had been captured; Louis XVI was forced to return to Paris. There were reports of a bloody slave uprising in Saint Domingue.

Finally, in the last week, the king had formally accepted the new Constitution. Marie-Anne hoped that would finally end the bloodshed and uproar, but nothing was certain. Not in these days.

Also during those two years, Verdette, the Lavoisier cat she had named after her daughter, was rapidly failing. Once an active mouser who could often be found prowling their rooms and laboratories, she now mostly slept in a reed basket made into a bed in Marie-Anne's small lab. She seemed to want only Marie-Anne's presence, and Marie-Anne would often look up to find the cat regarding her curiously as she mixed solutions and purified chemicals in the retorts.

Now, Marie-Anne paused as she held what she hoped was the true elixir, in a small, blue crystalline vial. She saw the mice in their cages; she could add a few drops to their food and observe what happened. Her notebook was already open, with an inkwell and two quill pens set alongside. This time . . . she was certain. She could sense it.

Verdette glanced at her and mewled piteously, as if in pain. That made her hesitate. She glanced at the cages of mice, then at Verdette. She went to the cat, scratching her behind her ears. Her fur was dull, as well as matted in some places; she'd stopped grooming herself a few months ago. Antoine had mentioned several times that Verdette probably would not be alive for the turn of the new year. "We don't really need immortal mice, do we?" Marie-Anne said to the cat, who was leaning into her fingers. "No, we don't need that at all. And if it only gives you a few more years, well, we'll take that too, won't we?"

In recent months, with Verdette's limited mobility, Marie-Anne had begun feeding her table scraps as well as the occasional mouse from her cages. Josette had brought in a lunch of a chicken breast; Marie-Anne tore a few small pieces from the breast and put it in Verdette's bowl. She uncapped the vial of elixir and let several drops fall onto the chicken. She put the bowl in front of Verdette, who sniffed at it suspiciously and looked at Marie-Anne. "Go on," she said. "Eat it, dear."

Verdette took a nibble, then attacked the meat more aggressively. Marie-Anne watched, nearly holding her breath—hoping that the formula was as exact as she thought it was, praying that the amount she'd given the cat was correct, afraid that something would go wrong and Verdette would be hurt. *It didn't hurt very long when I took it, and it didn't seem to be too painful for the mice.* The reassurance did little as she watched Verdette take the last piece of chicken and swallow.

For a few moments, nothing happened at all. Then Verdette gave a yowl and came up hard on her front legs. Marie-Anne could see changes rippling through the animal, the fur moving as if insects were scurrying around underneath. Marie-Anne was certain in that moment that she'd made a mistake, that the elixir was still flawed and that she had just condemned Verdette to a horrible, agonizing death.

Verdette yowled again, louder this time, and Marie-Anne reached down to pick her up, sobbing in sympathy and remorse. She cradled the cat to her chest; the cat felt heavier than she had only minutes before, and her fur—it was softer, thicker, and under Marie-Anne's fingers it reflected the lamplight in the room, glistening. Verdette finally settled as Marie-Anne stroked and cuddled her, purring now: a low, loud rumble that she felt more than heard. She set Verdette on the laboratory table: yes, this was Verdette as she had been as a young cat: all lean muscle and gleaming fur, her eyes bright and alert. Her tail twitched as she sniffed the air, then—in a single, fluid motion—she leaped from the tabletop to the floor and padded away, tail held high.

Grinning despite herself, Marie-Anne capped the vial of the remaining elixir. She picked up a quill and dipped the sharpened end in the ink. Crouched over her notebook, she began to write.

"I can't believe what I'm seeing with Verdette. It's literally a miracle; as if she's been reborn."

Antoine marveled to Marie-Anne at dinner that night as Verdette purred on a chair next to Marie-Anne. The servants bustled around the table, placing the soup course in front of the two. Since she'd given the cat the elixir, it seemed that the animal wanted to always be in the same room she was in—she followed Marie-Anne around more like a dog than a cat. The trait, so unusual in Verdette, made Marie-Anne worry about how the elixir might have otherwise changed the cat, but she managed to smile at Antoine.

"Not a miracle," she said. "I took some precipitate of mercury and heated it—you've always said that the air it gives off has wonderful restorative properties, and Verdette was failing so quickly. I collected the air and forced her to breathe it. I think it has given her back the energy she'd lost."

Antoine gave a short, skeptical laugh. "Then you may have stumbled upon a rejuvenation process to rival the accomplishments of all the alchemists of the past. You and I will have to do some further experiments along this line." He reached across Marie-Anne to stroke the cat, but Verdette hissed and slid backward in the chair, her tail puffing out and waving vigorously, the hair rising along her spine. She rose up and her front paws slashed at Antoine's hand, leaving behind a trail of four bloody furrows before he could draw it back. Droplets of blood spattered the tablecloth and the soup bowls rattled on their plates as he recoiled. "Merde!" Antoine said, staring at the injured appendage in disbelief. The cat snarled as Antoine wagged a finger at the animal.

"Verdette!" Marie-Anne scolded. The cat's head snapped toward her, the tail stopped lashing, and her fur relaxed again. She allowed Marie-Anne to scratch her ears without protest. Marie-Anne shook her head as the cat stepped from the chair and settled into her lap, obviously content again. "I don't understand, Antoine. Could she smell something from one of the experiments on your hands?" The cat had never been anything but placid with both of them, and for that matter, with anyone who deigned to show her affection.

"I doubt it. I washed them thoroughly before I came to dinner." Yet as Antoine tentatively reached for Verdette again, the cat stiffened in Marie-Anne's lap, giving a low warning growl as her ears flattened against her head. "Perhaps the mercury precipitate affected her."

Antoine pulled his hand back. He sighed and dabbed at the scratches with a napkin dipped in a water glass. "*Excusez-moi,*" he said to her, pushing back his chair. "I should bandage this . . ." He bent down to her, carefully watching Verdette, who peered at him suspiciously from Marie-Anne's lap, and kissed his wife's cheek. "I'll be right back, my dear. Finish your soup; I'll tell Josette to hold the entree for a few minutes. And perhaps Verdette should be discouraged from being at the table."

"Certainly," Marie-Anne told him. "Take care of your hand, and I'll see to Verdette."

As Antoine left the dining room, Marie-Anne looked down to see Verdette's green eyes staring at her placidly. The cat rubbed its head against Marie-Anne's hand. "What's going on with you?" Marie-Anne asked the cat as she rubbed under her chin, the cat lifting its head and closing its eyes under her caress. She could feel the throbbing of the cat's purr, but beyond that, the cat didn't answer.

She would discover over the next several days that Verdette would tolerate no one else's touch: not Antoine's, nor any of the household staff, nor that of strangers. She continued to try to be wherever Marie-Anne was. When Marie-Anne left the house, the servants told her, Verdette would vanish in the recesses of the house and not reappear until she heard Marie-Anne's voice again.

"*We both have to pay for what's been given us,*" Nicolas had said. Marie-Anne was afraid that she was beginning to understand what payment the elixir had demanded of Verdette.

She went to the laboratory, Verdette padding along behind her, and took the blue vial from its place on the shelf. She held it for a long time. She'd thought that once she knew that the elixir truly worked she might give it to others. Antoine would have been her easy first choice: a good and compassionate person, an intelligent one, her lover. The gift of an eternal life in his scientific pursuits: she could only imagine what he might accomplish, the heights to which he could bring his passion. Even if they ended up apart decades or centuries later, she would never regret giving him that gift.

But . . . At what cost? The elixir had chained her to the green soul-hearts, to the creative energy that nourished her and kept her healthy. That wasn't a horrible fate—she'd found love and companionship through that compulsion, and she could not say that she regretted it even in those times when the lack of a soul-heart around her made her weak and sick. But Nicolas—the elixir had done something even darker to him, binding him to pain and death and an irrational hatred of her.

And now poor Verdette, who had been so gentle and loving and who was still that way—but only with her.

The facets of the crystal dug into her palm as she squeezed the vial. *Do you dare to give this to anyone else without knowing more? Would you risk creating another Nicolas?*

She had no answer to that. Not yet. She took the vial and locked it in a small chest in the laboratory. Her notes she put together and bound up with a ribbon, placing them underneath the chest. She looked at the mice in their cages; their black eyes seemed to glare back at her accusingly.

Verdette jumped from the floor to the bench before which Marie-Anne stood. The cat rubbed against her, walking back and forth and meowing softly until Marie-Anne stroked her. "What did I do to you?" she asked the cat. "What did I do?"

~

Marie-Anne Paulze Lavoisier: 1793

A NOTHER FEW YEARS ON, and Verdette continued as she was without change. Not so the world around Marie-Anne and Antoine.

That world continued to deteriorate. Not long after Marie-Anne gave Verdette the elixir, food riots broke out in Paris. Austria and Prussia allied against France, beginning a war that France hardly needed, given its own internal turmoil. In the summer of that year, after the Prussian Commander, the Duke of Brunswick, issued a manifesto announcing that the allies would enter France to restore the monarchy of Louis XVI, the citizens of Paris stormed the Tuileries Palace, slaughtering the Swiss Guard protecting the king, and the royal family was taken into custody. In September, the kingship of France was dissolved and the First Republic proclaimed; in December, Louis XVI was tried, with Robespierre declaring that "Louis must die, so that the country may live."

On a cold, late January day in 1793, Citizen Louis Capet—formerly known as King Louis XVI—was guillotined at the Place de la Révolution. Marie-Anne heard with horror that many in the vast crowd ran forward to dip their handkerchiefs in the former king's blood as it gushed from his body. The two main political factions within the Republic, the Girondins and the Jacobins, began to tear at each other; in July the scientist and radical journalist Jean-Paul Marat, one of the Jacobin leaders, was assassinated. On October 18, Marie-Antoinette's head was also struck from her body, and with that final purge of the royal family, the political parties of the Republic began to look suspiciously at each other. The Revolutionary Tribunal, under the direction of Maximilien Robespierre, had already convicted several hundred if not thousands of citizens of treasons. Heads were being lopped from bodies by the dozens every day in the Place de la Révolution.

On the 10th of November (or, under the new Republic calendar, 20 Brumaire, Year II), Jacques-Louis David came to their house. Marie-Anne hadn't seen the painter for some months, not since he'd shown them his painting of Marat's death—a painting that Marie-Anne found disturbing both for the grisly subject matter and David's idealization of Marat's features. The Lavoisiers had met Marat in their scientific circles, and his face and skin were disfigured with a hideous blistering skin condition, yet his skin was unblemished in David's painting. "You've made him look like a martyred saint," had been Marie-Anne's reaction to the painting.

"*Oui*. That's exactly what he is," David had answered in his slurred speech. The growth on his scarred face had become more prominent in the last few years, further interfering with his speech and giving his face an even more lopsided appearance. Marie-Anne had no adequate answer to his statement; she'd remained silent.

Now David was back in their house, and his excitement was evident. Marie-Anne, with Verdette in her arms, met him in the foyer as Etienne opened the door for him and took his cloak and hat. "Ah, look at this small miracle!" David said. "Verdette, you look as young and fit as one of your daughters." He reached out toward the cat but Marie-Anne stepped back, shaking her head as she felt the cat stiffen in her grasp and growl.

"I wouldn't," she warned him. "Verdette's become . . . temperamental of late."

"Ah," David said. He looked at her and Verdette quizzically, but he withdrew his hand. "You and Antoine should come with me and Marguerite," he said. "Marguerite's waiting in a carriage outside. Robespierre is speaking at the Celebration of the Goddess of Reason tonight—it would be good for the two of you to make an appearance with us."

Marie-Anne nearly laughed. Earlier in the year, she knew, David had been named a member of the Art Commission as well as the Committee of Public Safety, making his opinion the preeminent one for painting. Marie-Anne had already heard David referred to as 'the Robespierre of the brush.' Now here he was at their door urging them to go see the genuine article. "Good?" Marie-Anne asked him. "In what way? Antoine and I have not been involved in politics; you know that."

"That is precisely why you should come," David answered. "Those who are not for the Republic are considered to be against it. And I've heard whispers . . ."

"Whispers, Jacques-Louis?" Antoine interjected. Marie-Anne turned to see her husband descending the stairs to the foyer, accompanied by Joseph Louis Lagrange, a mathematician, family friend, and possessor of a soul-heart similar to Antoine's. "What whispers have you heard?"

David gave Antoine and Lagrange a small bow. "I hesitate to say," he said to Antoine, glancing at Lagrange.

"You can say whatever you want in front of Joseph," Antoine said. "He's a friend of the family, as are you."

David gave another small bow. "The gossip is that the Tribunal is starting to look at the former members of the Ferme-Générale, Antoine, and that arrests might follow soon. I worry about you."

Marie-Anne gasped. "Is this true? Antoine did nothing—he wasn't one of those collecting taxes for the king, after all. He was just a low-level administrator."

"But all those in the Ferme-Générale profited from the taxes that were raised, and that, evidently, might be enough," David answered. "Come with me to the Celebration tonight—I know Robespierre well, and I can introduce you to him; he'll see you with me and know that you're loyal citizens of the Republic, as much as I am. Monsieur Lagrange can come with us, if he wishes."

Marie-Anne glanced at Antoine, who was frowning. "Antoine, perhaps we should listen to him. What could it hurt?"

"I've done nothing wrong," Antoine told them all. "All I've ever done has been for my family, my science, and for France."

"I know that," David answered. "But it's important that Robespierre knows this as well. He is a friend of science, as both you and Monsieur Lagrange should know. Have you met him yet?"

Antoine shook his head. "I certainly know *of* him, as does any citizen," he said, with a curl of the lips that spoke of his opinion of the man. "But Marie-Anne and I have had no occasion to be introduced to him."

"I'll do so tonight," David said. "Antoine, Marie-Anne, I tell you again—this is important for you. You can no longer hide away and pretend that all this turmoil will pass. France has changed; the world has changed. You must change with it or face the consequences. Please, get yourselves ready, and we'll go."

Marie-Anne glanced at Antoine, nodding slightly. Antoine took a long, slow breath. "Joseph?" he asked his companion.

Lagrange shrugged. "I've nothing else planned. It might be . . . interesting," he said.

"Then we'll go," Antoine said, "since you deem it so vital, Jacques-Louis. Don't leave Marguerite out in the cold; fetch her and wait for us in the dining room; Josette will bring the two of you some refreshment while we dress and make ourselves ready. Joseph, my closet is yours as well if you wish to change; we're of the same size."

"Excellent," David said. "And all of you—no powdered hair and no periwigs. Not tonight. This is not a night for you to appear to be putting yourself above others."

The Celebration of the Goddess of Reason took place at the Cathedral of Notre Dame on the Île de la Cité, though since the several laws enacted by the National Council forbidding religious affiliations, the great cathedral had since been re-dedicated as the "Temple of Reason." The initial ceremonies had already begun by the time they arrived; they could hear drums inside the cathedral and a choir singing the "Hymn of Liberty." The crowd outside was large and raucous; inside, the noise was tremendous, with the musicians and choirs and people shouting. The interior of the cathedral had been stripped of anything that spoke of the Church: all the crucifixes and images of Mary and the saints were gone. The high altar had been similarly modified: there was a throne set there and the inscription "To Philosophy" had been carved over the doors of the cathedral.

As they approached the cathedral, Marguerite took Marie-Anne's arm as they walked, letting the three men precede them. "I sometimes think this all feels wrong," Marguerite whispered, inclining her slender neck toward Marie-Anne. Her dark hair was tucked under a bonnet adorned with silken flowers, and her high cheeks were reddened by both rouge and the cold night air. "After all the masses I attended here—why, this feels like desecration."

Marie-Anne patted her hand. "I feel the same," she told her. "But those words would be dangerous to speak too loudly."

Marguerite had a short laugh at that, her fingers squeezing Marie-Anne's arm. "Even thoughts are dangerous in these days."

David took the lead as they entered through the wide, central double doors, escorting them through the throngs, hailing those he recognized and introducing Marguerite, Marie-Anne, Antoine, and Lagrange. He stopped midway up the aisle as trumpets sounded. At the high lectern, a short man dressed in black lifted his hands for attention, and the tumult under the great arched ceiling abated somewhat. "That's him," David whispered to them. "That's Robespierre."

Robespierre began to speak as the crowd quieted. Marie-Anne could barely see him over the top of the crowd and with the lectern in front of him—just a dark-haired speck at the far end of the temple, features indistinguishable in the dim light. "Citizens, we wish an order of things where all low and cruel passions are enchained by the laws, all beneficent and generous feelings aroused; where ambition is the desire to merit glory and to serve one's fatherland; where distinctions are born only of equality itself; where the citizen is subject to the magistrate, the magistrate to the people, the people to justice; where the nation safeguards the welfare of each individual, and each individual proudly enjoys the prosperity and glory of the fatherland; where all spirits are enlarged by constant exchange of Republican sentiments and by the need of earning the respect of a great people; where the arts are the adornment of liberty, which ennobles them; and where commerce is the source of public wealth, not simply of monstrous opulence for a few families."

Marie-Anne found his delivery to be slow and measured, but his voice was weak and she was doubtful that those to the rear could hear him at all, though he was interrupted often by applause, especially by those closest to the lectern. David took Marguerite's arm and pushed forward to hear him better; Marie-Anne, Antoine, and Lagrange followed. Robespierre's phrases were so long that every time he paused she thought that he had nothing more to say, but after looking slowly and searchingly over the audience, he would then add more adornment to his sentences. She wondered how such a person could have come to hold such power. David finally stopped when they were nearly underneath the raised lectern, his arm around Marguerite's waist, and Marie-Anne could see Robespierre's face clearly for the first time in the lamplight.

The sight nearly made her faint. She knew the face. Knew it far too well even though it had been long decades since she'd seen it. Robespierre looked again at the crowd, but he'd not yet glimpsed her. She started to back away. Antoine noticed her distress and looked at her quizzically. "Marie-Anne? What's wrong?"

"I'm not feeling well," she told him, turning her face away from the lectern. "Please, can we go home?"

Antoine's face reflected his concern. "Certainly, my dear," he told her. "Let me just tell Jacques-Louis and Joseph . . ." He took a step back into the crowd toward where David and Lagrange were standing even as Marie-Anne tried to stop him.

"Here, tonight, we celebrate the power of reason over the failed power of false faith," Robespierre was intoning in his pale, low voice. As Marie-Anne turned to Antoine to pull him away, Robespierre glanced down at the movement. She heard the intake of his breath and his dark, intense eyes met hers, then dropped lower down her body. Her hand came up involuntarily to her breast; she had worn the sardonyx pendant over her dress. Her hand grasped it, hiding it from sight. He seemed to smile at her, at Antoine, and at David. The pause before he began again was even longer. "We celebrate the true Supreme Being, the Goddess of Reason. Let us welcome her into our midst."

"Antoine!" Marie-Anne pulled at his arm, dragging him away even as he whispered to the others that they were leaving, even as she heard David say, "But wait, I wanted to introduce you personally . . ."

Drums and trumpets sounded, and the hymn began again even as Marie-Anne tried to push through the crowds. A processional was coming down the central aisle, moving toward the Altar of Logic. The crowd on the floor began to surge toward the procession, and Marie-Anne took the opportunity to move down the side aisle toward the door. She glimpsed the goddess on her palanquin—an actress from the opera, David had told them on the way to Notre Dame, would portray the goddess so there would be no question of idolatry. The hymn rose, the drums and trumpets clamored, and the procession with its lights and banners, proceeded into the church. Marie-Anne risked a glance back. Robespierre had left the lectern; she could no longer see him.

Maybe I was mistaken. Maybe he didn't see me, didn't recognize me.

She clung desperately to that hope as she pushed through the last of the crowd and outside. The knife edge of the cold in her lungs seemed a relief after the atmosphere in the cathedral. She took in great gasping lungfuls as she leaned back against the great stone walls of Notre Dame. Antoine reached her side and put his arm around her. She leaned into his embrace, putting her own arms tight around him. "Darling, you look so feverish, and you're shivering." He touched his hand to her forehead. "Let's find a carriage and get you home." He glanced back at the spires and gargoyles of Notre Dame, which seemed to mock her with their silent laughter. "The Goddess of Reason," Antoine nearly spat out the words. "There's no reason here. Only more madness."

The terror began the next morning with a crash of wood and an alarmed shout from Etienne, and the sound of many boots on the tiles of the foyer. "Where is Monsieur Lavoisier?" someone shouted. Even as

Marie-Anne came running toward the commotion—Verdette padding alongside her—she heard Antoine's voice answering.

"What outrage is this? How dare you men break into our house like this!"

As Marie-Anne reached the top of the stairs, she saw Antoine in the foyer already struggling in the grasp of two armed Guardsmen, with another quartet surrounding them, and an officer of the Guard looking at the papers in his hand. Old Etienne wrung his hands, with Josette gaping from the hall door. "Stop!" Marie-Anne shouted as Verdette growled at her feet. "What's the meaning of this?"

"Your husband is under arrest for treason, Madame Lavoisier," the officer replied. "We have orders to search the house and seize all material that might be pertinent."

Marie-Anne thought of all of the papers of Antoine's, the countless records of his experiments; she thought of the notes for her own experiments and the blue bottle of the elixir, still in her own smaller lab. "You cannot."

The officer held up the papers. "These say I can," he told her, "and I will." He gestured to the two soldiers holding Antoine. "Take the prisoner away," he said, then gestured to the others. "You know what to do."

"No!" Marie-Anne nearly screamed. She ran down the stairs to Antoine. Already her hand was on one of the vials in the hidden pocket of her belt. She took it out, ready to throw it, readying a spell at the same time: she could blind them all momentarily and fill the room with a choking smoke. She could snatch Antoine away and run . . .

Before she could act, a gray blur flashed by her head: Verdette, leaping from railing of the stairs. The cat launched herself at the officer, claws extended. Yowling madly, she raked her claws down the man's face, digging in. The officer howled himself, snatching Verdette away by the scruff of her neck and flinging her hard to the tiles. His boot lifted and stomped down on the cat's head as both Antoine and Marie-Anne shouted. Verdette went suddenly still. Blood dripped from the officer's face to his collar and onto the floor.

Marie-Anne lifted the vial high. But Antoine saw her gesture and shook his head as the two men holding him gripped his arms tightly, as the bayonet-tipped rifles of the other soldiers came down threateningly. "Marie-Anne," he called out loudly, "no, please! This isn't the way. I need you free and out here to help me. There's been some terrible mistake. That's all. You'll have to convince them." His eyes pleaded with her.

"Your husband is right, Madame," the officer said. He dabbed at his savaged face with a handkerchief—it was obvious he regarded the vial in her hand as no threat at all. "I've no orders to arrest you or the rest of the household. There's nothing you can do about this; we're simply doing our duty to the Republic, and if Monsieur Lavoisier is innocent, he will prove it to his judge. For now, he is under arrest." He gestured sharply to the men holding him. "Take him."

"Where?" Marie-Anne pleaded. "Where are you taking him?"

"He's to be taken to Port-Libre." The officer looked at the blood-daubed handkerchief and scowled. His foot lifted again as he glared at the motionless form of Verdette.

"No!" Marie-Anne half-screamed. The officer glared at her. "There's no need for that. Please," she said more calmly, and the officer lowered his foot slowly to the floor. "Let me say *adieu* to my husband, at least," she asked, and the officer shrugged. Marie-Anne went to Antoine, kissing him as the soldiers continued to hold him. "I'll get you out," she told him. "I promise. I won't let them hurt you."

Antoine nodded. She saw him try to smile for her. "We need to be brave for each other," he said as the soldiers pulled him away. "I love you," he said over his shoulder as they escorted him through the wreckage of their door. She saw a black carriage waiting on the street, with more soldiers around it.

"I love you," she called after him, then turned back to the officer and the quartet of soldiers still with him. "Do what you need to do," she told him. She bent down and gathered Verdette's limp form in her arms. She could feel the faint stirring of breath in her body and knew that the elixir's gift was already working inside to heal her. She didn't want the officer to see that, afraid of what he might do.

She needed to get to her own laboratory: the notes for her experiment were there, and the vial of the elixir. She had to hide them. With as much dignity as she could muster, she nodded to the officer and walked slowly up the stairs, stroking Verdette's body.

She wouldn't show her fear. She wouldn't weep for herself and Antoine. She wouldn't give Nicolas—if it had been Nicolas who had ordered this—the satisfaction of hearing she was afraid of him.

~

Marie-Anne Paulze Lavoisier: 1794

THE COPY OF THE ARREST notice that was given to Marie-Anne claimed that due to his actions in his former position in the Ferme-Générale, Antoine was a traitor to the Republic to be imprisoned at Port-Libre, a former abbey, and tried. That began months of turmoil for her, as she tried frantically to obtain his release.

She watched Antoine sink into a deep depression; she watched his green heart fade and nearly die in the foul air of his prison. Especially in the first days, she was tempted to cast everything aside, to take on a new identity and flee once again. That would have been the easiest and safest route for her. But she told herself that she couldn't abandon Antoine, whose soul-heart, encouragement, and unknowing help had allowed her to rediscover the elixir. She owed him that much, even if it meant that she remained in danger.

So she held back and remained in Paris. She went first before Monsieur Dupin, a former member of the Ferme-Générale, the person whose name had been on the warrant ordering Antoine's arrest. "Why?" she asked. "Antoine is innocent of crimes against the state; you know that best of all. Why did you sign the warrant? Who gave you these vile lies against him?"

Monsieur Dupin had shrugged. "My source was quite emphatic and persuasive about the seriousness of the charge, Mme. Lavoisier. My personal feelings about Monsieur Lavoisier don't enter into this. I'm sorry."

"Persuasive? Do you mean he threatened you? So this came from someone above you?"

Dupin pursed thin lips. "I've told you more than enough, Madame."

"Who was it?" she demanded. "Was it Monsieur Robespierre? Tell me." But he refused, and would talk to her no further on the subject.

Marie-Anne pleaded next to Jacques-Louis David. David agreed to meet her, almost reluctantly, at his studio—David now had three separate studios in the Louvre, an indication of his status as a painter within the Republic. The smells of turpentine and oils were strong in the air; David was painting in a shaft of sunlight from the windows: a self-portrait, Marie-Anne saw. The radiance of his soul-heart was wrapped tightly around him, glowing. She touched it with her mind, tasting it. "Your favorite subject?" she asked. Startled, David nearly dropped the brush he was holding.

"Marie-Anne! You startled me."

"We haven't seen you since the Celebration at Notre Dame," she said. "You've heard about Antoine?"

He didn't seem to want to meet her eyes; his gaze kept slipping around her face, looking somewhere beyond her or down to his palette. "*Oui*, I heard," he said. "I was utterly stunned by the news, of course . . ."

"Of course you were," Marie-Anne answered. "Antoine needs your help, and so do I, Jacques-Louis. We need you to speak to the Tribunal and tell them about this mistake they've made."

"Marie-Anne, I think you overestimate my influence within the Republic. I'm just a member of the Art Committee. I know you're devastated by what's happened, but I don't know what I can do to help."

"You told me that Robespierre is your friend."

David managed a shrug. "I know the man, yes, but on this . . ."

"Did you talk to him at the Celebration, after I left?"

David set down the palette, inserting the brush into a small jar of turpentine. Swirls of solemn umber danced through the clear liquid. "I did. He . . . well, he'd noticed you in the crowd, and asked who you were."

"And so you told him."

David looked at her quizzically. "Of course I did. After all, introducing you to him was the reason I'd brought the two of you to the Celebration. I told him who you were, and also told him how well I thought of both of you and how crucial you and Antoine could be to the Republic. He asked several questions about you, especially, and I told him how important you were to Antoine's work. He seemed impressed, and very interested in your laboratories and experiments. That's why I was as startled as anyone when I heard that Antoine had been arrested." His scarred head swayed from side to side. "I thought that if Robespierre saw the two of you with me it would keep you both safe, since I knew that the Tribunal was looking at those from the Ferme-Générale, but I never thought this—" He stopped. "I'm so sorry, Marie-Anne."

"It wasn't you, Jacques-Louis, and nothing you did. You owe me no apology. But you can do one thing for me."

He seemed relieved at that. "Name it," he said. "If it's in my power, I'll do whatever I can."

"I need you to use your friendship with Monsieur Robespierre," she told him. "He'll see you privately, will he not? Make an appointment with him sometime in the next few days—and I will keep that appointment for you. Will you do that?"

David was frowning. Over his shoulder, his half-finished portrait seemed to scowl. "Do you mean harm to the man?" he asked. "Marie-Anne, after what happened to Marat . . ."

"You think I intend to kill him?" She laughed. "I don't think that's possible. No, I only want to talk to him, but I doubt that he'd see me if I asked myself. Will you allow me that one small favor, for the sake of Antoine? You're married yourself; wouldn't Marguerite do the same for you if you were imprisoned?"

David caught his lip between his teeth, looking down at the floor.

Then his head came up again, slowly. "I'll do it," he said. "But you must promise me, Marie-Anne, that there will be no violence."

"I promise," Marie-Anne said.

She wondered if that was a promise she had any intention of keeping.

"Were you searching for me, Monsieur, or was it only terrible bad fortune that caused you to find me again?"

David had arranged to meet Robespierre at one of the taverns along the Seine on the Left Bank. He was sitting alone at a table against the wall, wineglass and some bread before him, his hat and cloak hung nearby. There was a quartet of men at a table by the door; she saw them watching her warily as she approached, and two of them had hands suspiciously in the pockets of their overcoats. *His men*, she decided, which is why she stopped short of the table and spoke.

Maximilien Robespierre—Nicolas—turned slowly in his chair to look at her. He smiled and rose politely, gesturing to the chair across from him. "Please, sit," he said. Marie-Anne hesitated, then took the offered chair. "I was expecting Jacques-Louis. I assume that you coerced him into setting up this appointment; that explains the tone of his note to me."

"Don't blame Jacques-Louis," Marie-Anne said. "He was feeling guilty for having brought us to the Celebration; he'd wanted to introduce me to you. Ironic, isn't it, Monsieur Robespierre? Or do you still prefer Nicolas?"

"Nicolas . . ." he said, seeming to roll the word around in his mouth as if tasting the syllables. "It's been a long time for that name—as long as it's been for you, Perenelle, or should I say Madame Lavoisier?" He smiled again, showing his teeth. "But yes, seeing you there that night was a shock for me. I wondered if you might not be back in Paris—in fact, I thought that perhaps you could be poor Jacques-Louise's wife, though that suspicion was dispelled as soon as I met Marguerite. I hadn't considered Antoine Lavoisier, though that makes perfect sense. A brilliant chemist—as you were yourself. It's a shame his days of experimentation are over now."

"This isn't about Antoine, any more than it was about any of the others. It's about you and me, Nicolas."

He was already shaking his head in denial. "We both know better. I can't kill you; you can't kill me. But even if I can't kill you or even permanently harm you, we both know that the pain of injury's still very real—why, it took me weeks to entirely recover from being shot back in Ferrara." He took a sip of the wine in front of him. "What I've realized is that I can hurt you more by hurting those you love. Yes, there—I can already see it in your face, my dear. You really should work on that. We're very alike, but also different, Perenelle. I know what you feed on, but *I'm* fed by something else. You've no idea how *delicious* your pain is to me—almost as delicious as the pain of others. I can taste it right now, as we're sitting here." He lifted the wineglass again, sipping it as his eyes closed momentarily. "Mmm, yes, this wine goes well with it. Red. Like blood."

"You're a vile, awful creature," Marie-Anne spat.

"I'm sure you think so, my dear," he replied calmly. "You probably always thought so—I'll admit that I did enjoy the beatings I gave you so long ago, too, if not in the same way, and killing Provost Marcel with my spell was sweet as well. But it was your elixir that finished the task. *That* made me the way I am; *you* made me the way I am. The elixir changed me, as it changed you—as it would change anyone, I know. Have you figured out how to perfect it yet, Perenelle? Have you given it to anyone else?"

She shook her head, but she was remembering her cat Verdette.

"That's a shame," he said. "That would an interesting experiment—if only to see how much pain and torture such a being can endure, and to see if perhaps I can find a way to actually kill them."

Marie-Anne shivered, hearing the eerily calm voice discussing such a horror. "You *can* do that," she told him. "You can have me. Let Antoine go; take me."

He laughed then, leaning back hard against his chair. "I don't mind killing mortals," he said. "That's all they're really good for—feeding me with their pain and the sweet, wonderful taste of their eventual passing.

But you and me . . . I *like* this, Perenelle. I like coming across you every now and then. You're a fine feast that I love having every so many decades, but a steady diet of you . . ." He shook his head. "No. It's tempting, but I don't want that. I hate you, Perenelle, and I know that you hate me in return. Our mutual hate nourishes and sustains me; if you were gone, that would be lost to me. Besides, one day you *will* perfect the elixir, and then I'll take that from you, too."

He looked at her with such hunger and ferocity that she pushed her chair back from the table. "Antoine?"

"Oh, he'll die." Nicolas shrugged. "His fate's already settled. I'll be there to taste his death, and to taste the fury and loathing that you'll give me as a result. It will be such a doubled pleasure."

"You're a monster."

"In your eyes, perhaps. But the truth is that I'm only doing what I need to do to live, just as you are. If that's a monstrosity, then everyone is a monster, yourself included."

"If Antoine dies, I'll find a way to bring you down," she told him. "I'll find a way to kill you, and I'll send you to hell."

He laughed again. "You've become so terribly dramatic, my dear. Do whatever you want. If you want to find me, all you need to do is go to wherever there's pain and turmoil and death. I'll be there, waiting for you." He drained the wine in his glass. "And now I have affairs of the Republic to which I must attend. I need to assign a judge to Antoine's case—one who understands the verdict I have in mind."

He pushed his chair back and rose, taking his coat and hat from their hook on the tavern wall. He brought the cloak over his shoulder. "If you're hungry, the food here's excellent," he said. "Have the waiter order you whatever you like—tell him to put it on my account. It was good seeing you again, Perenelle. I very much look forward to our future meetings."

With that, he bowed to her and placed his hat on his head. He turned, gesturing to the men at the neighboring table. She could have shot him then, could have discharged the pistol she carried with her, leaving him twisting in pain on the floorboards. She could have cast a vial at him, speaking a spell word so that the chemicals inside bloomed into flames to char and blacken his flesh.

But none of that would change anything. In a few minutes, a few hours, a few days or weeks or months at worst, he would be whole and unhurt again.

She couldn't stop him.

She watched him leave the tavern, safely in the midst of his companions.

Antoine's eventual trial before the Tribunal didn't take place until late April, but its outcome was certain from the moment it began. The judge refused to listen to Marie-Anne's appeal to spare Antoine's life so that he might be allowed to continue his experiments. "The Republic needs neither scientists nor chemists; the course of justice cannot be delayed," the judge said, after glancing once at the papers in front of him. No witnesses had been called; none, she knew, were necessary. "The sentence will be carried out in ten days." And with that, he gestured for Antoine to be taken away.

Marie-Anne went to see Antoine that night. The air of the prison was chill and damp; she could hear Antoine coughing as the guard escorted her to his cell. "A few minutes only," he told Marie-Anne as she pressed the coins of the necessary bribe into the guard's hand and Antoine came forward from the dark, fetid recesses of the small cell.

"You shouldn't have come," he told her as the guard left them. She could hear the stirring of the other prisoners in the nearby cells, could feel their gazes on the two of them. Antoine looked horrible: thin and emaciated, his hair matted to his skull and bruises mottling his face and arms. He had told her previously that he was questioned and beaten irregularly, that Robespierre sometimes attended the interrogations; it appeared that he'd experienced another beating since the travesty of his trial. She took his hand through the bars, pressing her face against the cold, rusted iron to kiss him.

"Don't give up hope yet," she told him. "You're well-loved, my darling.

There are those who are outraged at this verdict, and they've told me that they'll make their voices heard."

He nodded, but she saw the resignation in his eyes, bloodshot and dull. She wondered if he'd heard the lie in her voice: she had no hope now that anyone could change the verdict, knowing who Robespierre actually was. "Thank you," he said, and she saw that he was missing teeth, slurring his words. The fingers clutching hers were little more than flesh draped over bone, the ligaments visible underneath. "The laboratory? My notes?"

She shook her head. "Everything's been confiscated by the state, months ago: our house, the laboratories, all of our notes. Everything. It's all gone, I'm afraid. I didn't want to tell you."

He nodded again, as if he'd expected the news. There was no change in his expression, and she knew then how deep his despair had become, and how hopeless he felt. It steeled her resolve.

She'd thought for a long time about this. Expecting this, she'd burned the notes she had on the elixir—she didn't want Nicolas to have them. She made copies for herself and placed them where she could retrieve them at some later date, but left out the critical element: the blood that made the elixir work. That vital ingredient she would keep to herself. She wouldn't let Nicolas know that. Ever.

With the laboratories intact, she might have been able to do more. She might have been able to release him from Porte Libre as she'd once released herself from her Roman prison, though Porte Libre was far better guarded, and she had no idea where they could hide afterward. But it didn't matter; in the day following Antoine's arrest, their laboratories had been destroyed, the chemical stores and equipment taken away. Everything. Everything save one.

In her cloak, nestled in an inner pocket, was the blue vial. She'd managed to save that.

"We don't have long," she whispered to him urgently. "Do you trust me?" She passed him the blue bottle. "Drink this," she told him.

He stared at the bottle. "Marie-Anne, are things truly this desperate?"

She realized then that he thought the vial contained a poison, that she wanted him to commit suicide rather than face the guillotine. "You don't understand. This is to keep you alive, Antoine—no matter what happens." She could see the confusion in his face. "Trust me," she told him again. "Please."

He uncapped the vial. "I do trust you," he said, "no matter what this is." He upended the vial into his mouth; she saw his throat move as he swallowed. "Bitter," he said, grimacing. "And it burns all through me . . ." His voice cut off as he gasped and cried out in sudden pain, his mouth a wide oval, his eyes nearly as wide. She could see changes rippling through his body, his hair losing the gray it had acquired, his receding hairline surging forward like a rushing tide over his forehead, the lines of his face smoothing, his back straightening. He grunted, as much in wonder as in pain, holding his hands in front of his face: a young man's hands, the skin elastic and smooth. As she watched, the transformation ended, and his breathing became more regular and even, though he continued to stare at his hands. "Marie-Anne?" he asked, a dozen questions held in the query of her name.

"Look at me, Antoine," she said, whispering so that none of the others could hear her. "Look at me with someone else's eyes. Haven't you ever wondered why I haven't changed all that much over the years of our marriage? Haven't you heard people say how young I still looked, with a bit of puzzlement or even jealousy in their voices? Antoine, I don't age. I'm far, far older than you would believe if I told you. And my body heals itself: shoot me, cut my throat with a knife, snap my neck—none of that will end my life. I've just given you the same gift." But the elixir will also change you, as it did me and as it did Nicolas and Verdette. I don't know how, but it will. The elixir will demand an eternal payment for what it gives; for that, whatever it will be, I can only ask for your forgiveness.

She didn't tell him that. He would find out, soon enough.

"This is nonsense," he blustered, his eyes wild, though he touched his face in wonderment. "A fantasy. Even if it were true, why would you do this, when in a few days . . ." He couldn't speak the rest.

"I told you," she said. "Stab me, shoot me, and I don't die. And neither will you, my love. Neither will you." She patted his hand. "I know you don't believe me, but trust me."

Even as she heard the metallic jingle of the jailer's keys, she saw hope bloom in his eyes, even in the darkness of the cell. She kissed him again—his lips, young and pliant—as the guard entered the corridor for his cell and grunted at her.

"I have to go now," she said. "Trust me, Antoine. Believe in this. You will not die."

It was the 8th of May, 1794. She could not think of it as 19 Floréal, Year II.

The designation hardly mattered. No matter what it was called, this was the day she was to watch her husband lose his head. Even knowing that Antoine had taken the elixir, she found herself frightened. The guillotine: this was a different kind of death than any she'd experienced.

Joseph Louis Lagrange, alone of their friends, stood with her in the thin gathering around the Place de la Révolution. At the beginning of Robespierre's purge of anyone who might be against him, there had been enormous crowds for the executions, and the guillotine had become the favorite entertainment of the masses. The "People's Avenger," they called it, or "Madame Guillotine," or "The National Razor"—as noble heads fell and the crowds jeered and cheered. People would bring their children, placing them on their shoulders so they could watch the blade fall and see the heads tumble away. But as the grisly violence of the Reign of Terror lengthened, as untold thousands fell under the blade, it was no longer just the nobility, but the intellectuals, the politicians, and even the commoners and prostitutes who were executed in a continuing, endless bloodbath.

Even the spectacle of public death became boring. The crowds had begun to wane.

Marie-Anne and Lagrange, bundled in cloaks against recognition, approached the Place. Vendors called out to them, waving pieces of parchment with the names of the condemned printed on them as a program. There were a few hundred rather than thousands of people around the bloodstained device this morning. "Are you certain you want to be here, Madame?" Lagrange asked her. Marie-Anne had stopped at the edge of the crowd as the shadow of the guillotine touched her and sun sparked from the angled blade. "If you wish, walk away. No one would blame you in the slightest, Antoine least of all. Take a carriage and return to your house. I will stay as your witness and report back to you. No wife should have to see her husband suffer this."

"No," she told him. "I want Antoine to see that I'm here." She watched: as the long list of prisoners was called out one by one; as they were brought onto the platform; as they knelt down and their heads were placed on the blood-spattered board; as the blade was winched up and released, falling in an instant; as the severed, dripping heads were held up to the crowd's roaring approval.

It sickened her, watching this, knowing that Antoine would soon experience the same fate. And she wondered, as well, what the guillotine would do to Antoine or her, if even an immortal body could survive such terrible abuse.

Even as the thought passed in her mind, she heard Antoine's name called out. He ascended the steps to the platform, his hands tied behind him, his hair cropped short and the collar of his shirt loose. A murmur that quickly became a roar came from the crowd: Robespierre himself escorted Antoine, holding him by the arm. She saw Antoine look out over the crowd, saw him recognize her and give her a faint, brave smile. Nicolas saw her too, and his smile was broad and mocking. He pointed toward her, then made a gesture as if swallowing something from a cup or bottle. *He knows. He knows I gave him the elixir . . .* "We are conducting an experiment today," he said aloud, his voice faint over that of the crowd. "We shall discover if science can defeat the guillotine."

Nicolas helped Antoine to kneel down, and as he straightened again, he bowed in Marie-Anne's direction. Antoine's gaze was still on her as well; he must have seen her hands fly to her face in shock. But the executioner pushed Antoine's head down into the stock, then lowered the top board.

The blade began its agonizing, final rise.

Marie-Anne turned away, with a quiet sob, then turned defiantly back. She would watch, and wouldn't give Nicolas the satisfaction of seeing her fear. She watched the blade fall, heard the crowd's approval, felt Lagrange's hand on her shoulder. She wondered if it would have been better if it had been *her* head that had been separated from its body, but she knew that wasn't what Nicolas wanted.

"I hate you, Perenelle, and I know that you hate me in return," he'd told her. *"That mutual hate nourishes and sustains me; if you were gone, that would be lost to me."*

"Let's leave here, Madame," Lagrange said, not understanding her grief, her sorrow, and her regret. He gave a huff of indignation. "It took them only an instant to cut off his head, but France may not produce another such head in a century."

"I've made arrangements for the body," she told him. "I have to take care of that."

"Then I'll accompany you."

Most of the bodies were simply thrown into common mass graves outside the city. Two-wheeled tumbril carts collected them—heads in sacks, the bodies piled into the tumbrils until the cart was full. Those few bodies that were to be claimed were set aside briefly. Marie-Anne and Lagrange moved past a fully-laden tumbril from which thick blood was leaking. Large black flies buzzed thickly around the tumbril and the blood pooled on the cobbles of the Place, stirring as if in irritation as Marie-Anne and Lagrange, holding perfumed handkerchiefs to their faces against the stench, came near them: some of the bodies had evacuated their bowels and bladders during their execution. "Here," Lagrange said, moving toward a body stretched out on an unhitched tumbril a little away from the others. "Madame," he asked again, "are you sure . . . ?"

"Is it Antoine?" Marie-Anne asked, and Lagrange nodded silently.

Seeing him was worse than she'd thought possible. His head was in a canvas sack at the feet of the body, the fibers liberally soaked with his blood. The bed of the tumbril was tilted, so it appeared that the head-less body was leaning back against the bed of the cart. The wound on his neck was horrible to see, still seeping blood onto the linen shirt. The body was still and unmoving. For a moment, seeing Antoine's body, the world shivered around Marie-Anne as she remembered seeing Paolina's murdered body, and she thought that she would faint. She clutched the side of the cart and took several gulping breaths. She felt Lagrange's hand on her shoulder. "Come away," he said. "I'll deal with this."

She shook her head, steeling herself. She crouched down to the canvas sack and untied the twine holding it together. She forced herself to take Antoine's head in her hands, grateful that someone had closed the eyes. Rising, holding the gory mess away from herself, she placed his head against the body, where it rightfully belonged.

She heard Lagrange's hissing intake of breath as she became aware that someone else had approached the tumbril. She looked up to see Robespierre watching from the other side of the tumbril. She glared at him; he looked blandly back at her. "You have no idea what you've done, Monsieur," Lagrange spat out angrily.

Robespierre glanced at him. "I believe I know exactly what I've done," he answered. "And I would be careful, Monsieur Lagrange, lest you say too much."

Marie-Anne ignored Nicolas. She stared at the body, not certain what she was expecting to see: strands of muscles reaching out from body to neck, pulling it back together, bones and sinew and flesh knitting together, the heart starting to beat once more, the lungs to breathe, Antoine's eyes opening to gaze at her once more . . .

There was nothing. No response at all. The head remained stubbornly severed, the body unmoving. "He looks so strangely young," Lagrange said, then sighed. "Madame, we should leave." She didn't respond. She stared at Antoine, willing him to come back to life. She'd snapped the spines of mice in the laboratory before. They'd come back; surely the elixir could do that with Antoine.

But she'd never entirely severed the heads. She'd never removed the head from the body until all life was gone, *then* tried to restore them.

"Antoine . . ." she whispered. There was no answer.

"It would seem that the guillotine renders anyone mortal," Robespierre said. Marie-Anne glanced up to find his amused regard on her. "I'm sure we'll both remember that," he said.

"Monsieur," Lagrange interrupted. "I must ask you to leave. Allow Madame Lavoisier to grieve in peace."

"Grief is such a rich emotion," Robespierre answered. "It possesses such an exquisite taste." He shivered then, as if with a sudden chill, and took a step back. He bowed to Lagrange, to Marie-Anne. "We will meet each other again," he told her.

"The man is drunk with his power, and he'll come to a terrible end soon enough," Lagrange said as Robespierre left them, though he half-whispered the words so that none of the people milling around them could hear him. Marie-Anne nodded, but her gaze was still on Antoine. *Now*, she thought, *now it's safe, Antoine. Come back to me. Please come back, my love . . .*

But Antoine remained obstinately dead.

It would be two full days before she allowed him to be buried. When the body began to show irrevocable signs of corruption, she finally permitted the lid to be nailed on the coffin. As she watched the coffin being lowered into the grave, she thought of Nicolas.

I know how to kill you now. I know.

6:
THALIA

Camille Kenny

Today

AS THE FALLING sun painted ragged clouds with purple and red, they strolled over the Pont au Double toward Île de la Cité and Notre Dame, stopping to watch a puppeteer performing on the bridge.

"Mexico's beautiful this time of year, don't you think?" David laughed, though Camille managed only a smile at his jest.

At Camille's insistence, she and David had told their friends in New York that they were going to Mexico City and Acapulco. She'd dropped Verdette off with Mercedes with strict instructions to let her roam the house but not to try to pick her up or pet her.

But rather than going to Mexico City, they instead flew to Paris. She told David that the lie was "so no one can interrupt us, no one can find us, and we can surprise everyone when we come back," though that, too, was a lie. After Helen's murder, she was afraid that Nicolas would come after David next. She intended to spend a few days with him in Paris to make certain he was settled and comfortable, then fly back to New York alone on some pretext or another. She would deal with Nicolas; she would end the hunt.

Then, if she could, she'd come back for David. When it was safe for him.

"I'll pay for the trip from my trust fund," she told him. "It's rather flush right now. You don't need to worry; just make sure your passport's in order. Bring your camera—think of what you can shoot there: a whole new country."

Camille had thought that David might protest the subterfuge, especially given the continuing investigation into Helen's murder, but he'd given only a token protest, which told her just how stressed he was also. "It'd be nice to be alone," he'd said, "just the two of us. I've always wanted to see Paris, and that detective woman told me that I wasn't a suspect, so sure. Why not?"

Why not? That had been enough; Camille had booked them the flight the next day, not caring what it cost. *Time to go home. Time to think. Time to decide what I'm going to do.*

Camille tossed a euro into the puppeteer's hat as they walked on a few more paces. She leaned on the stone railing of the bridge, looking down into a Seine whose ripples glittered with the sunset's colors. Just downstream, another couple was sitting on a ledge near the water, arms around each other and basking in the remaining light. The towers of Notre Dame appeared golden in the late afternoon. A tour boat passed underneath them with a snatch of French from the guide. ". . . one of the most famous Gothic cathedrals, begun in 1160 and completed nearly two centuries later. Notre Dame was one of the first buildings in the world to use the flying buttress . . ."

She heard the click of a camera behind her, and glanced over her shoulder to see David taking pictures of her on the bridge with Notre Dame as the backdrop. "You know, there have been a few million pictures taken right here," she told him. "All of them are currently moldering forgotten in a few million albums."

He grinned lopsidedly at her. Since they'd come to Paris, much of the grief that surrounded him following Helen's murder had been overpowered by the scenery. He could manage to laugh and smile again, though the shadows still crept over his face at odd times. "Yeah, but none of them have *you* in them, and they weren't taken by me."

"Egotist," she told him. For a moment, she forgot her own quandary in the innocent, honest awe in his face as he gazed around at the scene in front of them, and she laughed. "Put the camera down and come here."

David had never been to Paris before, never been to Europe at all, and she could feel his eagerness and wonder at the sights, sending his emerald radiance to pulsing as he tried to absorb everything around them. "There's nothing like this in America," he told her. "Nothing. There's such a sense of *age* here. New York . . . Well, as wonderful as it is, it's so *new* and blandly modern compared to this."

She smiled and didn't contradict him, though she had little romanticism about the Paris she remembered from centuries ago. That Paris had been smaller, malodorous, and filthy, the air thick and dark, the houses smaller, more closely-set and poorly-built. *This* Paris had space and was far cleaner, yet the memory of the violent, periodic spasms Paris had experienced still lingered, sanitized like the rest of the inner city—pockets of ancient memories hidden in the midst of more modern structures. She could still see underneath the facade to a past that, sometimes, felt more real to her than the present. She stood arm-in-arm with David, basking like a cat in sunshine to the radiance of his green heart.

Only she could feel that. That pleasure was hers alone.

They strolled across the bridge to the Île. David marveled at the elaborate stone figures above the massive doors of the cathedral, gazing up at the gargoyles that leered down at them from the roof. "Can we go up to the top of the tower?" he asked her.

"Not tonight," she told him. "Leave something for another day. We've plenty of time to see everything, as much time as we want." She hoped that was true. "This evening, let's just walk around the city and pretend we're not tourists, just two lovers out for a stroll."

They did exactly that, walking across the Île to the Right Bank, past the grand facade of the Hôtel de Ville, turning west along the rue de Rivoli, with Camille giving him a running commentary on the sights. They came to the rue Saint-Denis and Camille stopped, overcome again with memories. The rue Saint-Denis had been called rue des Saints Innocents when she and Nicolas had lived there, close by. Nothing remained from that time, all of it obliterated by the glacial but inexorable march of centuries and decay. She could recall where their little estate had stood, but there were newer buildings there now, already a few centuries old themselves.

She'd been back to Paris several times over her long lifetime, but while she loved the city and felt that it was more "home" than any other place, each time she returned, the city saddened her as well. All these people around them: all of them felt so *temporary*, given such a fleeting existence that, to them, the city seemed solid, permanent, and largely unchanging in a way it could never be for her. To her, the city was ephemeral and constantly in a state of slow alteration.

And David, on her arm, was no different than any of them: to her, his life would be just as ephemeral and fleeting, unless she did with him what she'd done to Verdette, and that was something she wouldn't do without his understanding of all the implications the potion represented.

Nicolas would not have her hesitation.

It was as if his name generated the vision. She saw a man, dressed in dark clothes, approaching them from farther up the rue Saint-Denis. He was short, and the bulk of his body and the way he carried himself . . . For a moment, Camille's vision blurred and she saw the street as it once had been, with the cobbles and central gutter and their house set on the corner, with the neighbors she remembered moving around them.

He had found them, impossibly. She wasn't prepared for this; she'd intended to buy a small handgun here in Paris, but had not yet had the opportunity. There were a few vials of chemicals in her purse, ready to be set off with a small spell, but that was all. But *he* would be ready. Camille's arm tightened around David's; as she reached into her purse; he misinterpreted the gesture and smiled, leaning down to kiss the top of her head.

"I can see why you love this city," he said to her. She barely heard him, watching the man approach. He was within a dozen strides of them now, and she waited for him to take a few more steps, so she could fling the vial at his feet and shout the spell—if she was lucky, if Nicolas didn't stop her first, if he didn't send the black fire rushing toward her and David. A shielding spell—could she cast it quickly enough? She wondered how she could communicate her urgency to David, to convince him to run while he could, while she tried to deal with the threat. "Paris has the energy of New York," he was saying, "yet there's so much *history* here also. I can't wait to see more of it. How many times have you been here before, Camille?"

With the invocation of her current name, her vision cleared. The short man was but a few strides away, but now she saw his features and realized that he was not Nicolas. He was not anyone she recognized. Her fingers released the glass tube they were holding. The man felt her gaze on him, though. He nodded to her as he passed, smiling as he regarded the two of them, her arm still holding him tightly. *"Bon soir,"* he said. *"Appréciez votre soirée."*

"Bon soir," Camille answered. Then, to David, she said: "I've been here too many times. The city is inhabited by ghosts."

The next day, they left the Hotel de Notré Dame on rue de Maître-Albert, leaving their key with Dominique, the owner who also worked at the desk. Camille expected to do the normal tourist things, and they did: not for her, of course, but because David wanted to see them and it gave her pleasure to watch the delight in his face as he gazed at the Eiffel Tower and the Arc de Triomphe, the Jardin du Luxembourg and Jardin des Tuileries. David, never without his camera, took a massive number of pictures, though he complained that too many of them looked exactly like tourist shots.

David wanted to tour the Louvre as well, but she convinced him to leave it for another day, shepherding him instead to the Musée d'Orsay, with its incredible collection of mid-19th to early 20th century paintings, all in what Camille still remembered as the Gare d'Orsay, a train station built at the turn of the century.

She'd been there the day the train station had opened, during the Exposition Universelle of 1900. The current building overlaid her memories, dimmed.

Later that afternoon, they wandered the Musée de Cluny, close to their hotel. Originally built to house the abbots of Cluny, the building itself dated from the late 15th century and was constructed over the remnants of Roman-era baths, some of which had been excavated and were now visible again in the basement of the museum as well as in a rear court. David seemed most impressed by a room hung with the six tapestries of the *Lady and the Unicorn*, but Camille herself stopped near the top of the stairs leading to the tapestry room. There, on the wall, was a rectangular square stone, much weathered, with images of the sun and three men, two of them depicted as saints with a key and a book, the figures carved above a section of writing.

Her breath caught, looking at the stone—she'd forgotten that it was there. She remembered it; she'd last seen it in 1418, above an empty grave. "What's that?" David asked her, his touch on her shoulder startling her. He bent down, reading the card for the exhibit, printed in English and German as well as French. "Nicolas Flamel's tombstone? Isn't he that alchemist guy?"

"Yeah," she answered, surprised at the trembling in her voice. "That alchemist guy."

David chuckled. "It figures you'd be interested in that, given the laboratory you have in our apartment."

That evening, David came grinning into the room. "I was just talking with Dominique at the desk," he said. "I know where we're going for dinner."

"I do, too. We're going to the Petit Saint Benoit."

"Nope." He shook his head. "We're going somewhere else. I've already made the reservations."

"Where?"

His grin widened. "Not telling you," he said. "It's a surprise."

That evening, they took a taxi from the hotel. He still refused to tell her where they were going. The taxi moved across the Île and up the Boulevard de Sébastopol, finally turning right, then left again, then right once more before stopping. Well before then, she realized where they were heading, knew with a knot in her stomach. The street sign on the building proclaimed this to be the rue de Montmorency, though she remembered other names for the street. It was close to where she and Nicolas had first lived. As David paid the taxi driver, she peered at the small building sandwiched between two larger ones: *Auberge Nicolas Flamel*, it proclaimed, and a sign placed on the house itself proclaimed this to be the "House of Nicolas Flamel and his wife Perenelle," built in 1407.

She knew the truth: that "Perenelle" had vanished from Nicolas' life five years before, that Nicolas had never actually lived here. She managed to smile as David came up to her. "Look," he said. "Nicolas Flamel's house. Dominique said it's one of the oldest buildings in Paris, maybe even *the* oldest, and that the restaurant here is excellent." He stopped, looking at her suspiciously. "You already knew about this place, didn't you?"

"Yes," she told him, and the visible disappointment in his face made her sorry for the admission. "But . . . I've never eaten here before. And I think it's lovely that you would put this together." On her toes, she reached up to put her arms around his shoulders and kiss him: a long, lingering embrace that surprised even her with its intensity. She was surrounded by him, by his radiance; she felt complete, as she had not felt in more than half a century. "It's still a wonderful surprise, and I love you for the thought. Let's go in."

For a time, inside the restaurant, she could almost believe that she had dropped back in time: the exposed timbers, the carvings, the candles alight everywhere, the decor; all brought her back to another century despite the modern conveniences. She managed to put aside the fact that she was inside a house that Nicolas had built—though the waiter informed them, as she already knew, that this hadn't been his home. This was designed as a house for the indigent, who were given a drink and food in the tavern on the ground floor, then were taken upstairs to sleep, paid for with their prayers for the souls of Nicolas and Perenelle.

She had smiled tight-lipped at that. "Nicolas must have felt they truly needed the prayers," she said, and their waiter shrugged.

"Who knows?" he said. "Everything about the Flamels is mysterious, no?"

The dinner was as delightful as Dominique had advertised, and they lingered for a few hours. Afterward, in the cool evening, Camille had taken David's hand. "Come on," she said. "Since you're on this Flamel kick . . ."

They walked south for a few blocks, toward the Seine, and onto a narrow street set with shops and taverns, crowded with throngs of people. She pointed at the street sign: *rue Nicolas Flamel*. "Stand there under the sign," David told her, bringing up his camera. "I should get a shot of this."

"No," she told him firmly. "Take a picture of the sign if you want, but not with me."

He looked at her strangely, but shrugged, lifting the camera and taking a quick snapshot. She took his arm again and they strolled down the lane, weaving through the clots of pedestrians and looking in the shop windows. As they walked, she felt her mood darkening again. "So, is it true what our waiter said, that Nicolas may not really have been an alchemist at all, that it was all just a rumor?" David asked her.

"He was rich," Camille told him. "That much is certain. And he didn't get that way by selling books and working as a scrivener."

"So you think he was actually able to transform lead into gold?"

"Transmute, not transform," she told him. "And probably not gold. But mercury to silver . . ." Her shoulder lifted. "Maybe. Maybe he managed that much."

"And the rest? All those legends that he and Perenelle have been seen long after they were supposed to have died?"

She shivered. The street seemed darker now and more shadowed, and the laughter of the people easing around them was hollow and mocking. "Sounds like a total fantasy to me," she said.

David paused to take a picture down the street. He gave a small satisfied nod at the result, looking at the camera display. "Is that what you're looking for with all those chemicals you have?" he asked. "The secret of immortality? The chance to live forever?"

She didn't answer, instead responding with another question. "Would you want to live forever, David, if you had the chance?"

"I don't think most people in decent health really want to die," he answered. "And I think that if you thought you were going to live forever, the knowledge would change you—change the way you act and the way you think. Maybe pretty drastically."

"TANSTAAFL," she said, pronouncing the letters as a single word: *tan-staff-ull.*

"Huh?"

"It's an acronym. 'There Ain't No Such Thing As A Free Lunch.' Whatever advantage you gain, you have to pay for it in some way. If Nicolas and Perenelle managed to find the elixir they were looking for, then they're paying for it—and the bigger the payoff, the bigger the cost they're paying."

David shrugged. "Still, I can see wanting that. Though maybe what you find out is that eternal life doesn't automatically hand you eternal happiness. And it wouldn't stop the people you love from dying around you."

The remark brought her to a halt as the street dead-ended into another. "Yeah," she said. "I'll buy that. Are you thinking of Helen?"

He nodded. "She and I . . . well, she always said she'd wanted to go to Paris, and I said I'd take her there one day. Now it's too late for her." His lips pressed together, and Camille hugged him.

"It wasn't your fault," she told him. She pointed to a street sign across the way on the cross street: *rue Perenelle*, it said. "Maybe having to live forever wasn't exactly a blessing for them, either."

The night was suddenly full of ghosts again, rushing past her and whispering her names: all of them, the long succession of people she'd pretended to be. The ghosts tugged at her, hissing and warning her: *You can't stay here more than another day or two. Running has never been the solution. You still have to be the hunter; more than ever now that Nicolas knows your current identity. Leave David here, go back, and do whatever you must to end it.*

She shook her head. "David, can we go back to the hotel? I'd like to be alone, just the two of us."

She could hear David snoring in the darkness, but she couldn't sleep, her thoughts all in turmoil. Nicolas lurked in her dreams. She glanced at the clock on the nightstand; the LEDs glared that it was 4:30 in the morning; 10:30 at night back in New York. She threw aside the covers and quietly dressed, then wrote a terse note that she left on her pillow: *Went for an early walk. Back soon. Love, Camille.*

She left the room and rode the elevator down to the lobby, where a sleepy-looking attendant glanced at her from behind the desk. She slid him her room key but said nothing as she crossed the small lobby and went out the doors into early morning Paris. She walked quickly up the street toward the Seine.

Paris never sleeps: that was the saying, and it was generally true. Even now, in the predawn, there were people out along the main boulevards and traffic on the streets. Notre Dame was pinned in amber spotlights, gleaming against a night sky that was just beginning to lighten, while street lights plucked deep pools of illumination from the dark. Camille crossed the Quai de Montebello, walking past the shuttered booksellers' stalls, and taking the Pont au Double toward the Île. Halfway across the bridge, she stopped, leaning on the stone railing and staring down at the water of the Seine, shimmering with the reflected lights of the city.

This was the place she lived much of her long life. She wondered if this is where she would end it as well. All these centuries of being a muse for someone else—what had it gained her? All the centuries of inevitable loss, or moments of joy interrupted, of death and the decay of age.

At an all-night Internet cafe a few blocks from the hotel, she booked herself a plane flight out of Paris, leaving the following afternoon. This would be their last day together.

Maybe our last day together forever. She shivered at the thought.

Not long after dawn, after making a few discreet enquiries, she found a dingy shop open in an alleyway on the Left Bank that would sell her a 9mm handgun and a full clip without worrying about the legalities. She put that in her purse; the weight made her feel slightly less paranoid.

She'd also considered that here in Paris, it would be easy for her to walk away from David, to walk away from Nicolas and the attention of prying detectives like Palento for Nicolas' murders. She could vanish

again into the streets of the city she knew so well, take on another identity, and David would never be able to find her again. And Nicolas . . .
well, she could find him again, and begin the hunt once more.

The problem with that strategy was that it was becoming more and
more difficult to assume new identities. In a world laced together by the
Internet, in a world where anyone could reach into distant databases,
in a world where information had a potential shelf life of forever, where
communication was quick and easy and documents more and more
technologically difficult to fake, becoming someone else was a slower
and far more expensive game.

In the beginning of her long life, when people rarely traveled more
than a few miles from their home and communication was measured in
months or weeks rather than minutes, all she'd needed to do was take
an appropriate name and say that she was from some sufficiently distant
town. She could create a background and lineage that suited her, and
no one would particularly question it. Even up through the 19th century and through much of the 20th, claiming a distant home was safe
and forging documents was relatively simple.

Not now. Now it was easy to be caught and exposed. Even a relatively trivial run-in with the authorities could lead to issues and awkward questions. She knew that from her interaction with Bob Walters
and Detective Palento.

Worse, it was also becoming harder to escape through faking death
as well—she suspected that an embalming would not only be agonizing,
it might also truly kill her. Even if her body could somehow recover
from that abuse, which she doubted, coming back from it would be a
lingering and long torture. The modern world was no longer one from
which an immortal like her could easily escape.

No matter how tired of the game she might be, it was a game she
couldn't voluntarily quit without experiencing actual death. On the
other hand, the modern world was one in which it seemed there were
more ways for her to finally, truly, die. Cremation, embalming, an au-
topsy, electrocution, explosions and terrorist bombings . . . She wondered whether her body could survive any of those, whether she would

have died like thousands of others if she'd been caught in the twin towers during the 9/11 attack.

There was no way to tell without experimentation. Those were experiments Nicolas might have made with others; they weren't ones she was willing to test herself.

I don't want to do that. I don't want to abandon David.

If the previous evening had told her nothing else, it had told her that she did love David, loved him as she had so very few in her life. His green heart: it contained that rare lapis thread that she'd thought she might never taste again. With him, maybe, she could find in herself her own genius once again, and move her own creative endeavors forward. He could be *her* muse as she was his. Could she give that up once more, as Nicolas had forced her to do before?

Only four or five times before had she encountered a green heart like his, in all the centuries. She could not even think of that. She would not.

She lifted her body up, leaning well over the rail and staring into the Seine as if she could find answers there in the dark, swirling water. She heard two people approaching the bridge, talking. She let herself fall back onto her feet again. She took a long breath. In the east, the sky was salmon-colored and cloudy. She walked over the bridge to the Île, then over to the Right Bank. She wandered, not caring where her footsteps took her, just letting her thoughts move her. The sun rose, lifting itself slowly into a cloud-strewn sky and doing little to allay the early morning chill. Camille found herself at the east end of the Jardin des Tuileries, near the glass pyramid in front of the Louvre. There were already quite a few people out in the park in the early morning. She found herself rousing from her reverie at the sight of a gray-haired and mustachioed old man, wearing a set of horn-rimmed glasses and seated on a chair under the trees near the Place du Carrousel. He was dressed in a beige sport coat and dark pants, his shoes polished as if for church.

A paper bag was on his lap between his legs, and he plunged both hands into the bag before lifting them skyward. A few moments later, dozens of sparrows were fluttering and dancing around his outspread hands, landing on them momentarily as they fed, then rising again in twin, animated clouds. The old man watched them, a tight-lipped smile on his face as the birds cavorted around his hands. When they left, descending to the grass around him, he put his hands back into the bag and the aerial dance began once more.

Camille watched, not even realizing she was staring, until the old man turned his head slightly toward her. "They dance beautifully, do they not?" he said to her in French.

"*Oui*, they do."

"Would you like to try?" He held out the paper bag toward her.

"No," she said automatically, but his smile only widened.

"Come. You'll enjoy it," he said, and she found herself moving toward him as the birds scattered. "Bring that chair here," he said pointing to one of the chairs nearby. She dragged it over alongside him. "I'm Etienne," he said.

"Camille."

"*Enchanté*, Camille," he said. "You're a tourist?"

She shook her head. "I used to live here, once. But I live in New York City at the moment."

"Ah." He favored her with a small nod. "You speak French well, but not quite like a Parisian. I've never heard an accent exactly like yours. Now, you must be very quiet and very still. Put your hand in the bag; it's full of birdseed coated with just a little honey, so it sticks to your fingers . . ."

She gingerly placed her hands into the bag and pulled them out again. She could see bits of birdseed adhering to her skin. "Good," the old man said. "Now, just hold your hands out and wait."

She didn't have to wait long; first one sparrow fluttered around her fingers, then another, and finally the entire flock seemed to be in motion around her. She could feel the buffeting air from their wings, the occasional strike of them against her hands or arms, and their beaks plucking the seeds from her skin. Helplessly, she laughed. "It feels so strange," she said. "And yet it's so delightful. So *alive*. Do you do this every day, Etienne?"

The old man was smiling with her. Now that she was close to him, she could see the way his jacket was worn, the edges and seams frayed from long use. There was, very faint, a green soul-heart inside him. She could feel its quiet radiance: simmering there, content. She wondered what he did to feed that creativity, or perhaps it was this daily performance in the park. "When the weather's good, I come here," Etienne answered. "Charlene—my wife—always liked feeding the birds in the park. Ever since she died, I've been feeding the birds for her."

"I'm sorry."

"That's kind of you to say, but there's no need to be sorry. Charlene and I had a wonderful sixty years together, and we'll be together again, one day soon enough. Here, let me have more seed . . ." She handed him the bag, and he put his hands into the sticky birdseed, letting the sparrows flock around him once more. "You remind me a bit of our granddaughter," he said as the sparrows fluttered around them. "She has Charlene's enjoyment for life, I think. That's what I remember most about Charlene: how she relished every day we had."

The birds fluttered down to rest, and he brushed the seeds off his hands. A few pigeons cooed at his feet, their heads bobbing as they searched for the seeds in the grass among the sparrows. "You have someone that completes you the way Charlene did me?" the old man asked her. "A husband, perhaps?"

"A boyfriend," she answered. "But—"

"But?" His eyebrows lifted. "You love him? He makes you happy? He treats you well? He makes you laugh?"

"Yes, all of that. And more."

"Then it's simple," Etienne told her. "You should stay with him for as long as life lets you." He plunged his hands into the paper bag again and the sparrows lifted from the ground eagerly. Twin chirping gray clouds formed around his hands. "The birds know," he said. "You must grab for what you want while it is there. Otherwise, you may never find it again."

"Where have you been?" David said when she returned to the hotel. He was in the lobby, pretending to read a newspaper, even though it was in French. He leaped up as soon as he saw her approaching. His camera swayed on its strap around his neck. "I was beginning to get worried."

"You should have called my cell. But, I have breakfast," she said, lifting a paper bag of croissants. "Come on. It's a beautiful day; let's walk."

"You're in a good mood."

She grinned at him and grabbed him around the neck, pushing the camera aside so she could hug him tightly and kiss him. She saw Dominique—who had come on duty—smiling at the affectionate display from behind the desk. "I am," she told David. She took his hand. "Very much so. Come on. I want to you to meet someone."

They ate the croissants as they walked alongside the Seine in the shadow of Notre Dame. They strolled north and west past the Louvre and into the Jardin des Tuileries. Camille looked for Etienne, but his chair sat empty. A few pigeons scavenged around the iron legs. "Who did you want me to meet?" David asked.

"He was here earlier," she told him, "but he's gone now." She looked up the length of the park. "Maybe he's just moved. Let's just keep walking . . ."

It was a slow stroll, with a stop for ice cream, but an hour later they were at the western end of the park, standing at the fountain there with its black stone figures edged with bright gilt. They gazed out at the Place de la Concorde and the tall, gold-capped spire of the Obelisk of Luxor at the center of the square.

Staring up the long, rising expanse of the Champs-Élysées toward the Arc de Triomphe, Camille remembered an entirely different scene, when Place de la Concorde had been called Place de la Révolution, when rather than the obelisk, the bloody guillotine had pierced gray Paris skies near the Hôtel Crillon.

Nicolas . . . Pressing Antoine's head down onto the stock as the blade of the guillotine creaked upward . . .

"Camille?" David's voice brought her back to the present. "Hey, are you okay?"

She tried to smile for him as the scene snapped back to the present, as the vicious, eager roar of the crowd faded in her ears. She heard the click of a shutter and realized that David had been taking photographs of her. They were surrounded in an emerald glow so strong that she wondered that the people passing them didn't notice it.

"I'm fine," she said. "It's just that seeing this brought back some memories of another time I was here." She shuddered, suddenly and visibly, then grabbed David's arm again. "Thanks for walking with me. Sorry that the man I wanted you to see wasn't here."

"No problem. I love walking this city, and I love watching you. It's like you see the city as an old friend, one you've known forever, with all her quirks and foibles."

She laughed breathily, the sound almost unheard against the rushing traffic around the roundabout of the Place. "Yeah, it's something like that," she said.

"It's almost too bad we have to go home," he said, lifting up the camera again. "I almost wouldn't mind staying here forever. After what happened back home . . ." He grimaced suddenly, and she knew he was thinking about Helen—and that reminded her of Nicolas once more.

She remembered what Etienne had told her: *Then it's simple. You should stay with him for as long as life lets you. . . .* But it wasn't so simple, not for her. And not for David, as long as he was with her. "I wish we could, too," she told him. "And maybe we can, one day." *After I kill Nicolas. After he's really and truly dead.* "By the way," she told David, "I got a phone call early this morning. I have to go back to New York City tomorrow—some business with my accountant that I can't let slide. It'll only take a few days."

"Oh," he said, obvious disappointment in his voice. "That's too bad. I guess we'll have to come back some other time . . ."

"No," she told him. "I want you to stay here. There's no reason for you to have to come back with me. Stay here; see the city. Or take the train out to Chartres or the Loire Valley or Normandy. I'll come back and join you just as soon as I can."

"I don't know, Camille," he said, but his face contradicted his words. She squeezed his hand.

"You should stay," she repeated. "And maybe I'll bring Verdette back with me and we really will just stay here afterward."

They returned to the hotel late that afternoon. Dominique handed them the key to their room, then called out after them as Camille was pressing the button for the elevator.

"Oh, I nearly forgot. A package came for you while you were away, M'mselle. Here it is."

Dominique placed a small wicker basket on her desk. In it, nestled in rustling straw, was a bottle of tequila: *El Tesoro de Don Felipe,* the label on the clear bottle proclaimed. *100% Blue Agave Tequila.*

"Is there a note?" David asked over Camille's shoulder.

There wasn't. "Who brought this here?" Camille asked, probably too harshly, since Dominique's eyes widened.

"Why, a delivery man," she answered in her accented English. "One of the local ones."

"What did he look like?"

"I don't know. . . . An older man, his hair gray and balding here." She patted the top of her own head. "Taller than your boyfriend, and heavier." She tilted her head quizzically. "Do you think you know him, M'mselle?"

"Tall . . ." So it wasn't Nicolas. She felt the panic which had started to rise in her chest subside slightly. But not entirely. "No, I don't know him. What service brought this here? Do you have their address or telephone number?"

"*Oui, M'mselle,*" Dominique replied, though with a quizzical, concerned look. "Let me write it down for you . . ."

David was also looking at her strangely. "I get it, Camille," David said. "One of our friends has figured out we're not in Mexico, and sent us this as a joke. I'll bet it was Mercedes; that would be like her. She knows her tequila, after all."

Camille managed a half-smile as Dominique handed her a slip of paper. She was just as certain that it wasn't Mercedes or any of their friends, but Nicolas who had done this. *"Don't you understand, Perenelle?*

You're my passion." This was a message to her: he was watching, and he knew where she and David were.

David had picked up the basket. "Thanks, Dominique," he said, then hefted it in Camille's direction. "Guess we'll have tequila rather than wine this evening, eh? We can celebrate Paris with a bit of Mexico."

"We can do that," she told him. "Why don't you go on up to the room? I'll be up in a moment; I want to call my accountant and let him know when I'll be arriving . . ."

David shrugged. "Don't be long," he told her. She watched him enter the tiny elevator, then went to one of the couches in the small lobby as she pulled out her cell phone, placing the paper Dominique had given her on her knee. She dialed the number.

"Bonjour," she said to the woman who answered. "This is Camille Kenny, staying at the Hotel de Notré Dame on rue de Maítre-Albert. One of your drivers just delivered a basket with a bottle of tequila here for me."

"Oui, M'mselle. Is there some problem?"

"No. Not at all. I just wondered . . . There was no note, and I would like to know which of my friends sent the gift, so I can send a thank-you note."

"I understand. One moment . . ." Camille heard the buzz of the hold, her stomach churning in time to it, then the woman came back on the line. "The package was sent from a Dr. Pierce, of New York City."

"Was he *here?"* Camille asked. "Did he order it in person?"

"Oh no, M'mselle. The order came in through a long distance call from the States."

"I see." The acid threatening to rise in her throat subsided a bit. *He's not here. He's still in New York.* "That's all I need, then. *Merci beaucoup."* She ended the call, sitting on the couch with her eyes closed.

Her plans had just been shattered. Leaving David here wouldn't mean that he was safe: Nicolas knew where to find him, and even if Nicolas himself stayed in New York, Camille was certain that he still had contacts in Paris. He could reach David here, through them, or through a simple plane flight.

The best way to protect David now is to keep him near you. You know that. He's in danger because of you, but you're his best shield. You can't leave him; you know that from the past.

She couldn't leave him unless she was willing to accept his death. She couldn't leave him until she could rid her life of Nicolas: forever.

But she'd known that for centuries, and it still hadn't happened . . .

"David?"

He was lying on the bed in their room, an arm over his eyes against the light from the window. He stirred sleepily. "Yeah? What's up?"

"I want you to go back with me."

The arm lifted and David sat up, rubbing at his eyes. "I thought . . ."

"I changed my mind," she told him. "My accountant thinks it could be a week or more before we get things settled. If that happens, then you'd be coming back anyway. I'd rather not be away from you that long. I already booked us seats on a flight tomorrow afternoon. We'll come back to Paris later, maybe in a month or two."

"Okay," he shrugged. "Promise?"

"Promise."

Another shrug. David swung his feet off the bed. "Then let's make the most of the time we have left here," he said. "To hell with a nap . . ."

They stayed out the rest of the evening, seeing the sights a last time, watching the sun set over the city from the summit of Sacré-Couer and eating dinner in the Montmartre district.

Despite the pleasures of the day, Camille had been unable to shake the sense that they were being watched, and that somewhat spoiled the evening for her. The steep inclines and the twisting, crowded streets of Montmartre were tinged with the faint possibility of Nicolas being there, watching them, though whenever she glanced behind there was never anything there: no Nicolas, no stranger looking at them too intently, no faces she recognized from earlier in the day.

David's constant stopping to snap pictures wasn't as invigorating as it should have been; she found herself jittery. She kept looking at the entrance to dark alleyways, half-expecting to see someone there or the glint of a sword's blade striking for her neck. She glanced constantly behind them in the crowds, wondering if she would glimpse someone following them, and she kept her hand near the opening to her purse, ready to reach for the 9mm there.

All the paranoia was wasted: she saw nothing. They took a late subway train back to the hotel. By the time they returned to their hotel, she was exhausted and frazzled. She wanted nothing more than to fall into bed, as David had done, but she pulled the Tarot deck from where it was tucked in a silk scarf in her suitcase, intending to quickly lay out the cards and see what they told her. They could tell her where Nicolas might be, whether he was still back in New York. She switched on the desk light . . . and the bulb immediately flared and went dead.

She stared at the dead bulb.

"I can call down to the desk to have them send up a bulb," David said from the bed.

David's comment woke Camille from her reverie. "No," Camille said, her hand still on the switch, "it's fine. Leave it. It's our last night anyway."

She glanced down at the Tarot cards, but she left them wrapped in the silk. In her life, she had learned to believe in omens—the cards hadn't wanted to be read. That's why the bulb had burned out.

She undressed and lay next to him. When he moved to caress her, she demurred. "I'm sorry, David; I'm so tired . . ." He finally fell asleep, but she did not, her mind moving too fast, listening to his quiet snoring and feeling the warmth of his green heart. The tendrils of it wrapped around like a second set of arms, enfolding her.

In the dark, she took a long, shuddering breath, staring at the ceiling. David stirred in his dreams. His hand reached out. His fingers found her neck and the pendant there and stayed, warm and comforting.

She imagined killing Nicolas, his bloodied head rolling like some evil stone across a nameless floor, his mouth gasping for air like a fish tossed up on the back, his eyes wide with the shock of his decapitation. The image was terrifyingly sweet.

The tequila bottle stood unopened on the desk, the clear glass reflecting sunlight back to her. An accusation.

Camille stood at the window of their hotel room, looking off into a foggy morning. In a few hours, they would be flying "home" to where Nicolas was waiting. She felt the surge of David's green heart, its energy causing her to lift her head as she tasted the sweetness; she heard a camera clicking, several times, then the sound of David putting the camera down again. "What'cha thinkin'?" David asked her, coming up behind her and hugging her. She leaned back into his embrace, nearly sobbing with the luxurious feel of it, with the sense of complete connection.

With David, she had a chance of a full life. With David, if she dared one day to give him the elixir, she had a chance of having a partner who could share eternity with her. With David . . . if she could rid herself of Nicolas.

"Let's go out for a bit," he said to her, his breath warm against her ear. "Our last morning in Paris . . ."

They went out in to the fog, which was quickly burning off as the sun lifted over the city. Notre Dame cast its long, spired shadow across the plaza as they crossed the Seine. They wandered north, crossing the Seine again to the Right Bank, and turning eastward. "Where are we going?" David asked her.

"Nowhere," she told him. "I just want to see if someone's here . . ."

They walked through an archway of the Louvre near the pyramid, and turned right toward the Jardin des Tuileries. Camille found herself smiling: Etienne was there, with the sparrows creating their intricate ballet around his uplifted hands. "Look," she told David. "That's the man I wanted you meet yesterday."

David laughed with delight. He already had his camera out, zooming in on the image. "Now that's lovely," he said. "You know him?"

"A little," she said. They walked closer. "Etienne," she called as they approached, as the birds flitted away, startled. The old man turned his head. He smiled.

"*Enchanté*, Camille—good to see you again!" he said in French. "Did you come to feed the birds? Is this the boyfriend?"

"*Oui*, this is the boyfriend," she acknowledged, staying in French. "His name is David."

David heard his name and held up his camera. "Ask him if he minds if I take pictures."

Camille relayed the request, and Etienne shrugged, pretending to brush his white hair into place. "Tell David he should be careful. A face like this might crack his lens." Camille laughed gently; she nodded to David. He crouched down a few feet from them, as Camille dragged a chair to sit alongside Etienne, as he wordlessly handed her the paper bag with the honeyed birdseed. She dipped her hands in as the sparrows rose from the grass expectantly, fluttering around her fingers as she lifted them, as Etienne did the same alongside her, as she heard the click of David's camera.

"He loves you, you know," Etienne said as the birds danced in the air before them. "I can see that just by looking at him. See the way his eyes dance as he watches you, like he's afraid that you'll be gone if he looks away too long? The two of you are tied together. Don't you feel that?"

"*Certainement*," she acknowledged. She glanced at David through the flurry of sparrows. He looked up from the camera and winked at her, grinning. "I do."

"Then life is very simple for you," Etienne said. "You stay with him, and continue to love him, and you'll be happy." He nodded toward the birds. "It's no different with them: as long as they're fed, they're happy."

"As long as there's no cat waiting to eat them," Camille answered.

Camille could hear the melancholy coloring her voice, but Etienne only chuckled. "None of us can ever know when the cat will spring—so it's useless to worry about it, *n'est-ce pas?* You should pretend there are no cats."

"But there *are* cats," Camille protested. "Pretending they aren't out there doesn't make them vanish."

Etienne shrugged, sending the birds on his hands fluttering away momentarily. "Then I would remember that most birds are faster than any cat, and take comfort in that. Either that, or make friends with the nearest dog." He lifted his eyebrows at that, pursing his lips comically.

She allowed herself to laugh with him. The birds, startled, flew away as one as David's shutter clattered.

INTERLUDE SIX

Emily Pauls & William Blake

1814

Emily Pauls

1814

"WELL, AS SAMUEL Johnson reputedly said: 'What I gained by being in France was learning to be better satisfied with my own country.'" Blake chuckled grimly at that. "Our Mr. Shelley will undoubtedly discover that to be true as well. But perhaps you would know best, having spent as much time in Paris as you did, and by virtue of having a French mother."

Emily—as Perenelle called herself then—nodded to Blake at the admission. She'd maintained an erratic presence in Paris as Madame Lavoisier, especially after Robespierre himself was guillotined a few months after Antoine—she found it hard to believe that, after centuries, Nicolas was at last dead. But the habit of cultivating new identities was one she couldn't break—with or without Nicolas, she would always need other people to become. She'd moved to London as Emily Pauls, a student of the fine arts supported by a modest trust from her deceased parents: an English father and French mother, so as to explain her accent, which years in Paris had brought back.

There, as she had done before and as she would do in New York City almost two centuries later, she associated herself with a loose collection of artists and intellectuals of all description: the poet Lord Byron, the young Mary Wollstonecraft Godwin, daughter of the bookseller, the poet Percy Bysshe Shelley, and the painter JMW Turner among them.

Before, that strategy had always been used to evade Nicolas; now, it was simply because she'd not yet found a specific soul-heart that truly called to her, and until she did, she could subsist on several smaller ones. Eventually, she knew, she would come to crave the nourishment from a truly intimate relationship with a single person, a person whose green heart had potential that she could tap and expand, and take into herself.

Soon. She would have to find someone soon. Again. But not yet. She could wait. She could be patient. She would choose the right one—because *this* time, perhaps, it could truly be a relationship for the ages.

She had all the time in the world to make her decision.

Among those in her circle was William Blake, whose green heart was perhaps the most verdant of all of them, but also the most troubled. Even some of his friends referred to the man as "insane," and his recent trial for treason, accused of having cursed the king while assaulting a soldier, hadn't helped that impression even though he'd managed to be acquitted of the charges. Since then, however, Blake had found difficulty selling his books and illustrations, and the few reviews he'd had from critics were uniformly vicious.

Still, she found that she enjoyed the man's company and the temporary comfort his green heart could afford her, despite his sometimes loud raving about angels and visions, and his moodiness.

Adding to that was the presence of his talented wife, Catherine, who helped with the engraving and coloring of Blake's illustrations. Catherine's own green heart was quiet and small but solid, and the love she had for Blake was still palpable, long decades now into their marriage. Emily felt that the Blakes had what she herself wanted—at least partially. Catherine gave Blake unbiased support and kept him working despite the darkness in his soul. The couple was childless in their long marriage, but Catherine appeared not to be jealous of the attractive and young Emily, but instead treated her almost as she might a daughter.

In his late 50s now, Blake's hair had gone gray and receded well back from his forehead. His features had thinned as well, and the flesh of his hands was covered with fine wrinkles. But his dark eyes burned with intelligence and keen wit, and his observations were sharp. His passion for his work drove him despite the financial difficulties in which he and Catherine found themselves. For that alone, Emily wanted to be around him. She wanted to taste that green heart and make it glow even brighter; she wanted his soul-heart to lose its bitterness and rage.

Even if Emily had thought of having Blake as a lover, she would have changed her mind after a comment he'd once made to her, when Emily asked Blake if Catherine ever worried about her being around him. He'd snorted through his long nose. "A mistress never is nor can be a friend. If you agreed that we should be so, you and I could be lovers; when it was over, we'd be anything *but* friends. You're my friend, Miss Pauls. I intend for you to remain so, and Catherine fully understands that."

She liked and admired the relationship Blake and Catherine had too much to tear Blake away from Catherine, even though she knew she could.

No, she would not take Blake's green heart for her own. She would steal occasional nourishment from it, but Blake belonged to another muse.

Emily was in the Blake residence now. The cheap flat was full of books and paper. Blake's current project—a heavily illustrated book of his poem *Jerusalem*—was scattered about in various states of completion. She and Blake were sitting at a table; Catherine puttered about between their room and the kitchen.

But this was one of Blake's better days, and they weren't talking of angels or visions or his deep and dark moods. They were instead discussing the recent flight of Percy Bysshe Shelley from both London and from his pregnant wife Harriet, and the fact that sixteen-year-old Mary Godwin had accompanied the young poet into France. "I fear that Miss Godwin has been seduced by Mr. Shelley, or worse," Catherine said as she set tea down before them. The teapot was old, the painting on its sides flaking away, and the cups were chipped, but the smell of the tea was strong and good. Catherine poured them each a cup and passed them out. "Why else would he have fled so precipitously, and why else would she have gone with him? As for Mr. Shelley's poor wife Harriet, why, she's big with child."

"And the good Mrs. Harriet Shelley was, like Miss Godwin, only sixteen when *she* eloped with Shelley," Blake interjected. "Or so I'm told."

Catherine shook her head. "I never took Miss Godwin for that type of person. She seemed so innocent."

China rattled as Blake took a sip of the tea, drawing it loudly between his teeth. "Every harlot was a virgin once," he said.

"William!" Catherine said. "Such language in front of our guest."

"Well, it's true enough," he answered, scowling at the hand Catherine placed on his shoulder. "God can hardly scold me for speaking the truth, however baldly. Miss Pauls, have I managed to offend your delicate sensibilities?"

"Not as yet, sir," Emily answered with a laugh. "But I would counsel you not to contradict your wife, as she's far the wiser of the two of you."

"Ah!" Blake glanced from one to the other of the women. "It would appear that I am sadly outnumbered on the field and should now retreat for my own safety. However, that's not my inclination. I must say that Miss Godwin has made her bed and she must now sleep in it—which I suspect she is doing most enthusiastically."

"Honestly, William!" Catherine exclaimed.

"I take it, then, that you don't believe that there are times when one must retreat rather than stand," Emily commented to Blake. "Or that there are situations where a person must follow the inclinations of passion despite what others might think." She glanced pointedly at the pages of *Jerusalem* piled haphazardly across the table.

Blake caught the glance as Catherine chuckled and reached across to pour herself more tea. He scoffed. "I confess that I admire our Mr. Shelley's work, and I will acknowledge that he possesses a certain genius." Emily nodded in agreement as Blake spoke—Shelley's green heart was vast, if erratic and infected with other more earthly passions that made her wary of him. "However, I *cannot* condone his abandonment of Mrs. Shelley, no matter what passions Miss Godwin may have incited in him. He has obligations both legal and moral toward his wife, who is after all soon to be the mother of his legitimate child, and he has recklessly and shamefully abandoned both of them." He banged his fist softly on the table as he took a breath; crockery chimed in response. "Would you disagree?"

"I'm only saying that I can sympathize with our wayward couple. Mr. Shelley has never made it a secret that he was unhappy in his marriage. You and I have both heard his comments on many occasions, and we've also both seen how he and Miss Godwin found great comfort in each other's company. I understand why they would run off together and I find it hardly surprising. I would also point out that there is a considerable difference between understanding and condoning."

"If you don't mind my saying so, that's a very *French* attitude."

"As you've pointed out many times, Monsieur Blake," she said, allowing her accent to color the words, "I *am* half French."

"Which means you're half right in this," Blake retorted. "Mark my words: this will not end happily, and we will find Mr. Shelley slinking back to London and his wife very soon, leaving poor Miss Godwin behind and entirely disgraced, and perhaps with child herself."

"And being entirely *English*, no doubt you're entirely wrong about this," Emily answered. Catherine hid her laugh behind her teacup, but Blake was scowling again. Emily patted his hand, and—grudgingly—Blake managed a tepid smile. His gaze slipped past and above Emily's head and fixed there, his head tilting as if he were listening to someone the rest of them could not hear.

"I understand," he said, but he was still looking somewhere beyond Emily. Then he shook himself and his regard returned to her. "The angel says that it's better to murder an infant in its cradle than nurse an un-acted desire." Blake said. "So perhaps God agrees with you."

Emily pressed her lips together and patted Blake's hand again, glancing once at Catherine, whose expression had gone solemn and concerned. "God created France as well as England, so He knows everything," Emily answered lightly. "He also gifted us with the capacity to both love deeply and to create well, and we'd be poor worshippers if we didn't fully utilize those gifts. I trust that we all have a purpose in His world, even Mr. Shelley and Miss Godwin."

"And *your* purpose, Miss Pauls?" Blake asked. His eyes flicked away again, looking past her and back. Catherine's hands stroked her husband's shoulder comfortingly. Emily resisted the temptation to look over her shoulder, knowing she would see nothing there. "The angel would like to know if you understand your purpose."

"If your angel could tell me that, I would be happy to act upon it," Emily told him. "Perhaps one day I'll know."

Emily gave Byron a last kiss before leaving the bed, pulling her chemisette down as she lifted the covers. The cameo pendant on her necklace had fallen behind her on its chain; she adjusted it as she stood. Byron watched her languidly, a faint smile on his face as he contemplated her.

"What are you thinking?" she asked him.

"I'm imagining you with Shelley," he said. "Or Turner—I suspect you'd be able to tempt that recluse out from his shell. Or perhaps Blake. Yes, yes, old Blake is the one. You seem to like him well enough, and he's mad enough for you. You're Blake's lover also."

"You'll only have your imagination for that scenario, I'm afraid," she told him as she began to dress. "I would never dream of betraying Catherine."

"What about the good Mrs. Shelley? Did you betray her as Mary Godwin has? Ah, never mind—your blush gives you away, my dear. At least with me you needn't worry about betraying a wife."

"No," she said curtly, tucking in the red curls of her hair, "I'm not betraying a wife, only all the other women you've known." Byron's love affairs and his behavior had scandalized half of British society. Had she been cruel, Emily would have said something about Augusta Leigh, Byron's half sister, who had been delivered of a daughter only a few months earlier—the rumors were currently swirling concerning the true identity of the child's father. But she only smiled. "I'm well aware of your reputation, George. And as for your having a wife, I understand that you and Lady Milbanke have been seeing quite a lot of each other. You seem well suited; perhaps she'll become Lady Byron soon?"

"So you listen to that vile society gossip, do you? Why, I swear that I detect a certain tint of jealousy in that lovely voice of yours."

Emily laughed. She turned from the mirror. "Hardly. You may flatter yourself if you like, Lord Byron, but I have no designs upon you at all, other than for the moments we sometimes share." She slipped on her petticoat; with the new fashion, fewer women were using stays and corsets, a trend that Emily relished, though the English dresses were frumpy and frilled in comparison to those in Paris. The fashion in the embattled Napoleon's court was for simple, flowing, and high-waisted gowns.

"You, Miss Pauls, are entirely without shame or guilt."

She took her dress from where it was draped over one of the chairs in the bedroom. "Neither of those are attributes I can afford to have, I'm afraid, and since it's to your advantage, you should be glad of it. Here, will you help me with the buttons?"

"I am glad, indeed," he said as he slid out from under the covers. Emily looked at his body appreciatively; Byron was slim and well-toned, and the lines of his face were like those in a classical painting. And his green heart—his was a rare one, and in another time she might have been indeed tempted to make it hers alone, but she was afraid to commit herself so completely to one person again. With Nicolas finally gone from her life, she had promised herself that she would take her time and find the perfect match. "By the way," Bryon continued, "I have someone you really must meet: a friend of mine I met in Edinburgh who's studying to be a physician: John William Polidori. He happens to be in London and I have a luncheon appointment with him later today, if you'd like to come along."

"And why should I meet this man?" she asked.

"You have a propensity for talented people and handsome men, and he's both. He's intelligent, and he also writes—very strange tales, I must say—and he's intensely interested in the Arts. He professes that he wants to meet all the painters, artists, and musicians that he can. I think you would like him."

"Then I'll lunch with you and meet this paragon. Hand me my pelisse and bonnet, please."

After returning to her own rooms, Emily fed Verdette, who mewled piteously at her overnight abandonment but made up almost immediately as Emily scratched her ears. She went to sleep for a few hours, with Verdette curled up and purring contentedly in the curve of her waist. The German-made alarm clock on her dresser woke her with its noisy clanging just before eleven.

After dealing with her toilet and dressing, Emily took a hired carriage to the Dorset Park Hotel near Regents Park. "Lord Byron's table," she told the maître d'. As they approached Byron's table, she saw only the back of the other man at the table. Byron rose to seat Emily, but she froze as the stranger turned his face toward her.

She gasped, audibly, the shock freezing her when she wanted to do nothing more than turn and run.

It was Nicolas.

Yet that was impossible, for she'd seen him—as Robespierre—guillotined, watched his head roll from his body and the executioner pick it up by the hair to display to the crowd. She'd seen it, witnessed it, and—with some guilt—felt exultation at seeing it. Yet here he was, undeniable alive . . .

And if Nicolas had somehow survived the guillotine, did that mean that Antoine might have as well? Did that mean that she'd buried him while there was still a chance of recovery? Did he wake up in his coffin terrified and alone? My God, was he *still* alive and still trapped, two decades on?

Her stomach lurched with the rush of thoughts in her head. She swallowed hot, scorching bile. She stared.

She could not mistake that face, those eyes, his short stature, that mocking half-smile. Emily backed away from the table. She doubted that he'd do anything here, in public with Byron as a witness, but the temptation to flee was nearly compulsive, and she suddenly wished that she'd prepared a spell or brought one of her chemical vials with her before coming here, or had a drawstring reticule large enough to carry a pistol.

"Miss Pauls," Byron said, his gaze moving between them quizzically, "do the two of you know each other?"

"I regret to say that we do," she told him, hardly daring to speak, her regard entirely on Nicolas, who had also started to rise from his seat. He didn't appear to be as startled as her; it was almost as if he'd expected to find her. "I'm afraid, Lord Byron, that I must leave. I apologize." She started to walk away, aware of the stares from the other patrons in the hotel's restaurant, but Nicolas put his hand out to her forearm: gently, not grabbing at her, but only touching her arm.

I have to go back to Paris . . . Antoine . . .

"Please, Miss Pauls," he said. "You have every right to leave, and I would understand if you feel you must, but I beg you to stay. Please . . ." He gestured to the chair that Byron was still holding. Emily hesitated. Nicolas had found her again, but she'd gain nothing by running blindly from him, and in Byron's presence. Most importantly, she had to know how Nicolas had survived the execution, so she would know whether she had to disinter Antoine's body. *The agony Antoine has endured, the madness of being buried alive in his casket. What have I done to him?*

She took a long, slow breath, and allowed Byron to seat her.

"Well, this is rather awkward," Byron said as he took his own seat again. "Miss Emily Pauls, Mr. John William Polidori—though I take it that introductions are entirely unnecessary."

"We're rather well acquainted with each other," Polidori said. He was staring at Emily, though she found herself unable to decipher the emotions he might be feeling. "We knew each other, in France. I confess that I'm as shocked as Miss Pauls by seeing her so suddenly. I had no idea . . ." The tone of his voice indicated that he was genuinely stunned and unprepared to have seen her. There was a quaver in his voice as he shook his head. "I'm afraid, Byron, that I'm guilty of having treated Miss Pauls quite poorly in the past, and she is right to be loath to sit at the same table as me. In fact, I'm certain that she thought me dead—and I have to confess that she has every reason to have found comfort in that belief. I can only hope that she can find it in herself to somehow forgive me and let us begin to know each other again, as if our unfortunate past history . . ." Here he gave the slightest of smiles. ". . . did not exist," he finished.

"By Heavens, Polidori," Byron said, "you make it seem like you murdered her family or something equally foul. I must admit you have me curious."

"I've done grave disservices to Miss Pauls in the past," he answered, "but I'll leave it to Miss Pauls to relate the tale to you, or not, as she sees fit. Otherwise, that's all I will say on the matter, other than to remind Miss Pauls that I have something of hers that I assume she would like me to return, and I will do that as a token of my sincerity."

Does he mean my notebook from the Lavoisier laboratory? Emily toyed with the napkin on her table. If he'd actually used the notebook, then he knew that the formula she'd written there was deliberately flawed and that the notebook had little value at all. She wondered how many people he might have killed to discover that, relishing their deaths. "Indeed, Mr. Polidori," she said, keeping her voice flat, "returning my property would go some way toward amends. And there are questions I would like to ask you." She wondered whether he could really believe that she would ever forgive him. Nothing could change the deaths, the injuries, the pain he had caused: nothing could pay for that. Forgiveness would have to come from who or whatever waited for Nicolas in his eventual afterlife. Since the Reign of Terror, she had believed that he had already gone to the arms of that last judgment, and she had prayed to God that hell truly existed, for that's where Nicolas would have been sent.

"Then you and I should meet later," Polidori was saying. "I would leave that to your discretion, Miss Pauls, understanding that you may have reservations about such a meeting. Make whatever arrangements would make you comfortable; I will be happy to bend entirely to your wishes. It's my fervent wish to repair the rift between us, as much as that is possible."

"I wish I could believe that," Emily answered.

Polidori favored her with a wry, almost shy smile. "I wish you could, as well. Believe me, I am sincere."

"Sincerity is easily claimed."

"Then I ask you to meet with me again so I can demonstrate it to you. I'd . . . Well, after our last encounter, I've been actively looking to find you again. Since then, I've had time to regret my past actions toward you, and to repent my ways. Please, I pray you, let me demonstrate my sincerity. Set a time and a place, and I'll be there and we can talk further."

He sounded entirely genuine, and she could see no deceit in his face. "I'll consider that," she told him.

Byron, who had listened to their exchange with a bemused expression, stirred finally in his seat. "Well, since that's settled, we should eat." Byron smiled, patted Emily's hand, and gestured to a waiter leaning against the wall nearby. "I understand the roast pigeon here is quite exquisite."

But Emily rose from her seat. "I'm afraid that my appetite is quite lost," she said, "and I have much to think about. Forgive me, gentlemen." With that, she made her way from the restaurant, feeling her whole body trembling as she put her back to Nicolas.

"I say, Polidori, you really must give me this tale . . ." she heard Byron begin to say, but she was gone before Polidori could answer.

Emily made the arrangements through Lord Byron: she would meet Polidori in the garden of King's Square on Wednesday noon. Her thoughts still roiled with the implications of Nicolas' presence. Part of her had wanted to immediately book ship for France and Paris, to run to poor Antoine's grave. But she told herself to wait, that another week wouldn't matter against the quarter century already past, that she needed to know more before she permitted herself to panic.

She slept very little that night, so restless that even Verdette abandoned her usual spot next to her and instead curled up at the foot of the bed away from her thrashing. Emily's dreams were of being trapped in a coffin, her fingers clawing futilely at the wooden lid as she screamed and screamed and screamed in the darkness . . .

The Blakes had agreed to accompany her; she told them that she was meeting someone whom she didn't trust, and while she wished to speak privately with him, they weren't to allow her out of their sight. King's Square was busy at noon with people out in the gardens. If there *was* to be violence, it would be noticed, and people would come to the aid of a woman in distress, especially with the Blakes directing them.

She was as prepared as she could be. She was certain that, in public, he'd be very careful, but her reticule was very heavy indeed that Wednesday and much larger than was fashionable in order to accommodate the small, dual-barreled flintlock pistol that she carried. She knew it wouldn't kill Nicolas—as it appeared that even losing his head had not slain him—but it *would* stop him. She wore, as usual, the sardonyx pendant, but kept it hidden beneath the collar of her dress; she wasn't going to give him the satisfaction of knowing she still kept it.

Polidori was waiting in the park as Emily and the Blakes descended from the carriage she'd hired, rising from a bench on which he was sitting. "That's him," Emily whispered to them, clutching at Catherine's hand. "I'll introduce the two of you, but we have, well, *private* matters to discuss, so if you would just follow us . . ."

"Certainly, dear," Catherine said. "We understand, don't we, William?"

Blake merely grumbled. His gaze flew rapidly around the square: a King's Square address had once been the envy of everyone in London, though that time was now a century past. Fine houses still surrounded the open space and throngs crowded the square (and a herd of pigs that was being driven through the square toward London's markets). But the buildings surrounding the square were becoming more commercial than residential, and the nobility no longer sought to have an address here, as it had when Charles II's illegitimate son, the Duke of Monmouth, had his house here. The neighborhood of Soho was becoming crowded and dirtier; the garden park at the square's center boasted a now rather dilapidated statue of King Charles II, for whom the square had been named, and the garden itself needed attention. Emily wondered what Blake was seeing as he gazed around, whether there were angels or more demonic creatures lurking there for him. She squeezed

Catherine's hand again, took a breath, and walked forward toward Polidori.

He seemed genuinely relieved to see her. "Miss Pauls," he said, and his voice sounded pleased, though she noticed that his gaze slipped to her reticule and its obvious heft. "I was afraid that perhaps you might have changed your mind."

"As you see, I've kept my word," she told him, "as I hope you'll keep yours. I'd like to introduce you to my companions." She indicated the Blakes, who were hanging back a step. "This is Mr. William Blake, whose fine work you may know, and his wife Catherine. Mr. John William Polidori, a friend of Lord Byron's, and an old acquaintance of mine."

"Pleased," Polidori said, taking the hand that Blake offered and bowing slightly to Catherine. "I certainly do know your work, sir, and I'm most impressed by it. Byron showed me his copy of 'Songs of Experience' and I am in awe of your skill with words, as well as with your illustrations. If you have more copies, I would love to purchase one for myself."

That seemed to mollify Blake somewhat; he nearly smiled. "I'm glad you've found my small efforts pleasing," he muttered. Again, his gaze drifted away. "The Lord has given us a beautiful day," he said. "The gates of heaven are opened all around us, and the dead might come forth to speak."

Polidori cocked his head slightly, Catherine gave an indulgent sigh. "Yes," Emily said, hurrying to cut off Blake's comment as he paused to take a breath, and no longer quite so sure that she'd made a good choice of support with William. "Let us walk and enjoy the day, Mr. Polidori."

They began walking toward the garden area at the square's center, the Blakes a discreet few steps behind. Polidori said nothing at first, and Emily tried to pretend that she was looking at the flowers and shrubberies lining the short walk.

"Perenelle . . ." he began, and she stopped him.

"Don't use that name," she said. "Whoever I am, I stopped being your Perenelle years and years ago. I'm not Perenelle, not any longer."

"Fine," he replied, speaking to her in French, "if you want to play that game, we can, though I must say I find it silly. We can't pretend that we were never Nicolas and Perenelle. But if you wish: I won't be Nicolas Flamel but only his pale ghost."

"Fair enough," she answered in the same language—perhaps that was a way to be circumspect; there were fewer people who, if they happened to overhear them talking, would understand them. "I'll continue to call you Mr. Polidori, then; I find that more to my liking. The other name . . . well, I don't have good memories of it. You said that you were going to return something of mine—which I'm assuming is either a very old notebook, or a much newer one from the Lavoisier house in Paris. You don't seem to be carrying either."

"No," he said. "I didn't bring the notebooks with me, though I do have both. The older one's become rather fragile with time and usage, I'm afraid, but my intention is still to give it to you, along with the other. Of course, the formulae in both are flawed, as you know."

"How many people died for you to ascertain that?"

She caught the glimpse of a smile ghosting over his lips. "Those flaws, and knowing what happens to those who take that version, make it very strange that you chose to give Antoine that formula," he continued. "Unless, of course, there was something you neglected to put into your notes." The mention of Antoine made her stomach roil again. Polidori made a sound as if what he saw confirmed his suspicion. "I know what's been in your thoughts since you saw me," he continued. They were walking past the fountain, with the statue of Charles II set in the middle. She glanced at the monarch, at the black soot stains marring his figure, at the white rivulets left by the pigeons on his shoulders and down his bewigged head. "I can *taste* it. But you're making a wrong assumption, Per—" He stopped. "Miss Pauls," he said, instead.

"What do you mean?"

"You have a weapon in your reticule, don't you?"

She nodded.

"Good. Then I want you to reach into your reticule, place your weapon in your hand so you feel safe, then look up at good King Charles again," he answered.

She stared at him; he nodded. She slipped her hand into her handbag, curling her fingers around the wooden stock and putting her finger on the cold metal of the trigger, pointing the hidden barrel toward Polidori's chest. Polidori paused as they passed the statue, and she saw his hands moving as he spoke words that she recognized as Arabic. Her finger tightened on the trigger against the spell she was afraid was to come, but she glanced up at the statue and stopped.

King Charles' stone visage seemed to melt. Instead, the face there became that of Nicolas—Polidori—looking sternly out across the square, his face not stone but flesh. The statue's new face glanced down at her; he winked and smiled. Behind them, she heard Blake cry out in surprise; he was looking at the statue also. Polidori immediately stopped the chanting, his hands fell back to his coat, and the statue's face was merely a stone replica of King Charles again. A few strides behind them, Catherine shushed Blake, taking his arm firmly.

"So it *wasn't* you the guillotine took," Emily husked out.

"What?" Polidori said in mock outrage, pressing his hand to his breast. "Why, certainly it was. You saw Robespierre's head held up and displayed to the cheering throngs. Ah, the cheers that arose then . . . I distinctly remember the look of pleasure on your face, even though you tried to hide it—and I know the part you played in bringing down poor Robespierre, even though you might deny it." Then his tone changed, and his lips tightened. "People believe what they see, Miss Pauls. The evidence of their eyes is all they need. I suspect your friend Blake is an excellent example of exactly that. If one sees angels and hears them talking, how can you fail to believe in them? If you witness the guillotine taking Robespierre's head, then the deed was done. No questions. No suspicions."

"Only another innocent man killed in your place."

"Oh, the poor man was *far* from innocent, believe me," Polidori chuckled. "Why, even you might have found him to be a fitting substitution. And it was far from easy for me, as well. That spell wasn't as simple as putting a face on a statute for a few moments. I not only had to make my poor companion look like me, but I had to make my own face unrecognizable. I had to maintain the spell for *hours* and there were times when it very nearly failed me. I had to shoot the poor man in the jaw, so that he couldn't speak and ruin my deception. The effort of that enchantment kept me in my bed, helpless, for days afterward. But you don't care about my little sufferings—let's return to Antoine. I'll ease your fears, Miss Pauls. I assure you he is well and truly dead, though I'll admit that part of me would rather continue to revel in your fear and guilt."

"Then why are you telling me this?"

"Because I believe the two of us have made a mistake in being enemies."

"You hardly gave me any choice in the matter."

"I'll grant you that. But look at how you prepared today. I could have done the same. I could have placed a pistol in my coat—a better and more devastating one than you probably have in that bag—and you know already that I can disable you with a well-placed spell. If I wanted to hurt you in that way, I could have done it the very moment you arrived; I could have brought people of my own with me, as well, to ensure that I'd have the opportunity to escape. I could have shot you, and in the confusion afterward, have hacked off your own head with a sword. Why, I could have killed your Lord Byron yesterday after luncheon, just so you couldn't feed from him anymore, after he'd told me about Blake and Turner and all of the rest of them around you. They could be dead if I wanted it so. I could have forced you to run once more, hungry and desperate and still guilty about what you may have done to poor Antoine, if that were truly my desire. Will you grant me that much?"

She lifted her chin but didn't answer.

"I've been Polidori for several years now," he continued. "As Byron told you, I've been attending medical school in Edinburgh and will graduate next year. I'm learning so much, and I intend to learn more. Byron's told you that I've been writing?"

"He said they were strange stories."

Polidori laughed. The sound of his amusement nearly startled her; she couldn't remember when she'd last heard him laugh so easily. "Certainly they are strange. My, or should I say 'our,' experiences undoubtedly would seem odd to someone outside them. You've heard the folktales about the creatures called vrykolakas or strigoi or vampyres? I've been thinking of working on a story concerning them, since they have, well, a certain affinity to our own situation."

"I fail to see how."

He laughed again. "Then perhaps you'll let me explain all this to you. Meet me for dinner tomorrow night, Miss Pauls. You choose the location. Take whatever precautions you feel necessary. Just—" he glanced meaningfully behind them—"don't bring along guests this time. I want to demonstrate that I can be trusted alone with you. Perhaps it can be the start of a new beginning between us. We will never be lovers again, I suspect, but perhaps we *can* be allies."

She started to refuse, but the look he gave her was so open that she couldn't say the words. There was no green heart to Nicolas, or perhaps she couldn't sense it because of the elixir they'd shared. "You'll bring my notebooks?" she asked. "You'll give them to me then?"

He shook his head. "No," he said, almost sadly, then hurried to speak before she could say anything else. "As I told you, Perenelle's old notebook is in a fragile condition, and I'm loath to move it more than I need to. They're both together, but I need to recover them from their current location. They're currently in Edinburgh, not London; after all, I'd not expected to actually meet you yet. I *will* give them to you, but later. Perhaps by then you'll understand that I'm no threat to you. Tomorrow night, Miss Pauls?"

She hesitated, but she knew that she'd already made the decision. She hoped it was the right one. "I'll meet you," she said. "I'll send word to Lord Byron this afternoon as to where."

He smiled then, fully, and bowed to her in an old-fashioned manner. "*Merci beaucoup*," he said. He tipped his hat to her and to the Blakes. "Tomorrow night, then."

"Is he French?" Blake asked her, and Emily nodded, watching him hailing a carriage at the end of the square. "That explains much," Blake said. "The angels don't like him. They say he makes them weep."

"He has that quality," she answered. "In abundance."

Verdette slid sinuously between Emily's legs, rubbing against her stockings under the long skirt and watching Catherine warily as Blake's wife arranged Emily's hair. "Really, I can put her in her cage," Emily said, looking at Catherine in the mirror of her dresser. "She's so badly behaved with other people . . ."

The image of Catherine in the mirror smiled over her head. "Not to worry," Catherine answered. "I'll just stay out of Her Majesty's way and we'll get along famously."

Emily had to admit that, as people went, Verdette tolerated Catherine like no other. No, she wouldn't allow the woman to touch her, and she hissed if Catherine accidentally came too near, but she allowed Catherine to be within paw's reach without immediately lashing out at her. To Emily's mind, this was a tremendous act of approval on the part of Verdette, one with which she agreed wholeheartedly. Catherine had become a true friend in the time she'd been here as Emily, and the obvious mutual respect of the Blakes for each other was a model for marriage, in Emily's opinion.

When I find someone about which I feel that way . . .

"You've lovely hair," Catherine said as she brushed. "So strong and so soft, and such a gorgeous color. I swear that mine has become little better than straw, and more gray than brown. What's your secret?"

"I've just been fortunate," Emily answered, "and I think your hair is exquisite. Mine flies everywhere in this weather. At least yours behaves itself."

Catherine laughed, a rich contralto that seemed to almost shimmer in the air. "This Polidori," Catherine said. In the mirror, she caught her upper lip in her teeth momentarily as she worked at a knot. "William's feelings can be strange sometimes, but I've learned to trust his intuition. When he said the angels didn't like Mr. Polidori, well . . ."

"And you, Catherine? What did you think of him?"

"I thought he was handsome enough, but every so often there was something in his face that made me look away, as if I'd glimpsed something I didn't want to see."

"I think you're the angel to which William was referring."

Catherine laughed again at that. "Still, are you certain you're doing the right thing, going to see him this evening?"

"I'll be in public," she answered. "That will be enough." She knew it for a lie. She'd laid out the Tarot earlier this afternoon, before Catherine had arrived, and the cards had given her hints of problems, with swords predominating both of the readings. She'd spent time in the small laboratory she rented a few blocks away, making certain she had protections against attack, though she worried about how quickly she could respond to a spell from him. She had her own spells prepared as well, but she knew that played to his strength, not hers. Being in public was no panacea, either, not if he were willing to risk exposing himself and having to change his identity once more—and that was something they'd both done often. She'd even toyed with doing the same: a bribe to the maître d' to place a package under the table for her, and she could discover whether an immortal could survive an explosion, and she could be gone long before the police came looking for her. "I'll be safe," she said, though she wasn't nearly as confident as she pretended to be.

"I won't be comfortable until I *know* you're safe," Catherine said. Verdette mewled at that, as if agreeing with Catherine's comment. She bumped hard against Emily's shin; she reached down to scratch the cat's neck. "Promise me that you'll call on us tomorrow morning."

"I promise." Emily leaned back against Catherine, who rested her hands on Emily's shoulders. In the mirror, she saw Catherine press her lips to the crown of her head, a touch she barely felt. "Thank you, Catherine," she said. "You don't know how much your friendship means to me."

Catherine's lips curved upward. Her brown eyes found Emily's green ones in the mirror. "Somehow, you remind me of William when he was younger," she told Emily. "You're so full of hope and light, and you've brought so much comfort to both of us. Please promise you'll be careful. William believes the angels never lie to him, after all."

"I know," Emily told her. "And I will."

Lord Byron had made arrangements for Emily and Polidori to dine in a small room off the main dining room of the *Society of Eccentrics*, a gentleman's club with a Covent Garden address, of which Byron was a member. Women were not permitted to either join the club or to enter its chambers, but this particular room, attached to the club, possessed a separate outside entrance and was sometimes used by members who wished to converse with a woman—often a mistress with whom the member didn't wish to appear in public—over dinner. The waiters knew to be discreet, and there would likely be other diners in the room with them.

Byron intimated that there were other, even more private rooms just off the dining room that could be hired if she wished, as well. She assured him those wouldn't be necessary.

Emily arrived a quarter hour after their arranged time, telling the coachman to wait for her. She stood for several long breaths on the street outside, arguing internally with herself. She'd tried—again—to read the Tarot before coming; again, the reading was confused and muddled, and rife with the dangerous swords. Eventually, she hefted her reticule, heavy as before with her pistol as well as a few vials, and went to the door. She lifted the knocker in the shape of an owl and let it fall once, the resulting thud sounding like a cannon shot. She could imagine the passers-by on the street staring at her and speculating as to the type of woman she might be.

A waiter opened the door for her. There were two other couples in the room, each in their own corner at candlelit, small tables. In the corner just to her right, she saw Polidori, already rising from his seat to greet her. He was smiling, and the expression on his face seemed to be relief at her arrival. "Good evening, Miss Pauls," he said as the waiter seated her. "I'm glad we could arrange to meet."

"You may thank Lord Byron," she told him. "And as to being glad . . . well, that remains to be seen. I still don't have my notebooks."

"Ah." Polidori's lips tightened into a compressed smile, "as cautious as ever, but I can assure that the notebooks are now on their way to London. But we have time tonight, and don't need to immediately discuss business. Was your journey here comfortable? I love the evening air this time of year—I find it bracing . . ."

The waiter brought the soup course as they discussed the weather and how long they'd each been in London. Polidori seemed to be familiar with Shelley's latest scandal as well, and mentioned that he bought one of Blake's illustrated works from a bookseller on Pall Mall. It wasn't until the second course, with the bottle of wine between them half-emptied, that Polidori put his elbows on the table and leaned forward.

"We should work together," he said softly, pitching his voice so that the other diners in the small room could not hear his words. "I have ability with magic that you don't possess, and you . . . well, you have the better aptitude for the science of our twinned goals. We could work together as we did before."

She nearly laughed at the audacity of the remark, the wine fumes in her head clearing as if they'd never been there. "*We* never worked together. Antoine and I worked together. With you, I worked on my part alone, when you weren't forcing me to translate scrolls and work for you. I worked *for* you. Never *with* you."

He leaned back again, and there seemed to be confusion in his gaze. "Was it truly that bad?"

"It was worse. You just never saw it because things were exactly as you wanted them to be."

His cheeks had the grace to color slightly under the stubble. "I didn't understand, back then. It was a different time, with different mores and different attitudes. That was *centuries* ago."

"I assure you that you still don't understand." The waiter arrived again, placing a slice of lamb with carrots and a mint sauce before them. Any appetite that Emily had had vanished. Polidori leaned forward again.

"You have to admit that we two have abilities that none of the sheep around us possess."

"I don't think of them as sheep." Emily stared at the plate in front of her; her fork scraped at the pattern around the rim of the china as she set it down.

"Not all of them, but many of them are little better than that, and about as intelligent. Think, Perenelle . . ."

"Mr. Polidori, I'm sorry, but that's not my name, and I'd appreciate it if you didn't use it. As I've already told you, I'm no longer the woman who once possessed that name and I've tried very hard to forget that time."

"Miss Pauls, then, if you want to use the niceties of *this* time." His knife sawed at the lamb; he placed a bite in his mouth; she watched him chew and swallow, closing his eyes momentarily. "I truly don't care," he continued. "If you want to know why I wanted to meet with you, this is it. Think of what we could do together: we could create a group of immortals like us—people who would understand us because they would share the same qualities. We could lead them. The possibilities are staggering: why, once in place, we would never die, never lose our youth, never have to be replaced. I ask you to consider this: what if the great leaders of history could have remained in power forever: Alexander, Julius Caesar, Queen Elizabeth, Napoleon. Can you imagine the grandeur they could have achieved, the empires they could have built? That could be *us*. That could be forever us."

"Nothing lasts forever. Not even us. Not any longer. We both know that: Antoine taught us that we, too, can die."

He smiled as he cut another slice of the lamb, his knife grating against the plate. He speared the piece on his fork, lifting it to his mouth. "Which means that we can control the immortals we create. We can end their long lives as easily as we create them." He placed the lamb delicately in his mouth.

"You want to establish a Reign of Terror, only one that lasts forever—because that will feed the part of you that was affected by the elixir. You see *yourself* as this great leader. You want to be the elite of the elite."

He shrugged and dabbed at his mouth with his napkin. "We both need to feed. Any immortals we create will also have their own peculiar needs. You and I, we are the true vampyres, feeding not on blood but on emotions and passions. Your Antoine, had he survived the guillotine, would have had his own requirements; we'll just never know what they might have been." Polidori's words made Emily think of Verdette, back in her rooms. "For that matter," Polidori added, "think of what *you* could do: all the artists and writers and scientists would come to beg at your feet for your help, and the creative arts would flourish as they never have. You could gorge on the Arts as never before. You could have all the resources and all the time you needed for your own research and interests; you could become the equal of any artist or scientist who ever lived. Yourself. Imagine that world. All we need to achieve it is the true formula. Give me that, and the world is ours. Ours alone."

She sniffed. "Now we come to it. You want the formula. What if I tell you that I've not yet discovered it?"

Polidori took another bite of the lamb. "I wouldn't believe you. I know you. You have it; you wouldn't have given Antoine the flawed version."

She forced herself to continue to stare into his eyes. "Even if that were true," Emily told him, "and I'm not saying that it is, I wouldn't give it to you."

He put down his utensils on the tablecloth, leaning back until his chair creaked in protest. His handsome, dark eyes regarded her from their deep-set sockets. "Of course not—in your position, I would say the same, because if you give me the formula, then I have no reason to leave you alive except for the pleasure I receive from your anguish. I'm assuming that you won't divulge the formula to me." His forefinger stabbed at the tablecloth, so hard that his plate rattled. "However, I don't need the *formula*, only the elixir itself. Keep your secret, if you must, as your protection. All you need do is produce the elixir for us to use together. Examine yourself, honestly. Tell me you're not tempted, even just the slightest bit. Tell me that you don't want to stop hiding from the world because it won't accept you. Tell me that you haven't felt lonely and alone. The world is changing, more than it has at any time since our beginnings. The time of royalty and kings is gone—what happened in France has proven that, as does the defeats Britain is suffering in their new American war. The world revels in its Napoleons now and desires rulers and emperors who don't come from royal stock. That's us: you and me. This is our time—we should grasp it."

She could feel the passion in his voice, and couldn't deny that some of it spoke to her as well. *Why else did you labor so hard to recreate the elixir, if not to be able to share it with others, to have companions whom you wouldn't have to watch age and die so fast?* Yes, she shared a portion of that desire with him, but she shook her head, denying it. "Napoleon is in exile now, and the British haven't yet given up on their American war. There are still kings and queens all over Europe and the East. No. That's the only answer I can possibly give you."

A scowl replaced Polidori's terse smile. His voice became louder, enough that Emily noticed the other couples in the room staring at them. "You're making a mistake, Miss Pauls. You're making a very bad mistake."

"It's my mistake to make. Not yours," she retorted, nearly at the same volume. The room became very still.

"This is why I hated you. You always thought that you were better than everyone else."

"If I was arrogant, you easily matched me in that."

Emily pushed her chair back from the table, the legs scraping against the parquet floor. She stood, taking up her reticule.

"You're making a mistake," Polidori insisted. "I've offered to make peace with you; what happens if you don't will be your fault."

"Don't threaten me." She leaned forward, pitching her voice low once more. "I know how to kill you, if it comes to that. Don't think that I won't do it. I will." With that, she straightened and began walking away from him.

His laugh was boisterous and mocking at her back. "Leave, then. Anything that happens now is on your head."

She continued walking, reaching the door before the waiter that scurried to open it for her. She turned the handle and left the room.

When Emily arrived, Blake was nearly frantic.

"I don't know where she is," he began as soon as he opened the door for Emily. Their rooms were in a mess; papers were scattered everywhere and food was cooling on the table, with a few desultory flies picking at the stew. "A message came while I was sketching, and Catherine said she had to go out, that you wanted to see her and she'd be back soon. I waited but she never returned. Then at dinnertime, another message came." He handed Emily a leaf of fine cream paper, his liver-spotted hand trembling as he gave it to her. The message had been written in a fine, though somewhat cramped and small hand—one she'd seen before.

Tell Ms. Pauls that I have her where horses make beer. At sundown, I'll give her my own elixir if I don't have hers.

"What does that mean?" Blake was asking before she had even finished reading the message. " 'Where horses make beer?' What elixir? Who sent this? Is it that Polidori man? The angels have been shouting his name all afternoon and I can't get them to be quiet."

"Just be calm," Emily told Blake. "I'll find her; I promise you. Don't worry yourself. Just stay here and do your work, and I'll bring her back. There's been some confusion, that's all."

It took several more minutes for her to calm down Blake enough that she felt safe leaving him, precious minutes where the questions that he'd asked burned in her own mind. Polidori's version of the elixir was deadly; it would kill Catherine—not immediately, but inevitably and painfully. Emily had no doubt that Polidori would hold to his threat, but she also was fairly certain that his apparent kidnapping of Catherine was intended to draw her to him; that she was the quarry, not Catherine.

She left the Blakes' rooms in a rush. There wasn't much time—a few scant hours until the sun set over London. She hurried to the nearest tavern. There were only a few patrons there; they stared at the intrusion of daylight as she opened the door. She went to the bar, placing a silver crown loudly on the scratched wood to get the barkeep's attention. The man strolled leisurely over to her: balding hair, jowls the consistency and color of bread dough, and a dirty apron draped over a large paunch. The ruddiness high on his cheeks and the redness in his eyes suggested that he sampled his own wares rather profusely. "Miss?" he said, in a voice that suggested that he rarely had female clientele who looked respectable. "How can I help you?"

"I was given a riddle to solve," she told the man, holding down the crown with her forefinger, "and I was hoping that you might know the answer."

He scratched at his paunch with fingers that looked like plump, pale sausages. "Well now, I can't say that I'm good at riddles, Missy." He glanced at the silver visage of King George III under her finger. "But I suppose I could give yours a listen."

Emily lifted her finger, and a sausaged hand made the crown vanish. "Where do horses make beer?"

"Where do horses make beer?" the man repeated. He lifted rheumy eyes to the tin-stamped ceiling, as if the answer might be written there. "Where do horses make beer? I must admit that I'm completely graveled. Charlie!" he called out suddenly to one of the patrons a little down the bar. "A riddle for ye. Where would horses make beer?"

"Is there a brewery at the track, Sammy?" the man answered, looking up from his porter and cackling. "I imagine any mare could do a better job a-pouring a full pint than you."

Sammy waved a fat hand at the man. "Ah, you're daft and drunk besides." He scratched again at his apron as Emily started to turn away. "Wait a moment, Miss. For aught I know, ol' Charlie might have sparked a thought despite hisself. There's that brewery near Tottenham Court and Oxford; the Horse Shoe Brewery, it's called. They make our porter, in fact. Could that be your answer?"

It was an answer at least, and a better one than she'd expected. Emily felt her heart racing, and she nodded to the two men, putting another crown on the bar. "Thank you both," she said, "and the next round's on me."

She prepared as best she could in the time she had. She had no illusions about her ability against Polidori's magical skills. Her only hope was that he underestimated her own ability as a chemist, as he had her skill at alchemy, and she could only pray that he hadn't already harmed Catherine. There were warding spells that she remembered from her studies; she set them in her mind as well as she could. From her chemicals, she put together an explosive mixture, sifting the resultant orange powder into three ceramic flasks that she placed in the inside pocket of her over cloak. She loaded the two barrels of her pistol and prepared extra packets of balls and powder.

The sunlight was climbing the wall of her rooms as she worked, the sun setting faster than she thought possible. She had no more time; what she had would have to do. Rushing outside, she hailed a hansom on the street and gave him the address.

The Horse Shoe Brewery was in St. Giles, a slum district sitting uncomfortably near the more respectable houses around King's Square. The brewery was located near the southern end of Tottenham Court Road where it caressed the northern part of St. Giles, the building nestled amongst the hovels and shanties close to the corner of Great Russell Street and Tottenham Court Road. The area was overcrowded, filthy, and noisome, though the street near the brewery wasn't particularly busy. A clot of barefooted and raggedly-clothed urchins chased each other through the trash and black filth on the cobbles; a trio of shawled women hurried toward the end of the street where a butcher's sign beckoned, the hems of their dresses dirty and frayed; a few workingmen in stained clothing sat on the stoop of a boarding house.

Emily found that she wanted to put a perfumed handkerchief over her nose against the stench of the place, but her dress and bearing, and the fact that she'd arrived in a hansom (which had taken off as hurriedly as it had come) were already attracting too much attention.

There was evidently a wake underway in a building across the street from the brewery, with people in mourning dress descending a stairway liberally draped with cheap black crepe.

There were two men leaning against the supports of the open brewery door with their arms crossed over their chests. They pushed off with their shoulders and started purposefully toward Emily at the same moment that she noticed them. They, like Emily, were dressed too well for the area, both of them wearing worsted suits with collars and ties, and fashionable bowler hats. Their shoes were polished. The eagerness in their eyes as they approached made her stop. She reached into her reticule and pulled out her pistol. She deliberately and showily cocked the weapon, pointing it at the nearest of the two.

At the sight of her brandishing the weapon, the men on the stoop stood up and hurried up the steps; the children stopped their play and pointed. But the two men both laughed. "Are we supposed to be afraid, Miss Pauls?" the closest one asked. He spread his hands, exposing the starched white shirt with a waxed collar under his coat. "Don't you know you can't kill me with that."

Her answer was to press the trigger. The pistol bucked in her hand with a puff of noxious smoke and the smell of gunpowder assaulted her nostrils. The man clutched at his chest as blood bloomed on the white shirt. He looked at her startled, and went down. She cocked the second barrel, sliding her finger down to its trigger. "Your turn," she said to the other man as he hesitated, looking at his companion; she fired again. He crumpled to join his companion on the street. She reloaded the pistol as she walked over the bodies toward the open door. There, she hesitated. The smell of hops, yeast, and alcohol was nearly overpowering in the dim room beyond, crowded with tall vats and teetering racks stacked with bags of barley, various malts, and hops. After the gunfire, there was no need for stealth. "Polidori!" she called into the brewery. "Nicolas!"

She heard movement behind her and laughter above. A shoe scraped wood at the doorway and she turned. Both of the men she'd just shot were standing there, their shirts bloodied, their jackets and pants filthy from the muck in the street, but very much alive. Again.

She knew why: Nicolas had given these men the version of the elixir written down in her ancient notebook. As it had for her mice, it rejuvenated them if injured—at least for a time.

Which was one of the reasons she'd reloaded her pistol. She cocked it again even as she turned, firing once, then recocking and firing again, her wrist sore from the savage recoils. Both men staggered and dropped once more, and she looked around the brewery quickly, not certain what she was looking for but knowing when she saw it: an ax, leaning against the wall near one of the racks, the blade gleaming from having been recently sharpened. She lifted the ax, grunting at the weight of the steel, and went over to where the two men lay. One's eyes were still closed and he didn't yet appear to be breathing; the other was groaning and glaring at her. He spat at her as she approached. "You're a fool," he told her. "You can't kill us."

She shook her head at him, sadly. "If that were true, there'd be no hope at all," she answered. "Forgive me."

He tried to rise up, but she swung the ax at the same moment, the massive weight of steel driving into his neck even as he tried to turn. Blood spattered out as the head lolled on the shoulder, half-shorn from the neck. She could see the white of the spine in the deep wound. She raised the ax again and brought it down with all the strength she could muster. The blade bit into the wooden floor as the head rolled clear. The amount of blood surprised and horrified Emily, much of it flying back to spatter on her clothing. She could smell it: an iron tang in the air. The severed head gaped at her, the mouth open in a silent scream. Most horrifyingly, the eyes blinked once at her before closing forever.

Emily felt the gorge rising in her throat, burning. Her stomach turned and she had to hold back the vomit that threatened to spill. She retched, spitting. The head lay at her feet like an accusation.

Emily sobbed as she lifted the ax again in arms that now seemed leaden and uncooperative. She stood over the other man, wondering if she could really do this again. She brought the ax down hard. This time, one stroke accomplished the feat: the head rolled away a few feet as blood fountained and spilled in a great, dark mass on the floor, dripping through the gaps in the floorboards. She left the ax there, the handle at an angle and the blade stuck in the planks of the floor.

She could come back for it later. For Nicolas.

Deeper within the brewery, someone applauded, the sound echoing down the open staircase at the rear of the building. Emily moved that way, her hand now on the small flasks in the pocket of her cloak. "Nicely done . . ." Nicolas' voice seemed to shimmer in air as she reached the bottom of the stair. She looked up to a large, high-ceilinged room crowded with massive wooden-slatted vats and piping, and the huge casks upwards of twenty feet in height. "They were such exquisitely nourishing deaths, too," he added as she began to climb, the stairs creaking under her weight. "I didn't think you were capable of such savagery, my dear." As she approached the top of the stairs, Emily prepared the simple warding spell in her mind—certain that Nicolas would attack her quickly as soon as she was in sight, before she could do anything with her own preparations. She hoped it would be enough to turn whatever spell he cast; the preparation had been exhausting enough for her. She reached the top stair. She caught a glimpse of a chair and a woman tied there: Catherine, though there was something wrong with her appearance that Emily couldn't quite place. Catherine inclined with her head toward the nearest vat.

"As I told you, we're quite alike." With the words, Nicolas stepped into view from behind the vat. She heard him speak a quick phrase in Arabic and lift his hands. Emily spoke the warding spell in the same moment and raised one of the flasks to throw toward him, but her barrier couldn't hold against the rumbling darkness that slammed into her and bore her down.

"No, she's not dead, Mrs. Blake," she heard Nicolas' voice saying as she returned to consciousness. "You needn't worry yourself. It will take more than that to kill her."

Emily opened her eyes enough to look through her lashes but remained still. Nicolas was standing next to the chair to which Catherine had been tied. Emily saw now what had made her wonder at Catherine's appearance: her graying hair was now a rich, dark brown, and the wrinkles around her eyes and mouth had vanished. Emily felt despair at the implications: Nicolas had already given Catherine the elixir—*his* elixir. He had given her youth, but he had also guaranteed her an agonizing death.

The black lightning had burned and scorched Emily's clothing; she could feel that her skin was blistered and raw, and the stench of brimstone and smoke filled her nostrils. Now that she was fully conscious again, it was difficult not to scream from the pain that she felt. Her hand was trapped underneath her body, near the flasks. She tried to unclench her fingers, to lift herself enough to put her hand in the pocket without Nicolas noticing.

The pain of movement was a new fire. She couldn't keep inside the shriek that tore from her throat, echoing among the huge vats.

"There, you see, Mrs. Blake?" Nicolas said casually. "She's returned to us already. Miss Pauls, you seem somewhat charred, my dear. I do apologize, but I had to make my point."

The cloth against her skin felt like she was dragging her hand over a steel file as she reached into her pocket, still trying to hide the motion from Nicolas. She could barely feel the smooth ceramic of the flasks or the cork that stoppered them. She wondered whether she could summon the flame spell that would also be necessary, whether she could drag the words from a mind overwhelmed with just trying to deal with the pain.

"What have you done, Nicolas?" she managed to grate out. Her throat was raw, as if she'd swallowed fire. "You promised me that you wouldn't harm Catherine if I came here."

"Harm her?" Nicolas answered. "Why, I've given her back her youth, haven't I? She'll have that for the rest of her life, even if that's unlikely to be all that long." He laughed again. "We're the same, after all. We're both beyond promises, Perenelle. We're beyond *any* morality and any laws. We needn't bow to any mere mortal's concept of right or wrong."

"You're mortal, Nicolas," Emily spat. "*I* know how to kill you."

She forced her hand to close around one of the flasks. She wondered whether she could throw it hard enough to break it.

"As you've just demonstrated with my friends downstairs," Nicolas acknowledged. "But we are decidedly not 'mere,' my dear. We are extraordinary." He moved to stand alongside the chair to which Catherine was bound. "What's also extraordinary is the amount of torment someone can withstand before they simply go mad from the experience. Perhaps your friend would care to demonstrate for you." Nicolas produced a folding razor from underneath his jacket. "Why, now that she's tasted the elixir herself, I could flay Mrs. Blake alive, ever so slowly, timing each cut so that the first is starting to heal even as I start the next. Can you imagine how that might feel, Perenelle, knowing that the torture could conceivably last for as long as I wish it to last?"

She saw Catherine's eyes widen. "No," the woman breathed, the word nearly a sob. "Please, in God's name, don't."

Nicolas smiled down at Catherine as Emily watched. "I love it when they beg. It only makes the pain sweeter." Then he looked at Emily. At Perenelle. "I asked you to give me the true elixir," he said. "Have you changed your mind, my dear?"

Emily shook her head. "I can't." She looked more at Catherine than Nicolas, desperate.

"Can't? Oh, I'm afraid that's the wrong word. You mean you won't—because it *is* a choice you're capable of making. Very well, then; I'll see if I can change your mind." He lifted the razor and placed it against Catherine's neck. He slid it slowly downward, a thick line of red following, her skin parting and gaping in the wake.

"No!" Emily pulled her hand from the pocket, ignoring the pain. She brought her arm back and threw the flask. It landed several feet away from Nicolas, near the foot of one of the vats, breaking into several pieces. She could see the dark powder spilled on the floor.

Nicolas chuckled, glancing back at the flask. "A poor throw," he said. "Really, I thought better of you . . ."

He stopped as Emily spoke a single Arabic word: *"Nahr!"* A small flame bloomed in the palm of her hand, and she threw that as she'd thrown the flask: as Nicolas dropped the razor, as he started his own counter spell. The flame hissed in the air and touched the powder on the floor.

The flash blinded her, the concussion made her scream again. As Emily blinked, as she forced herself from the floor, she heard the groan of the metal supports around the vat, heard the *ping-ping-ping* as rivets shot away from the over-stressed iron bands. Then, in a moment that seemed to stretch impossibly, the slats pushed outward, the entire floor groaning as the vat collapsed, as the heavy weight of the thousands of gallons of porter it contained struck the vats alongside it, and they too collapsed like a line of bone stick tiles on a gaming table. Nicolas, nearest to the first vat, was overwhelmed in a foaming brown flood, his arms upraised. The building shook and seemed to shriek as if mortally wounded as the remaining vats went with the first. A wave of seething porter engulfed them all, the floor collapsing underneath them, the flood bearing Emily away. She fought for air, her mouth and nose full of the stench of beer. In the torrent, she glimpsed Catherine, still bound to her chair, and she reached for her, caught the chair with a hand and managed to hold on as the new, raging river battered them. They struck something—one of the shelves from the lower room?—and she very nearly lost consciousness again. Emily was shouting, but she couldn't hear her voice against the sound of the flood . . .

. . . She glimpsed light; she gulped air, then went under again. Rocks (cobblestones? Were they in the street?) tore at her dress and skin. Catherine's chair hit something hard, breaking off one of its legs. The world rushed by them, or they were hurled through it, bouncing and rebounding from buildings and carriages, battered and beaten. Emily felt her right arm strike a metal pole, heard the snap of bone, and she screamed, taking in a mouthful of beer. She couldn't breathe, could no longer hold onto Catherine or the chair . . .

. . . But the tumult was passing, depositing her broken and gasping on the street two blocks away from the brewery, the street still running with an ankle-deep stream of beer. The world slowly came back into focus: she could hear people screaming and shouting all around her, and the shrilling of police whistles. The street reeked of porter; it pooled in the cobbles, potholes, and gutters of the street. Several of the houses nearby looked to have been destroyed; one of them was afire despite the flood; in the light of the flames, she could see bodies on the street around them: limp and drowned. People were dragging themselves from the rubble. She could see the chair and Catherine, across the street. Emily forced herself to stand, to limp over to her. "Catherine?" She thought for a moment that the woman wasn't breathing, then Catherine's eyes opened and she took in a deep, gasping gulp of air before throwing up an immense quantity of beer. Emily tore at the remnants of the woman's bonds with her good hand. She helped Catherine up: her clothing ruined, drenched, her hair plastered to her face, the wound inflicted by Nicolas' razor still gaping and flowing red, but already starting to close.

"Alive . . ." Catherine gasped. "Is it . . . ?"

"Yes," Emily told her. "Without the potion he gave you, you'd be dead."

Catherine looked around wildly. "Polidori?"

"Doubtless alive, also," Emily told her. "Somewhere."

The streets were beginning to fill with the denizens of St. Giles, some of them with pots and pans in hand to scoop up the pools of porter in the street. She saw police arriving as well. "Come on," she told Catherine. "We should leave here while we can . . ."

The carriage rocked and swayed as it made its way from the flooded St. Giles district. Emily stayed next to Catherine, her arm around the woman, who alternately sobbed and sighed. She kept looking at her hands, turning them in front of her in the dim light of the carriage's lamp. Emily knew what she was marveling at: the smoothness and elasticity of the skin, the strength that had returned to fingers once stiff with swollen joints. She touched her face with those smooth hands also, as if in disbelief.

"Am I . . . ?" she asked Emily as the carriage turned onto Tottenham Court Road.

"Yes," Emily told her. "The elixir that Nic . . ." She pressed her lips together. ". . . Mr. Polidori gave you restored your youth."

"And you?"

"I've taken a similar potion," Emily admitted.

Catherine's face turned toward Emily. Her eyes searched Emily's face. "How old are you?"

"Older than you could imagine," Emily told her. "Centuries. But . . ." She bit her upper lip, then said the words. "Catherine, you won't live as long. I'm sorry. Polidori's potion, what he gave you, is flawed. Incomplete. One day . . ." Emily stopped. She remembered her mice: youthful one day, then their age exploding back onto them suddenly, their bodies writhing in agony as they aged and died in minutes. That was Catherine's fate also.

Unless . . .

Outside, she heard the carriage driver call to his horse, heard a newsboy's cry as he sold his papers on a corner. The carriage swayed as they turned left; the sound of the wheels changed underneath them. She took Catherine's hands in her own. "Catherine, the elixir you took removed the burden of your years from you, and it will hold them back—but only for a time. One day, all those years will come rushing back, and many more besides." She told her then about her failed experiments and the mice. She told her about her own potion, how it had worked when the other had failed, though she didn't tell her why. Catherine's eyes widened with the tale.

"How long?" she asked. "How long will I live?"

"I don't know," Emily answered, hoping that Catherine couldn't hear the lie in her voice. *Not long. A few years, a decade. Maybe as short as a few months.* "No one can know."

"Why?" she asked. "Why would he give me this elixir?"

"The potion—either one of them—changes you in other ways, Catherine. It gets into your mind, makes you *need* things. Polidori—he needs pain. He feeds on torment and anguish; it nourishes him. The thought of your eventual agony pleases him, and knowing that he has hurt me by hurting you . . ." Emily shrugged. "I'm afraid that pleases him most of all."

Catherine pulled her hands away from Emily; she released them reluctantly. "What about you?" Catherine asked. "He said the two of you were alike. What do *you* feed on?"

"The soul-heart," Emily breathed. "I need creativity, in all its forms. I was doomed to be a muse. A daemon."

Catherine sunk back into the corner of the carriage as it jounced and turned again. Her hands were pressed against her sodden blouse, over her heart. "And me?"

Emily shrugged. "I don't know what it's done to you. But you'll know. Soon enough."

"So I'm going to become a monster like Polidori? And I'm going to die a horrible death as well?"

"Am *I* a monster, Catherine?" Emily asked, but Catherine only shook her head without answering. "And as for the other problem," Emily continued, "there may be a solution for that. You could take *my* elixir. The true one."

She saw Catherine's face as the woman grasped for this small hope. "That would save me?"

Emily shook her head. "Save you? No. It will change you just as certainly as the other one has; worse, I can't honestly tell you *what* will happen to you, since I don't know anyone who's taken the potion twice, nor have I made such an experiment myself. You'd be stepping into unknown territory. But it might mean that you'll live. Even possibly forever, if that's what you want."

Catherine blinked. She stared. She cowered against the wall of the carriage.

"I'll send the elixir to you," Emily told her. "You can choose what you wish to do."

She didn't seem to hear that or understand it. "Polidori—he'll come after me again. He'll hurt me the way he hurt you."

Emily started to pat Catherine's hand, but she drew back, placing her hand at her side where Emily couldn't reach it. "No, he won't," she told him. "He won't because I'm leaving London, Catherine. I'm going elsewhere, taking another name, becoming another person. It's me he truly wants, not you. When I'm gone, he'll leave also."

Emily wasn't certain she was telling Catherine the truth. She didn't know that Nicolas would indeed leave the Blakes in peace after she left. He might still try to hurt them, figuring that the news would in turn upset her. But she didn't *know* that. In her mind, there was a good chance that "Emily's" disappearance would give them a respite from Nicolas' machinations, and in any case, her saying that would at least give the Blakes hope that the terror was over.

She would have to hope herself that it was the truth.

The carriage lurched, and they heard the driver call "Whoa now!" to his horse, then the driver opened the flap at the top of the carriage. "23 Hercules Road," he called down to them. Emily looked out. The door to the Blake house was open; she could see William outlined against the lamplight inside, peering out. "You should go," Emily told Catherine. "He's waiting for you."

"What am I going to tell William?" The question was a mere breath, nearly inaudible.

"Tell him that the angels have touched you," Emily told her. "He'll believe that."

"Emily . . ."

"Go on," Emily told her. "Don't make him wait."

Catherine nodded. She reached over and opened the door of the carriage and stepped out. She ran toward the house without looking back.

Emily would return to her own rooms and pack. She would leave London that same evening, but not before she sent a small package to the Blake house.

She never knew whether Catherine used it or not.

7:
TERPSICHORE

Camille Kenny

Today

Gina Palento, her detective's badge draped over the breast pocket of her suit, was waiting for them as Camille and David walked out of the Customs area at LaGuardia. Camille saw the woman detach herself from a wall and stride toward them as she and David started to roll their luggage toward the escalator to the public transportation area. "Miss Kenny," she called out, stopping several paces away from them. To their right, Camille saw a man in a dark suit station himself near the head of the escalator: Palento's partner, she was certain, cutting off any possible escape. "Did you have a good time in Mexico?"

Camille glanced at David. "Give me a minute," she said. "Watch the luggage." She went over to Palento, who favored her with a slight smile as she approached. "Now, it could be that we just took the long way home, via Paris," she said to the detective.

"Uh-huh. And I'm just here picking up my Aunt Sally. But I'm not worried about why you went to France instead of Mexico, like you told me and your friends. You gave Bob Walters ten thousand dollars a few days before he was killed. Why?"

"Have you caught his killer yet? Or Helen's?"

Gina shook her head. "Uh-uh. That isn't how this works. I ask the questions; you give me answers. Ten thousand dollars? That's a lot of money—especially for someone who doesn't seem to actually have a job."

Palento was staring at her, the woman's gaze unblinking and hard, and Camille struggled not to show the thrill of fear she felt. *I should have never allowed myself to become involved with David. It's happening again. I'm going to have to become someone else before all the lies fall apart completely, and when I do that, I'll lose David, too.*

She glanced over to David, tried to give him a smile as if her conversation with Palento was entirely casual. "I have a trust fund, Detective," Camille answered. "That's how we could afford to go to France. We told everyone—including you, and I'm sorry about that—we were going to Mexico because I didn't want my stalker to be able to follow us. And as for the ten thousand, which also came out of that same trust fund—Mr. Walters said he needed the money to get some information. I had the sense that what he was going to do wasn't exactly legal."

"Must be a big trust fund." Palento continued to stare and Camille forced herself to lock eyes with the woman. After a few breaths, Palento seemed to shrug. "All right, play it that way if you want, Ms. Kenny. For what it's worth, here's what I think. I've seen the pictures you gave Bob, and I know Bob believed Dr. Pierce was your stalker. Bob kept excellent, if rather cryptic, notes about what he was doing with all his clients. For your information, he paid nearly all of that ten thousand to someone else. When we talked to that guy and leaned on him a bit, we found out that he'd hacked into Helen's ISP and her computer, and then into Beth Israel's ISP and specifically Pierce's computer. That's what Bob was going to tell you, anyway. Strange coincidence, isn't it, that both you and Pierce are now bound up in the same two separate cases?"

"I didn't kill Mr. Walters, and I didn't kill Helen, either. I wasn't responsible for either of those two murders."

A shrug. "Maybe not. I'll grant you even probably not. But I also think you know Dr. Pierce better than you've told either me or Bob—I took your advice and looked into his background, and Pierce isn't the guy's name, and I'll bet he's not actually a doctor, either. So what *is* his name, Ms. Kenny?"

Camille shook her head. "Honestly, I don't know. He's used lots of names in the time I've known him—that's why I wanted Mr. Walters' help finding him. You've found and arrested him?" she asked hopefully, but saw the answer in Palento's face immediately.

"We'll arrest him when we find him," she answered, and that told Camille that Nicolas had most likely shed the Pierce identity and gone underground again. But he was still here in New York. She was certain of that. Now that he'd found her, now that he had flushed her out, he wouldn't leave. Not yet.

"Do you think Pierce killed both Mr. Walters and Helen? Do you think Helen's murder wasn't just a robbery?"

That netted Camille another shrug from Palento. "I'd say that we're questioning whether the robbery was meant to cover up something else. What do you think, Ms. Kenny? You were talking to Pierce at Mrs. Treadway's visitation. Was he your stalker or not? And what was he talking to you about?" Palento tilted her head as she looked at Camille. Her stare never wavered; the radiance of her soul-heart was as cold and steady as her gaze.

"Yes, he's my stalker," Camille told her. "When you heard us talking, I was telling him to stay away from me. As to whether he's Mr. Walters' murderer or if he had anything to do with Helen's death . . . Yes, I think he's involved." Palento's eyes narrowed at that, and Camille hurried to add: "I just don't know why." *Liar. Look at how she's looking at you. She knows you're holding back the truth.*

"You might not, but *we'll* know. Soon. I promise you that," Palento said, then her gaze flicked away from Camille toward David. "Your boyfriend's looking anxious," she said. "I suppose he wants to get home."

"I do, too," Camille said. "We're both tired and jet-lagged."

The detective lifted her chin: half a nod. "Yeah, I hate long flights myself. Go home, take a shower. I hope you don't have any more trips planned?"

Camille shook her head.

"Good," Palento said. "I'd advise you to keep it that way for the time being. Have a good day, Ms. Kenny." The detective gave David a wave and Camille a final nod, and walked away. Camille watched her

leave, the man at the escalator hurrying over to join her. She heard
David approach from behind her.

"Isn't that the detective who's handling Helen's case? What'd she
want?"

"It wasn't about Helen," Camille answered. "It was about my stalker.
She thinks . . ." Camille hesitated, not certain she wanted to say it. *He'll
know eventually; you'll have to tell him anyway.* "She thinks that Pierce
was also my stalker."

"Pierce?" For a moment, he just gaped at her. She felt the tendrils of
his soul-heart pulse, lifting from her momentarily before embracing her
again. "That's just too weird, Camille."

"That's what Detective Palento thinks also. And I don't blame her."
She took David's arm. "I'm too tired to think about the whole mess
right now," she said. "Let's go home. I need to rescue poor Mercedes
from Verdette at least."

As Camille walked into *Annie's*, she heard a loud and plaintive yowl:
Verdette, in her carrier, which was sitting on the tabletop in the nearest
booth, with Mercedes alongside it. Camille waved to Mercedes and slid
into the booth. Camille set down her handbag on the tabletop next to
Verdette's carrier; it made a muffled but heavy noise. Mercedes glanced
at the purse as Camille slide onto the bench seat across from her. "Jesus,
what've you got in there? A brick?"

Verdette yowled again, and pawed at the wires of the cage's door.
Camille stroked the paw, which was withdrawn and replaced by Verdette's muzzle. The cat's raspy tongue scraped at Camille's fingers.
"Thanks for taking care of her while we were gone. I really appreciate
it. Did she behave for you?"

Mercedes laughed and held out her hands to Camille, palms
down. Camille could see scratch marks on both, and she grimaced.
"I'm sorry. She's really a one-person cat. I really appreciate you looking after her."

"That's what friends do." Mercedes pulled her hands back.

"That may be, but lunch is definitely on me, and more." She noticed that there was coffee in front of Mercedes, and an iced tea near the carrier. "Have you ordered yet?"

"I have, and I've ordered your usual." Mercedes slid the iced tea in front of Camille. "That okay?"

"Absolutely. Thanks." Verdette had stopped licking Camille's finger and settled down in the carrier where she could see Camille. Her purring was audible. Mercedes shook her head.

"That's one weird cat. Okay, let me get this straight. You told us that you and David were going to Acapulco, but you went to Paris instead? Is that what I'm hearing?"

Camille glanced at her in surprise. "Who told you that?"

"Is it the truth?" Mercedes shook her unruly mane of black hair and sipped at her coffee, looking at Camille from under her lashes.

Camille sighed and nodded. "It didn't have anything to do with you guys," Camille told her. "There was someone that we wanted to keep our location from, and I was afraid that he might come asking the group where I'd gone—so I made up a little white lie. You're not angry, are you?"

Mercedes shrugged but said nothing, which told Camille more. "'He.' So it's a guy you're trying to avoid, huh?" Mercedes said, rather than answering Camille's question. "Are you talking about Morris?"

"No, not Morris. But, yeah, it's someone Morris knows. So who told you that David and I were in Paris?"

Mercedes gave a lift of her shoulders. "Morris came to the *Bent Calliope* once while you were away. He told us that the benefactor who was funding his last sculpture had vanished all of a sudden, though he's still working on the piece. He asked about you, too. Seemed disappointed that you weren't around. And, yeah, he said that he'd heard you two hadn't gone to Acapulco, but France, though he didn't tell us how he knew that." Mercedes raised an eyebrow. "That what you wanted to know?"

"Some of it. I was just wondering." So Morris was still working on the sculpture that Pierce/Nicolas had sponsored. She doubted that Morris would be continuing with something that would be so expensive to cast without one of two possibilities being true: that he truly felt the work would be so compelling that some other collector would purchase it, or if Nicolas were *still* funding the project and funneling money to him, even though "Pierce" had vanished.

And if it *was* the second of those possibilities, as she suspected, then Morris might know how to find Nicolas. Thinking of that, she nearly missed Mercedes' comment.

"Damn, woman, we've been lovers and friends for how long now? Doesn't that give me the right to the juicy gossip?—because I can tell, *mai*, that there is some. I promise you, I won't talk about it to anyone else, though"—she grinned at Camille—"if it's *really* good, I won't promise not to put it in a book sometime. Properly fictionalized, of course."

"You have the right, Mercedes, more than anyone I can think of besides David, but . . . I can't. I really can't. Maybe later."

"I'm a writer, so let's use the right word. It's not that you *can't*, it's that you *won't*," she said. Mercedes' hand, lined with scratch marks, snaked across the tabletop to touch Camille's. Verdette, in her carrier, growled at the touch. "Look, now that you have David, you don't have as much need for the old gang, all of us revolving around you like you're the sun that gives us all light. Am I right?" Her half-smile took some, but not all, of the sting from the words.

"That's not fair."

"Didn't say it was fair." Mercedes gave a scoffing laugh. "The right word, remember? Fair isn't a synonym for true." Mercedes continued to look at her; Verdette continued her low growl.

"David hasn't changed how I feel about the group."

That earned her another sigh. "Girl, you need to learn how to tell the truth. Really, you do. I love you dearly, I do, but you aren't very good at being honest and open with people who genuinely care about you. You and I both know that David gave you in one person what you were trying to get from all of us. I don't quite know what that something was, but it's obvious how *everything* changed for you and the group once you found David. Morris knows that, too—and so does the rest of the group."

That was another truth Camille couldn't admit. Not openly. She would need the nourishment of David's soul-heart, and perhaps those of the others, if she were going to take on Nicolas.

Mercedes was still holding her hand, and now Camille trapped it with her free one. Mercedes looked down at their entangled fingers as Verdette growled again. "Do you want to go to my apartment and talk more there? You could read the new chapters in my novel and tell me what you think." She paused. Smiled. "I don't have any etchings."

"I'd like to."

"But . . . ?"

Camille inclined her head toward the cat carrier. "I should get Verdette home, and David's expecting me. I could come over this evening, maybe . . ." She stopped. "But reading the novel and talking is all we'd be doing. Would that be enough?"

The waitress, with a tray and stand, was approaching their table. Mercedes pulled her hands back as the waitress opened the stand and set the tray alongside their booth.

"Guess it's gonna have to be," Mercedes said. She sat back against the booth's cushions. "So, tell me all about Paris, why don't you?"

Camille felt Morris' energy long before she saw him. She stood in the hallway outside his studio for several minutes, leaning back against the wall and just tasting the emanations of his green heart and gazing at its colors. A wash of aggressive, driving hip-hop music filled her ears, the bass line causing the plasterboard wall to vibrate with every beat.

Nicolas was still involved with Morris; she was certain of it. She could taste it in the new bitterness of his energy, in the paleness of it, in the way it wanted to coil around her like a noose.

Yes, Nicolas was still in contact with him.

Camille took a breath, pushing herself off from the wall. As with the last time she'd been here, she could sense that Morris was utterly absorbed in his work. She walked to the open door of the studio, peering into the large, high space. Morris was sitting on a stool, leaning forward as he worked in a shaft of sunlight spearing through the huge southern-facing windows. What had been mostly an empty armature when she'd last seen it was now a full-fledged clay sculpture nearly ready—she suspected—to be prepared for casting.

Vengeance. That was the title Nicolas had given Morris to work with. Now she stared at two nude figures, male and female, locked in a titanic physical struggle. Like most of Morris' figures, they were pre-ternaturally thin, nearly skeletal, as if their god had stretched them on a cosmic rack. The man's hands were locked around the woman's throat while she pushed back on his chest and neck, tendons standing out in her arms. One of her legs wrapped around his hip, the other was trapped between the man's legs, and she was bent over backward by the force of his attack. Their faces were what drew her the most: his was snarling with manic energy, and yet there was a softness to his eyes as he stared at the woman. And the woman: her mouth was open in a silent scream. There was terror on her face but yet that expression was also tinged with acceptance.

And it was *her* face. While the man was no one that she recognized, the woman's features were definitely Camille's. She had no doubt that was a deliberate choice. She wondered who had decided on that: Morris, or Nicolas.

The scene was violent, yes, but it was also strangely erotic at the same time, as if on some level the anger the two figures felt toward one another was also a manifestation of a subverted and twisted love.

Nothing Morris had ever done before had quite the same power as the sculpture she saw now. He'd done something the old Morris wouldn't have been capable of. This was his masterwork. It seemed that anger might be as powerful a daemon as herself.

"That's very impressive," she said loudly into the room, pitching her voice to cut through the music. Morris' head snapped toward her, a double-ended clay-shaping loop in his hand. At first his face looked furious, then he seemed to fold up the expression and put it away, the lines of his face smoothing. He placed the tool on the tray next to him and touched the iPad connected to the stereo system; the music died suddenly, leaving behind an aural void.

"Hey, Camille," he said. His lips twisted as if he were deciding whether or not to smile. He ran a hand over his shaved skull. "Back from Mexico, eh?" He put far too much emphasis on "Mexico."

"We went to France instead," she told him.

"Yeah, that's what I heard."

"The tequila was a nice touch, though."

He looked at her quizzically. "What are you talking about?"

"Nothing." She entered the studio fully and walked around the sculpture in front of him. He watched her as she moved, his gaze never leaving her. "I wasn't joking: this is a powerful piece, Morris. Really impressive."

"I know," he said. It was simply a statement of fact with no sense of braggadocio or ego. If anything, he sounded more reverential than anything else, as if he were more in awe of the accomplishment than anyone.

"It's going to cost a fortune to cast, though."

Now his gaze snapped away from her, looking aside. "Yeah. Well, I'm not worried about that."

She nodded. *Yes, Nicolas is still involved.* "You're nearly done."

"Just doing the final touch-ups, then I'll be prepping it." His nostrils flared with a breath. "Why are you here, Camille? You didn't come to see the sculpture."

"Actually, I did. Mercedes told me you were still working on it. I thought that after Pierce disappeared you might have given up on it."

A shrug. "You obviously thought wrong, then."

"He's still paying you to complete the work, isn't he?"

He regarded her with his head tilted sideways, still seated on his stool. "Why does that matter to you one way or the other? Why do you care?"

"Because I'd really like to get in touch with Pierce, or whatever he's calling himself now."

"Why? You thinking like the cops, now? You figure you might get a reward for turning him in? You think he offed your boyfriend's wife?"

"What's between Pierce and me is personal. We've known each

other for a long time. He's the one who told you to use my face on the sculpture, isn't he?"

A smile ghosted across his lips. "You noticed, eh? Yeah. He did. Not that I minded. Seemed a good choice. I don't think Pierce likes you much—which takes us back to my last question. Why do you want to contact him? You planning to mess him up? You hoping that then I won't have the money for this?" He gestured at the sculpture. "I didn't think you hated *me,* too."

"I don't hate you, Morris. I never have. I think you're incredibly talented." She glanced again at the sculpture. "I think you're more talented than I realized, actually."

He nodded as if considering that. "Well, wouldn't matter anyway. I've already been paid what I need to finish this. And you gave me inspiration," he said with a bitter laugh. "Even gone, you managed to do that."

"Then pay me back for that," she told him. "Let Pierce know that I want to meet with him. I promise it's not about any payments to you, and I promise it's got nothing to do with the cops. Can you tell him that much?"

He shrugged. "Maybe. Are you telling me we're friends again, Camille? Are you telling me that things are back to the way they were?" His voice had lost its edge of anger and gone soft. His hand lifted as if he wanted to touch her, then fell back again. She took a step toward him; he remained seated on the stool. Her legs nearly touched his knees.

"I won't lie to you. I'm with David, Morris. Only David. Right now, that's the way it has to be—I can't look any further into the future to know when or if that might change. I'm sorry."

"Yeah. So am I," he answered.

"You don't know how to get in contact with Pierce? You don't have an address, email, phone number, anything?"

Morris shook his head. "Sorry."

She nodded and stepped back again. That was it, then. She could hire another private investigator to watch Morris' studio in case Nicolas came there, or maybe she could call Detective Palento, let her know that Nicolas might be in contact with Morris. But knowing Nicolas, that would be dangerous for Morris—if Nicolas noticed the police watching, he might think that it was Morris who tipped off the police, and she knew what Nicolas tended to do with people who got in his way. "It was good seeing you, Morris," she said. "It really is an incredible work you've done here. I hope it brings you the recognition you deserve. I mean that sincerely."

He said nothing. He was staring at the sculpture, not her. She started to leave the studio, her footsteps loud on the worn planks of the floor.

"Camille," Morris said behind her, "how can Pierce get in touch with you? If I do hear from him, that is."

She stopped. Turned. "Tell Pierce that I'll check in at my old apartment regularly. He can send a message there, or to my e-mail."

"It might be awhile. It's not like I see the guy much. But he said he'd be back, to look at the sculpture when I got this part done."

She smiled. "Thanks, Morris. I appreciate it."

He nodded. He touched his iPad again, and the music thundered in mid-phrase. He picked up one of the tools from the tray.

Camille watched him for a few minutes, then left the studio without another word.

Camille felt the touch of the woman's soul-heart as she stepped onto the sidewalk outside Morris' studio. "Detective Palento," she said, without turning around. "Somehow we keep bumping into each other."

Palento was leaning against the corner of the building as Camille turned. She saw her partner across the street in a parked car. The detective pushed her sunglasses over her short hair as she approached Camille. "It's strange how that keeps happening, isn't it?" she said. "Strange, too, how you'd show up at the studio of a guy that Pierce dropped several large ones on."

"You're following the money."

Palento nodded. "And here it's led me to you. Again."

"I told you, Detective, Pierce is the guy who was stalking me; you'd

have to expect him to be around people that I'm also around. I don't
think that's so strange. Besides, it saves me having to call you."

Her eyebrows lifted slightly. "How's that?"

"Morris told me that Pierce said he'd be back here to look at the
sculpture sometime soon; he wants to see the completed clay model
before he gets it ready to cast. If you and your friend stick around here,
he might show up." She didn't tell the woman that she doubted that
Nicolas would be stupid enough to simply walk into Morris' studio
without taking precautions: she remembered how he'd used a spell
to make someone else appear to be Robespierre, how he'd shown her
the same enchantment on the statue in King Square. She assumed
he'd be able to do the same again for long enough to stroll into the
studio looking like someone else entirely. Worse, he'd have other, far
more dangerous spells prepared, though he'd be less likely to use them
in public. "The two of you need to be less obvious, though," she told
Palento. "If you do see Pierce, I'd be extremely careful. He's a very
dangerous man."

"We'll do that," Palento said, but her tone indicated to Camille
that she considered Pierce no more dangerous than any other person.
Camille wanted to warn her that such an attitude might cost her more
than she'd wish to pay, but the appraising look in Palento's eyes made
Camille press her lips together.

"Good," she said, curtly. "Are we done, then?"

Palento gave her a frosted smile from lips touched with pale red,
and stepped back, theatrically waving along the sidewalk. "You're free
to go, Ms. Kenny," she said.

Camille started to pass the detective, who stepped into the street,
ready to go back to her partner's car. Camille stopped. She found Palento's gaze and held it. "I meant what I said," she told the woman. "Please
don't take Pierce lightly. I'm afraid that's what Mr. Walters might have
done."

"Are you saying now that you're *certain* Pierce killed Bob? Do you
have any evidence or proof of that?"

Camille shook her head. "No, but if Mr. Walters knew some of what you know and confronted Pierce, then Pierce would do whatever he needed to do to keep his identity intact. I know him well enough to say that, and I can tell that's what you think, also."

Palento gave her the faintest of nods. "Ms. Kenny, look, if there's *anything* you can give us regarding Pierce . . ."

Camille wanted to smile. *Nothing I'd tell you would be anything you'd believe.* "Just . . . be very careful with him. I can't prove it, but I'm certain he's responsible for both Mr. Walters' and Helen's deaths. He can't . . . won't hurt me, but those around me . . . They're not entirely safe right now."

For the first time, Camille thought she saw a trace of sympathy in Palento's eyes. "Ms. Kenny, why don't we sit somewhere and just *talk.* You and me, as two people, not as detective and suspect. Tell me all about Pierce and your history with him. Maybe there's something in that to help us, something you don't even know is important . . ."

Camille was already shaking her head before the woman finished. "No," she said. "Maybe sometime, but not right now. If I think of something, I'll call you. I promise."

Palento sighed audibly. "Ms. Kenny, I have lots of practice at reading people. You're pretty good at hiding what you're feeling—better than most, actually—but I can still tell that you're scared and worried. Why not let me help you?"

For a moment, Camille was tempted. She *wanted* to unburden herself, to share with some other person all the centuries of fear and pain that she'd experienced. She could feel it all inside her, wanting to burst out, and Palento's soul-heart tugged at her, drawing her toward its warmth and sustenance.

But she couldn't. Shouldn't. She shook her head doggedly. "I'll call you if I think of something," she said again. "Just be very careful." With that, she started to walk quickly away, almost expecting that Palento would call after her, or maybe try to stop her.

But she didn't. She could feel the woman's appraising stare on her back as she fled.

*   *   *

She'd started Vivaldi playing on her stereo system; the soothing, intricate counterpoint of L'estro Armonico washing over the apartment. She'd picked up more of her clothing and personal items from the apartment, stuffing them into a laundry basket which was now sitting near the door, ready to take them over to David's apartment.

She sat on the couch in her apartment with Verdette on her lap, one hand scissoring her pendant between her fingers. On the wall across from her was a framed reproduction of one of Blake's paintings: The Temptation And Fall Of Eve. There, the tree stood between Adam and Eve; Adam had his back turned, while the serpent coiled around Eve's naked body, the fruit held in the snake's mouth and pressed against Eve's open mouth. It was strangely erotic and dangerous at the same time. Camille stared at it as she stroked Verdette's fur.

Verdette purred, her eyes closed while her front paws kneaded Camille's thigh. "Ouch," she said, disengaging a claw that had become hooked in the fabric of her jeans. "It's time for a trimming, girl. I know you hate it."

Camille heard a knock at the door. "Just a moment," Camille called out. Verdette, irritated at the interruption, leaped from Camille's lap as she rose from the couch, putting the pendant back under her T-shirt. No one had buzzed for entry, so it was probably Mrs. Darcy from the other side of the hall wanting to borrow something. Still . . . She glanced toward the table in the breakfast nook; her purse was there, with the Ladysmith in it. She thought for a moment about retrieving it. No, Nicolas wouldn't knock; he'd be less subtle than that. For that matter, he wouldn't need to knock.

As she walked toward the door, she felt a soul-heart's presence, one that made her want to simply pull the door open and fall into the embrace waiting for her. She put her eye to the door's peephole. In the distorted fisheye image, David's visage peered back at her, his camera bag, as usual, slung across his shoulder. He waved, and she unlatched the chain and pulled the door open. She hugged him hard in the hallway.

"Hey, what's that for?" he asked, chuckling.

"Just because," she told him. "How'd you get in without buzzing me?"

"I waited until the guy downstairs brought in his groceries and followed him when he opened the door. He likes you; said it was good to have you here, but if I were planning to take you away to live with me, to tell you that his second cousin's daughter in Jersey is looking for a sublease in the city. Told him I'd let you know. You ought to think about it."

"I need to talk with him," Camille said.

"About that sublease?" David asked, with an uneasy smile. The smile slowly faded. "Guess not, eh? Don't be too angry with him—he thought he was doing you a favor letting me in; besides, he's seen me before, so it's not like he was letting a stranger get inside."

"And you knew I was here how?"

"You weren't at my place, and Verdette was gone, too. So I figured you'd come back here to grab some other things, and had taken Verdette because you were feeling guilty about having abandoned her for Paris." He glanced over at the laundry basket. "Looks like I was right, too. You gonna let me in or are you ready to go now? I can just grab that basket for you."

"Not yet," she told him. "Come on in . . ."

Once the door was closed behind them, he kissed her, a kiss that promised more, but Verdette bumped up against Camille's legs, obviously annoyed at David's presence. David bent down to pet her, but she hissed, flattened her ears, and fluffed the hair on her back. "Fine," he said, withdrawing his hand. "I can take a hint." He glanced at Camille, raising one eyebrow. "How about you?" he asked. "Can you take a hint?" The arms of his soul-heart were as tight around her as the embrace in which he held her.

She wanted to give in to his invitation, but the afternoon visit with Morris intruded, dampening her emotions. She remembered the urge she'd felt to tell Palento everything. She felt that urge again now as she looked at David. She wanted someone close to her who understood. Understood everything.

She wanted David to be that person, but she was afraid. She knew what Nicolas could do. She knew what Nicolas *would* do. Still . . .

Tell him, or don't. Decide.

"Do you love me?" she asked him.

"Yes," he said, without hesitation. "In fact, let me prove it . . ."

He took her hand, obviously intending to lead her into the bedroom, but she didn't allow him to pull her away. She sat on the couch, patting the cushion next to her. "Sit, please," she told him. Verdette climbed onto the coffee table, pacing the polished wood with her tail lashing. David looked askance at the couch.

"Uh-oh. This sounds serious." He set his camera bag on the coffee table; Verdette glanced at it and hopped back down to the floor. "All I know is that we were terrifically happy in Paris. If something's happened since we got back that changed things for you, I want to know what it was. If it's something I did, something I can change, then I'll make it go away. Or is it that detective woman?"

She stopped him with a hand to his arm. "You didn't do anything. There's nothing wrong between us."

"The detective, then? What happened?"

"Sit," she told him. "Do you want something to drink? I know *I* need something . . ." She got up and went into the kitchen, pouring two tumblers half-full of Redbreast Irish whiskey, putting an ice cube in each. She handed one to David, and took a long sip of hers, relishing the burn down her throat. He sat where she'd been sitting, on the couch; she moved to the chair opposite the couch, staring at him over the coffee table, over the camera bag. She felt the radiance of his soulheart dim, pulled inside away from her.

"You're not going to believe what I have to tell you, David." Her vision shimmered in a wash of salt. She wiped angrily at her eyes for their betrayal. "That's just fair warning. You're going to think I'm crazy. But listen to me, please—this is hard enough to talk about. I . . . I haven't been entirely truthful with you, David."

"What do you mean? Are you saying there's someone else? I already know about Mercedes and Morris and the others, and I told you that it didn't matter."

"No." She shook her head quickly. "It's nothing like that. It's about me. About my background. Where I came from. And where Pierce fits in."

"Pierce?" He nearly spat the name. On the cushion, his free hand fisted on the leather. "What about that guy?"

Verdette curled her tail around Camille's ankles, meowing. She ignored the cat.

"I've known Pierce for a long, long time. And that's dangerous for you."

He seemed to stifle a laugh, but his face seemed far more angry than amused. "You can't just say something like that without an explanation, Camille. It doesn't make any sense. How can I believe you?" He was irritated now; the whiskey shivered in his hand, the ice rattling. He set the glass down on the coffee table. "Goddamn it, if you want to talk, then *talk*."

"How old do you think I am?" she asked David.

"You told me you were twenty-four," he answered. "Was that a lie?" His eyes suddenly widened. "God, you're not telling me you're underage, are you?"

She laughed, bitterly. "No. But I *did* lie."

He stared, silent. And with a deep, slow breath, she began. "I'm much *older* than twenty-four, and my name isn't really Camille . . ."

The tale took hours to tell, even in the condensed version she gave him. After a while, she thought David had stopped really listening to her. He was nodding and making the appropriate noises, but he was no longer asking questions and there was almost a panic in his eyes, as if he'd been trapped in a closed space with an insane person.

Their tumblers had been drained, refilled, emptied, and refilled yet again.

"So this Nicolas Flamel is your stalker, and he's been chasing you for centuries. Not only that, but you're saying that he's also Dr. Pierce, and that *he* killed Helen?" His voice sounded dry and almost strangled. He took another long sip of the whiskey.

"Yes," she told him.

He nodded, but she knew that it wasn't comprehension, only a reflex. He was staring somewhere past her. She saw his gaze snag on the Blake print. "You knew Blake. Vivaldi. Bernini. They were your lovers."

She gave him a silent, quick nod. "Blake, no, but Vivaldi and Bernini, yes. Among others."

He started to speak, then shook his head, taking another sip of the whiskey. "And you *feed* on artists."

"It's not that one-sided, David. Yes, an artist's creative energy sustains me, but I can also help a creative person reach his or her full potential. I can enhance the creative flow, let you tap deeper into what's inside you. And that energy . . . it allows *me* to follow my own creative endeavors. I'm a muse, not a leech. A daemon, not a demon."

"And you chose me because I could sustain you better than the others."

"You make it sound so cold-hearted, self-serving, and cynical, David. It's not like that."

"Then what *is* it like?" He slapped a hand on the couch; she saw dust fly up from the cushions. Verdette hissed and fled the room. His dark gaze found her; he studied her as if he were peering through his camera lens. "My God, Camille—or Perenelle or whatever I should call you—how am I supposed to actually *believe* any of this? It's insane."

"I told you that it wouldn't be easy, David. You're supposed to believe it because I told you, and you know that I wouldn't lie to you about something as complicated and strange as this."

He stared at her, silent and grim. She rose from her chair, went to the kitchen, and came back with an 8-inch chef's knife. David's eyes widened as she put the knife on the coffee table in front of him. "Stab me," she said. "Stick that right in my gut. Do it—try to kill me. Go ahead."

"Camille, I'm not going to stab you. Are you crazy?"

"I'm not crazy. You won't do it because you haven't believed anything I told you."

"That's not fair. Look, if you're really insisting on something like this, just cut your arm or something—you say you heal fast, right?"

She shook her head doggedly. The room swirled around her with the motion. "No," she insisted. "That won't be enough. You'd pass it off as some kind of trick. C'mon, David. I'm asking you to do this for me. For us. Go ahead."

"I don't know *what* to believe," he told her. "But I'm not going to stab you with that thing. Chris'sakes, that really *is* insane . . . and, hell, what if you're wrong . . . ?"

"You don't believe me," Camille repeated, "or you wouldn't have said that."

The knife glistened on the polished wood. *You have to prove it to him.* She knew part of it was the liquor talking, that her mind was fuzzy with the whiskey fumes, and that she wouldn't be thinking this way if she were entirely sober. She wondered if she could do it anyway, knowing the pain she'd feel, knowing the agony she'd have to endure to prove herself to him.

Do it!

Before she could change her mind, she snatched up the knife, placed the point against her stomach, and pushed in hard with a cry. David shouted in panic, reaching for her. The pain was worse than she'd imagined: her mind had blanked the memory of the other times she'd had to endure such severe wounds. Blood soaked her T-shirt and poured down the blade, slick and hot. Her hands, slick, slipped on the handle as she tried to pull it out and the blade moved inside her. She screamed at the agony as the blade twisted, doubled over and gasped. Verdette came running in from the other room, hissing and ready to protect her. David was up now, alongside her, the cat slashing at his jeans.

"Take it out!" she managed to say. "Please, David! Take it out!" and she cried out again as his hand pulled the blade from her body. He dropped it on the carpet and helped her sink to the floor. Her vision was fading; she saw David's hands, red with her blood. She heard him fumbling for his cell phone. "No!" she told him. "Don't call anyone. Just wait. Be patient. This is important."

"Damn it, Camille. You're losing blood fast, and you need help. I have to call 911."

"No! Wait! Please . . . Please . . ." Already it was becoming easier to speak. She lifted her shirt, showing him that the blood flow was easing, that the far edges of the deep wound were already beginning to slowly, reluctantly close. David stared, his phone still in his hand. She took a breath, forcing her voice to sound calm and slow. "David, I'll be fine. I just needed to show you, to prove it to you."

She sat up, which caused fresh blood to flow. "A towel," she said to David. "In the kitchen."

He broke from his stasis, hurrying into the kitchen and returned with one of her dishtowels, handing it to her. She pressed it against the wound and extended a hand to him. "Help me up."

He helped her get to her feet, biting her lips to stop from crying out. Verdette growled from under the coffee table. Her insides seemed to pull and tear with the movement, but she could move. Blood was clotting quickly along the wound; she carefully peeled the sticky dishtowel away and refolded it to press clean cotton against her abdomen. David still held her arm. Camille forced herself to straighten fully, despite the protest of her body. A distant part of her looked at the dark stain on the rug and thought, *I'll have to get a new one. That'll never come out . . .* "See," she told him. "I was telling you the truth, David."

His face was pale. "You didn't have to do *that.*"

"Yes, I did," she answered. "You wouldn't have believed me otherwise. Look now . . ." She pulled the cloth away again. The wound was nearly half-closed, and visibly less wide and deep than it had been. It was no longer seeping blood, though the center of the wound was still wet and dark. She wasn't certain what emotion she was seeing in David's eyes. "In a few days, it'll just be a scar which I'll have for a month or two, then even that will vanish. I was telling you the *truth,* David. The truth—which I haven't shared with anyone I've ever been with. None of them. You're the first and only one I've ever told everything, all of it, and if that doesn't tell you just how much you mean to me, then I don't have any other way to demonstrate it to you." She could feel tears burning in her eyes, and she blinked hard, sniffing.

"Camille . . ."

"No, let me finish. When I tell you that you're in danger, that's the truth also. Nicolas—Pierce—wants to hurt me, and he knows that what would hurt me most is losing you. Don't you understand? That's why I took you to Paris, so you'd be safe, but then the tequila came and I knew that he knew where we were . . ." She stopped, taking in a long, shuddering breath. The pain in her abdomen was beginning to recede. "We, and you especially, need to be very careful until I deal with him, or until . . ." She glanced at the long table in the corner of the room, with its cages of mice, the jars of chemicals, the alchemical equipment. He saw the direction of her gaze.

"Until you give *me* the elixir? Is that it?"

She nodded.

"What makes you think that I would take it if you offered it to me?" he asked her.

The question furrowed her forehead, made her eyebrows climb. "You wouldn't want immortality? You wouldn't want several lifetimes to perfect your craft?"

"Yeah, artists want immortality all right, but the immortality we're after is the kind you don't know you achieved because you're dead when it happens. It's the *work* that's supposed to live forever. Not the artist."

A wry smile lifted one corner of her lips. "I know that better than anyone," she said. "Believe me." The self-inflicted injury and her body's efforts to repair the damage were sapping her strength. She fumbled for the chair, sitting abruptly. David watched her with concern, but he didn't move to her or touch her. His soul-heart's radiance stayed inside him when she most needed it.

"Look, you said the elixir cost you your skill in alchemy; it forced you to seek out people with these 'green soul-hearts' to keep you healthy," he said. "Is that right?"

Camille nodded.

"And you said that it turned Nicolas into someone who feeds off death and pain. He claimed that all the mice you injected became compulsive and obsessive about *something*. That's why Verdette is the way she is."

"Yes, but . . ."

He shook his head at her protest. "What would the elixir cost *me*?" he asked. "Would it take away the gift I have with photography? Would it make me a half-vampire like Nicolas, finding my pleasure in pain and blood? What kind of eternity would that be for me? For us? Could I even *be* what I want to be if I take your elixir?" He swept a hand through the air, as if an invisible moth fluttered in his face. "I gotta go," he said suddenly, then grimaced. "You're sure you're all right? I can take you to Urgent Care or the ER . . ."

"I'll be fine," she told him. "I promise. David, where are we now, you and me?"

"I love you, Camille," he answered. "I do. But right now, I really don't know. I . . . I just have to think. Alone. I'm going to go home."

Muscles and tendons pulled inside her as she tried to stand again. She closed her eyes, refusing to cry out against the pain. She let her mind touch his soul-heart, take some of the energy inside herself; she needed it—needed him. David shivered, as if he noticed. "All right, then," she told him when she could speak. "But let me go with you to your place. All I need to do is get Verdette and take the stuff I put together." Something inside her moved painfully; she felt the wound pulling as it knitted itself.

"No," David said, surprising her. "Why don't you just stay here tonight and let yourself recover. Use a spell, or however you do it."

The undertone of sarcasm in his voice bit at her even as she tried to ignore it. "David, I'm worried that it's not *safe* for you. Give me a few minutes . . ."

David was already shaking his head. "I'll watch out for the little bastard." He was already at the door. As he turned the handle, he looked back at her. "I'll be fine, Camille. Right now, I just want to be by myself for a bit."

"That's fine, and I'll give you that space. Just let me be sure that you're safe in your—our—apartment. I love you, David," she told him, trying to smile. "Let me walk back with you, then I'll come back here. Please."

He pressed his lips together, then opened them with a long sigh. "Fine."

They walked together, slowly, Camille holding onto his arm heavily at first, then less so by the time they reached the studio apartment and climbed the stairs. He opened the door. "See?" he said. "All safe. Now . . ."

"Okay. I'll call you tomorrow morning, okay? I'll bring Verdette and the rest of my stuff over, and we can talk some more. We're going to be good, aren't we, David?"

"Sure. I just . . ." He sighed again. "I have to process all this." He leaned in and touched his lips to hers; it was the kiss a brother might have given her. Reluctantly, she released his emerald tendrils, let them fall around him like an unseen cloak. She stepped back into the hall, and he closed the door behind her.

She left. Without David's energy to speed the healing, she could feel the throbbing from the wound in her abdomen all the way home.

INTERLUDE SEVEN

Gabriele Tietze &
Gustav Klimt

1891

Gabriele Tietze

1891

"**D**O YOU LOVE ME?"

Gabriele smiled at the question. "No," she told him. "I revel in your talent; I bask in your radiance. But love? No, Gustav—you love yourself too much for that. Besides, you already have more lovers than you can handle."

"You let me . . ." He stopped, grinning at her and leaving the rest unsaid.

"I do, and I enjoy it, too. But that is sex. Love is something else. You have sex with many women, but you don't have to *love* any of us. You love the one you *won't* bed—and you know who I mean. Isn't she a little young for you, Gustav? She's what . . . all of seventeen? And your sister-in-law besides."

"You evidently know as little about love as you do about painting," he retorted.

Gustav Klimt was dressed in his painting smock, a pleated gray robe that covered him from neck to feet, dotted with flecks of color from his brushes; below the smock, she could see his bare ankles and his feet encased in paint-spattered leather sandals. She was not dressed at all, reclining nude on the bed in the studio, holding the pose he'd given her. He'd sketched her lightly in charcoal on the gessoed canvas, and was beginning to add washes of color to the painting now, blocking in her figure and the light. He peered at her through his viewfinder: an ivory rectangle the size of a hundred-kroner banknote with a square hole cut in it. She could see his eye through the hole, staring.

His soul-heart was a luscious, delicious green, the color of wild spring grasses, and it flowed wonderfully from him, seeming to light up the studio for Gabriele. She had already touched in him a dozen new pathways for that creative energy, and in the few months she'd been here in Vienna, she already saw his work changing and growing under her influence.

He would be one of the great ones, she knew.

He would also be her bait.

She'd come here chasing Nicolas, knowing after their London encounter with the Blakes that she must now become the hunter, not the hunted—because that was the only way she could ever guarantee her own sanity and safety. Eight innocent people had died in the flood of porter from the Horseshoe Brewery—she had *caused* them to die, and the guilt stayed with her. *To kill him, must you also have to become like him?* That was a question that troubled her.

After the debacle at the brewery, she left London entirely for a few years so that Nicolas/Polidori would have no reason to further torment the Blakes—when "Polidori" didn't vanish suddenly, she watched him to make certain that he left the Blakes alone. She'd followed Polidori's brief career as a hanger-on in the Lord Byron/Shelley camp; then, in the spring of 1821, she returned to London herself to track him down. She intended first to disable him, then to cut off his head to kill him forever, no matter what the cost. She was near to doing exactly that, but somehow Nicolas realized that she was tracking him: Polidori "died" suddenly in August of 1821—evidently via the same enchantment that had saved Nicolas as Robespierre, since a body with his face was identified. Not surprisingly, perhaps, within two days the doctor who pronounced him dead and the mortician who buried the body also died mysteriously.

Nicolas vanished again, wrapped in some new identity. She knew his obsession, and knew what drew him—wherever there was death and suffering in plenty, he might be there. Since then, she'd nearly caught him twice more: in 1846 in Roscommon County, Ireland, as over a million Irish peasants succumbed to starvation in the midst of what the Irish called *an Gorta Mór*, the Great Hunger; in 1866 after the end of the Caucasian War in the West Caucasus, as the victorious Russians slaughtered untold numbers of the native Circassians. In both cases, Nicolas managed to slip the traps she'd set for him and vanish under a new identity.

Last year, she'd read about a sequence of strange deaths and suicides in Vienna, including that of Crown Prince Rudolph and his paramour. The suicide rate in Vienna, it was whispered, was higher than anywhere else in Europe despite the city's prosperity, and the city was also said to be obsessed with death. The accounts were compelling enough that she'd come to the city again after a century and a half away. She was certain he was here; she was certain she could feel it in the strange, morbid, churning energy of the city in this last decade of the 19th century. She saw it in the Tarot whenever she laid out the cards to read them.

He was here. He was living amongst the gentry somewhere.

She knew that what had most often brought her to Nicolas' attention in the past had been her relationship with a single prominent artist. She was vulnerable when she was with someone who stood out and who had a rising reputation with his or her creative endeavor— that was the spoor that called to Nicolas. After London, she countered that as she had before: avoiding the truly massive soul-hearts and great talents, instead taking what sustenance she could from groups of lesser talents and diminished soul-hearts. It left her feeling hungry and tired and irritable, but they could sustain her while she searched for Nicolas.

But now . . . She wanted to bring him out from wherever he was lurking—and one way to do that was to make her own presence known. And of the burgeoning artists in Vienna, just beginning to make their reputations, none was better known that Gustav Klimt. It was easy enough to become one of the many models he hired. It was easy enough to seduce him. It was easy enough to take the vast soul-heart within

Klimt, already radiant with talent, and begin to fully release the potential inside him.

The satisfaction she felt in blending with a soul-heart this full after so long was nearly enough to drive away the guilt that plagued her for using him so callously.

Do you have to become like him to kill him?

"I've done all I can do today with this," Gustav said to her, setting down his palette; one of the boys he employed as an assistant hurried over to take away the palette, the jars of pigments, and the brushes, stealing several lingering glances at Gabriele's reclining figure on the bed before leaving the studio. She heard him in the small prep room off the studio, a rattle of glass and the scent of mineral spirits as he cleaned the brushes. Gustav cocked his head, staring at the painting before draping it with a cloth. He went to the door of the prep room and closed it as Gabriele stretched muscles tired and stiff from maintaining the same position for so long.

Gustav unbuttoned his painting smock and let it fall over his shoulders. He stepped out of the pool of paint-spattered cloth; underneath, he wore nothing at all, and she could see his arousal. He hung the smock on a hook, unbuckled his sandals, and came over to the bed as Gabriele sat up. He leaned over toward her. He kissed her, a hand on either side of her face, and she curled her arms around his neck, pulling him down on top of her. "You're so beautiful," he gasped when he finally lifted his face from hers. The glow of his soul-heart wrapped her like a second body, arousing her more than Gustav himself.

"Not as beautiful to you as *she* is," Gabrielle whispered in his ear.

"Be quiet," he answered, his voice gruff. His hand cupped her breast, then drifted lower. She gasped. "Be quiet . . ." he repeated more softly, then his lips found hers again.

Pauline Flöge ran a dressmaking school just off the Ringstrasse, the wide boulevard that encircled old Vienna and which also served as the promenade for the wealthy and royalty of the city. It was there that Gabriele bought most of her dresses: the prices were reasonable, the quality excellent—Pauline ran her school with a strict overseeing of her pupils' work—and unlike the more proper clothing establishments, all Pauline cared about was that Gabriele paid well and often for the dresses produced by her students. It didn't matter to her that Gabriele was a model who often posed nude for the Klimt brothers—one of whom, Ernst, had married Pauline's sister Helene only two months ago, while the other, Gustav, paid an inordinate amount of attention to the youngest of the Flöge sisters, Emilie.

Pauline didn't treat Gabriele as a common cocotte, but as a valued customer.

Pauline tucked a curl of stray ash-blonde hair back into her coiffure as Gabriele entered the house that served as the school, looking up from a dress pattern laid out on a table. Emilie, her sister, stood alongside her: a smaller, thinner image of her older sister, with delicate features and a body still rounding into full womanhood. "Ah, Fräulein Tietze," Pauline said. "You've come to try on the dress you ordered? Emilie, please escort Fräulein Tietze back to the fitting rooms and help her try it on. I'll come and check the fit in a few minutes."

Emilie nodded. "Fräulein, if you'll follow me . . ." Gabriele followed Emilie from the front room and up the stairs. They passed open rooms where women were sewing at treadle machines, marking dress hems on forms, or stitching intricate embroidery patterns. At the end of the hall, Emilie opened the door of one of the rear fitting rooms. Gabriele's dress was hanging there, next to others made by the school: a décolletage in white tulle, a fichu made of brilliant white lace, and a faille dress with dark-red roses on curling stems, the flowers matching the color of her hair and nearly vibrating against a saturated green background that was the color of a soul-heart.

Emilie closed the door and gestured to the brocaded screen in the corner. "If you wish to undress in private . . ."

Gabriele nearly laughed. "I just came from Herr Klimt's studio," she said, removing her shawl and starting to unbutton her blouse in front of a large, freestanding mirror. "Modesty is hardly an issue of mine." She paused. "Unless *you* prefer that I disrobe behind the screen."

"No," Emilie breathed, then repeated the word again with a shake of pale, fine curls. "No." Gabriele saw a hint of color in the young woman's cheeks, and she looked quickly away from Gabriele. "How is Herr Klimt?"

Gabriele smiled at the woman as she removed her blouse. "He is painting madly," she said. "Now that the *Kunsthistorisches Museum*'s staircase paintings are done and he's joined the *Künstlerhausgenossenschaft*, his work has become so much more expressive and free. I think it's wonderful."

"You must be an excellent subject for him." Emilie took the dress from the hanger and held it open for Gabriele to step into. Gabriele could see Emilie's face in the mirror. "You were the model for 'Girl From Tanagra,' weren't you?"

"I was."

"It's a beautiful painting. Very different from his other work. Perhaps he needed you as his muse."

Gabriele could hear the hint of jealousy in Emilie's voice, and she shook her head. "No, my dear. He has a much prettier daemon than me. In fact, Herr Klimt showed me his portrait of you the other day."

That garnered a helpless smile from Emilie. "It's finished?"

"Yes. And it's very striking. I imagine Gustav will show it to you tomorrow." Gabriele pulled her arms through the sleeves of the dress as Emilie began to button the rear closures. "I watched him working on it for hours, so gently, as if his brush were his hands stroking your own face and caressing your neck. When he's with me, I sometimes wonder if he's imagining you there with him instead."

She heard Emilie's intake of breath, felt her hands stop moving at her back. For a moment, in the mirror, their eyes met. "Fräulein . . ." she gasped, but her voice was neither as shocked nor aggrieved as it might have been. Emilie's gaze fell away again, and Gabriele felt her tug harshly on the dress as she began to button it once more.

"I'm sorry, was that too forward of me? I do apologize. I know Herr Klimt is never anything but respectful and proper toward you, as he should be, nor does he ever express anything but admiration for you to others. But I also know his deeper feelings toward you—and those are identical to what his brother feels toward your sister Helene."

Emilie's head came up, and again found Gabriele's eyes in the mirror, though this time there was no protest, only a hopeful look. "*Die ist die Wahrheit*," Gabriele whispered to her.

"What is the truth?" another voice intruded as Pauline entered the fitting room.

Emilie's eyes had widened in the mirror, her mouth open as if to protest. Gabriele swept a hand down the side of the dress. "The truth is that I believe your students are blessed to be working and learning with you, Fräulein Flöge. The dress is exquisite. Far more beautiful than I expected."

"I'm so pleased, Fräulein Tietze," Pauline answered. "You flatter me." In the mirror, Emilie's mouth closed again, and her head ducked down as she finished buttoning up the dress. Pauline walked slowly around Gabriele, her mouth pursed as she examined the dress, occasionally plucking at the fabric to test the fit. "The dress works very well for you, I think," she proclaimed at last. "That green is a wonderful color for your complexion and hair. Very striking. You will turn heads at the balls." Pauline clapped her hands together in satisfaction. "I don't see where any alterations need to be made, though of course, we'll do them for you if you wish. Emilie, if you would assist the Fräulein in removing the dress and box it for her, I'll have it sent over to her apartments and prepare the bill."

With that, Pauline curtsied politely to Gabriele and left the room. Emilie moved behind her once more. "Emilie," Gabriele said, daring to use the young woman's given name, "you should know that I'm not a jealous woman, and I'm not in love with Gustav—nor is he with me. We're simply, well, *convenient* for each other. All you need do is tell when you want me to step aside, and I will. It's you he wants—at least for the moment."

"You are very . . . *modern*, Fräulein Tietze."

Gabriele laughed gently at that. "Please, call me Gabriele. And no, I'm not modern at all. These ideas of morality people call modern are mostly old ones that have just been rediscovered. Gustav is a good man, but I'm afraid that if you're genuinely interested in him, you're going to have to be 'modern' yourself. I'll also tell you this: he won't be faithful to you, no matter what he says, and I say that only so you know what awaits you. He is a fascinating person, a loyal friend, and a fabulous talent, but when it comes to women, he's only the weakest of men. He'll be yours and yours alone in everything but physical intimacy—and you will need to accept his flaws as well as his virtues if you wish to keep him."

Emilie had unbuttoned the dress, and Gabriele turned to Emilie as she slipped the sleeves down her arms. "Gustav wants you, Emilie, more than he wants anyone else." Emilie was staring at her. Gabriele reached out to softly touch her cheek, as an older sister might. "What is most important is whether *you* want *him*. That's what you need to decide."

She let her hand drop, and Emilie blinked. "I'll pack the dress for you, Fra—" She stopped, gave a shake of her head. "Gabriele."

"Thank you," Gabriele said. "I'll tell Gustav that you're looking forward to seeing your portrait, if you'd like."

"Do," Emilie said. "And thank you, Gabriele, for talking with me."

Gabriele laughed again. "We muses must lean on each other," she said. "Otherwise, it's a lonely life."

Vienna, as it approached the 20th century, could have supplied a thousand muses like Gabriele with sustenance. The old fortifications of the ancient city had been demolished, replaced by the wide boulevard of the Ringstrasse, fringed with grandiose public buildings and private palaces, a magnet for Vienna society, where all flocked to see and be seen.

It was as if the destruction of the last vestiges of Vienna's medieval past had somehow ripped open its artistic consciousness to expose riches buried underneath. Creative endeavors flourished everywhere in the rich humus of the Austro-Hungarian Empire. Even as the empire floundered in unstable European politics, even as her people continued to mourn the terrible death of their beloved Crown Prince Rudolph two years previously, boundaries in the arts were being pushed and bent and shattered: in the Fine Arts, Gustav Klimt was very popular, certainly, but no less was his brother Ernst and their usual companion Franz

Matsch, as well as Koloman Moser, Max Kurzweil, and dozens more. The architects Adolph Loos, Josef Hoffmann, Joseph Maria Olbrich, and Otto Wagner were bringing a new vision to the buildings being designed and built. In music, there were always the old lions Johannes Brahms and Johann Strauss, Jr., the Younger, but there were also the new lights in the musical landscape: Gustav Mahler, Anton Bruckner, and Richard Strauss, whose operas seemed to recapture the muscular strength of Richard Wagner. In literature, many of the writers of Vienna gathered in the Café Griensteidl: Arthur Schnitzler, Hermann Bahr, Felix Salten, Karl Kraus. There was the new alienist, Sigmund Freud, whose theories on the mind were fascinating many of the intelligentsia.

Vienna was a Muse's dream city, as vibrant and alive as Paris. Perhaps, for this moment in time, even more so.

Another aspect of life for which Vienna had no significant rival at all was its balls. There were well over a hundred significant balls during the course of the carnival season. Every guild and group had its ball: the Vienna Skating Club, the Industrialists, the Hotelkeepers, the Danube Steamship Company, the Physicians, the Master Bakers, the Cobblers, the Laundrymaids, and the various artists' associations with their "Gschnas" balls—the "false magic" balls which were always fantastical and strange.

It was already late in the ball season, which began with the New Year's Eve Imperial Ball, the first major ball of the year. In early March, the last of the balls in which the *haute bourgeoisie* might reasonably expect the appearance of some of the aristocracy was the Opera Redoute Ball, where the ladies were expected to come masked and mysterious, at least until the grand unmasking at midnight—after which the ball would continue to rollick on until a new dawn painted the eastern sky over the Ringstrasse. Gustav was making a rare appearance at the ball—despite his publicly stated distaste for them—and he'd asked Gabriele to attend as his guest.

"And why have you decided to grace the Opera Redoute with your presence?" Gabriele asked Gustav as she stepped into the carriage he'd hired.

"There's a man attending that I wish to meet," Gustav replied. Sitting across from her, he looked rather elegant in his coat and tails, a brushed and shiny top hat on the seat alongside him. Gabriele raised her eyebrows at that. Under her fur-trimmed long coat, she was wearing the dress that the Flöges had made for her. She held her mask on her lap for the moment: a black domino adorned with peacock feathers and a green satin ribbon. "He said he can supply me gold foil for my paintings at half the price of my current supplier."

"Half the price? That's impossible, Gustav—at least legally."

"Indeed. But he says he can do it, nonetheless, and entirely within the bounds of the law. He had a certificate from the Ministry of Commerce, and a letter from Archduchess Gisela herself recommending him." Gustav shrugged. "Why not talk to the man?"

Of late, Gustav had taken to decorating his canvases with pieces of gold foil, incorporating them into the painted work and lending the compositions a shimmering allure. He was also beginning to abandon the strict realism of his earlier work, lengthening and distorting his figures. Gabriele wasn't certain yet that she entirely approved of the changes he was making, but she could feel the passion and fury in the energy of his soul-heart. Whatever he was doing, it was at least partially due to her influence and the artistic expression within him that she had unleashed. So she smiled and reached over to pat Gustav's knee.

"Why not?" she answered. "Will the Flöge sisters be there as well? It was Emilie and Pauline who made this dress; I should like them to see me in it."

He didn't look directly at her, but stared out into the night through the carriage's door. "I believe they will be," he said.

"Fräulein Emilie is delightful and enchanting, I think. You captured her well in her portrait."

Gustav grunted in reply, still seemingly fascinated with the scenes along the Ringstrasse. *You should have asked her to accompany you, not me*, Gabriele thought, but kept the admonition to herself.

They arrived at the Redoute in a line of carriages and fiacres disgorging the bejeweled and dazzling well-to-do of Vienna. Gustav tied the mask's ribbon carefully around Gabriele's upswept coiffure, and they descended from their carriage to join the crowd. Few people arrived on foot—that was simply not done, no matter how close one lived. The opera house was brilliant with electric lights, and a new parquet floor had been erected over the opera seats, while on the stage none less than Eduard "Edi" Strauss, son of Johann Strauss the Elder and younger brother of Johann Strauss, Jr., led his waltz orchestra. Gabriele took Gustav's arm as they entered the crowd and gave their tickets to the white-tailed doormen, who pointed them toward the entrance to their room.

Gustav was stopped several times by men wishing to speak with him; she noticed he deliberately never introduced her to anyone. She could see them peering at her and her masked features, wondering who the well-known Klimt might be escorting: some well-known person, perhaps: she heard one man whisper to his companion that she must certainly be Adele Bloch-Bauer, the wife of Ferdinand Bloch-Bauer, the wealthy industrialist.

The masked women smiled openly at Gustav, and to Gabriele as well; afraid, perhaps, that they might be slighting someone whom they wouldn't wish to anger. Until the grand unmasking, this was a night of anonymous flirtations, both in play and in earnest. Here, her identity hidden by her mask, a woman could dare to touch a man's face with her gloved hand, or place that hand on his arm—several women did so with Gustav. He was besieged, and—making excuses—made his way quickly to their table in a room just off the main dance floor. Franz Matsch was already seated at the table, escorting Theresa Anna Kattus, daughter of a wine merchant—several bottles of her father's sparkling wine were already chilling in ice buckets on the table. Gustav's brother Ernst was standing to one side, watching the dancers with his wife Helene. With him also were the other Flöge sisters, Pauline and Emilie, both unescorted and both masked. As Gabriele and Gustav entered the curtained-off room, with its far end open to the dance floor, Gabriele could see Emilie's mouth frown slightly under her blue domino, adorned with red glass spangles.

The orchestra was just starting a quadrille; out on the floor, groups of couples bowed to each other as they began the dance. Gabriele disengaged her arm from Gustav's as he greeted Franz and Theresa, and Gabriele went to stand next to Emilie as the bright strains of the quadrille shimmered in the air of the hall. "You look lovely tonight, Fräulein Tietze," the young woman said. Her eyes glittered behind the mask, but the mask hid whatever expression they held.

"Call me Gabriele," she reminded Emilie. "And if that's true, it's mostly due to your wonderful dress." She swayed her hips in time to the music so that the dress swirled out, displaying the embroidery. "Gustav keeps remarking on how talented you and your sisters are." Under the mask, Emilie smiled momentarily at that, and Gabriele leaned toward her, whispering so that only she could hear. "I think you should ask him to dance with you. He won't be able to refuse."

"You wouldn't mind?" Her voice was light with hope.

Gabriele laughed. "I'm only here because he didn't dare ask you. On the way here, he asked me three separate times if I thought you'd be here. Can't you see him staring at you now, even while he's talking to Herr Matsch?"

Emilie glanced back into the room, and Gabriele saw her smile widen slightly as she quickly glanced away. "His look makes me shiver," she said.

"It's him that's shivering," Gabriele said. "Tonight he's in *your* world. You're his empress. You control him, not the other way, and don't let anything in the world tell you differently. Listen—the quadrille's nearly over and they'll be calling a new dance in a moment. Go and ask him to take you out to the floor."

Emilie stared at her for a moment through the mask, then nodded once. Gabriele watched her walk up to Gustav, who bowed as she approached and took her hand. They spoke for a few moments, then Gustav looked up and found Gabriele's eyes. She smiled at him and gestured with her open fan to the dance floor. Still holding Emilie's hand, Gustav moved past his brother, Helene, Pauline, and Gabriele and out into the ballroom. Gabriele watched them go (and felt Pauline and Helene's gazes on her also), taking a place with several other couples as another quadrille began. They bowed and entered the formal turns and steps of the dance.

Gabriele watched, and applauded when the dance ended. Gustav and Emilie remained on the floor, their heads inclined toward each other. Gabriele could feel the long, bright tendrils of Gustav's soul-heart bending toward Emilie, her own grasp on them now stretched and thin. It was difficult to keep down the flash of jealousy she felt, watching them, but she forced it away. *I'm only using him; I don't want him that way. She's his true muse, not me . . .*

As Emilie and Gustav conversed, Gabriele saw a man approach the two. She couldn't see his face, but something about him, about the way he walked and the way he held himself . . . She *knew*, knew without seeing that face. Her breath left her, making her feel light-headed. Her stomach churned, and she could taste bile in the back of her throat. Then the man turned to profile, and she knew for certain.

Nicolas.

Despite the fact that this was what she'd wanted, she wasn't ready. Not tonight. She had nothing with her to protect herself, and she didn't wish to talk with him or let him know she was here. Not yet; not until she could do so on her own terms and in a place where she felt safe. He couldn't *know* she was here; not yet. He would suspect it, might even be relatively certain, but he couldn't *know*, not until he'd seen her with Gustav. They were still talking, and she saw Gustav introduce him to Emilie; she thought she saw disappointment cross Nicolas' face. Gustav waved a hand; he gestured in the direction of their open room, and Nicolas looked that way.

Gabriele took a step farther back in the room, happy for the mask that hid her features and shielding herself behind Ernst and Helene. "I'm afraid I'm not feeling well," she said to them. "Tell Gustav that I'm taking a fiacre back to my rooms. I'll talk to him sometime tomorrow."

They murmured polite noises, though she knew that they were both thinking that this sudden illness had something to do with Emilie. She hurried from the room, took her coat from the checkroom, and hurried

into the lobby, telling one of the doormen to summon transportation
for her.

*He's here. You've found him. You've sighted your quarry; now you can
plan the kill.*

The realization made her simultaneously thrilled and frightened.

Verdette purred on her lap as she worked, dressed in her nightgown.

Even when she'd been Perenelle, she'd often wished that she possessed Nicolas' affinity for spells. While she'd been able to master some
of the spells in the books and scrolls they'd acquired, she'd never managed the ease and power he'd been able to acquire. After taking the
elixir, she'd been able to use only the most simple of spells. She'd hoped,
with the centuries of practice open to her, that she could match him,
but it seemed that part of her mind had been burned and scarred by the
elixir. While her skill with alchemy and chemistry had slowly returned
and even blossomed, while she still found the Tarot to be a useful tool,
she remained eternally a novice with magic and spells.

The new explosives she'd developed were at least as potent as Nicolas' magic, but more . . . comprehensive. Nicolas could select and kill
a single person in a crowded room with his black lightning; she'd seen
that. She could control the timing of an explosion from the chemicals
she mixed either through an infused timing cord, a watch mechanism,
or even via the small store of spells she was capable of learning. But
while she could ensure that an explosion would take out Nicolas, it
would do the same to everyone—innocent or guilty—within several
strides of him, and potentially wound dozens more with shrapnel or
simply the concussive force of the blast.

She wanted Nicolas dead, but she wasn't willing to take other lives
with him, no matter how much she desired to remove him.

I won't be like him. I won't.

Still, this was her best defense against Nicolas: that and a handgun,
which were becoming more reliable and more powerful with each passing decade. She'd purchased a Gasser-Kropatschek Officer's Revolver,
made here in Vienna—a weapon in use throughout the region. If she

could stop Nicolas, render him unconscious or helpless for just long enough to strike his head from his body . . . and for that, she had a meticulously sharpened officer's saber in her apartment. That would serve.

Verdette meowed on her lap, glaring through the archway of the small workroom into the reception room and the door of her suite. She heard a knock a moment later. The sound startled her and she grabbed for the revolver, already loaded on the table, before she felt the touch of the soul-heart outside. "Gustav?" she called. "Are you alone?"

"*Ja*," she heard him reply, his voice muffled through the wood.

"A moment . . ." she called out. Verdette grumbled as she rose from the chair and threw a sheet over the table laden with chemicals, retorts, and measured vials. She put the revolver in the pocket of her robe. She retied the sash of her nightgown, stained here and there with the splash and stains of chemicals. She brushed her hair back with her hand as she went to the door. "You're alone?" she asked again as she put her hand on the chain.

"I've already told you that," Gustav answered, irritation coloring his voice and the hue of his soul-heart. Gabriele unfastened the chain and clicked the lock, turned the door handle as she opened the door enough that he could slide in, her hand on the revolver's wooden grip and her finger on its trigger. It was only Gustav; she let her hand slide from the weapon as she closed and locked the door again.

"I'm sorry, Gustav," she said, "but I wasn't dressed . . ."

He looked at her and grunted. "So I see." Without asking her permission he shrugged his coat from his shoulder and draped it over the nearest chair. He plunged a hand into the side pocket of his jacket. "You left the ball the other night so abruptly, and you haven't been to the studio in two days. You're truly ill?"

She shrugged. "Not anymore. I'm feeling much better now. How was the ball? Was Emilie a sufficient substitute for me?"

He smiled momentarily at that. "I don't think you're as subtle as you think you are, Gabriele. But *ja*, she and I got along very well. And you aren't jealous?"

"I've already told you, Gustav. I love you, but I've no interest in being *in* love with you. She already is. Are you with her?"

"You're impertinent."

"I'm truthful," she answered. "And I wasn't ill. I was just giving Emilie the room she needed. I like her, Gustav. She's the one you need, much more than you need me." Gabriele pulled the robe tighter around her shoulders as Verdette rubbed against her ankles. She bent down to pick up the cat, making certain that she held her front paws in case she decided to strike at Gustav. Verdette purred, but her eyes were on Gustav and her tail lashed angrily. "The man you wanted to see at the ball—he was the one who came up to you and Emilie after the first quadrille?"

"Yes. Herr Anton Srna, who is here for the Amateur-Kunst Photography exhibition, where he's displaying some of his prints. A photographer must know silver, so why not gold also?" Gustav pulled his hand from his pocket, displaying a small cardboard box; he opened it and showed it to her. A packet of several sheets of tissue paper lay inside, and he lifted the top sheet to show her a delicate rectangle of gold foil nestled between the sheets. She could see the gleaming edge lift with her breath, like an impossibly-thin autumnal leaf. "A sample: easily half the price I would have paid at Mörtenbock's or Heldwein's. I had it assayed and it's genuine—and as finely hammered as any foil I've seen. The man wasn't lying. He says he can supply me with as much as I like. I'm meeting him tonight at *Gösser Bierklini* to finalize the deal."

"How do you know that the rest will be as good as the sample?"

"It will, or he'll live to regret that mistake," Gustav said. The grin he gave then was ugly; Gabriele knew Gustav's predilection for picking fights when he was drunk. He seemed to enjoy the pounding of fists into flesh and the blood that followed. More than once he'd come to the studio with eyes purpled and swollen from having been in an altercation the night before, too sore and hungover to paint, but strangely happy.

Gabriele rubbed Verdette's ears. "Be careful, Gustav. You don't know this man."

"He'll need to be the careful one, if he thinks he can cheat me." Gustav sniffed. "Oh, and I nearly forgot. He mentioned that he also wanted to meet *you*, my dear."

The statement made her shiver, as if the chill March wind had found its way into her room. Her arms tightened around Verdette, who mewled inquiringly. "Me? He said that?"

Gustav shrugged. "He said he would like to meet the model for 'Girl From Tanagra.' He told me that he found the painting intriguing, and that he particularly likes women with red hair. Perhaps you'd like him, as well, eh? A man who can afford to sell gold for less than it's worth? Maybe you could love him but not be *in* love with him also." Gustav laughed.

"What did you tell him?" Gabriele asked. "About meeting me?"

"I told him that you'd be at my studio tomorrow. You will be, won't you? I need you to model."

A momentary fear ran through her, and she had to remind herself that this was what she'd wanted, what she'd planned for, and that settled her once again. She smiled at Gustav and released Verdette, who padded away. "Of course," she said. "Tell Herr Srna that I very much look forward to making his acquaintance. Tomorrow. At the studio."

Gustav laughed. He took a step toward her, one hand touching her face. She kissed his palm as his other hand untied the sash of her robe and let it fall open. Chill air touched her. "What do you have in your pocket?" he asked. "Your robe is so heavy."

"It's nothing," she told him as his hands roamed her exposed body. "Gustav, your meeting tonight . . ."

"That is hours away yet," he said. "Let me spend one of those hours, at least, with you . . ."

The *Gösser Bierklini* was a tavern and restaurant located at Steindlgasse 4, near the Palais Obissi. It was one of Gustav's regular stops, she knew—he'd taken her there several times in the year she'd been his model. The area around the tavern was fairly well-traveled, though after midnight it was far less so.

She knew Gustav well enough that she was certain he would stay drinking with Nicolas far into the night, and that Nicolas' manner toward Gustav would be soothing enough that there'd be no altercations. After Gustav left her, she dressed and followed him to his house—he lived with his mother and his sister—and had the carriage driver wait until she saw him leave for the tavern. She had her driver follow his fiacre, stopping the carriage well down from the tavern and waiting as Gustav entered the establishment. Several minutes later, she saw Nicolas, walking down the street from the opposite direction toward the *Bierklini.* She watched him go in, then paid her driver and stepped out onto the street as well.

In the early evening, the avenue was relatively crowded, with carriages passing by and people walking the streets. A few young boys moved among the better-dressed citizens, begging for coins. Gabriele walked toward the tavern slowly, thinking. When one of the boys approached her, she caught him by his thin shoulder. "How would you like to earn five kronen tonight?" she asked.

He looked at her with a strange melding of eagerness, suspicion, and greed as he wiped a dirty sleeve over a slightly dirtier face. "And how might I do that?"

"Nothing too hard, and nothing that will get you in trouble with the gendarmerie. What's your name?"

"Andre."

"Well, then, Andre . . ." She described Nicolas and Gustav to the boy, handing him a one-krone coin. "That's your advance. The rest I'll give you later. Now, I want you to go inside and look for the two men I've described. They should be drinking together. I want you to see their faces so you know them. Then come back out here and I'll give you the rest of your instructions."

The boy returned several minutes later, chewing the remnants of a pastry he'd either stolen or bought with the krone. "I saw them, Fräulein. Herr Klimt I recognized; the man with him is dark-haired and short, with sharp eyes and hands that won't stay still. They're sitting at a table on the balcony outside the Steindl Room with steins of beer and plates of *schmankerln.*" He grinned and licked his lips of the pastry crumbs. "It didn't look like they'll be going anywhere soon."

Gabriele patted the boy's head. She pointed to the corner just down the street, where a carriage went jangling by. "There's an inn just around the corner there. You know it, Andre?" He nodded his head vigorously. "That's where I'll be. I want you to stay here and watch; if you see either Herr Klimt or the other man leaving, run and get me. Otherwise, I'll return in two hours, and I'll pay you the rest of your fee."

At one in the morning, after fending off several offers by well-lubricated customers to escort her to their rooms, she paid her bill and left the inn, going back to the *Gösser Bierklini*. Andre was still there, leaning against the pole of one of the gas lamps that dotted the street. "Herr Klimt and the other man are still inside," he told her. "I just checked again only a few minutes ago. But their plates have been collected and the bill is on the table."

Gabriele thanked him and paid him the remaining kroner for his troubles. She found a shadowed spot at an alleyway entrance half a block up the street and kept watch herself; perhaps fifteen minutes later, she saw Nicolas emerge from the tavern with Klimt. The two conversed for a few moments, then Klimt turned left and Nicolas right, back the way he'd originally come and moving toward Gabriele. The street was now otherwise deserted, and she stepped farther back into the alleyway, drawing the Gasser revolver from her handbag, and putting her back to the wall closest to where Nicolas would pass. She whispered a phrase in Arabic before he could reach her, accompanying it with a wave of her free hand: in response, the night suddenly went eerily silent around her; she could not even hear Nicolas' footsteps on the stones of the avenue. She saw the elongated form of his shadow, thrown by the gas light, then Nicolas himself, walking quickly down the street.

She raised the revolver, aimed directly at his back. She pressed the trigger and saw the flame, but there was no report echoing from the flanks of the buildings around them, only silence. Nicolas stumbled, his head craning to look back, his mouth open in a shout, though she could hear nothing: she fired again into the eerie silence, the chambers turning, then yet again, and he went down hard onto the cobbles. Gabriele looked quickly around—the street was still empty. She thrust the revolver back into her handbag, then ran to grab the limp body by the lapels, pulling Nicolas deep into the alleyway, well away from the street. As she did so, the spell of silence vanished; the sound of Nicolas' body being dragged along the stones sounded impossibly loud, and her breath seemed a roar. Panting, she leaned over the body; the mingled, sharp scent of blood and gunpowder wrinkled her nose, overpowering the other odors of the alley. Her hands were stained with red.

Nicolas didn't appear to be breathing, but she knew that already the elixir would be working in his body, repairing the damage and returning him to life. She set down the handbag and removed from it a long, wicked butcher's knife—she'd left the saber behind as too heavy and obvious to carry in the streets. The butcher's knife would make the work more difficult and messy, but that didn't matter. She knelt down on the greasy stones of the alley.

A carriage rattled past the entrance of the alley; she hesitated, ready to flee, but it didn't stop.

As she placed the blade against Nicolas' throat, his eyes flew open and he took a long, shuddering gasp. *Do it. Do it now . . .* She knew she should move before he could speak, but it was already too late. "Perenelle . . ." His voice was weak, little more than a croak. He moaned, then, and that made her draw back a little. His eyes found hers. "You don't need to do this."

"You left me no choice, Nicolas." She pressed the blade hard enough that a line of blood trickled down his neck. He was staring at her, watching her. She could feel her hand trembling. She imagined how it would feel: the blade slicing muscle and tendons, severing veins and arteries so that the blood would spurt, slick and hot on her hands. She would hit the cartilage of the esophagus and push through, Nicolas' life gurgling out, his dying breaths causing the blood to bubble. And finally reaching the bone of the spine, where she would have to saw her way through, with both hands pressing down on the knife to separate the head from the body, as the guillotine had done to Antoine.

Then it would be over. He would no longer be able to torment her.

"It tastes good, doesn't it?" Nicolas grated out. "Like a warm slice of just-baked bread, slathered with butter. I understand." He gave a hideous, liquid laugh that flecked his lips and cheeks with spots of blood. "It's the way *I* am."

"No," she said. "I'm not like you at all."

He laughed again. "You are now," he said, and that angered her enough that she started to press harder on the knife as his hands flailed helplessly on the stones. Blood began to flow.

"No!" she shouted at his contorted face. "I'm not like you! I'm saving the world from you, from all the rest that you'll end up killing."

"Phah!" he spat. His ruined voice was nearly inaudible. "At least have the courage not to lie to yourself. You're doing this for yourself."

"Hey! What's going on here?" The shout, from the end of the alleyway, brought Gabriele's head up. A trio of men stood there, outlined against the light of the gas lamp across the street. They were pointing toward her, and already one of the men was stepping fully into the alley.

"Help me!" Nicolas' shout was more a harsh whisper, but it carried. "Murder!"

All three began to move. Gabriele pressed down hard on the butcher knife, but she couldn't cut all the way through his neck. She dropped the knife and reached for her handbag, bringing out the revolver. "Stay back!" she told the men. Drunkenly, they stumbled to a halt; one retreated entirely, shouting for help. Gabriele placed the gun directly over Nicolas' heart. His eyes were open, staring at her above the new red mouth that was his ruined throat. "Remember the pain," she told him, "and leave me alone from now on."

She pulled the trigger, the report muffled against Nicolas's suit jacket. His body jerked and went still; his eyes closed again. She could hear a gendarme's whistle tearing at the night, and the sound of running feet. The two remaining men shrunk back in alarm as she brandished the smoking barrel toward them. "Get back, or I shoot!" she shouted at them, and they retreated hastily.

Then, turning, she gathered her bloody skirts and fled to the far end of the alley, where it emptied out onto the next avenue.

Back in her rooms, she found herself shaking as she cleaned herself of Nicolas' blood. A quick charm had masked the blood from the gaze of the casual passers-by as she'd made her way home, but the spell had failed as she'd neared her apartment, and she'd been lucky that no one had seen her as she'd run the last few blocks. Verdette watched from a perch on the sink, then padded over to her and jumped into her lap when she finally sat, exhausted and still trembling with emotion, on the couch. She stroked the cat, talking to her as if she could understand. "It was so much harder than I thought it would be. To kill someone—even Nicolas—when he's looking at you, face-to-face . . ." She shuddered, remembering, and choked back a sob. "I had him, Verdette. It was over, and I . . . I waited too long. I failed. I had the opportunity and I couldn't just *do* it. I failed."

She pressed down too hard on Verdette's back as she stroked, and Verdette mewled in protest, rising and settling again. "I'm sorry," she told Verdette, told the air. "I'm sorry."

She fell asleep there, finally, with Verdette still on her lap.

The next morning, she went to Gustav's studio. He was already there, working with his assistants on preparing a canvas, and when he turned to greet her, she knew that she was already too late. The certainty was there in the smoothness of his skin, in the way his hair had darkened and regained the shore of forehead it had abandoned. "Gustav . . . What have you done to yourself?"

"Done?" he answered. "Herr Snra said you would know immediately. Last night over dinner, he told me how you were actually much older than you appear to be, and that you were once lovers, years ago. He said it would be a gift from him to you to have me take the same elixir, rare as it is. I must admit that I feel twenty years old again. I feel utterly marvelous. Oh, he also said to tell you that he wouldn't be stopping by today; he had another appointment he'd forgotten."

So he's gone . . . "Gustav, why would you take such a thing from a man you barely know?"

His eyebrows crinkled quizzically and his head cocked slightly. "Ordinarily, I wouldn't. But he seemed genuine enough, and it was obvious he knew you, and we were drinking, so I wasn't exactly as cautious as I might have been . . . Gabriele, why are you crying? I would have thought you'd be happy for me."

I should have killed him. I should have done the deed, but it was already too late for Gustav . . . She sniffed and blotted her eyes with the sleeve of her coat. Her handbag was heavy on her arm, the weight of the revolver an accusation. "I'm glad you feel so well, Gustav. The elixir . . . I should thank Herr Srna personally. Do you know where he's staying? I want to meet him again."

He was staring at her strangely, but he shrugged. He obviously hadn't heard of the attempted murder of Srna the night before, though she was sure that he would, soon enough. "*Ja*, I have his card. Let me see . . ." Gustav went to the desk in the corner of the studio. "Here it is," he said, handing the linen rectangle to Gabriele. "You'll pose for me? I feel such energy to work today."

"Later this afternoon," she told him. "I really must see Herr Srna now, before he leaves."

Gustav's eyebrows rose, but he only shrugged under his painting smock. "Then tell him that I wish to buy more of his gold foil at the price he suggested. I'll send one of my assistants to him tomorrow with a note from my bank. Will you tell him that?"

She nodded. "I'll tell him," she said.

"And you'll come back then and pose for me."

"*Ja*, Gustav. I will." She stretched out her hand and touched Gustav's cheek. His skin felt impossibly smooth. Youthful. But he wouldn't stay that way. Not for long.

And it was her fault, and she was the only one who could do anything about it.

The address Gustav had given her was for rented rooms in a building outside the Ringstrasse, a neighborhood that had once been rich but was now slowly declining. The building had originally been a single residence but had more recently been converted into spacious flats. Gabriele checked the gun in her handbag as well as the vials nestled in cotton wool there.

The concierge at the door was an old man who looked as if he'd been at his post for decades. A bronze tag on his uniform proclaimed that he was Franz. The wrinkled landscape of his face creased into sorrowful folds when she told him that she was here to see Herr Srna.

"That poor man," Franz said. "He was nearly murdered last night."

"Truly?" Gabriele tried to look appropriately concerned. "So he's in hospital? Do you know which one?"

"Oh no, Fräulein, he's not in hospital, though he probably should be. It was terrible. When they brought him here, his clothing was soaked in blood and he looked near death. He couldn't walk or talk; they'd had to hire men with a stretcher. He had insisted that the gendarmes bring him here. They woke me up, and my wife and I helped Herr Srna up to his rooms with the gendarmes and the stretcher men. I thought we would be calling for an undertaker within the hour at first. But my wife, she spent most of the night tending to his wounds and bandaging him—he had terrible wounds on his neck. She tried to convince him to call for a doctor, but he wouldn't let her. He sent her away after she bound up and cleaned his wounds. She's asleep now, poor dear."

He sighed dramatically. Gabriele had the feeling that Franz would talk for hours if she allowed him.

"If I might go see him since we're old friends . . ." she began, but Franz shook his head dolefully.

"Why, just a few hours ago, Herr Srna left us. He said he had to leave Vienna suddenly on urgent business—and I must say that thanks to my wife's ministrations, he already looked far better than he had last night, though he was still so weak that he could barely walk with his cane. I had to help him into the carriage, and I could see that he was still in great pain, and his face was nearly as white as my shirt. A hired carriage came and took him away with a few trunks of clothing and possessions; I heard him tell the driver to take him to the train station. He said I'm to sell the furniture he bought, and that my wife and I could keep any pieces that we fancied, in gratitude for our services." He shook his head sadly. "I'll miss him. He was a good man, and so talented—did you know he's a photographer? I can only hope he survives."

"I don't think you need to worry about that," Gabriele said, rather more sharply than she intended, and the concierge glanced at her strangely.

"Forgive my asking, Fräulein, but your name . . . ?"

"I'm Gabriele Tietze," she told him: it didn't matter anymore. *I won't have that name for very much longer.*

"Ah!" Franz exclaimed. His face brightened. "In that case, I have something for you. Herr Srna gave me this as he left." He reached inside his jacket and produced an envelope of thick ivory paper, holding it out to her. "He said you'd be here sometime today."

Gabriele took the envelope. Her name—her current name—had been written on it in a shaking, uncertain hand. "Thank you," she told Franz. She found a krone in her coin purse and gave it to him. "For your trouble."

Franz gave her a stiff Austrian bow. "My pleasure, Fräulein."

Gabriele took the envelope and walked across the avenue to a small park. She sat on a bench there, turning the envelope in her hands for several minutes before opening it. Inside was a folded piece of paper, written in French in the same shaking hand. She read the words there.

Perenelle—

> *I realize that except for an accident of fate, last night would have been my last. You had me, and I should be finally dead. The realization has changed me. As I lay in the alley with that knife against my throat, as I waited for your final thrust and the black oblivion that was to follow, I found myself a changed man.*
>
> *Your Gustav is already dead. By now, I expect you know that. He has at best a few years left to him before the flawed elixir takes him. That will have to be my small vengeance, accomplished before I made this decision. I won't insult you by saying that I'm sorry. I'm not. I've not changed that much.*
>
> *But you have. As I told you there in that bloody alleyway, I saw myself in your eyes. I hope you can live with that, Perenelle. I hope it causes you pain.*
>
> *However, I do believe that it's time for us to call a truce in our*

long war. I will bow to you and acknowledge that you've won our final battle. You'll be pleased, I suspect, to know that I have never before endured such pain as I am currently experiencing. I'm leaving Vienna in order to recover privately, and I'm also leaving behind Anton Srna, so you needn't bother trying to find me that way.

In fact, I urge you to not try to find me again at all, and I tell you in turn that I won't seek you out again, Perenelle. I leave you to your addiction, if you'll leave me to mine. Forget me, and I will endeavor to forget you.

After all, we should each have a long time in which to forget.

It was signed, simply, "Nicolas."

She sat on the bench for some time, reading the letter again and yet again, trying to find in its words some solace, some sense of triumph, some satisfaction. "I am not like you," she whispered to the thin, erratic writing on the page. "I am *not* like you." But there was no answer.

She folded the letter and placed it back in the envelope, then put it in her handbag to nestle next to the revolver there. "I don't believe you," she said to the air, as if he were still there to hear her. "I want to, but I don't believe you. You've lied to me too many times."

She glanced around the park, at the pigeons feeding there, at the couples strolling through the grounds, at the buildings of Vienna around them.

She knew what she had to do.

"Forgive me, Emilie," she said. "I don't mean to intrude, but I need to talk with you. It concerns Gustav."

Emilie opened the door to the rooms she shared with her sisters with a quizzical look on her face. She led Gabriele to a sitting room just off the entrance. The apartments were hardly lavish, set above the dressmaking school and store that the sisters operated. "May I get you some refreshment?" Emilie asked, though it was obvious that she was surprised at Gabriele's attire, so obviously dressed for traveling. Gabriele shook her head, remaining standing even as Emilie sat in one of the embroidered chairs.

"I can't stay," Gabriele told her. "I came to tell you that I'm leaving Vienna."

"Oh?" Emilie said in genuine surprise. "Gustav must have been upset to hear that; he won't want his favorite model to abandon him."

"Gustav doesn't know yet," Gabriele said. "I haven't told him. In truth, I *won't* be telling him. You will—because you need to be his muse now."

She'd felt she had little choice. She didn't believe Nicolas, didn't believe what he'd said in his letter even while she'd hoped it was true. It would be too easy for him to simply take another identity, now that he knew where she was, and wait for the right moment to attack her as she'd attacked him, springing out when she was vulnerable. The letter might have been sincere—she still *hoped* it had been sincere—but it might as easily been a tactic to put her off her guard and make her stop hunting him while he searched for her.

No, the only way to be safe was to leave Vienna, change identities herself, and wait. He would no more be able to ignore his compulsion than she was. She could wait and see where he was likely to be—following the spoor of violence, torment, and death—and reset the trap for him.

If he had told the truth, the trap would never be sprung. If he had lied, then she would be prepared.

She saw relief struggling with Emilie's surprise at Gabriele's announcement; the young woman's hands fisted in her dress, gathering the fine cloth. She seemed to want to rise from her chair. "Here," Gabriele said. "I have something for you."

From her purse, she gave Emilie a small vial of thick, blue liquid in a stoppered cut glass vial. "What is this?" Emilie asked as she took it. The liquid moved sluggishly behind the facets. She didn't know if her elixir would help Gustav or not, didn't know if it would give him immortality, or increase the length of his life from Nicolas' flawed potion, or do nothing at all. But she owed him that chance, as she had owed it to Catherine Blake. She suspected that Catherine had taken the potion: *her* potion, the right one. At the very least, Catherine had lived longer than the few years that Nicolas expected of those he'd given the flawed elixir; she had survived William, who had died in 1827, some thirteen years after Nicolas had given her the potion. Supposedly she had died herself in 1831, but Gabriele hadn't been there and she often wondered whether Catherine had—as she herself had several times—arranged for a false death and burial as she took on another identity. Catherine might be even now somewhere in the world, living another life, with her own obsession, whatever that might have been . . .

It was a chance she would take with Gustav as well, if for no other reason than the guilt she felt. She'd thought of telling Emilie to take the potion herself as well, but she couldn't do that, not knowing what changes and what personality alterations it might wreak on her. Nicolas wouldn't hesitate, but she couldn't play with her life that way. "Gustav's been given a potion by Herr Srna," Gabriele told her. "But I know that Herr Srna's potion is incomplete. Gustav must take this one as well or there will be dire consequences for him. I need you to give it to him."

"A 'potion'? A potion that does what?"

"Gustav will tell you—in fact, you'll witness its effects when you next see him. Give this to him. Please . . . please tell him I'm sorry, but I can't stay." Gabriele smiled down at Emilie. "As I've told you, he's always been yours, not mine. Now that will truly be the case. Be good to him."

Emilie nodded, staring at Gabriele, who took a long breath. "I'll miss Vienna," Gabriele said to her after a pause. "I feel like the world is about to change, here."

"Where will you go?" Emilie asked.

"Paris, first," Gabriele told her. "Then . . ." She shrugged. "Perhaps it's time to see an entirely new world for a time. I don't know. I'll go where I'm needed." She smiled again at Emilie.

"And you," she told her, "are needed here."

8:
URANIA

Camille Kenny

Today

THE NEXT MORNING, before she went back to David's, she went to Morris' studio, knowing that finding Nicolas first was vital. She had to remain the hunter.

"Have you heard from Pierce yet?"

Morris whipped his head around at Camille's question. Hip-hop music swirled around him, and, almost savagely, he punched a finger at the iPad attached to the stereo. The music died in mid-sentence, a late slapback reverberating from the far wall. She could smell the sharp scent of melted rubber, and noticed that Morris had sectioned his original clay sculpture into four pieces and was applying rubber to the clay to make a mold. One of the four sections had already been coated, then surrounded with plaster—the next step in the bronze "lost wax" process. From here, she knew, Morris would take the pieces to the foundry, where the pieces would be recast in wax in preparation for the bronze pour.

The energy of his green heart glowed around him, but it darkened and changed color as soon as he saw her, going to smoke and ash. And there was something more—something else different in the energy radiating from Morris that she couldn't identify. He didn't *feel* the same. Camille puzzled over that as Morris dropped the thickly coated brush into the pot of melted rubber on its burner. "Camille," he said. "I'm surprised to see you here."

"Why?" she asked. "I don't have a grudge against you, Morris. I told you—I'd like to remain friends."

"Sure, we can do that, at least for as long as you're getting what you want out of it. That's how it is for you, isn't it, Camille?" He said it with a certainty and viciousness that puzzled her.

"That's not fair, Morris."

"Maybe not, but I really can't discuss it right now. It's not a good time for me. I'm kinda busy." He gestured at the sculpture.

"I can see that. I won't stay. I just came by to see if you'd heard from Pierce, if you knew how I can contact him."

On the way into the building, Camille had seen Palento's partner parked across the street, though she hadn't seen Palento herself. She'd waved at the man, who had a long-snouted camera up to his face. She wondered how many pictures of her they had, and whether Nicolas was on one of them.

Morris sniffed. He dragged a hand over his forehead. "Yeah, I've talked to him. He stopped by yesterday, in fact, and I told him how you wanted to meet with him. He thought that was rather humorous, and he told me a hilarious tale about you, as well."

"Oh?" Camille felt the self-inflicted knife wound in her abdomen pull as she straightened—it hadn't healed anywhere near as fast as it could have; it was still seeping blood and she'd had to bandage it. *You'll be with David again in an hour. Maybe less. That will give you the energy to heal.* She hoped that was right, but after her revelation the night before, after the strange way he'd sounded when they'd left, maybe she'd lost . . . No, she wouldn't think that. She wouldn't let herself.

Morris was staring at her. His face was like a dead thing, as cold and rigid as one of his sculptures, and there was that strange, almost rusty hue to his soul-heart. She looked more closely at him: Morris was in his early thirties, and before she'd noted the beginning of wrinkles around his eyes and a few speckles of gray starting in his wiry hair. But now the wrinkles were smoothed away and his hair was unrelieved, lustrous black.

Camille found herself taking in a breath that made her wound ache, afraid that she knew what else had happened when Nicolas visited Morris yesterday.

"Yeah," Morris was continuing as she stared at his face, at his muscular hands, "he tells me that he's known you a *long* time, that you seem to think you're some kind of artistic muse, God's own gift to creative types, and that you get off being around people like me—that's your kink. You like to fuck 'em, too, if they'll have your skanky ass. And when you find someone that you think has more talent, you're off to be with them and you don't give a damn what kind of wreckage or pain you leave behind. That sounds like a goddamn familiar pattern to me."

The unbridled anger in his voice and expression wasn't like the Morris that she knew. Morris could be prickly and too concerned with his own place in the universe, but *this* Morris had those qualities on another, more alarming, level, and she was afraid that she also knew the cause of that.

Nicolas, what have you done?

Camille felt her face reddening as Morris spoke, angry at Nicolas for having told Morris about her, embarrassed at the way in which Morris threw it back at her, but most of all growing more frightened at the implication that Nicolas would have given Morris the flawed elixir. She imagined Morris, curled on the floor in agony as the elixir burned away at his mind and body, decades passing for him in a few minutes, dying horribly—and Nicolas there to feed on his agony.

"Pierce said that's why you tossed us all off after you found David," Morris rattled on. "The bunch of us together at the *Bent Calliope* weren't fucking *talented* enough for you, but David was, all by himself. More talented than all of us put together. He could satisfy you when none of us alone could."

"Morris—"

"Tell me it's not the truth," he spat out. "Look at me and tell me that."

She returned his stare as steadily as she could, one hand over the healing wound under the T-shirt. "Where can I find Pierce?" she asked.

"So you're not going to answer?" Camille waited, and finally Morris shrugged. "Well, Pierce said to tell you that he'd find *you*. It'll be very soon, too—he added that especially. And he also said to tell you that this time it'll be final. He said you'd know what he meant by that." Morris took a step toward her, and she retreated the same amount. She felt the heft of metal in her handbag; it gave her little comfort.

"Morris, did Nicolas give you something? A blue liquid?"

Morris grinned at that. "What's the matter, Camille? Jealous? Worried that you're going to have me to deal with forever? Well, you won't. Nicolas will take care of that."

Yes, Nicolas gave him the potion, and Morris doesn't understand how . . . Camille's shoulders sagged. "Oh, Morris . . ."

" 'Oh, Morris'," he repeated, mocking her voice and tone, the ridicule nearly as painful as a knife stabbing into her belly. "You're a bitch, Camille. You know that?" He was walking toward her as he spoke, and she continued to retreat. "You're a bitch and a slut who'll spread her legs for anyone who asks, and David can fucking have you. You're nothing. Worthless."

He advanced toward her, and she retreated again. Her back found the wall near the door, and he took another step in her direction. She could see spittle fly from his lips as he cursed at her. "Bitch!" She wondered whether she could shoot him if he tried to hurt her, though she knew that it wouldn't kill him—no, she could taste the elixir in his radiance. Still, the sight of the pistol might be enough; he wouldn't be certain yet of his immortality, though she would have bet that Nicolas had "shown" Morris how he could recover: he'd have done that just for the pleasure of Morris' pain. She started to reach for her handbag.

"You're a stupid cunt, and you have no fucking *idea* just how goddamn talented I am." Morris pounded his chest with a fist. He was inches away from her, glaring down at her, his hand still fisted and too near her face. Her hand touched the polished wood handle of the Ladysmith as he swung his arm; she felt the breeze of its passage a scant hair's breadth from her nose. "Get the fuck out of here!" he shouted at her. "Go on, before I decide to do Pierce's job for him."

She left, squeezing against the wall as he continued to stare at her, her hand now curled around the gun though she hadn't pulled it from her purse and the safety was still on.

She found the door and fled.

She'd stopped back at the apartment to pick up Verdette and her clothes before going over to David's apartment, but found herself pacing the floor there after the confrontation with Morris. Verdette watched from her perch on the coffee table, the cat's gray head moving back and forth as Camille stalked past her. Nicolas' cameo swung on its chain with each step, pounding against her chest like a slow hammer.

She couldn't sit still.

It had all gone wrong, so quickly and so badly. Nicolas had vanished; he could be anywhere in the city now, under any name he'd managed to prepare beforehand. Now Nicolas had turned Morris, giving him the elixir that would kill him before his time—unless she gave him her own elixir, if she could even convince him to take it, considering his attitude toward her.

The wound on her stomach pulled underneath the bandages as she walked. *You're letting him win.* The accusation burned in her gut, underneath the new scar from the knife.

"What am I going to do?" she asked Verdette, who stared back at her. "How can I fight him if I can't *find* him?" *I should leave here.* The thought came again, as it had in Paris. *I could lose myself as I have in the past—once I'm gone, once Nicolas knows that I'm no longer attached to him, David will be safe. I can start over again. I can track Nicolas down once more, and maybe this time . . .*

It was only a self-soothing rationalization, and she knew it even as she tried to convince herself. David wasn't safe, nor was Mercedes or any of the others; none of them were safe while Nicolas was still in New York. Nicolas could—would—torment them for the sheer pleasure it would give him. Verdette meowed plaintively, and Camille stopped to scratch her neck. Verdette pressed her head hard into Camille's fingers.

"I know," Camille said. "I shouldn't stay here. After what he's done to Morris . . ." She stopped, suddenly afraid. Who else in the *Bent Calliope* Group might Nicolas have contacted? Who else might he have told; to who else might have he slipped the elixir with his sweet-tasting lies and frosted promises?

Verdette bumped her hand again and Camille started from her reverie guiltily. "I'm an idiot," she said aloud, looking at Verdette, who gazed back placidly. "This is how Nicolas wants me to feel, wants me to react. He's counting on me giving up and running, to put things off until another time. Well, that's not going to happen. One way or another, it ends here."

She grabbed her purse from the corner of the couch where she'd tossed it; the Ladysmith was heavy in the bottom, but her Tarot, her chemicals, and her katana were at David's place, not here—and she needed to check on him anyway after their quarrel the night before, needed to make sure the two of them were still good, needed his energy so she wouldn't fall into illness and lethargy herself.

"Let's go," she told Verdette. "I have a lot I need to do."

"David?" she called as she turned the key and opened the door, but there was no answer. She half-dropped the basket of clothing on the couch so she didn't have to bend down with the wound; she put Verdette's carrier on the end table and opened the wire door to it. Verdette padded out, mewling querulously.

"David?"

Camille walked through the apartment, Verdette following her. David wasn't downstairs; he wasn't in his studio. Sudden worry grabbed her stomach, as painful as the plunge of a knife. Panicked, she spoke a quick charm, but there was no sense that Nicolas had been here, which meant—hopefully—that David had gone off on his own.

"Fuck," she grunted. "Where the hell *is* he . . . ?" She wanted to believe that he'd just taken a walk or maybe had a meeting with Prudhomme, but she couldn't keep the worst scenario from invading her mind: images of Nicolas with David, of Nicolas forcing David to take the flawed elixir then torturing him, knowing that David's body would heal quickly and allow Nicolas to torment David again and again and again . . .

She called his cell: no answer; that only increased her paranoia. She left a message: "David, please call me. I want—no, hell, I really, really *need*—to talk to you. Please. Call." She texted his cell as well, with the same basic message.

She called Jacob Prudhomme's office and talked to the secretary there: no, David wasn't with there and Jacob didn't have any pending appointments with him on the calendar. Jacob was out on a client lunch, but she'd have him call Camille when he returned.

She called Mercedes next. "Hey, Camille," Mercedes said. Her voice was cool and removed. "What's up?"

"Mercedes," she said, trying to keep the desperation and fright from her voice, "you haven't seen David, have you?"

"David? No. Why would I? What's the matter?"

"I'm not sure." She needed to find David, but she also needed a soul-heart. She could feel the weariness in her body, a physical listlessness that threatened to overwhelm her. "Listen, can I come over?"

The hesitation said more than any words. She heard Mercedes take a breath, then another heavier one. "Sure," she said. "You hungry?"

"Right now, I don't think I could eat."

"I am. I'll call for pizza. See you in twenty?"

"Sure," Camille answered, the banality of the conversation scraping against the urgency in her head.

"*Ningún problema*," Mercedes said. "Veggie all right?"

"That'll be fine. See you in a few."

She checked her cell again after she ended the call, though she hadn't heard it indicate there'd been another call while she was talking with Mercedes. No voicemail. No return text.

"Watch the place," she told Verdette. "I'll be back as soon as I can."

*   *   *

Mercedes met her at the door with a plate holding a pizza slice and a look on her face that Camille couldn't quite decipher. The woman's soul-heart was wrapped tightly inside herself, not allowing Camille to fully touch it. Camille was reluctant to try to breach that reserve, as much as she wanted to for the solace it would give her, uncertain of what Mercedes' reaction might be. At least Mercedes' green heart tasted no different—there was no hint of Nicolas' elixir.

"Well, you look like hell," Mercedes said, handing Camille the plate as she held the door open for her. Camille took it, but set it down again almost immediately on the end table of the couch.

"I can't stay. I have to find David. But I had to . . . needed to . . ." She stopped. The wound in her abdomen burned under the bandages. Mercedes looked as if she wanted to come to Camille, to fold her in her arms and hug her, but she didn't. She seemed closed and almost angry.

Mercedes' apartment was small; her desk sat in one corner of the living room. The pizza box gaped open on the couch; a paper plate and two frowning crusts sat on the corner of the desk. Mercedes locked the door behind Camille and sat at her desk, swiveling around to face Camille. The light of her computer monitor lent her hair an angelic nimbus, and Camille could see Mercedes' novel open on the screen. "How's it going?" she asked. The question seemed silly and irrelevant amidst the roaring in her head.

Mercedes glanced back over her shoulder and shrugged. "Not bad for someone with only a mediocre talent, I suppose," she said. "Not enough talent to satisfy you all by myself."

The words chilled the air. Camille blinked, feeling the sting. That explained the closing of her soul-heart.

Her wound should have healed far more than it had; it *would* have done so had she been with David. Even as Mercedes' comment made her hear Nicolas' voice in hers, a lethargy also swaddled her, a weariness that made her want to do little more than sleep and conserve what little energy remained to her. But Mercedes' gaze was searing, and her accusation cut deeper than the knife wound.

"Oh," Camille said. "You've talked with Morris, then."

Mercedes didn't answer. Not directly. "Is it true?"

"Is what true?"

"What this Pierce guy is saying about you."

"Not the way he told Morris it was."

"Then *how* is it, Camille? You tell me. Make me understand, be-cause what Morris said and what he hinted at . . ." Her lips clamped shut. Her dark eyes smoldered.

"I don't know that I can. I don't know that if I told you that you'd even believe me, or if you'd just think I was crazy. And I don't know if I have *time*. I really need to find David."

The screen saver on her computer kicked on. Behind Mercedes, a swirling light like the borealis swept across her screen: green, but not the same hue as the heart within her. "Try me," Mercedes said. "I might believe you more than you think. Have you *seen* Morris in the last few days, how he looks? Or Kevin and Rashawn, for that matter? I might just believe you, no matter what you tell me."

"Oh, God—Kevin and Rashawn, too?" Camille felt as if an immense weight were pressing down on her chest, making it hard to breathe. "Did Pierce . . . ?"

"*Sí*, Pierce," Mercedes said. "He called me, too, but I blew him off, told him I had to think about things. So—tell me, Camille. *Dígame la verdad*. Tell me the truth, or I'll go to him and let *him* give me the story, however he wants to tell it."

"It's a long story, and it didn't go so well the last time I told it."

"I've got all day, and you don't look like you've got the energy to go looking for David anytime soon."

It was strange: all these centuries, and for the first time, she felt trapped by circumstances, felt that she *had* to tell the truth where lies had always sufficed before. *If you run* . . . the voice inside nagged at her, and she nodded. Yes, if she ran, she could say nothing. If she ran, she could keep all the lies. But if she ran, she would lose everything she had here. "All right," Camille said. "I'll tell you . . ."

Camille watched Mercedes' face carefully as she spoke, trying to gauge what the woman might be thinking. She saw the flush of disbelief when she started, telling Mercedes that she'd been born in the 14th century, and relating the beginning of Nicolas and Perenelle's story. She gave her an abbreviated account of her journey, of the long war between her and Nicolas. She saw Mercedes wince as she tried to explain why the group that had coalesced around the *Bent Calliope* was important to her, and what she'd felt when she'd met David.

"You have to understand, Mercedes," she said, desperately. "What I feel in the soul-hearts . . . it doesn't mean anything about how well you'll succeed or what you'll be able to do, or whether people will love your work or not. I've seen people with huge potential who were never known or never became famous at all despite producing incredible work, and people with what I thought were small hearts who became famous and successful in their time. What I can do—well, it has little to do with fame or money."

"Now you're trying to placate me," Mercedes said. "You know what, that sucks. Just say it. What you're really trying to tell me is that you don't think I have enough talent for you." She glanced back at the computer again. Camille saw Mercedes bite her lower lip and squeeze her eyes shut once before turning back to her. "So that's what Pierce, or Nicolas or whoever the hell he is, offered to Morris and the others: the elixir. The chance to be like you."

Camille shook her head. "No. I'm sure that's what he told them, but it's a lie, and it's vital that you understand that. The elixir will do nothing but shorten their lives and result in them dying in agony. Please, you have to believe this, Mercedes. If Nicolas offers you the elixir, you have to refuse it. For your own sake. For mine. He wants your pain and your death—that's what *he* feeds on."

"I think you should leave, Camille. Please."

"Mercedes, don't do this. I don't want to hurt you. I never, ever wanted to hurt you. You especially. You're my friend, my lover, someone I care deeply about. Of all of the *Bent Calliope* Group, you . . ." She stepped toward Mercedes, arms open, and the woman backed away.

"Stop it," Mercedes barked. Her eyes narrowed, glaring. "Just . . . Stop it."

"All right," Camille said. "I'll go. Mercedes, I hope . . ." Her voice caught in a sob. "I hope you can forgive me. You mean so much to . . ." She couldn't go on. She sniffed hard, trying to force back the tears, but she couldn't. With Morris, she'd simply been furious and frightened; with Mercedes, she felt as if she'd been ripped open as surely as with the knife. She hugged herself, her hands folded under her breasts. Mercedes wouldn't look at her, staring instead somewhere past her.

Camille went to the door. She picked up her handbag from the table, feeling its weight as she slung the strap over her shoulder. "Camille," Mercedes said behind her, and Camille turned, hoping to hear her ask her to come back, to try to mend the rift between them.

"I don't think you should come back to the *Bent Calliope* again," Mercedes' clear voice said. "You won't be welcome there anymore."

Camille nodded. "Mercedes, I'm telling you: if Nicolas comes to you, don't listen to him. He'll lie. He'll say anything he thinks you want to hear, but it's all to hurt you. To hurt me through your pain. Please believe me. I've told you only the truth."

Mercedes didn't answer. She swiveled her chair around to face the computer once more and moved the mouse. The screen saver vanished. The words of her novel burned on the screen.

The buzzer woke Camille from a troubled, restless nap on the couch in David's apartment. She'd spent the day well into the evening searching for David: calling on acquaintances; going into shops he tended to frequent; checking her own apartment, just in case he'd gone there; aimlessly walking around the East Side near their apartments until her feet and leg muscles ached.

The buzzer sounded again before she fully awakened. Verdette growled angrily and jumped from Camille's chest, where she'd been sleeping. Camille felt a sudden thrill of adrenaline—*David?*—but she couldn't feel his soul-heart, and she was certain that even from the distance to the front door of the building she'd be able to feel him, though there was a green heart there, fainter and less defined than David's. Rubbing her eyes, she staggered to the door and the panel set there, leaning heavily against the wall as she pushed the button.

"Yes?"

"Ms. Kenny, this is Detective Palento. Do you have a moment to talk?"

Camille thought of saying no, but that would only lead to more conversation. She touched the pendant under her sweatshirt from long habit, then, without answering, she pressed the buzzer to open the front door. She turned, still leaning against the wall, and surveyed the apartment with bleary eyes: she hadn't cleaned since the conversation with David. Her clothes were strewn about; dirty dishes from a hasty dinner sat on the coffee table in front of the couch. She caught a glimpse of herself in the mirror on the opposite wall: dressed in rumpled sweats and socks, her hair a sleep-mussed horror. She ran her fingers through her hair, trying to make it halfway presentable as she heard footsteps in the hallway, then a knock on the door. She unlatched the chain as Verdette hissed and fled into the kitchen, and opened the door. Gina Palento stood outside, dressed impeccably as usual; behind her lurked her partner, dressed in a well-used dark suit; older than Palento by a good decade or more, Camille guessed, his face lined and somewhat sallow, his dark hair retreating from his forehead, though thin strands of it still clung to his scalp.

"Ms. Kenny," Palento said. If Camille's appearance startled her at all, it didn't show on her face, which remained noncommittal and serious. "You remember my partner, Roger Compton?"

Camille nodded. "I've seen him around. Come in—sorry, the place is a wreck. I was just . . . napping."

"Don't worry about it," Palento said as she passed Camille, who could see her gaze traveling quickly around the room. "This looks like *Good Housekeeping* compared to some of the places we normally see. Right, Roger?"

"Yep," Compton agreed. "Seen lots worse." Camille caught a whiff

of stale cigarettes and coffee as he entered. She shut the door behind
the duo, running her fingers through her hair again.

"I'm going to make some coffee," she said. "Would either of you like
a cup?"

They shook their heads in unison. Neither of them was looking at
her, but rather at the apartment. Camille was aware of the Tarot deck
laid out on the small table in the kitchen area, visible from the front
room, and of the shelves of labeled chemicals behind the table, of her
half-finished paintings stacked against the wall leading to the upstairs
studio, of her purse sitting on the couch with the Ladysmith revolver
inside.

"Sit wherever you like," she told them. "Just move stuff aside." She
went into the kitchen, half-surprised when neither of them stopped her.
She grabbed a coffee filter from the cabinet over the sink and spooned
coffee into it, then rinsed the carafe, filled it with water, and poured it
into the coffeemaker. She pressed the button, listening to the gurgling
and hissing as it dripped water onto the grounds. She grabbed a mug
from the shelf and held it, staring at the coffee rising slowly in the carafe. Her hands were trembling.

"I'm afraid we haven't found Pierce yet," she heard Palento say,
and half-turned to see her at the table, staring down at the Tarot array,
one fingertip extended and nearly touching the cards. Her soul-heart
pulsed and Camille nearly allowed her mind to reach out to caress it.
Almost as if in response to the impulse, Palento turned her head to look
at Camille, her blue eyes more gray in the light in the room. "He seems
to have vanished pretty effectively. You wouldn't know some way we
could get in contact with him? Have you heard from him? You went to
see Morris Johnson today . . ."

"I did," Camille said. "And Pierce had been there a few days before me."

Her eyebrows arched, her forehead wrinkled. "You're sure about
that?"

"That's what Morris told me. You guys missed him." Camille could
have told her why, as well—remembering Paris and London: *because he*

can change his face for a short time if he needs to. He knew you'd be watching the studio.

"That's not possible," Palento said, then scowled. "Okay, it's *possible*, but we've had Johnson's studio under surveillance since we knew that Pierce was giving him money for a sculpture. You're sure?"

Camille nodded. *Yes, and Morris is going to die as a result.* Again, she held the words. The coffeemaker hissed as the last of the water left the pump. Camille poured herself a mug, lifting it toward Palento. "Sure you don't want any?"

The woman shook her head. "What happened there?" She gestured to Camille's midriff. Camille glanced down; her sweater had risen up when she'd reached for the coffee filter, exposing the bloodstained bandage. She pulled the sweater back down.

"An accident," she said. "I caught myself on a piece of jagged metal. It's nothing important."

Palento's gaze held her for a long moment, then she glanced down again at the Tarot, then into the front room where her partner stood holding Camille's purse, looking at the two of them. Some sort of unspoken signal seemed to pass between the two detectives. Palento nodded, but whether to Camille's answer or to her partner, she couldn't tell. "Is Pierce going to try to come at you now?"

Camille took a sip of the coffee. "Yes," she said, tersely. "He is. And after my friends, also."

"Hopefully, we'll get him before that happens. He can't hide forever."

Camille almost laughed at that, the mug shivering in her hands. "If you *do* happen to find him," she said, "you should call me before you try to arrest him."

Palento looked again toward her partner. "Why?" she asked. "So you can use the gun in your purse?—which, by the way, I assume you have a permit for."

"I do," Camille told her. "And no, that's not why. You don't know what Pierce is capable of."

"Why don't you tell us?" That was Compton, coming into the kitchen from the living room. "Or are you figuring on taking care of him yourself? Maybe with the Ladysmith?" He still had Camille's purse in his hand. He dropped it on the table on top of the Tarot cards; it landed hard. Camille winced.

"I have the gun for protection," she told them. "That's all. And it's legal. My carry license is in there with it."

"Uh-huh," Compton said. He went to the shelf of chemicals, staring at the labels. He plucked a jar of comfrey from the shelf, unscrewed the lid, and sniffed at the contents before replacing the lid and putting the jar back on the shelf. His thick fingers prowled the rest of the jars. His eyebrows lifted as he stared at the nearly human form of a mandrake root. "So when we find Pierce, what is it we have to know that's so vitally important?"

Camille only stared at him. She heard Palento sigh. "Roger," Palento said, "why don't you give me a few minutes with Ms. Kenny? Maybe you could call the station and check to see if they have any leads on that 187 we caught last night?"

Compton grunted. "Yeah. Sure. I guess I can do that." He was still glaring at Camille, then finally broke his gaze and trundled out of the kitchen. They heard him on his cell phone in the front room.

"Okay," Palento said. "Camille—can I call you Camille?—look, I just want to help you here. We're on the same side: do I think Pierce killed your boyfriend's wife? Yeah, I suspect he was behind that, even if he didn't do it himself. Do I think he killed Bob Walters? Yeah, I think he's good for that one, too, given the time line of things—and as it turns out, the people at Beth Israel have lots of questions for this guy, too: it seems that too many patients that he had contact with ended up dying when they shouldn't have—and I can see from your face that doesn't surprise you, either. I really *want* this guy, maybe as much or more than you do. Bob was my friend and first partner, after all. But . . ."

Palento smiled at her, and her voice was sympathetic and warm as her soul-heart pulsed. "Camille, I've looked you up in the system, too—and I have the suspicion you wouldn't want me to look any further than I already have. I'm sure Bob checked out your story, too, as he should have to do the best job for you, and I also know from reading his notes that he liked you and trusted you. He redacted most of the stuff he found on you—shredded it, probably. Bob would only do that for someone he thought was a good person at heart, and the man always had great instincts. So I'm not going to go poking around for more, *if* you tell me what the hell's really going on."

Camille wanted to believe the woman, wanted to let the story pour out for the third time in two days, but she could only shake her head. "I can't. It's not . . . believable."

"Why don't you try me." She said it flatly, without the interrogative lift at the end.

Camille ignored that. "Pierce is more dangerous than you think, Detective. If you do come across him, don't even give him a chance to speak—if you do, it'll be too late."

"Because . . . ?" Palento prompted.

"You don't want to hear it. Just remember how Mr. Walters died—do you know of any weapon that could have done that? Don't give Pierce the chance to do the same to you. All he needs are a few words and gestures, and he can burn you the same way he did Mr. Walters."

"Are you suggesting *magic?*" Camille could hear the disbelief in the woman's voice, and she remained silent. Palento glanced at the cards underneath Camille's purse, then at the shelves of chemicals. Camille thought Palento was going to press her further, but the woman didn't. Palento's hand stroked her chin; she adjusted the collar of her blouse. Behind Camille, Verdette hopped up on the counter, nudging Camille's arm.

They all heard the scrape of a key in the apartment door's lock then, and the slide of the deadbolt. Camille grabbed for her purse; Palento slid her service pistol from underneath her blouse, and Compton was already in stance, his gun pointed at the opening door.

The door swung wide, and David was gaping at them, a camera draped on a strap over one shoulder

"David!" Camille dropped the purse on the table again and ran past the two detectives to David, who was raising his hands tentatively. She hugged him hard, relishing the feel of his body and his soul-heart. She wrapped his energy around her, gratefully. "I was so worried about you . . ." She stopped then, and pounded gently on his chest with her fist. "Damn it, where the hell have you been?"

David's arms came around her slowly, then more tightly. She felt his lips touch the crown of her head, kissing her softly, and the aura of his soul-heart brightened, opening to her. She nearly gasped with the feel of it. "I'm sorry, Camille," he said to her. "I was just out walking, and thinking. I'm sorry."

"David?" She lifted her face to his; he bent his head down and kissed her lips.

"I shouldn't have walked away from you like that," he said softly. "I never wanted to hurt you, especially after . . ." She saw him glance at Palento and Compton, both of whom had holstered their weapons. ". . . After you were so honest with me," he finished. He hugged her again, then closed the door, still holding her hand. "Detectives," he said. "Sorry to startle you. Is there something I can do for you?"

"Not right at the moment," Palento said. "Ms. Kenny, thanks for the talk." She pulled her card from her suit jacket and handed it to Camille. "In case you lost the last one," she said. "Call me if you hear from Pierce, or if you have something more to share with us. We want the same thing; we really do. Remember that."

With that, Palento touched her forefinger to her forehead, almost as if she were saluting, then inclined her head to her partner. "Hey, Roger," she said. "Let's get out of this couple's hair. It looks like they have things to discuss."

"What was all that about?" David asked her when the door had closed behind Palento and Compton. Camille had gone to the window, looking down at the street from behind the sheer curtains as the detectives went to their car. Otherwise, no one seemed to be watching: the few pedestrians on the sidewalk walked past without a second glance at the building.

No Nicolas. She turned back to David. "They were letting me know that they haven't found Pierce yet."

David nodded. "You look exhausted," he said. "That's my fault. I'm really sorry. I know you said you were coming here this morning, and I should have waited for you before I took off. But really, I . . . I've just been doing a lot of thinking."

She nodded. "You didn't see Pierce?"

"You mean Nicolas?" He sniffed, as if mocking his own words. "No. I didn't. You?"

She shivered and let the curtains fall back over the window, turning back into the room. "No, but he's been around. David, he's given Morris and some of the others at the *Bent Calliope* the flawed elixir. He contacted Mercedes and tried to do the same with her, but she didn't accept, thankfully. Still, he's been telling them things—about me. Lies. He's turning them all against me."

"You tell the cops this?"

Camille shook her head. "Not all of it. Just that Pierce is still out there and that he's after my friends and me, but the cops can't help. Not with him."

David sniffed. "Yeah. 'Cause he has magic and stuff." A trace of skepticism still colored his voice. She ignored it. "What do we do now, Camille?" he asked.

I have to find him, and I have to kill him before he hurts anyone else I love. She didn't say that. Instead, she smiled wanly. "So, in all that walking and thinking, did you give any more thought to what I told you?"

He gave a short, ironic laugh. "I couldn't exactly think about much else, frankly. And I'm still not sure how to feel about the story you gave me, or how I'm supposed to know what's true and what's not in it. I went to the library and looked up books, got on the computers there and went all over the Internet, looking up those people you said you were and those you said you were with, trying to imagine that it was *you* and not someone else. It's all so . . ." He shook his head. "It's still all so *impossible*. Frankly, it'd be easier to think you're some kind of psycho than to believe you're telling the truth. But then I look at the photos of you on my camera, and I remember what you did with that knife, and how you knew everything about Paris and those people you said you were and were with . . ." Another head shake. "I still don't know."

She went to him and took his hands. She pressed her fingers into his. "I love you," she said. "You can believe whatever you want, David, but that's the final truth."

"You love me, or you *need* me?"

"Both," she answered honestly. "I need you, too—and yes, you know why. I can't say this any more simply or truthfully, David. I need you, because . . . because everything else . . ." She could barely get the words out. She took in a long breath that shuddered audibly. His expression softened, and he leaned toward her until her forehead was against his chest. "*He's* still out there," she continued. "I've placed you in terrible danger, and I'm afraid that I won't be able to protect you. Maybe the best thing I could have done for you would have been to leave you and New York altogether as soon as I knew Nicolas had realized who I was. That might have saved poor Helen. But I couldn't. Maybe that's just me being selfish, but I couldn't." She was crying, uncaring that he could feel her weeping. His arms came around her once more; the radiance of his soul-heart was a cloak over them both. "I love you," she said again.

He didn't answer, not directly. Instead, he asked her, "Were you in love with the others the same way?"

She nodded, sniffing. She pulled back a little from him, wiping at her eyes with her fingertips. "Some of them, yes. Not all."

"If you could had given them the elixir, would you have stayed with them?"

Her shoulders lifted and fell. "I can't answer that for you, David. With some of them, the ones I thought I truly loved, yes, I would have tried. But people—mortal people, normal people—fall in love all the time and promise to stay together 'till death do we part' and often enough that doesn't work out, does it? Sometimes people grow apart, or they find that one or the other's love fails. I've told you this before: forever's a damned long time." She looked at David, at his posture, at the way he gazed at her, at how his hands fisted and unfisted on his thighs. "Is *that* what you want? The elixir—*my* elixir? The real one?"

"No." He said it too quickly, and he looked away from her as he spoke.

"David, I'll give it to you if you ask. I will. Tonight. That's how much I love you. But you have to know it will change you."

"Yeah," he said. "I've met Verdette, remember?" He smiled as if he were saying it as a joke, but it came out too harsh.

"You can make light of it all you want, but it's a serious decision—and one that you can't back out of once you make it. I *will* give it to you, David, both because I do love you and because it would give you some protection from Nicolas. But you'll change as a result and I don't know how. And that . . . that might not be a good thing for you."

She took in a breath as a sudden thought came to her: *You've never tried to feed from someone who's taken the elixir. What if that's not possible? What if you'd then still need to seek out someone else for your own needs? How would that change your relationship?* She shook her head, trying to banish questions for which she had no answer. "All you have to do is ask," she told David again.

"No," he told her again, but this time the refusal came after a silence and was softer, and this time he was looking at her as he said it. "At least, not right now, anyway. And to answer the question you haven't asked me—there is one thing I realized in all that thinking and walking: I love you, too."

She nearly sobbed again at that, her eyes burning with threatening tears. "Then we're good? I can stay here? I need to be with you."

"Yes," he said. "Of course you can stay here."

He came to her, and she saw the tears overflowing his own eyes. She allowed herself, finally, to let her emotions take control. She cried in deep, racking sobs, though she didn't know if it was relief or fear or both that brought the tears. She clung to him, and she let his radiance cover, comfort, and begin to restore her.

"I love you so much," she told him after they made love that night, and he whispered back in her ear the same words as he held her.

"I love you, too."

She smiled, touching his cheek with her hand. The stubble of his beard dragged at her skin. "Stay with me," she told him.

He laughed. "Forever," he said, then seemed to realize what he'd said and just held her more tightly in the velvet darkness. She didn't correct him, only whispered back to him:

"Yes," and again, "yes."

For the next few days, she began to believe that everything could be as she wanted it to be. The reconnection with David was fast and satisfying. Her exhaustion vanished like a morning snow in spring; she felt whole and complete once more, and the knife wound on her stomach healed over completely, though the scar was still visible as an angry red line. David swept Camille up in his photography; he had her pose for him, clothed and unclothed, and put the prints up on the walls so they could critique them together. They made love; they talked. She told him details of her long life that she'd never confided to anyone else; she answered any question he asked—and he had many.

She felt, again, complete. Except for the lingering sense of unease due to Nicolas, they could have been in Paris again: alone together and happy. There were moments, even hours, where she could fool herself and believe that it could stay this way.

But she knew that this was only a respite. The Tarot cards told her; her heart told her. Nicolas was a thunderhead looming on the horizon, crawling toward her on legs of jagged lightning. The storm was inevitable.

She could hear the thunder of the storm in her dreams.

She put a small fire spell on a glass flask of explosive powder and gave it to David, teaching him the single word and gesture that would release the spell. "If you see Nicolas, throw the flask at his feet and say the spell word. The explosion should at least give you time to run; at best, it might incapacitate Nicolas long enough for you to do more."

She'd told him about Antoine and the guillotine, and what that had taught both Nicolas and her. She didn't know if David would actually cut off the man's head if Nicolas were lying unconscious in front of him, but at least he knew.

Camille hunted Nicolas, desperate to find him first. She spread out her cards for some hint of where he might show up next, but the array was cloudy and uncertain, as if something or someone was actively interfering with her reading. She might as well be playing Solitaire with them, for all she learned. Her Ladysmith and vials of chemicals in her handbag, her katana hidden inside a hollowed-out walking staff, she watched Mercedes' apartment, studying each person who entered the building: Nicolas could put another face on his own, but he couldn't change his height or general build. She spent time outside the apartments of the rest of the *Bent Calliope* Group, hoping that she might be lucky enough to see Nicolas. She called Palento every day, asking if they'd found Pierce yet; the answer was always the same: we'll let you know when that happens.

She saw no sign that Nicolas was watching her, though she often found herself peering out the window. She made excuses so that David wouldn't go out alone without her, and though he knew that the Ladysmith was snuggled in her handbag every time they left the apartment, he made no objection.

She called Mercedes, who didn't answer her phone. "Mercedes," she said after the beep. "I want to apologize. I don't want to lose you as a friend. Please call me back. I'm so sorry. And please, remember what I said about Pierce . . ."

She didn't hear from her. She didn't bother to call any of the other *Bent Calliope* regulars.

On the third day, she went back to the apartment to get more of her things. She stopped at Mrs. Darcy's apartment and told her that she was moving in with David for the time being, and that if she knew of someone who might want to sublet the apartment for a few months, to put them in touch with her. Camille took her time as she packed the essentials from her apartment, wondering whether she should put additional alchemical materials into the boxes she'd stored in her closet and bring them over as well, or if some of her older paintings should go with her too. If she did that, she'd need to call for a cab.

In the end, she packed up most of the things but left them there, taking only a small suitcase of clothing. She walked the several blocks to David's apartment. The day was warm and she walked slowly down Delancey, glancing back over her shoulder now and again, and watching the other side of the street as well.

Holding the suitcase she'd brought, she buzzed the apartment rather than trying to excavate her keys from her purse. She waited; David didn't respond. She buzzed the apartment again; once more, there was no response. He'd said something about working, so Camille figured he was in the studio loft and couldn't hear the buzzer. Grimacing, she set down the suitcase and fished out her keys.

The key ring jangling in her hand, she walked down the hallway—if David was engrossed, he wasn't going to hear her knock, either. But as she came closer, she slowed: if he was working, she should *feel* him, and there was nothing. No stirring of the green heart, no warm, grassy tendrils spilling from the apartment. A few more steps, and she saw the door of the apartment: it was slightly ajar.

Camille set down the suitcase again. She reached into her handbag for the Ladysmith. Her pulse pounded so loudly in her ears that she was certain anyone inside the apartment could hear it. Shielding herself on the wall, she pushed the door open with a foot. She waited, but there was no response and she heard nothing at all from within the apartment.

Taking a long breath, she slid inside. The large main room looked much the same as when she'd left. A coffee mug sat on the table in front of the couch and she could see the dark circle of the brew halfway down the side. She touched the cup; it was warm, but not hot. "David?" she called out tentatively, then more loudly: "David?"

Verdette came padding down from the upstairs studio, yowling angrily and curling around her feet. "David?" she called out more loudly. "Are you up there?" Could he have gone out? Maybe he was just around the back of the building, putting out the trash—that would explain why he left the door open. He'd be back in a few minutes, laughing at her panic.

She saw it then: the folded piece of paper behind the coffee mug. She snatched up the note. Underneath was the explosive flask she'd given David. On the paper itself was a crude sketch of a guillotine, and two brief sentences in French: *Je l'ai. Attente des instructions.*

I have him. Wait for instructions.

INTERLUDE EIGHT

Anaïs Dereux &
Charlotte Salomon

1941 – 1943

Anaïs Dereux

1940—1943

AFTER SHE LEFT VIENNA AND KLIMT, she reset the trap . . . and Nicolas didn't take the bait.

She'd gone back to Paris, which was still the center of the art world, and stayed there for several years. She thought Nicolas would certainly find the Great War compelling, and so she became—openly—a lover of several of the notorious Parisian writers and artists of the time, but Nicolas never appeared.

Camille began to have some small hope that Nicolas would keep his word, that he would no longer trouble her. When the Great War ended, she traveled to the United States for the first time. As "Alice Small," she spent time in California on the fringes of Group f/64—the informal club of photographers that included Edward Weston, Ansel Adams, Imogen Cunningham, and Sonya Noskowiak, feeding on the green soul-hearts that nurtured her most. Still, the incestuous crowd and their interminable affairs eventually soured on her. She traveled eastward across the continent, first to Chicago, then to New York, remaining a few years in each city, occasionally allowing herself to be prominently committed to one person: again, the trap always remained unsprung.

By the 1930s, she began to think that Nicolas would indeed abide by their truce. She found herself no longer looking constantly over her shoulder or avoiding places where she was alone. She found that she liked New York and the feeling of being immersed in the cutting edge of culture—but, achingly, that city with all its energy and vitality reminded her too much of Paris.

Meanwhile, Europe seemed to be undergoing its own new social paroxysms. She found that she wanted to be there, afraid for her old home.

Late in 1938, not long after British Prime Minister Neville Chamberlain returned from his talks with Adolf Hitler and declared he had obtained "peace for our time," she decided to return to France, taking on the identity of Anaïs Dereux. She traveled by ocean liner to England in early 1939, then eventually over the channel into France. She didn't return to Paris except to pass through the city on a train. She continued south to Nice, arriving in February as Prime Minister Chamberlain declared in the British House of Commons that any German attack on France would be automatically considered an attack on Britain.

She wondered then whether she'd made a mistake returning to Europe. The sense of dark and boiling storm clouds looming was palpable, even under the bright Mediterranean sky.

By the time that German troops entered Bohemia and Moravia, incorporating Czechoslovakia into Germany, Anaïs was well-ensconced in the Nice art community. Most of the talk in Nice revolved around the deepening German threat, with some holding out hope that Hitler could be appeased and a peace negotiated, while others scoffed at the idea of a German invasion of France. "The Maginot Line," the French military commanders stolidly declared, "will keep them out. No army is capable of breaching those defenses."

On September 1, 1939, the German army crossed the Polish border; two days later, France and the UK declared war on Germany, and the continent trembled on the blood-red precipice once more.

Anaïs could have left then, before the German army turned and invaded France, making a mockery of the Maginot Line, but she did not. She stayed. She stayed because of yet another soul-heart.

*   *   *

Anaïs had settled into one of the old quarters of Nice on the rue Neuscheller, a steep lane high above the Mediterranean, bordered by the
remnants of shabby old mansions from the 19th century that had been
parceled out into gloomy and musty apartments. Rue Neuscheller was
inhabited largely by families whose fortunes had declined sharply during
the economic upheaval of the 1930s, and also by an influx of Jews fleeing the rising oppression in Germany. Refugees had been coming to
France since the mid-30s, but the violence of Kristallnacht—the 9th
of November in 1938—had transformed that trickle to a flood. It was
becoming common to hear German or German-accented French being
spoken as one walked along the street.

The final week of April of 1940 was warm, with a briny sea breeze
wafting inland off the coast, sweeping the hills that spilled down into
the azure waters. Anaïs walked slowly down the avenue, enjoying the
feel of the sun on her face and the ocean's scent, and anticipating what
she'd buy at the market there—bread, certainly, and early vegetables
in from the local farms, if they were available, and maybe some fish for
dinner. Unfortunately, good food was becoming harder to find and more
expensive to buy. As she neared the square with its little shops, she
glimpsed a young woman in a blue sweater sitting on one of the benches
in the grassy central park, hunched over a tablet of drawing paper and
sketching furiously with a pencil.

Anaïs had found artists enough in Nice, most of them with talents pale and subdued. Collectively, they represented enough food
for her, but a feast that was bland and without sharp flavors: a gruel
of mediocre art. They could sustain her, but couldn't rouse in her
the flame that Lucio or Antoine or Gustav had. Ana was drifting
in the currents without making headway, and she knew it: in fact,
she intended it. The world was at war, but that was still possible to
nearly forget in Nice, which hadn't been touched by the screaming of
bombers and the chatter of gunfire. Still, it was safer to put down no
roots at all in an uncertain world and be attached to no one so that
she could flee at need. Nice pretended that it remained a destination
for the tourists; that people came for the sea air, for the dramatic

views, for relaxation and leisure. Nice pretended that nothing had changed.

It was a pretense that fooled no one, but the mask remained stubbornly in place despite the news.

Ana understood that. She pretended such things herself, pretended that she had eluded Nicolas forever, pretended that she would never see him again, pretended that she could sip from weak soul-hearts and be content. But Ana couldn't alter her character, couldn't fail to pay attention to the hunger within her for more, more, more. She saw the young woman and she stopped: the soul-heart within the girl . . . It was coiled tightly inside, held as closely to her as her body language might have suggested. Yet it glowed even in the sunshine, the potential of it stabbing deep within the girl, the coils writhing as if aching to be released.

And Ana found herself aching in concert with them. Give her enough time and she could unleash everything inside this one; she could let those coils pulse outward to find the inspiration and expression that this mossy potential wanted so desperately. This was not like Gustav's talent; no, Gustav's energy had been constantly in motion and could barely be contained: the taste and feel of this young woman's was different, but it was no less solid and real. Her soul-heart had already known pain, had been nearly suffocated and lost entirely. Ana tasted the radiance with her mind; the heart tightened even more in response, as if frightened.

Ana's fingers slipped between the buttons of her blouse to briefly touch the cameo. The sardonyx felt slick under her touch. *Do I dare do this again?* Then: *It's been over three decades since you've seen Nicolas. He's done what he said he would do. You're safe.*

Standing behind the girl, she glanced down at the sketchpad. There, reproduced in gray, firm pencil strokes, were the shops across the way, with a flurry of quickly-sketched figures moving along the sidewalk. "That's a nice rendering," Anaïs said, and the girl started dramatically, nearly dropping the pencil and grabbing at the sketchpad that threatened to tumble from her knees to the ground. She gaped up at Anaïs, her eyes wide. She was plain in features, with undistinguished brown hair cropped at the shoulders and pulled back with a pale blue ribbon from her face.

She appeared to be older than Anaïs had first supposed, maybe about twenty; her body was thin and waif-like, and perhaps that had contributed to the impression. "I love the sense of movement in the sketch," Ana continued into that face's apprehensive stare. "I can feel the people scurrying about."

"*Danke*," the young woman began, then swallowed hard. "I mean, *merci*. I'm glad you like it." Her French was good, but flavored like so many others with a slight German accent. That alone told Ana that she was one of the refugees.

Ana came around the front of the bench, though she didn't sit. "I'm Anaïs Dereux. I live just up there," Anaïs said, pointing back up the rue.

"I'm Lotte," the young woman said. For a moment, Anaïs thought that it was all she would say. She clutched her pad and pencil and seemed prepared to bolt. She shivered, visibly. "Charlotte Salomon," she said finally. "I live with my grandpar . . ." Again she stopped. "With my grandfather," she finished. Anaïs was certain Lotte had been about to say "grandparents," and that sparked a memory of an article in the local paper a week or so ago: a Jewish refugee from Germany, an older woman, had fallen from a high window and died, the story freighted with the heavy intimation that the incident had been no accident but a suicide, though that was never directly stated in the newspaper report.

"May I see your other sketches?" Anaïs asked. "I'm sorry; I shouldn't bother you, but I'm curious . . ."

Ana thought that Lotte would refuse. She hugged the sketchpad to her skinny frame, clutching it with a strange desperation, then abruptly handed it to Anaïs. Ana took it gently, and looked pointedly at the bench; Lotte scooted over to make room for Ana to sit next to her. Ana set the sketchpad on her own lap, carefully lifting the page, nodding as she went back through the sketches: landscapes with the trees of Nice and views of the harbor, a few sketches of buildings, and a larger, more finished portrait of an old woman, who appeared to be sleeping while her likeness was captured.

That one made Ana pause. The curled fingers near the head, the shadows of wrinkles on the face and down the neck, the quiet relaxation of the figure, the lines of her nightdress, the blanket wrapped to her waist: the portrait was evocative and stunning. "Who is this?" Anaïs asked Lotte.

The young woman glanced quickly at the paper and away. "That's Grossmama—my grandmother."

"It's a lovely sketch of her. Does she like it?"

"I never showed it to her."

"You should."

Her mouth tightened, and she looked away from the sketch. "I can't. She . . . died."

"That happened recently?"

The response was the ghost of a nod from Lotte, and Anaïs was quietly certain that her suspicion was correct.

"I'm very sorry," Anaïs said. "That's hard, losing someone you've known all your life. I didn't mean to pry. I'm sorry for that, too."

That earned Anaïs another nod, but the green heart remained wrapped tightly inside and Anaïs could only barely feel it now that Lotte had stopped drawing. Had she not felt it earlier, she might have missed it entirely. "It's all right," Lotte said. "She . . . She wasn't happy. Being here was hard for her."

"I've read the papers," Anaïs said. "I understand." The vitriol in the newspapers toward the Jews was increasing, with articles claiming that the German refugees were in fact a "fifth column" responsible for the loss of French troops against the onrushing German army in Denmark and Norway, and angry letters insisting that the government must do something about the traitorous Germans on their soil. Posters for the propaganda film *Jew Süss*, depicting a lecherous Jew defiling a pure Aryan girl, adorned the walls around Nice. To be German was bad enough; to be Jewish and German was worse.

Ana let the pages of the sketchpad fall back and handed it to Lotte. She pressed it to her chest as if she'd never expected to have it returned to her. "Do you paint, too?" Ana asked her.

A shrug. "Sometimes. I have some landscapes and some figures that I've done recently."

"I'd really like to see them," Ana said. "I might even want to buy one. Could we meet so I could look at them, maybe tomorrow? I could come to your house, perhaps."

The green heart throbbed once. Ana plucked at its tendrils, prying them loose and tasting them at the same time. Her own mood brightened with the feel of them. "That would be fine, I suppose," Lotte told her, and the corners of her lips twitched with a hint of a shy smile.

For the first time, the young woman made full eye contact with Anaïs, and the smile finally widened. It made her features suddenly and strangely radiant, and in that moment, Ana felt herself connect, momentarily, with Lotte's green heart. She gasped with the shock of the contact and with the depth of its potential.

"I think I like this one," Anaïs said. "How much do you want for it?"

The gouache painting of the steep, green hills outside Nice, falling down to an angry, storm-wracked sea, was competent but not overwhelming, little better than that of a hundred other artists working in the region. Ana could feel no stirring of Lotte's green heart as the young woman looked at the painting: this was not a work of the heart; this was intended to be purely commercial, a piece for the tourists to buy so that Lotte and her grandfather could eat.

Except that a German Jewess' paintings were not particularly coveted by the French tourists in Nice.

"Ten francs?" Charlotte's voice was tentative, and the end of her sentence lifted into a question. Ana shook her head.

"My dear, you undervalue yourself far too much. I'll give you twenty, and I'm still getting a bargain."

Lotte smiled at that and nodded. They were in Lotte's room on the second floor of the villa l'Ermitage, where her grandfather still lived even after the death of his wife—she was briefly introduced to the man, and she thought him both broken and unpleasant. Lotte's room was small but airy, with white chintz curtains that swayed in the breeze off the Mediterranean. Her bed, with a coverlet embroidered with a trellis of vines and roses, was pushed against a wall, as if afraid to intrude too far into the space. A battered chest of drawers lurked in a corner. In the space that remained, Lotte had set up an easel, and her paintings were stacked against or pinned to the walls. To Ana, the room smelled of Lotte: of paints and perfume.

Ana placed the landscape, unmatted and unframed, on the bed. She counted out twenty francs from her purse, and laid the bills on the coverlet. "There," she said. "Now we're both happy, *oui?*"

Lotte smiled at her. "*Oui,*" she answered.

"Good. I'll have this framed; it will look lovely and dramatic on the wall above my bed. I can look at it and imagine I'm a gull flying in that storm. Do you often go to the beach to draw and paint?"

"Sometimes," Lotte said, "or I'll go to the market, or up into the hills. There's so much beauty around here, and so many artists. I'm such a poor talent, compared to some of the others."

Ana took a step toward Lotte, taking the woman's hands in her own. Their gazes caught, held. Ana could feel Lotte's soul-heart, the emerald tendrils of it rising and curling toward her. She took them in her mind, let herself taste them, let herself strengthen them so that the radiance filled the air around them like sunlight through new leaves. "No," Ana said. "You mustn't say things like that. Lotte, you have no idea of the talent inside you."

She smiled at Anaïs, and Ana felt herself want to take the woman in her arms and hug her, but Lotte pulled her hands back shyly. "It's nice of you to say."

"It's the truth. I've known many painters, and . . ." She took a breath. "You've something few of them have, Lotte."

She turned away, though she looked at the paintings on the wall. "*Arrête, s'il vous plaît.*"

"I mean that sincerely. I'd like to go with you tomorrow, and watch you draw and paint. Would you let me do that? I promise I won't interrupt you." She put her hand on Lotte's shoulder, feeling the soul-heart reach out toward her touch. Lotte turned.

"I think I'd like that," Lotte said.

*   *   *

They would meet the next day, then often during the following weeks. Lotte seemed to enjoy the attention that Anaïs lavished on her. Ana had the sense that Lotte had few other friends, of her age or any other. Ana never pushed her to talk, never probed too hard about her past or her feelings. She'd linked herself with several women artists over the centuries; she'd even found the relationship becoming sexual as well: with Artemisia Gentileschi, with Paolina's mother Maria, with Radclyffe Hall. Those she loved, she loved without reservation. But she had the sense that if she pushed Lotte for that kind of intimacy, she would find Lotte pulling away.

If it happened, it would happen.

Instead, Ana concentrated on Lotte's green soul-heart, letting herself sink into that energy so that she could loosen it and allow it to grow outward. That was enough; she found that, slowly, over the days, Lotte began to talk to and eventually confide in her. She would lean against Ana's side as they conversed, or her hand might touch Ana's tentatively. Lotte began to paint more furiously, portraits and landscapes that were more experimental and less commercial: images that seemed to spring out from the deep well inside her.

For her own part, Anaïs pulled away from the group of artists on which she'd been feeding. Lotte was enough for now, and she found herself far more comfortable with Lotte alone than with all of the others. For the first time in a few decades, Anaïs found herself with the desire to buy chemicals and continue her quest for the second half of the Philosopher's Stone, to pull out her own paints and brushes, or to play the piano and find the songs inside herself.

Lotte's green heart began to slowly pull Ana from her own fallow period.

"I worry that I'll end up like Momma and Grossmama," Lotte confided to Anaïs one late May morning in 1940 as the two of them ate a picnic lunch on a cliffside overlooking Nice harbor and the lighthouse there. "I'm afraid that I'll give in to despair and just leap out of a window like they both did."

Sitting near the steep, boulder-strewn edge tumbling down into the blue water below, Anäis moved closer to Lotte and put her arm protectively around the young woman's shoulders. She could feel the young girl trembling, though she wondered if it wasn't the intimacy of the contact. "You're not your mother, or your grandmother," Ana said. "Because *they* did something doesn't mean that you must also end up the same way."

Lotte nodded, almost furiously. Her shivering stopped, and yet she made no move to leave Ana's embrace; instead she leaned her head into Ana's shoulder. "I understand that. I do."

The bright Mediterranean sun warmed them, and Lotte snuggled deeper in Ana's embrace. Ana could smell the fragrance of her hair, and she bent her head to kiss Lotte where her hair was parted. They remained there, caught in the lazy sun, in the salt breeze, in the susurrations of the waves against the rocks far below, for a long time: not moving, not speaking, just enjoying the feel of each other's closeness.

They climbed back down to the city a few hours later, and Ana walked with Lotte back to the house where she and her grandfather were staying. He must have been waiting for her; as they approached, he came toward them leaning on his cane, waving a piece of paper that snapped angrily with his gestures. "Have you seen this?" he half-shouted in French, ignoring Ana. "Twenty years I have been here in France, and this is what our world has come to, this is how I'm to be treated."

"What are you talking about, Grosspapa?" Lotte asked, glancing back at Ana with a worried look.

"Here! Read!" He thrust the paper in her face and stalked away, the paper fluttering nearly to the floor before Lotte managed to catch it. Ana watched her scan the words there, unable to read the print. She heard Lotte gasp.

"Oh," she said. Wordlessly, she passed the paper to Ana and went to her grandfather, who was sitting in a frayed fabric chair, muttering to himself. Ana watched Lotte crouch beside him, whispering to him in German, then she turned back to scan the paper. The words threatened to blur as she read them. *All foreign-born Jews in the Côte d'Azur must report for internment instructions in the next week . . . transport to an encampment beyond the Pyrenees . . . compulsory . . .*

Ana glanced over to Lotte, stricken. "I don't know what to say. This . . . this is horrible. There must be some way to fight this."

Lotte's grandfather sniffed derisively. "You're not Jewish," he said to Ana. "You don't understand. Ask Lotte; she's seen the infection first-hand in Germany. Now it's spread here, and soon it will be everywhere. Everywhere in the entire world."

Anaïs glanced at Lotte, who nodded as she clung to her grandfather. "He's right," she said. "I'm sorry, Ana. He's right."

"No," Ana insisted. "I won't accept that. There's something we can do. You'll see. There has to be . . ."

Ana tried to halt the deportation. She contacted everyone she could in Nice and the surrounding villages, but few in authority would even listen; if they pretended to do so, they only shook their heads sadly and shrugged thin shoulders, lifting their hands palms upward. "You must understand that it's this terrible, terrible war," they would say. "These measures are for our own protection, and for theirs as well. If the Jews are held in camps, then no one can accuse them of doing anything against us. It's only temporary, only temporary. You do know that some of them are helping the Germans as fifth columnists, don't you? Besides, they'll be treated better there than they are here. *C'est la vie.* It's for everyone's welfare . . ."

It was the same story everywhere, repeated from a dozen throats. Anaïs could feel the emptiness of the words. No one would do anything to stop the removal from taking place. If anything, Nice seemed pleased to have the "Jewish problem" removed from them; they would gladly give their fate into the hands of others.

This is only what you deserve, a part of her railed inside. *This is your punishment for letting yourself become involved this deeply with someone once again. Even without Nicolas, the fates punish you. You shouldn't have let yourself get this close and this vulnerable. Have you learned nothing at all over the centuries?*

She had no good answer to the internal accusation. *I do it because it makes me feel whole.* That was the only response she could give. *I do it because this is my addiction. I do it because I must.*

The world was prepared to mock her. The morning that Lotte was to be transported, Anaïs angrily snapped open her paper to see if the orders might have, miraculously, changed. On the front page was a photo of SS officers at a meeting in Berlin. She wouldn't ordinarily have done more than glance at it, but the grainy, black-and-white face of one of the German officers snagged her gaze and stole her breath. The man was short—the shortest of those in the photograph—and there was the way he peered at the camera lens with his head slightly tilted to the left, as well as the heavy-lidded contempt that seemed to radiate from him. She *knew* who he was, knew by the unseen fist that grabbed her intestines and twisted them violently, that turned the croissant to ash in her mouth. Her mouth voiced his name silently: *Nicolas.* She scanned the picture's caption: he was identified as SS-Hauptsturmführer Alois Brunner, but she knew he was no more Alois Brunner than she was Anaïs Dereux.

She found that she was not surprised to see him there, to find him among the SS in Germany. She thought she could hear the fates laughing at her at the serendipity on this day of all days, and it was also altogether fitting that Nicolas would be enmeshed with the Nazis, whose cruelty was already being whispered about. It was as if Nicolas, somehow, could interfere with her even when they were in countries at war with each other, even when, for half a century, he had seemingly abided by his promised truce in Vienna and left her alone.

The voice inside her laughed bitterly. Ana crumpled the paper in her fist, as if she could remotely obliterate Nicolas with the gesture. She pushed herself away from the table, leaving her breakfast untouched. She left the house and hurried down the hill to l'Ermitage, wanting to be with Lotte. *Needing* to be with her.

A hired car was idling in the driveway, but she found Lotte still there. Lotte was sitting in the dreary and dark communal dining room, with a single, ancient valise at her feet and a frayed, thin coat draped over the back of the chair in which she sat. Farther back in the house, Ana could hear Lotte's grandfather quarreling with someone over the disposition of the remaining furniture—the owner of the house, Ana supposed.

"Lotte?"

The young woman looked up, her face drawn and wan. She managed the barest of smiles for Ana, who knelt in front of Lotte and took her hands in her own. "You didn't need to come, Ana," Lotte said. The young woman's soul-heart was wound so tightly inside once more that Ana could barely pluck at its ends, could only sip at its potential richness.

Ana was suddenly frightened, afraid that this was the end, that she would never see Lotte again, never be able to taste the fullness of her creativity, never again feel her talent lifting Ana's own potential. She might never feel the softness of Lotte's touch, hear her surprising laugh when she was amused, never catch the floral scent of her hair nor linger next to the heat of her on a cool day.

She would never witness Lotte fully unleashing the gift inside her.

"I'll go with you," Ana said, clutching at Lotte. "I'll follow you. I'm a French citizen; they can't stop me from traveling. I'll find some way to get you out, you and your grandfather. Lotte, there's so much you have inside you. You can't ignore that. I won't let you."

"Ana," she said, and there was a finality in her voice. She leaned down, enveloping Ana in her thin, frail arms. "You've been such a sweet, kind friend; more than I could ever have wished for and more than I even knew I wanted. I love you for that. But this . . . You can't stop this."

"Of course we can't, if we're not willing to try," Ana answered. "Lotte, you could stay with me. We could buy new identity papers, ones that say you're only German, not Jewish. For you and your grandfather both. We could go somewhere else, where you wouldn't be known . . ."

"You want me to deny myself and my faith?" Lotte gave a small shake of her head, her brown hair swaying around her face. "Then I *would* be lost, Ana. No. We have to go. And it's time."

She stood, and Anaïs rose with her. "Grosspapa!" Lotte called out into the interior of the house. "The car is ready!" Then, more softly: "Ana, I will miss you most of all. You've been such a good friend. I never thought I . . ." She stopped and hugged Ana suddenly and hard. Ana's arms tightened around Lotte. She tried to memorize the feel of her, the smell. Emerald tendrils sparked and flared, wrapping about Ana like a second set of arms. Anaïs blinked back tears.

"I'll go with you to the station at least," she told Lotte, but Lotte was already stepping back from her and reaching for the handle of her valise.

"No," Lotte said. For a moment, Ana thought Lotte would cry, but the young woman sniffed and straightened. "Ana, please don't. It would be too hard, for both of us. Just let me remember you this way, right here."

"I won't give up on you, Lotte," Ana said furiously. "I won't."

"You must," Lotte answered, stroking her cheek with her free hand. She let the hand drop then and picked up her coat. "Grosspapa!"

Her grandfather came from the other room. He grunted at Ana, then pulled at Lotte's arm. Ana watched them leave, walking with them out to the courtyard where the hired car sat.

Lotte waved to Ana as she got into the car, before sliding in and closing the door behind her as her grandfather entered from the other side. Lotte pressed her hand against the glass in a last farewell.

Ana found herself terrified that this would be her last image of Lotte.

In the end, it would not be, though it would take nearly every *centime* that Anaïs could scrounge to ensure that.

She did follow Lotte, eventually, but first she went back to the familiarity of Paris. Anaïs had a few of Klimt's canvases squirreled away there, thinking that—a century or more later—she might be able to sell them for large amounts. She sold some of them now instead, though she received far less for them than she had hoped; with rumors that the Third Republic's days were numbered and that Marshal Philippe

Pétain, the great Victor of Verdun in the first Great War, would head a new government and sign an armistice with Germany, there were few buyers for luxury items like paintings. Still, the sale put funds in her pockets, money that could be used to grease her way into bureaucratic offices, to retain lawyers who could decipher the byzantine regulations that governed the relocation of foreign-born Jews, to pay the bribes necessary to see high-level officials in the government and to convince those officials to follow their own rules.

There were other bribes she had to pay as well, ones that involved no money at all. She did what she needed to do, as quickly as she could, telling herself that she been with enough men that these encounters meant nothing at all. In the midst of it, she imagined Lotte's face when she brought her out of the encampment.

It took until August and several negotiations with the Vichy government under Pétain, but Anaïs was finally able to leave Paris with a sheaf of stamped, official documents to deliver to the French Commandant in charge.

The internment camp was near the town of Gurs, in the Aquitaine region. The facility had been built in 1939 to house Spanish refugees fleeing Francisco Franco's regime, many of them combatants in that struggle. A year later, at the start of the German hostilities, the camp contained not only the Spanish, but German prisoners and those from the other Axis powers, as well as French nationals suspected of being Nazi sympathizers. When the Vichy government signed their armistice with the Germans, the war prisoners had been released, though the camp still held many Spanish refugees.

And now . . . The Vichy government held foreign Jews here, along with others suspected of being troublesome: leftist union organizers, pacifists, even ordinary criminals.

Gurs was a sleepy village alongside a river snaking through the foothills of the Pyrenees. The encampment was placed well away from the village, like someone holding a soiled diaper at arm's length. The smell hit Anaïs as soon as she left the car she'd hired in the village: the ripe scent of human excrement and corruption. She felt a growing disgust as she approached the administrative building for the camp, looking at the crowded facilities beyond the doubled barbed wire perimeter. There was a single paved street, on either side of which the land was divided into parcels, which were in turn packed with several small triangular huts. The ground was soaked from the frequent rains off the Atlantic, which turned the earth into soupy clay. She could see the inmates: they were everywhere, ragged pants soiled to the knees with the gray spatters from the ground, many of their bodies thin and skeletal. The men were separated from the women and from the entrance, Ana could only see the males; she could only hope that Lotte was somehow being treated better.

The French Commandant peered myopically at the documents that Ana presented him, harrumphing and stroking his bearded chin as he read the words, and glancing up at Ana from time to time. "These do appear to be in order," he said finally, tapping the paper with a thin forefinger, "but M'mselle must understand that there are many people here. To locate this grandfather and granddaughter and complete all the reports necessary, well, there is only so much time that I have and so many responsibilities. And in this time of national crisis . . ." He clucked his tongue, shaking his head sadly.

"I understand the times, Commandant," Ana told the man. "If it would help the Commandant, I am willing make a substantial donation to your camp operating funds. Perhaps then the Commandant could find the resources necessary to expedite this? A hundred francs?" She watched his face. "Or perhaps two hundred? I could give you the funds directly, Commandant: in cash today, so you can put the funds yourself into the proper hands . . ."

Half an hour later, a thin and pale Lotte was ushered into the Commandant's office. Her hair was matted and dull, her cheeks hollowed, but her face brightened as she saw Ana. Her green heart was nearly brown and vanished, wrapped far inside her and covered over. Yet Ana felt it stir, still alive, as the two embraced. Ana whispered the words of a small charm she remembered to stir the energy, subvocalizing the Arabic words so that Lotte wouldn't hear them, and sighed as she felt the energy connect again to her.

"You're free," Anaïs said to her. "You've been released so you can care for your grandfather back home in Nice."

"You did this?" Lotte asked Ana, who could not stop herself from grinning in delight at Lotte's gratification and pleasure. "How?"

"That's not important," she told her. "What's important is that you can go home, and you can start working again."

With that, Ana felt Lotte's green heart pulse once, lifting almost as in relief from its burial place inside. "Good," Lotte said. "I know now what I need to do. I've been thinking about this."

In the wake of the Vichy armistice, the Germans had taken direct control of northern and western France, with the Vichy shadow government controlling the so-called "Free Zone" of southern France, but Nice and the Côte d'Azur had been placed in Italian hands. There were swirling, wild rumors of mass numbers of German and French Jews being arrested and handed over to the Nazis by the French Vichy government, of the Jews in the Gurs encampment being emptied into a greater camp outside Paris called Drancy, run by the Gestapo Office of Jewish Affairs, and of those interned in Drancy being ferried eastward to forced labor camps in Germany.

However, the Italians seemed more tolerant and *laissez-faire* than the Germans—though there were demonstrations against the Jews in the Côte d'Azur, there were no reprisals and no mass roundups, and the Italian military permitted the Jews to remain in their homes. The gossip that Anaïs heard was that German Foreign Minister von Ribbentrop was complaining loudly and often to Mussolini that "the Italian military lacks a proper understanding of the Jewish question." Unlike the Jewish population of Vichy France or Germany, no Jews here were forced to wear the Star of David on their clothing as identification.

It was almost as if, for the moment, Ana and Lotte could ignore the war—if one could forget the short food and gas supplies and the barrage of news, both good and bad, coming from the various fronts.

Lotte's grandfather, already querulous and difficult to live with, only became more so after their return to Nice, and Ana was able to help

Lotte move away from his sour, negative presence to the La Belle Aurore, a hotel a few towns away from Nice toward the Italian border. Ana also moved to the La Belle Aurore to be with Lotte, and it was there that Ana was able to finally and entirely unleash Lotte's green heart.

Lotte had told her some of what she wanted to do as they'd returned to Nice from the Gurs encampment, though Anaïs hadn't understood half of it. The project had burst from Lotte almost as soon as she moved to La Belle Aurore—as if a volcano had finally been unleashed from deep inside her. Lotte began working furiously, so focused that Ana was almost frightened by the intensity—and, she had to admit, almost jealous of the attention that Lotte lavished upon her project. "No, I can't go to the beach today," she would say, if Ana suggested that the two of them relax together. "I want to finish this painting. Maybe tomorrow . . ."

But tomorrow there would be a new excuse, and the next day as well. Lotte barely noticed Ana bringing her food, or sitting down to watch her work.

Still, Ana reaped the benefits as well: she and Lotte grew increasingly close, and Lotte's creative energy fueled Ana's own efforts. She had set up a laboratory in the village and her experiments were proceeding well—she was trying to reproduce her and Nicolas' previous success in turning mercury to silver. Ana was painting also, in the same room as Lotte, and if she wasn't entirely pleased with the results, she found them satisfactory.

If Lotte and she were still not lovers, well, she was with Lotte nearly every day. That was pleasure enough. Had it not been for the war, she might have been happy.

"What *is* all this?" Ana asked her, shuffling the sheaves of paper on Lotte's table in her room. "I don't mean any criticism, my dear—these are wonderful images—but what exactly are they *for*?" The paintings were rough but yet evocative, bold strokes of gouache with a muted palette, sometimes with words painted directly on them. There were notes on presentation, notes on music: Ana couldn't decide whether this was a series of paintings or the storyboard for a play or movie. There were nearly two hundred of the paintings already, in less than a year; Lotte seemed to be interested in little beyond her feverish work.

Ana felt Lotte standing directly behind her, watching her as she examined the paintings, and she reached back with her hands to Lotte's hips, pulling her closer to her. Lotte laughed once, kissed the nape of Ana's neck, and took a step back, as if the reverse embrace were too intimate for her. Ana turned to face Lotte. "Tell me," she said. "Tell me what you're doing with all this."

"This is my life," Lotte told Ana earnestly. "All of it. Everything. If all the ghosts in their lives drove Momma and Grossmama to suicide, then I'm not going to allow them to do that to me. I'm going to capture those ghosts and bind them. I'm going to put them down on paper where they can't be hidden. I'll silence them by bringing them into the light—every last one of them, the good and the bad." Lotte reached out to Ana's neck; she took the gold chain there and gently pulled the sardonyx pendant from underneath the collar of Ana's blouse. She held it for a moment, looking carefully at the piece of jewelry. "Why do you wear this?" she asked Ana.

"You already know; I've told you before—it's to remind me of what I went through in order to become who I am, so I never forget."

"Well, just as this helps you to keep your memories fresh in your mind, that's what I'm doing with this. If I paint my memories, then they can't ever leave me, but they also can't ever hurt me again. I'll have rendered them harmless by binding them in paint. Do you understand?"

"No," Ana admitted. "Not entirely, anyway." She picked up a thick sheaf of the paintings and started looking through them, one by one. There: two male faces crowding the right side of the page, rendered in warm oranges and red; on the left, a female face protrudes, done in cooler hues, and in the middle, the words "Lieben sie mich eigentlich?" *Actually, they love me?* And here: as if the painter were hovering from a point well above and looking down, a family of men and women around a table, with a meal and bottles of wine set around them as they talk in groups. Many of the paintings had brushed dialogue or commentary accompanying them. "But my question still stands," Anaïs continued. "What are all these paintings *for*? What are you planning to do with them?—I don't see you trying to sell them individually. And you've made all these notes about music, presentation, and stage directions; it's like you're putting together a performance. Is that what this is?"

"Maybe." Again, Charlotte gave that musical, self-deprecating laugh. "I really don't know. It's just . . . since I've left Gurs—and since I've been around you, Ana—I feel like chains have dropped away from me. Everything inside me is flowing out and it's all I can do just to capture the vision before it's gone, it's coming so fast. I've never felt this way before. I'm burning inside and the only way to keep the flames from taking me is to paint and paint and paint . . ." She stopped, breathless and panting. "It's so wonderful, Ana. Wonderful and frightening and terrifying all at once. Do you understand that?"

Ana could only shake her head. "No," she said simply. "I wish I did. But I've seen it before. And I wish . . ."

I wish that it could be me that has that passion, that drive, that intensity. I have some talent, and I've had centuries to work, but I'm not one of the great ones. That's not my task, that's not my fate. I'm mostly the daemon, the channel, the one who can take the soul-heart inside and make it all it can be, as long as that soul-heart is in another person. Sometimes, yes, I wish that I could for once be the great artist rather than the artist's muse, the creator rather than the inspiration, but that's not the gift that was given me.

"I've seen it before," she repeated, and she took Lotte's hands in her own, pressing her fingers on hers, staring at them as if she could see the genius inside her glowing through the sinews. Lotte's soul-heart wrapped around her, shining as it never had before, so strong that Ana gasped at its touch. At that moment, she wanted more than ever to bring Lotte to her, to kiss her lips, to touch her . . . But she didn't. She only smiled at her and pressed her fingers. "It's enough for me that I've been some help to you," she finished.

She wondered if Lotte could hear the double lie in the words.

* * *

For nearly a year, the war had remained a semi-distant distraction for the Côte d'Azur. But the world would change twice for Anaïs during 1943.

"I love you." They'd both said those words to each other over the months, but Ana had always known that they meant something different to Lotte than they did to her. There'd been no physical intimacy between them beyond innocent cuddling and a few kisses such as two friends might naturally share. Yet they were together nearly every day and even some nights.

"I love you." To Ana, that meant that there was no one else, no one else alive in the entire world to whom she could say those words and mean them. But though she felt Lotte's green heart stir toward her when Lotte spoke those same words to Anaïs, there was always a reserve there.

They didn't define love the same way.

In February, Lotte's grandfather died, and Ana helped Lotte struggle with her grief. Around the same time, Lotte stopped working on the grand project of her life. "It's done," she told Anaïs finally. She showed her three simple, large cardboard boxes, stuffed with over a thousand individual gouache paintings on thick paper, some of them double-sided due to the war-caused shortage of painting supplies. "I've finished it."

Ana picked up the last paper that Lotte had done, on top of the pile in the final box. It showed a woman in a green bathing suit kneeling on a beach, her back to the viewer as she painted on a strangely transparent pad on her lap. On the woman's bare back, words had been painted in German: Leben? oder Theater? *Life? or Theater?* It was as if Lotte were questioning herself and her own reasons for having thrown herself into this obsession. The papers rustled as Ana laid the painting carefully back in the box. "And what now?" Anaïs asked Lotte. "What do you do now?"

"I've been painting, still, but . . ." Her shoulders lifted in a shrug. "There's something else I'm supposed to do now," she told Ana. Her eyes were bright and eager, her lips curling upward. Ana felt the green heart lift and pulse with the words, surrounding Lotte in the glow that only Ana could see. *Yes, there's something else . . . if I can help her find it.* "I just don't know what it is yet, but I can *feel* it in here." Lotte touched her heart, her breast. "There's something else, but it's just not ready to tell me what it wants to be yet."

Ana loved her more in that moment than she ever had.

After *Life? or Theater?* was finished, not long after her grandfather's death, Ana saw less of Lotte, though they were still together often. She moved back to villa l'Ermitage, where she'd stayed with her grandparents when she'd first arrived, and Ana also moved back to Nice, so she could be closer. Ana would walk up to l'Ermitage to find that Lotte had gone for a walk by herself, or she might be gone for a few days without having told Anaïs that she was leaving. Ana could feel Lotte pulling away, the energy inside her no longer as drawn to Ana's presence or to her coaxing of it.

Ana found herself, as Lotte had said she was also, waiting to see what her soul-heart wanted her to do.

When Lotte came to see her unexpectedly at the end of May, Ana wasn't entirely surprised, but the sober expression on Lotte's face was worrisome, as was the perfunctory hug that she offered and the catch in her voice when she answered Ana's "*Comment vas-tu?*"

"*Ja vais bien.* Mostly."

Ana tried to coax out her soul-heart, but she felt it resisting; it would only let her taste it, not fully allow her to take it in. "I haven't seen you very much." The energy seemed strangely thick and low around Lotte's waist, and colored with the azure blue that Ana had sometimes seen with the artists who had also been in love with her: the color that she associated with a true bonding. The hue hung in Lotte's soul-heart, but it wasn't connected to Ana, but inside.

"I know. I'm sorry." She wouldn't look up from her hands, folded on her lap as she sat in the chair across from Ana.

"Lotte, what's wrong?"

"It's that obvious?"

"*Oui.* And more." Lotte nodded. Her head lifted, and Ana could see that she'd been crying recently, her eyes rimmed with red. Ana knew then, suddenly; knew why the azure lurked in Lotte's soul-heart and why she couldn't touch it. "You're pregnant," she said.

Lotte's eyes filled then, and a sob caught in her throat as she tried to breathe. She gave another silent nod. "You're certain?" Ana asked her.

"Yes. I saw a doctor today. I just came from there. He said it's certain."

"Ah." Ana fought to keep her face from showing the betrayal that she felt. *You knew she didn't feel the same way about you . . .* But even knowing didn't stop the hurt and the odd sense of betrayal. She tried to smile, leaning forward to pat Lotte's hands. "And the father? Does he know?"

Another nod. "He does. He . . . he says he wants to marry me."

"Is that what *you* want?" Ana asked.

With that, Lotte managed to smile, the pain in her eyes clearing momentarily and the green heart inside her rising with its bands of sapphire, and her expression tore at Ana more than anything Lotte could have said. "I love him. I do. Yes, that's what I want."

The words hit Ana like velvet-wrapped fists. The emerald glow slid from her grasp, and she sat back, her own smile frozen on her face. "Good," she managed to say, then, more emphatically: "That's good, then. Who is he? Do I know him?"

"I don't think so. His name is Alexander Nagler. He lives at l'Ermitage also; I actually met him when I first came here, but he was with someone else then, though he's broken up with her since." Her smile widened. Some of the tiredness left her voice. Her green heart flared. "He walked me here. I'd like to introduce you to him; he's waiting for me out in the street. I want him to know you, because of everything you've meant to me. He should know my one true friend."

Ana had no choice. She forced another smile to her face and touched Lotte's hands again. "Yes, I'd love to meet him. Go call him, why don't you?"

While she went to the door, Anaïs went into the kitchen of her apartment and turned on the teapot on the stove, putting out three cups. Then she hurried to her study and opened a drawer there, taking out an old scroll she'd acquired in Paris. She scanned it quickly, her lips moving as she memorized the words there, which kept threatening to slip away from her mind. *If you had Nicolas' skill with magic, this would be so easy* . . . She heard Lotte and Alexander entering and placed the scroll back in the drawer, going into the main room. ". . . .really wants to meet you, and I want you to meet her," she heard Lotte saying. "She's been ever so important and so good to me. I wouldn't even be here if it weren't for her. Oh, there she is. Anaïs, this is Alexander."

The man extending his hand to her was thin and sallow, and she could see a mottled, large scar on his right ear and neck. Still, his face was handsome enough; she could see the attraction that he might have held for Lotte. "It's good to finally meet you," he said. "Lotte's spoken so often about you that I almost feel I already know you."

Ana didn't like his handshake; it was limp and quick. She waved the two toward seats in the room. "So," she said, "the two of you are engaged?" She watched his face more that Lotte's. She saw the way his lips pressed together before the obligatory smile; she noticed that he didn't look at Lotte, though she glanced at him. It was Lotte who spoke first.

"Yes," she said. "We're both very happy."

He nodded then, as if he had no choice. "Yes," he echoed. "Very happy."

The kettle began to whistle in the kitchen. "Lotte," Ana said, turning to her. "I've started some tea in the kitchen for us. Would you mind?"

"Certainly," Lotte said, getting up. Her hand lingered for a long moment on Alexander's shoulder. "I'll be right back."

Ana waited until Lotte had left the room. Alexander was carefully staring at the curtains beyond Anaïs. There was nothing of a green heart within him that she could sense. "Listen to me, Alexander," Ana told him. "I'm going to say this once, and once only. If you truly love Lotte, then marry her. But if you don't, if you're doing this only because you feel obligated since she's carrying your child, then you should leave—because in the long run that would be better for Lotte than a miserable marriage. Leave right now, this instant, and you can stay free. But if you don't . . . I'll tell you this: if you hurt Lotte, if you make her unhappy, then I'll consider it my personal task to make your life a hell twice as bad as whatever Lotte is feeling. And I have the means to do that."

Ana spoke the phrase she'd memorized, her hand describing a pattern in the air, and Alexander jumped. The room seemed to darken despite the sun outside, and sweat suddenly beaded on his forehead.

"Yes, you feel that, don't you?" she told him. "The terrible heat, the discomfort, the beginning of pain. Why, in a few seconds, Alexander, your clothing will catch fire and the flames will start to blister your flesh. You'll scream, and you'll try to tear the clothes away, but that won't stop it. Can you feel it, Alexander? Is the heat already searing you? Is that the first scent of smoke you smell?"

Ana knew that the spell was only a trifle, an illusion that would last only a brief few minutes and couldn't actually harm the man, no matter how much he believed that a heat was rising around him. Alexander had risen from his chair, his face red and frightened, his mouth open and gasping. Frantically, he started patting at his clothes, rivulets of sweat pouring down his face, his hair matted and dark with it. Ana spoke another phrase, waving her hand once again, and Alexander gasped again, this time with relief. The room returned to brightness, a cool breeze entering from the open window.

He sat abruptly, staring at Anaïs, a finger sliding along the collar of his shirt as if to pry it away from his neck. "How did you do that?" he asked, his voice choked and uncertain. "What *are* you?"

"I'm someone who will do whatever I can to protect my friends," she told him, "by whatever means I have available to me, and I have means you can't possibly imagine. Now, I want your decision, Alexander. Quickly, before she comes back. Do you love her? Do you *really* love her?"

He nodded his head. He wiped at his forehead with the back of his hand, but the sweat had already dried.

"Good," Ana told him. "I'm pleased to hear that. Then you and I will get along well. Ah, here comes Lotte with the tea . . ."

*   *   *

Lotte and Alexander were married on June 17, 1943. Ana was among those who gathered at l'Ermitage in Villefranche to toast their marriage and celebrate with them, though she found the moment at best bitter-sweet. It hurt her to see Lotte clinging to Alexander, and Anaïs was bothered by the guilty pleasure she felt whenever Alexander glanced her way apprehensively. She saw little of Lotte in the days and weeks that followed, and she realized that she had lost the green heart that had meant so much to her for the last few years. All of Lotte's attention was focused inward, swaddling the child in her womb. When Ana tried, once, to talk with her about the creative project that Lotte had said was still waiting for her to begin, Lotte only laughed, and her green heart barely stirred from where it hung around the child in her womb.

"Oh, I'll paint again. I know I will, but that's for later," Lotte said. She patted her stomach. "For after the baby comes, eh? I can't think of it now, Ana. I can't. If you were a mother, you'd understand."

Ana couldn't answer. *A daemon isn't meant to nurture someone that way . . . That's something I can never understand. Before the elixir, there was Verdette, but in all the centuries since, all the men I've lain with, I've never conceived a child. The elixir took that part of my womanhood away.*

The excuse sounded empty and hollow in Ana's mind.

By late July, Ana had begun to recontact the local artists, feeling empty, lethargic, and exhausted from the lack of Lotte's energy. Feeding from them was like subsisting on stale bread and water after having spent years dining in fine restaurants, but it was all she had.

Lotte was all but lost to her. The few days she could spend with her were almost painful, because they reminded her of all she was missing, and Lotte's visibly rounding belly was almost an accusation.

That was the first change.

The second would come later: on September 8, 1943.

On that day, Italy surrendered to the Allied forces, and Nice and the surrounding region came fully under German control. That changed everything for the Jews gathered there. Suddenly, the Côte d'Azur was plunged into the foul, rotting heart of the war; suddenly, they were the focus of intense German interest. The papers were full of stories and articles praising the great work of Germany and the obvious superiority of the Aryan race.

Among the newspaper articles was a sentence that sent a spear of ice through Ana's heart. The SS was sending a trusted operative to deal with the Côte d'Azur "Jewish problem."

That man was SS-Hauptsturmführer Alois Brunner.

Nicolas.

Anaïs cried aloud, reading that. *You should have gone to Germany when you first saw him. You should have been the hunter. Now he's coming here, and you're not prepared for him.* With the war, with the restrictions, leaving Nice and France wasn't a good option, even if she could stand to leave Lotte behind.

For the next week, Ana did what she could to prepare, crafting flasks of explosives, memorizing the fire spells that could set them off, and purchasing on the black market a rusty, Great War-vintage French Pistole Revolveur handgun with a handful of bullets.

On September 15, 1943, the papers reported that Hauptsturm-führer Alois Brunner would be arriving in Nice the next morning. Ana stayed in her apartment, not venturing outside for fear that somehow she might run into him in the midst of the city. He would recognize her immediately, after all. It wasn't that she was afraid of him; she felt at least some confidence that he might abide by the truce they'd come to—after all, he hadn't followed her to France, or to America; he'd been in Germany at the start of the war and his assignment here was only a strange and unfortunate fluke of fate. Still, she didn't want him to see her, to know that she was here and that she knew Lotte or the rest of the artists in the area.

She would protect herself from him if she had to. She would kill him if she had to—but she had some hope that wouldn't be necessary.

Still, she feared for Lotte as a Jewess, and that sent her back to her chemicals and the notes she'd made when she'd worked with Antoine in Paris—the work was difficult and laborious, especially given the problems finding appropriate supplies due to the war, but the effort consumed her. Within a week, she had a new vial of the elixir. She was determined to give it to Lotte, to convince her to take it even if she had to lie. Yes, it would change her; yes, it might destroy her as an artist; yes, Ana had no idea what taking the elixir would do to the child in Lotte's womb. But Lotte might live then, no matter what the Nazis might do to her—Anaïs couldn't bear to think of the alternative.

It was September 24th when she finished.

The rounding up of Jews in the area around Nice began that same week, the effort unexpected, sudden, and ruthless. When Anaïs, ensconced in her rooms, finally heard the rumors flickering like pale flames among the other residents, she set aside her own fear about Brunner and went to l'Ermitage.

Lotte and Alexander were no longer safe at l'Ermitage; that seemed clear. Anaïs hurried there, rehearsing in her mind what she might say to them and how she might respond if Nicolas himself was there, going over dire scenarios in her mind. She would give Lotte the elixir, saying as little about it as possible, knowing that Lotte would trust her and would take it. Then, perhaps she could help Lotte and Alexander escape along the coast and into Italy itself, where they might be able to get behind the Allied lines, or maybe they could find sanctuary among the mountains to the north. Perhaps Ana could take in the couple herself, claim that they were German cousins of hers, but not Jewish.

Nothing prepared her for what she found.

She could hear agitated voices as she approached, and she found the residents of the villa out in the courtyard, talking loudly among themselves with wild gesticulations. "Ah, M'mselle Dereux!" Madame Moore, the owner of the villa called as she approached. "It is horrible! Just horrible!"

"What is horrible?" Ana asked, dreading that she already knew the answer.

"The Nazis—they came in trucks just a few hours ago, and they took Lotte and Alex. The *bâtards* snatched them up and took them away. They wouldn't listen to us, wouldn't tell us where they were taking them. They forced them into the trucks, and Lotte, the poor girl, they practically had to drag her in, she was so distraught, and pregnant as she is . . ." Madame Moore's eyes widened suddenly. "Oh, I nearly forgot. Lotte, as they were taking her away, she said that she wanted me to be certain to give you something. She said it was vital that you have it. Come with me, come with me . . ."

Ana shook her head, wanting to run after these trucks and find Lotte (if not Alexander). But she impatiently followed Madame Moore, who escorted her up to Lotte's room in the villa and pointed to three cardboard boxes in a corner. "Those," she said. "She said she wanted to make certain that you had them."

Ana didn't need to open them: she knew what was in them—the paintings that Lotte had worked on so feverishly, the opera of her life: *Life? or Theater?* "I'll need a car for the boxes," she told Madame Moore. "Please, could you call one for me? And are you certain that they didn't say where they were taking Lotte and Alexander?"

Madame Moore didn't know the answer to that last question, nor did any of the other residents of l'Ermitage, but the driver of the car who drove Anaïs back to her rooms with Lotte's boxes thought he did.

"The Nazis have taken over the Hotel Excelsior in Nice," the driver told her. "I've heard that they're holding the Jews there until they're processed, then shipping them out by train for Drancy in Paris. And after that . . ." The shrug he gave then was more eloquent than words.

After Ana and the driver had carried Lotte's boxes into the apartment, after she'd paid the driver and had opened one of the boxes to look in at the sheets of Lotte's work, Anaïs had taken out her battered, old Tarot and laid out the cards. The reading had not been optimistic, and she could see Nicolas' influence throughout it. Angrily, she pushed the cards away on the tabletop. She took out the few old scrolls she'd gathered over the centuries, laying them out and trying to memorize the most effective spells there, knowing that none of them could match Nicolas, if it came to that. She placed the flasks she'd already prepared in her coat jacket. She couldn't concentrate; she was shaking and trembling and the vials rattled in her hands as she thrust them into the pocket. The vial of elixir for Lotte she hid in the broken heel of her shoe, gluing a strip of rubber over the hole she'd worn there. She thought of slipping the pistol into her handbag, but she was certain that she would be searched and to bring an obvious weapon would only result in her own arrest before she could get to Nicolas.

We agreed to a truce back in Vienna. He'll keep to it. She repeated the thought, over and over, as if sheer repetition could make it true. But at least part of her feared that would not be the case. *All the centuries, has he ever shown that he would stop?*

To that she had no answer. To that, there *was* no answer.

A few hours later, she was standing in front of the Hotel Excelsior, staring at the guards loitering at the entrance and the blood-red swastikas draped over the building's facade. Ana felt cold, as if a winter wind from the mountains had invaded the coast; all the fine hairs on her arms were standing up and her stomach roiled. She could taste acid at the back of her throat. She thought she could feel eyes—Nicolas' eyes—staring at her from the windows of the hotel. Almost, she turned and fled, but the thought of Lotte somewhere inside made her plant her feet and swallow hard. She strode up to a cluster of uniformed guards near the entrance.

"I wish to see Hauptsturmführer Brunner," she told the man in broken German.

"Your papers, M'mselle?" the guard asked, holding out his hand. He spoke passable French. His gaze was cold and appraising, his gaze traveling from her face down to her shoes and back, touching each part of her body as intimately as a hand. He took the identification that Ana handed him. "You're a French citizen?"

"*Oui,*" she told him. "I am."

"And your business here?"

"That is between me and the Hauptsturmführer."

The sniff of disdain, or perhaps amusement, was audible. "The Hauptsturmführer, I regret, takes very few appointments with citizens. If you could perhaps tell me more, I might be able to direct you to someone who might help you."

"Tell Hauptsturmführer Brunner that Perenelle wishes to see him."

The guard looked puzzled. "Perenelle? But your name . . ."

"Tell him that," Anaïs said. "I promise you that you won't get into any trouble. He'll want to talk to me. I guarantee you."

The guard stared hard at her for several seconds before calling over another officer and telling him something in quick, guttural German while handing him Ana's identification papers. She heard the name "Perenelle" repeated. The other man saluted and hurried off into the lobby of the hotel while the guard waited with Anaïs. Several minutes later, the officer returned. He looked at her strangely. "I'm to search M'mselle Dereux for weapons, then take her to the Hauptsturmführer's office," he said.

The search was thorough and humiliating, and Anaïs was glad that she'd decided against bringing the pistol. They took her into a small office in the hotel and made her strip to her underwear in front of them, then brought in a female adjunct to search that. Her vials were discovered nearly immediately; they looked at them strangely, shaking the powder inside, then put them in a small box and carried them away. Though they looked at her shoes, they missed the vial of elixir.

Afterward, the officer of the guard allowed Ana time to put her clothing back on, then walked alongside her through the east wing of the hotel. Hauptsturmführer Brunner's office was in one of the airy suites bordering the courtyard. The officer walked Ana between an array of desks hastily set in the hotel's wide corridors and past several guards into one of the rooms of the suite. Music was playing softly in the room from a phonograph in one corner; Ana felt the chill traverse her spine as she recognized the melody: the Spring allegro movement from Vivaldi's *The Four Seasons*. And the painting on the wall to her left: it was one of Klimt's portraits of her.

The doors to the room's balcony were open, the gauzy folds of the curtains billowing in a breeze. A short man stood there with his back to them, dressed in a crisp SS officer's uniform. He was smoking a cigarette and staring down from the balcony of the apartment into the court. Ana saw her papers open on his desk, and the flasks that had been taken from her. The officer clicked polished, booted heels together and raised his arm in the Nazi salute. "Hauptsturmführer," he said over the music, "the woman who wanted to see you."

The man on the balcony turned, and Ana was staring once more into Nicolas' face. He drew in a long inhalation from his cigarette and blew smoke from his nose as he tossed the cigarette over the balcony rail. He smiled as he entered the room, putting the bulk of the desk between himself and Ana, though he didn't sit. His forefinger rolled one of the glass vials across the blotter. "*Sie können gehen,*" he told the officer. *You may go.* The officer saluted again and left the room, closing the doors behind him. "I wonder what you intended with these," Nicolas said, switching to French. "I thought we came to an agreement in Venice." He clucked his tongue, shaking his head. "Why, I might think you didn't trust me."

"We had a truce," she agreed. "Forgive me if it seems I didn't entirely trust you to keep it."

He grinned at that, lifting his finger from the flask. "Well, my dear, this is a most unexpected pleasure."

"Irony really doesn't suit you, Nicolas," Ana told him. She glanced pointedly at his uniform, at the insignia of the SS pinned there. "But it looks as if this war has."

His smile broadened. "Oh, indeed, it has," he answered, and she could hear a terrifying satisfaction in his voice. "Quite well, in fact. This war and the Reich have given me the chance to do good work. Important work. Work I find . . ." He seemed to consider the words. "Deeply and intensely satisfying on many levels."

"Good work? Sending Jews to forced labor camps? Stealing their houses and their money from them, just as you did so long ago?"

The smile twitched. "You mean, forcing them to make justifiable reparations for what they have stolen from the people of the world?" he answered. "And making certain that they will never rape our people again? As I said, mine is very satisfying work and very necessary, no matter what you might think. You were always too sympathetic; it was one of your many faults, Perenelle. Or should I say . . ." He tapped the papers on his desk and peered at them. "Anaïs. You *do* surprise me; I truly hadn't the slightest idea that you were here. I would have thought you'd be in a safer place like the Americas. I'll admit that I'd put out feelers, looking for you after . . ." He grinned then: a jackal's grin, a hyena's amusement. ". . . after Vienna, poor Klimt, and our agreement. I promised to stay away, but I didn't promise to never know where you were and who you were with. The people I hired told me that you went to the United States, but then they lost you there; I thought you were *still* there. Yet here you are, presenting yourself to me all unasked for. And conveniently disarmed, it seems. I must ask: why?"

"You have someone in your custody. I want her released."

Brunner/Nicolas gave a loud, uproarious laugh at that. He slapped the top of his desk hard enough that the vials rattled. "Truly? So I've accidentally snatched up your latest artist and lover, all unknowing—is that what you're telling me? Now there's irony for you, Perenelle. Priceless. And 'her,' too." He chuckled, shaking his head. "So *modern* of you, and she's evidently a Jewess besides, or I wouldn't have her . . . Why, Perenelle, you've become positively decadent. So tell me, why should I do what you ask and release this person for you?"

"Because you made a promise that we would end our long dance. Because I spared your life in Vienna. You can pay me back for that now. Release her—let her go."

"And the name of this paragon?"

"Charlotte Salomon," Ana told him. "Or rather, Charlotte Nagler now. Your people took her and her husband earlier this morning."

"She has a husband, too." His eyebrows rose, wrinkling his forehead. "Another Jew as well. You *are* surprising. So you're begging me for the life of a worthless Jewess, after all these long centuries?"

"*Oui*," she told him. "Or rather, I'm not begging you; I'm telling you that you owe me that much and more because you're still standing here and not buried headless in Vienna—though looking at you now, I have to question my slowness then. How many people have died because I didn't move quickly enough?"

He sniffed; it might have been a laugh. "Feeling guilty, are you, *ma*

cherie? So you want me to release this one woman to appease your conscience? Not the husband, too?"

"It's Charlotte I'm concerned about," Ana told him. "But yes, I'm
asking you to release Alexander also, because of what it would mean
to Charlotte. Then I'll leave and you and I can go our own ways." The
Vivaldi movement reached its quiet, resolute conclusion.

"Ah, so there's coldness in you still," Brunner said. He seemed almost
delighted. "And do I hear some jealousy as well toward the husband?"

She ignored the jibe. "You'll do it, then? You'll let her go?"

Brunner seemed to almost sigh. "Once, your offer would have been
a delight. Why, even just fifty years ago . . ." He shook his head. The
phonograph needle hit the last groove of the record; she could hear the
repeated impact of the needle as the turntable continued to turn. *Hiss,
thump. Hiss, thump.* "So you haven't given this lover of yours the true
elixir? No, you haven't, or you wouldn't look so worried. You wouldn't
have come here to beg me for her release." He shook his head in mock
sadness. "Just as with poor Antoine, just as with me, you've been too
slow."

"Nicolas—"

He raised his hand, stopping her protest. He moved from behind
the desk and went to the door of his office. She heard him speaking to
one of the guards in the next room, and he heard the name "Charlotte
Nagler" in Brunner's quick German, then the sound of heels clicking
together. Nicolas came back in the room. He went to the desk again,
standing behind it and rolling her flasks idly across the blotter with a
forefinger. He didn't speak for several seconds, then looked up at her.

"I imagined the moment of finally killing you for so long, Perenelle.
Especially after our last time together in Vienna, I've thought how delicious it would be, seeing your head roll from your shoulders and watching the blood pulse from your body, seeing your mouth gaping as if to
speak and your eyes finally, finally going empty and dead. Forever dead,
the way you wanted it for me." The tone of his voice made Ana shiver
again. She heard the needle of the record—*hiss, thump*—and Nicolas
moved to the phonograph and lifted the needle.

"Yet when you had *me*, when you could have killed me and I saw you hesitate, when you agreed to our little 'truce' . . ." He lifted his shoulders and looked past Ana to the door of his office. "Ah, but here's our little Jewess, and *pregnant*, too . . ."

Ana turned and saw a haggard, frightened Lotte at the door. Brunner gestured, and the guard holding her pushed her into the office and closed the door again behind her. Lotte stumbled, and Ana caught her. They hugged each other tightly. "I thought I'd never see you again, Ana," Lotte said. "When they came . . ."

Ana kept her gaze on Brunner, but took Lotte's hand. "Shh. Come on. We're leaving."

"No," Brunner said. "The door's locked, and I'm afraid I've misled you, Perenelle. Promises mean very little to me. For both of us, our entire lives are snared in lies. Both of us are required to lie to stay alive, aren't we?"

Lotte pulled at Ana's arm, speaking to her softly and desperately. "What does he mean? Why is he calling you Perenelle?"

Ana didn't answer. Brunner started to come around the desk toward them, and Ana put herself in front of Lotte as they retreated, their footsteps hushed in the deep carpet of the suite. "I've had a long time to think about you and me since Vienna," he said, almost casually, "and you know what I've realized, Perenelle? We both seek out what gives us the most pleasure: you and your artists; me and, well, you know what I enjoy." Another step; another retreat. "I've been wondering if you and I aren't irrevocably connected; that when we took the elixir, the universe demanded balance. You became what you became, and so I became what I am, in order to maintain equilibrium." Step and retreat. "I came to realize that what I want isn't your *death*, Perenelle; it's your anguish and your agony, your guilt and your sorrow. And I want it *forever*."

The last word was a harsh whisper, the very lack of volume deepening the threat.

Another step, and now Lotte's back was to the wall of the room. Ana heard the frame of Klimt's painting rattle on the plaster as Lotte made contact. Brunner was still three steps away from them; as she watched he took another step. "Stay away from me," she told him. "From us."

He laughed. "No," he answered. "I'll never do that entirely, my darling. Fate has brought us together yet again, and who am I to deny fate?"

Ana's mind was in a fury. The small vial of elixir in her shoe seemed to burn underneath her. *If I can stop him, even for a minute, I might have enough time to get the elixir, to make Lotte drink it, and she'd be safer . . .*

As Brunner started to take a final step, Anaïs moved away from Lotte and raised her hands, shouting a phrase in Arabic. Blue flames huffed into existence, flying away from her in a hissing, shrieking ball that engulfed Brunner and sent him staggering backward. But though she expected the fire to sear away his uniform and his flesh, to send him crumpling to the floor, she heard him shout in the same language in return; with a wave of his hands, the fire vanished, leaving him untouched. He brushed at a few dark singe marks on the brown uniform.

"That was well played," he told her. She could see rage pulling at the muscles of his face. "I didn't expect *magic* from you, and you nearly caught me. But you were never very good at magic." Ana saw him lift the flap of the holster on his wide belt and slide his Luger from its leather nest. "Tell me, do you have magic prepared against this?"

The report of the pistol was loud and sudden, and Ana screamed as the bullet tore into her knee, ripping at bone, cartilage, and muscle and sending the other spells she had prepared flying away in her mind. Ana collapsed to the floor, blood pouring from the wound, writhing on the carpet, the pain blocking out everything else. She saw Lotte rushing toward her, but Brunner pointed his Luger at her and Lotte backed away to the wall again, hands cradling her stomach as if she could protect the baby inside. Lotte was sobbing and moaning, sinking down the wall to the carpet herself. Brunner walked up calmly to where Ana lay. She looked up at him, at the tendrils of smoke still trailing from the muzzle of his Luger.

"Let me tell you what will happen now, Perenelle. I'm going to watch you die. Again—because I know the torment that coming back will cost you." The weapon barked and jumped twice more, the bullets this time tearing through her stomach and abdomen. Ana shrieked in pain, in concert with a wail of terror from Lotte. She felt Brunner's hand unbuttoning her blouse; his fingers lifted the pendant on its chain. He laughed at that and dropped the pendant again. The muzzle of the Luger pressed hot and hard against her left breast. "Stay awake, *ma petite colombe*. Listen to me so you know what happens next. I've a new promise for you: I will make certain that your Charlotte gets very special treatment."

She heard him speaking through the roar of blood and the pain, but her vision had gone red and she could no longer see him clearly. Lotte cried in the background.

"There will be no forced labor for her," he continued. "No, no. Instead, I'll make certain that she learns firsthand what Auschwitz does best. Remember that, Perenelle, when you come back; your failures killed her. And here's another promise: next time I'll have you watch your lover die first before I take care of you. Won't that be exquisite? There's something for you to look forward to in your next life. It won't be soon—maybe thirty years, or fifty, or another century entirely. But I'll find you again, because you have a weakness I don't have, *ma cherie*. You actually care about people, and I don't. Now . . . say good-bye for a time."

Ana heard Lotte scream, then the report of the Luger against her chest, then nothing at all.

9:
MELPOMENE

Camille Kenny

Today

IT WOULD TAKE HER over a month to fully recover—physically, if not mentally—from what Nicolas did to her that day. She saw him only once after that: Nicolas visited her the day after their encounter to tell her, smugly, how he'd personally enjoyed Charlotte, how after he'd finished with her, he'd sent Charlotte and Alexander on to Drancy with orders for both to be shipped eastward to Auschwitz.

By the time Ana was well enough to leave the hospital, Brunner had left Nice and returned to Germany, his work done.

In early October, Lotte and Alexander had been transported to Auschwitz, where the two had been separated. As a pregnant woman, Charlotte had been sent to the gas chambers immediately; Ana would learn, later, that Alexander had survived forced labor until early 1944, when he, too, succumbed.

"Alois Brunner" vanished in April of 1945, during the Allied invasion of Germany. She was hardly surprised; Nicolas had long practice at becoming someone else at need. From that time on, they were engaged in a mutual hunt: he to torment her; she to end the torment forever.

She couldn't allow him to escape again. She could have no mercy, no compassion for him. Not if she still was to live in this world.

"Next time I'll have you watch your lover die first before I take care of

you." That's what Nicolas had told her, and now he had David. She had
no way to know where Nicolas had taken him, no way to find them.
She called Morris with no expectation that he'd help her, afraid that he
wouldn't answer when he saw it was her cell calling. But he was the only
person she knew who had actual contact with Pierce, who might have
be able to offer her a clue. His phone rang four times, then she heard
the click of the connection and his low voice. "What the fuck d'you
want, Camille? Can't you take a goddamn hint?"

"It's Pierce," she said in a rush over Morris' profanity-laced com-
plaints. "He's taken David, and he's going to kill him. I have to find
them, and I don't know where to start looking. You have to help me,
Morris. Please."

She could hear the desperation in her own voice, and, worse, she
knew Morris could hear it as well. She was certain he wasn't going to
answer, that she'd hear the click of his disconnection in the long silence
that followed. She heard him breathing, then a clearing of his throat.

"You're thinking I'm gonna help *you*? Are you fucking kidding me?"

"I don't believe you want David to die, Morris, no matter how you
feel about me."

"Yeah?" he answered, and she thought that she might as well hang
up when his voice softened slightly. "Look, Camille, I don't know where
Pierce is," he said. "I haven't seen him since . . . well, since he told me
about you. He always came here to my studio; I never went to him and
he certainly never told me where he's staying now. And now, with the
fucking cops watching my place, he ain't likely to show up here again,
either." He gave a short, mocking laugh.

She felt her shoulders sag. "Pierce hasn't picked up the sculpture?
He didn't have you send it somewhere?"

"No. It's been cast and I've been going over to supervise the final
construction of the pieces, but Pierce hasn't told me where he wants it
shipped yet. All I know is that he said it'd be local." Again, there was
a pause. "Camille, look, I don't have anything more to tell you. I hope
you find David, okay? If I hear from Pierce again, maybe I'll see what I
can find out." He sounded sincere.

"Thanks," she told him. There was nothing else to say. She had nothing more to go on than she had before. "I appreciate it."

He didn't answer that at all. She heard the click as he disconnected the call. She sat with the phone in her hand until she heard the recording telling her to hang up.

She waited, because she had no choice though it tore her apart to do so. A long afternoon faded slowly into a damp and dark evening. She pulled out her scrolls and began memorizing the spells and hexes there, trying to cram them into her memory. She went to the display of chemicals on their shelves and mixed several pungent and odoriferous vials. She laid out the Tarot cards on the table next to her laptop and scanned their familiar, scuffed, and faded faces, hating what the array told her: *danger, trouble, despair.*

At the center of the array stood the Tower card, to Camille the most frightening card of the Tarot, signifying sudden cataclysmic changes and a drastic upheaval. She went back to the chemicals and made more preparations, then finally fell asleep in a chair, exhausted and worried.

Verdette, purring on Camille's lap, leaped up in annoyance as Camille's computer chimed, announcing that she had e-mail. Camille pulled the laptop toward her and clicked on the Mail icon as Verdette fled the room; she didn't recognize the sender's name or the address in the inbox, but the subject line made her stomach lurch. *David*, it said simply.

Taking a long, slow breath, she clicked on the message.

She was greeted with a grainy image of David, seated in a battered old wooden chair with his hands duct-taped to the chair arms and his legs also taped together. He was staring at the camera with an expression of bewilderment on his face. Below the image, there were a few words: an address near the East River, and a warning in French—*Come alone or he dies immediately.* The message itself was unsigned, but it needed no signature.

She put her hands in the pocket of her jeans; her fingers touched a piece of cardboard there: Detective Palento's business card. She pulled out the card and stared at it for a long time before dialing the number.

It rang once, then went to voicemail; she listened to the short recording and Gina Palento's gruff voice. At the beep, she nearly hung up, but gathered herself.

"Detective Palento, this is Camille Kenny. Pierce . . . he has David. He says he's going to kill him if I don't come to where he's holding him, but I have to come alone. I want you to know, just in case . . ." She stopped. She could hear her breath ragged in the speaker. "Here's the address, but please, don't send any squad cars or Pierce will kill David. By the time you get there, it'll probably be over, one way or another." She gave the address, then ended the call.

Camille made certain that the Ladysmith was loaded and in her purse along with her several test tubes. She took the katana from its stand in her bedroom and wrapped it in a tablecloth. She picked up her cell phone again and dialed another number in its memory. The call went to voicemail. "Mercedes," Camille said at the beep. "If you're there, please pick up. I . . . I really could use your help." She waited; after a few breaths, she started to press the End Call button when she heard a click and Mercedes' cautious voice.

"Camille? What's going on? You sound really upset."

Camille told her quickly about Pierce's abduction of David and the e-mail. "I'm at David's now and I know I don't deserve any help from you. I was going to just call a cab, but I thought . . . I hoped . . ."

Mercedes didn't let her finish. "I'll be there in a few minutes. Just let me get dressed and I'll drive over. I'll honk when I'm outside."

"Mercedes, thank you. You don't know what this means."

"Shut up, girl," Mercedes answered. "You're wasting time. Get yourself ready to go."

Camille found Verdette and spent the time stroking her, wondering if she would see the cat again, wondering if David was still alive. He couldn't be dead, she told herself; not yet. She would somehow know if that were the case. Nicolas *wanted* her to come, after all. He wanted her to witness David's death; Nicolas would keep him alive until she was there.

When she heard the horn blare on the street outside, she hugged

Verdette again, who mewled in protest. She grabbed for her purse and the katana.

"I'll see you soon, Verdette," she said. She hoped that wasn't a lie.

"Okay, I *really* don't like this," Mercedes said.

She also hadn't liked the fact that Camille had entered the car bearing weapons. She'd given Camille a severely raised eyebrow when she learned that the long, thin bundle was a sword, and the other eyebrow had gone up when Camille admitted that she had a gun in her purse.

The address was an old building on East 10th Street near Avenue D. The front was boarded up, and as Mercedes slowed her ancient Volvo to a stop across the street she shook her head, glaring at the building as if she could demolish it with her scowl. "This isn't good, Camille," she said. "This looks like the place where someone finds a decomposing body six months after the murder, or that's crawling with crack addicts who would kill you for the change in your pockets. You're *sure* this is where Pierce said you were to meet him?"

Camille nodded; she glanced down at the scrap of paper in her hand, then at the address spray-painted on the facade and visible in the gleam of the streetlamp. "Yeah. This is it. Drive on past—park somewhere farther up where Pierce can't look out and see you."

Mercedes drove to the middle of the next block and pulled over. "We should call the cops," Mercedes persisted. That had been her plea through most of the short drive to the location. "You can't just go in there."

"I left a message with the detective who's handling Helen's murder," Camille said, a bit wearily. "But if Pierce sees cops, he'll just kill David immediately and he'll get away again. Mercedes, you have no idea what the man can do. No idea. This is something I have to do myself."

"No, you don't. I'll come in with you." She didn't sound quite so certain of that, but Camille smiled for a moment hearing her say it, even as she shook her head.

"He said 'alone.' That's the way I have to do it. All I'm asking is for you to drop me off. That's it. I don't want to expose you to anything more."

Mercedes scowled. "Well, I'm not a taxi and I'm not just dropping you off and leaving you," she told Camille. "I'm staying parked here until you come back out—and if you're not out fast enough, I really don't give a damn what you say; I'm calling 911."

"Don't get involved in this, Mercedes. I don't want you to get hurt, too."

Mercedes sniffed. "Then why the hell did you call me? I'm already involved, or haven't you noticed? You think your detective won't check your phone records and see that you called me? You think she wouldn't ask me what that call was about; you think the garage won't tell them that right afterward I took my car out? Look, if you don't want me to go in with you because you think that's dangerous for David, then fine. But I'm staying here; you just need to tell me how long to wait before I call for the cavalry, because that's what I'm going to do."

Camille took a long breath, considering her options. If she failed, if Nicolas killed both David and her, at least there might be a chance that the police would catch Nicolas. A chance, though not much of one . . . "Twenty minutes," she said. "That should be enough. And Mercedes . . ." Camille fumbled in her purse and pulled out a cork-topped test tube the length of her forefinger. In the faint light of the instrument panel, a thick, dark liquid moved sluggishly at the bottom. She took a pencil from the glove compartment and scribbled quickly on the address paper, handing it to Mercedes. "Can you say these words: *alnar aldhahabia?*"

Mercedes glanced at the paper, shrugged and repeated the phrase. Her pronunciation was poor, but the words were vaguely recognizable; Camille decided that it would have to do. "What language is this?" Mercedes asked.

"Arabic," Camille answered. She handed Mercedes the vial. "If you see Pierce, if he starts to come toward you, throw this at his feet hard enough that the glass breaks, then speak those words while striking the fingers of your right hand in your left palm like you're striking a rock with a piece of flint, and then run." Camille showed Mercedes the hand motion. "Just run and don't look back. Do you understand that?"

Mercedes took the vial gingerly, watching the liquid slosh inside. "Alnar aldhahabia," she said again, and moved her hands in imitation of Camille. "Umm, nothing happened," she said.

"Nothing *will* happen until the stuff in that tube is exposed to air," Camille told her. "Your pronunciation was rough, but I think it'll still work."

"You *think* it'll work . . ." Mercedes repeated, skeptically. "Do I want to know what's supposed to happen?"

"I don't think you'd believe me," Camille answered. "Just remember those words and the gesture—the stuff inside won't do anything without them."

"This is some of your . . . magic?" She said the last word as if she were tasting a rotten lemon. "Camille, I don't believe in magic—at least, not this kind."

Camille allowed herself a small smile. "Do you believe in science?"

Mercedes nodded. "Yeah."

"Then think of it as a science experiment that requires an incantational component, because that's what it actually is. If Pierce comes after you, you'll be glad you have it." Camille hoped she was telling the truth; she was doubtful that Mercedes could successfully work the spell words and gesture without a lot of practice, but she couldn't give her the Ladysmith. Mercedes gripped the test tube a little tighter. She nodded. "All right, I'm going now," Camille said. "Twenty minutes?"

"Twenty minutes," Mercedes repeated. "Good luck. And please be careful, Camille."

"I'll try." Camille opened the door and stood in the cool night air. There was no one nearby on the street, though she saw people moving a few blocks up. She unwrapped the katana from the tablecloth and untied the strings of the *saya* from the weapon, placing the sheath under the belt of her jeans at her left side and shoving the strings into her pocket. She took the Ladysmith and attached the holster at the back of her right hip, then slung her purse around her shoulder so that it also lay on her right. She stared at the building; she spoke a small charm, and felt a tingling that told her, yes, Nicolas was nearby. Nicolas would certainly feel her coming as well. She crossed the street at a jog, then entered the alleyway behind the building.

The rusted fire escape she dismissed immediately—even if it would hold her weight, it would creak and groan and alert Nicolas exactly how she was approaching. There was a crude plywood door a little farther down; she went to that. The wood was tagged with swirls of blue-and-orange spray paint, and the cheap hinges bled rust down the side. The hinges looked less than functional in any case; the door was nailed shut, the nail heads also rusted and pitted. It had been a long time since someone had come in this way.

Camille rummaged among the test tubes in her purse, pulling one out. She poured the thick, pale liquid inside over the door hinges and onto each of the nail heads before capping the vial again. Tendrils of smoke curled away from the metal, and she could smell an iron tang in the air. She stepped back.

She heard the sound of footsteps as she did so, someone coming at heavy run. She turned and drew her katana from its sheath in a single fluid motion: a testament to the years she'd studied martial arts. The draw of the sword was also the attack. The blade slid hard across the oncoming attacker's abdomen, cutting deep into the muscles and flesh there: she saw the man's intent as he held the tire iron high over his head to strike her. Then he doubled over as she continued to turn her hips, the blade ripping out of his body with a shower of blood droplets. The tire iron clanged against the pavement, dropped from his hands. She heard her attacker gasp as he sank to his knees, doubled over.

She didn't hesitate: this would be another of Nicolas' dupes, thinking they were immortal. If she left him here, he might just rise again like a zombie and follow her. She stared down at the man's back as he groaned and blood pooled on the blacktop. *Let the blade do the work . . .* Her teacher's words. The katana hissed through the air as she sobbed, a downward-angled cut. Despite having practiced at cutting reed bundles in her study of the art, she was surprised at how easily the head separated from the body and rolled away, at how the body remained upright on its knees for a few seconds before toppling.

She glanced at the head which had come to rest a few feet away, its face toward her . . . and she recoiled in horror, cursing. She knew that face, those features: it was Kevin from the *Bent Calliope* Group. He was younger in appearance, his long hair ash-brown rather than touched with gray, but it was him. The mouth was open in a soundless wail, the open eyes staring at nothing. Blood drooled from his neck. "Oh, Kevin," she said. "Why?"

But there would be no answer for that. Not now or ever.

God, please don't let me find Morris with him, too, or any more of the others . . . Her vision shimmered with tears, and she blinked them away. *You can't break down now,* she scolded herself. *You can't think about this at all. David needs you. Go help David.*

She brought the blade around in a quick *chiburi* motion to fling the blood from the blade, then sheathed it. She tried not to look at the body or Kevin's head as she moved back to the door. The acid had already done its work; the nail heads had vanished and the hinges no longer held the door to the frame. The plywood moved easily as she tugged at it, falling away from the doorframe. She caught it and lowered it to the ground; beyond was a corridor moving away into blackness. From her purse, she took a small LED flashlight and turned it on.

She entered the building.

She had to forget Kevin. She could deal with that guilt and grief later. She put David in her mind, and Nicolas.

Camille slid the Ladysmith from its holster; somehow the weight and bulk of the gun felt more reassuring than the spells coiled in her mind, the test tube vials still in her purse, or the newly blooded katana at her side. At the end of the dark hall, where it turned toward the front of the building, a lone, naked light bulb dangled from a cracked socket on the ceiling, illuminating stairs leading up to the second floor. There was no door at the top, only the yawning cavity of the frame with darkness beyond it, though she thought she detected the wavering, orange-yellow light of a flame flickering dimly beyond. She could smell Nicolas' presence now: the scent of chemicals, mixed and bubbling in their glass retorts. Her own laboratories had always had the same characteristic stench.

He was here; this was his lair. She was certain of it. She listened, thinking she could hear rustlings and burblings above. "Nicolas?" she called out in French. "You know I'm here. I'm alone, the way you said it had to be."

Faint laughter answered her and a light went on in the room beyond. She could see shadows moving on the walls, but no figures. "I knew you were here before you killed our little friend in the alley," Nicolas answered. "That was delicious, my dear. Thank you. A nice appetizer for the feast to come, eh? You're just in time. I was nearly ready to start the main course without you."

She swallowed the bile that threatened to overspill her stomach. "I want to see David."

"Oh, I very much want you to see him as well," the voice answered her. "Just come on up."

"Not until I know that's he's still alive."

In response, a harsh, white light kicked on, throwing a tight, dusty beam toward the top of the stairs. In the haze, she could see the outline of a man seated in a chair, and another man moving alongside. The shadows stirred, and she heard a gasp of breath. "Camille?" David's hoarse, desperate voice called out. "Get out of here. He's . . ." The voice cut off abruptly, the remaining words muffled and indistinct. She heard Nicolas' laughter once more. Shadows slid in the glare above her.

"He's so noble and self-sacrificing," Nicolas said. "And he has such love for you. Why, it nearly makes me want to weep." He laughed again.

"Nicolas, this is between me and you. Let David go, and we can finish things."

"You tried that argument with me half a century ago, Perenelle. It wasn't true then, and it's not true now. You know I'm not going to let him go. So come up if you intend to try to stop me, or just stay where you are and listen to him die. It's your choice—but you need to make it now."

She knew that as soon as she was visible at the top of the stairs, Nicolas would attack her, if only because he knew she would do the same. She closed her eyes, letting the spells in her mind rise to the forefront. She put the Ladysmith in her left hand, using her right to slide another test tube from the purse, this one full of a dark powder.

She tossed the vial in her hand up past the top of the stairs, shouting a word in Arabic as she heard the tinkling of breaking glass, closing her eyes and putting her right hand over an ear. White light and smoke erupted with a shattering, sharp explosion of thunder. She ran up the steps, two at a time.

By the time Camille reached the top, staying close to one side of the stairwell, the smoke was clearing but still acrid. Her left ear rang with the explosion's echo, deafened, and her eyes whirled with bright afterimages fading slowly through the hues from bright yellow to purple. Through the aural and visual fog, she saw David off to one side, trussed to a chair, and Nicolas standing before a workbench littered with test tubes and retorts, the shelves behind stocked with glass canisters of chemicals and alchemical ingredients, and what appeared to be her old journal propped up on a reading stand, along with several parchment scrolls. Nicolas was standing still, as if stunned, his hands—strangely—at his hips to either side. He didn't move, didn't speak, but she heard him cough.

She didn't give him the time to utter his spells or to counter her attack. She quickly brought up the Ladysmith in both hands. With a cry, she fired the weapon: once, then again. She saw at least one of the bullets strike him, his body turning violently with the impact, bending him backward over the table so that he crashed hard into the racks of test tubes behind him, smashing them underneath his weight. Camille tossed the Ladysmith aside when she saw him fall, drawing the katana and rushing toward him as she raised the blade.

She imagined his head rolling across the table like an ugly, misshapen ball. Like Kevin's head.

Nicolas lolled on the table, his face a rictus of pain as blood spread on the white shirt he wore; she had struck him in the side of the abdomen, though the other shot seemed to have gone wide. She saw this in the three steps it took to reach him, and in those three steps, she also found her mind wondering at the fact that he wasn't responding, that his hands were still splayed out at his sides, at the fact that his body seemed taller . . .

She remembered a statue in King's Square, remembered Robespierre's head tumbling into the basket below the guillotine's blade . . .

She brought the blade down hard, but at the last moment, she turned her hands. The blade sliced deep into the workbench, shearing through the wild brown locks just above the man's skull—whose features now flowed as if they were melting wax.

Flowed into David's features, and settled. It was David staring at her, his hands working against the ropes that bound him to the workbench, his eyes terrified, his mouth working as he spoke her name. "Camille . . ." Blood flecked his lips.

She released the katana with horror. The weapon quivered in the wood. Behind her, she heard sardonic, mocking applause through the ringing in her ears. "Bravo," she heard Nicolas say. "And here I thought I'd set it up perfectly for you to kill David yourself—though you probably have anyway. Guns are such ugly but effective weapons . . ."

Nicolas was standing in front of the chair that she had assumed held David, the ropes uncoiled at his feet, his features no longer David's but his own. His hands still applauded her softly. "You *have* killed him, you know," Nicolas said. "I didn't give him the flawed elixir for just that reason, though it was tempting. He'll bleed out, very soon. Look, he's already going into shock."

Camille glanced down. Nicolas was right. In the mess of broken glass and spilled chemicals, David's face had gone white and pale. His eyes were staring somewhere beyond her; his hands clenched and unclenched against their bonds. She shouted denial: "No!"

"We could save him still, you know," Nicolas said. "If I gave him *my* elixir, why, his body would heal itself. Or you could give him yours—but I see by your face that you didn't bring that. Were you too afraid that I'd take it from you? A shame. Still . . . Tell me how to make the true formula, and I'll give David mine in the meantime. That's all you have to do, and he lives. A fair bargain, I should think."

Camille looked at David. His eyes had closed; he didn't appear to be conscious. "Nicolas . . ."

He held out his hand; a crystalline vial glistened there. "I've given you my terms, wife. The rest is up to you."

She took a step toward Nicolas, and his fingers closed around the vial as he pulled his arm back. She stopped. "I'll tell you. Let me have that," she said.

"Tell me first."

She took a long breath that held back a wail. Defeat tasted like acid, smelled like rotting meat. Defeat was the brush of a corpse's hand against her face. "It's blood," she said. She couldn't look at him; she stared instead at David. "Human blood. That's what was missing. When you hit me that day, you made my lips and mouth bleed. My blood mixed with the potion when I drank it."

His dark, scornful gaze searched her face. "You're telling me the truth?"

"It's the truth," she told him, and he laughed.

"Really? So it was an accident all along? *I* caused the elixir to work for you? Oh, that's precious."

"Nicolas, please . . . The vial . . . David . . ."

Nicolas' hand opened like a slow, pale flower. The crystal gleamed in the light, the elixir a sapphire inside. "I suppose I don't need this anymore," he said. He flung the container at the near wall. It shattered there, spilling blue down the plasterboard.

Camille screamed in blind fury. She plunged her hand into a pocket and pulled out the last of her test tubes, an explosive, but she saw Nicolas react, his hands moving too quickly for her to have any hope. She dropped the vial and instead uttered a warding word, her hand chopping through the air. Nicolas' voice barked out his own quick phrase. Black fire erupted along her right side; the ward took most of the heat, but the force of the spell still rammed its way through the psychic shield of the ward, throwing Camille hard against the bench alongside David's body. Glassware rattled and shattered; she heard items falling from the shelving behind her. Something hissed and she smelled gas; yellow flame bloomed, reflected along the walls as smoke slid past her head. She tried to rise. Nicolas barked another word in Arabic and a giant's fist hit her: a fist of air that swept aside the smoke and smashed her down to the floor at David's feet. Fire was beginning to crawl up the wall behind her, licking at the bench that held Nicolas' alchemical experiments.

She heard Nicolas' laughter as she rose up on her knees, trying to clear the confusion in her mind and the pain from her scorched body. She felt more than saw Nicolas walking past her and wrenching the katana from where it had been embedded in the bench. "Very nice," he said. "You may have been the better alchemist, Perenelle," he said, "but you were never the better wizard. Such a shame. We could have been the perfect duo, you and I. Can you imagine what we might have accomplished, together? The power we could have held . . . But it's too late for that. With the fire, we don't have much time." He lifted the sword, let it hiss through the air. She raised her head to see him facing the helpless David. "You get to watch him die, Perenelle, just as I promised. Will you scream, I wonder? Will you cry out when his blood spatters over you and his head rolls at your feet? Let's find out, shall we? Then, since you've given me the secret of the elixir and I can make someone else to take your place, it'll be your turn."

He lifted the sword again, and Perenelle did scream: a hoarse, wordless, throat-tearing denial. She forced her legs to push her up as the sword—clumsy in Nicolas' untrained hands—rushed down, interposing herself between Nicolas and David as the sword threatened. She felt the blade slice into her side under her upraised arms, felt the steel catch on her ribs and turn, heard the crack of bone and the ring of iron. The intense pain followed an instant later, a searing blue tsunami that took her breath so that she couldn't shout or cry out. Nicolas yanked the blade from her body, and she mewled with the agony, hot blood pouring down her side.

"You were always the one for useless gestures, Perenelle," Nicolas said. "Now what did that gain you but more pain? It certainly won't save him, will it?" He brought the sword up again—she could see her blood bright on the steel, heavy droplets flying away in seeming slow motion. She tried to rise once more but her body wouldn't cooperate. As she tried to hold herself upright, she saw the blade begin its descent.

Shadows moved in the smoky room. She heard the pop of gunfire: three quick shots, and she saw Nicolas' body jerk with the impacts. That was followed by the bright sound of breaking glass at Nicolas' feet, and a voice calling two words—"Alnar aldhahabia!"—as Nicolas started to respond, too slowly. Camille threw herself over David's prone body: as heat exploded at Nicolas' feet and along her own side, flames as bright as molten gold climbing over his body.

Nicolas screamed. It was an ugly sound, a demon's shriek. Perenelle screamed with him, the golden fire touching her as well, the heat of it spilling over her as her body shielded David. Nicolas dropped the sword; his hands waving as if he were trying to conjure up a new spell to extinguish the fire, but the flames choked him. He breathed them in and exhaled them again as his clothing fell from him in shreds of sparks, as his skin blackened under the relentless, pitiless chemical fire.

Nicolas collapsed to his knees, his mouth open and working soundlessly. He slid sideways to the floor as the golden flames guttered and went out.

Camille picked up the sword in hands that shook, her skin blackened and blistered. "No," she heard someone say—Palento's voice. "Drop the sword, Ms. Kenny."

She paid no attention. "You goddamn son of bitch," she said, standing over Nicolas. She brought the blade up, and sliced downward as hard as she could.

Then, finally, she let herself fall.

There was a voice in the darkness, speaking words that slid through the filter of pain like shards of broken glass.

"We need a couple buses and the fire department to East 10th and D. The place is about to go up. Make it quick."

Her first breath was a gasping horror, and the rattling, terrible cough that followed was worse. "*Madre de Dios*, she's alive," she heard Mercedes exclaim, and fingers moved through her hair and brushed her cheek.

"David . . ." she managed to say.

"I have ambulances coming for both of you," Palento replied, "but we gotta get out of here—the building's on fire."

Camille shook her head. She blinked, trying to will the room into focus. The walls were lurching around her, the light was erratic and the room too hot, and she couldn't decide if her vision was blurred or if it was the smoke. She could see Mercedes kneeling next to her, and Detective Palento standing nearby. She was untying David from the workbench, which was alive with flames that engulfed the back wall. Camille's body felt like it had been pounded, sliced, then broiled. She forced herself to sit up, and Mercedes hissed at the movement. "You shouldn't . . ."

"I'll be fine," she told her. "Just help me stand, then take care of David. I can make it . . ." She felt Mercedes' arm underneath her, and she nearly screamed with the pain as the sword's wound ripped open again as Mercedes pulled her to her feet. The room threatened to go away, and she forced herself to remain standing, to breathe, to let the world settle again. She fought not to cough with the smoke, afraid of what would happen if she did. "Help with David," she repeated to Mercedes, and she started toward the stairs, glancing first to where Nicolas lay. His head was a hand's breadth from the blackened, charred body, the katana snagged in the floorboards between them. He seemed to stare at her in eternal surprise.

Grunting with the pain of the movement, she kicked the head even farther away.

She thought she should be feeling triumph, but instead felt nothing but blinding pain. She took a limping step, then another, then yet another, willing her body to move, holding the edges of the terrible wound together with a hand. Behind her, she heard Palento and Mercedes taking David between them.

She would not remember the descent, only the bite of the night air outside and the blessed purity of the breath she took then. She leaned against the wall of the building opposite. Kevin's body was still there in the alley, another accusation. She saw Palento and Mercedes exit the building with David, smoke billowing out from the top of the open doorway. Through the boarded windows above, yellow-and-orange flames were visible. She could hear the crackle of the fire now, almost as loud as the sound of approaching sirens. Palento and Mercedes laid David down on the alley's pavement near Kevin's body. Camille looked at Palento in mute question.

"He's still breathing," she said, and coughed. "I don't know about the gunshot or how much blood he's lost. He needs that ambulance, fast. And so do you."

Camille shook her head. The blood from the long, deep cut had already stopped, and the cool air soothed her burns. "No," she said. "I'll be fine on my own. It'll just take time."

Palento was shaking her head, but Mercedes put her hand on the detective's shoulder. "She's right," Mercedes said. "She'll heal on her own. The hospital's not the place for her."

Palento stared at both of them, at Kevin's body, at the flames beginning to appear between the boards of the windows. The sirens grew louder, echoing from the street's buildings. "Can you get her home?" she asked Mercedes, who nodded. Palento shook her head, as if arguing with herself. "I shouldn't, but no one's going to believe much of this anyway. Okay, get her out of here—now, while I get the ambulance crew and talk to my people. And neither of you two were ever here. Do you understand?"

They both nodded this time. Mercedes put her arm around Camille. Together, they limped away as Palento pressed the button of her radio. "Around the back," she said into the mic. "In the alley. Make it fast—I've a GSV who's bleeding out bad . . ."

Camille tried to smile at Mercedes. They were in David's apartment. Verdette was curled up on Camille's lap as she sat on the couch. Mercedes sat near her, wearing a set of Camille's pajamas and sipping coffee—Mercedes had cleaned up the worst of the blood, bandaged her wounds, and gently draped a soft nightgown over Camille's burnt skin, sighing in distress the entire time and wiping back tears at the sight of Camille's injuries. "I'll be fine," Camille kept telling her. "I need to know what's happening with David . . ."

Palento knocked on the door several hours after they'd left the scene, arriving as the sun was starting to rise. "David?" Camille asked her immediately, and Palento shrugged.

"He's alive, and out of surgery. Seems he was shot with a .38, same caliber as your Ladysmith, but whoever shot him had either really lousy or really good aim. He lost some of his liver and his spleen, his intestines were perforated, but they've patched him up, removed the bullet fragments they could find, and given him a transfusion. They think he'll probably make it."

Camille closed her eyes. The tears were hot on her cheeks. "Thank you," she said.

"Don't thank me; thank the docs." Palento sat on the chair across from the two women. She looked at Mercedes. "Would you mind giving us some time alone?" she said, and stared hard at Camille as Mercedes gathered herself and left the room. They heard her begin to wash dishes in the kitchen. "You were dead," Palento said at last. "I felt for your pulse, and there wasn't one. You weren't breathing. You were halfway sliced open with a fatal wound, and there was more blood than I've ever seen anyone lose before and live—and I've seen dozens and dozens of dead people. You were one of them . . . but you're not now. How is that possible?"

Camille remained silent, stroking Verdette. After a moment, Palento continued, leaning forward in the chair.

"You don't exist, either. There really isn't a Camille Kenny, any more than there was a real Timothy Pierce. You killed two people—in evident self-defense, I know—but then you took the time to decapitate them afterward. I saw things last night that defy explanation. You got one for me?"

Camille pressed her lips together. Verdette growled softly, glaring at Palento.

Palento sighed. "You're not making this easy. At least tell me this much. Is Pierce the guy who killed Bob?"

"Yes," Camille said. "He did. And he's the Black Fire murderer, too. He admitted it to me. Hell, he bragged about killing Mr. Walters."

At the last words, a look of pain briefly touched Palento's eyes. "How?"

"You saw what he did to me," Camille answered, lowering the shoulder of her robe to expose the blackened, crisp skin, already flaking away to show pink underneath. "That's what he did to Mr. Walters and the other victims."

"You're telling me that it's magic." Palento sat back in the chair again. She ran her fingers through her short-cut hair. There were dark circles under her eyes; she looked exhausted. "You're saying it was *magic* that Pierce used, and magic that you're still alive and looking far healthier than you have any right to look. I don't believe in that crap."

"Then don't," Camille told her. "Would you like some coffee? Mercedes could bring some in."

Palento's gaze flicked toward the kitchen and the sound of dishes. "No, I'm going home and I'm going to collapse. It's been a long night. Pierce killed Helen Treadway also?"

"Yes," Camille answered. "Or rather, he had people do it for him." It was hard to keep her eyes open; she was also exhausted, and Mercedes' soul-heart could only nourish her so far. "What happens now?" Camille asked Palento. "Am I going to be charged?" *And if I am, then it's time to leave again . . .* She suspected Palento knew that as well.

But the detective shook her head. "You weren't there, remember?" she said. "Neither was your girlfriend. I got your call about David being kidnapped, and you gave me the address. I was almost too late getting there. David had been shot and the place was going up in flames when I dragged him out." She shrugged. "Lots of chemicals there that didn't help. There were a couple explosions about the time the squad cars got there. The place is pretty much gone; there isn't much left for Forensics to dig through."

"And the decapitations?"

"There was obviously another person there we didn't catch. We're looking for him—because I have a witness who saw a man running away from the building. I've already taken David's statement; the whole evening is hazy to him, understandably." Palento rose from the chair, looking down at Camille. Verdette cowered back against Camille's stomach, her back arched as she hissed up at the detective. "She's gray, not black," Palento said.

"I'm not a witch," Camille answered. "I'm more a scientist."

Palento grunted. "After this," she said, "I don't ever expect to hear from you again. If that turns out not to be the case, then I'll do what I'm paid to do. I'll look into everything about you, and I will follow what the law tells me to do. I promise you that."

"I understand."

Palento straightened her jacket and brushed imaginary dandruff from her blouse. She moved toward the door without looking back.

"Detective Palento," Camille called out, and the woman turned, her hand on the knob. "Thank you for what you've done for me."

Palento shrugged. "I didn't do it for you. I did it for Bob and what he meant to me. You can thank him."

She lifted her chin as if in salute, then opened the door.

"You look like hell."

"Oh, yeah? Have you looked in a mirror lately?"

Camille could feel the hesitation in David even as she stared at him in the hospital bed. His face was still pale, though both eyes were circled in dark, ugly bruises. The stand next to his bed held a quart of saline, plasma, and a morphine demand-drip; alongside, a monitor graphed his pulse, heartbeat, and BP readings. A catheter tube ran out from under the bedsheets to a plastic bag. His body was wrapped in bandages, and he grimaced as he moved his arm to raise the head of the bed slightly. She reached for his soul-heart, but he kept it inside himself, wrapped tightly around a ball of ugly scarlet that might have been his pain. She plucked at it, but she couldn't get the energy to release.

"What happened there?" David asked. "I don't remember much of it after . . ." He stopped.

"After I shot you?" Camille ventured. "You know why that happened, don't you? I didn't *intend* to shoot you."

He closed his eyes as he took a breath, grimacing. "Yeah," he said. "I figured that. Speaking of mirrors . . . Pierce . . . he showed me my face, how I looked like him and he . . ." Another pained breath. ". . . looked like me," he finished. "Bastard."

Camille ventured a smile. She sat on the chair next to his bed. She put her hand on his. "How are you?"

"Pretty lousy, if you must know. The docs say that I'll be here awhile, and there's still some worry." His eyes closed again, and he took another few breaths before opening cracked lips to speak again. "I'm looking at another surgery or two to get stuff they couldn't take care of in the emergency operation. They said it'll be a long recovery."

"I can change that for you," Camille said. She lifted her hand from his and reached into her purse. She took out a small glass tube, placing it on the sheet over his chest where he could see it. A deep blue liquid nestled inside the glass.

"Is that . . . ?"

"Yes," she told him. "All you have to do is drink it."

"Then what?" he asked. His eyes were darker bruises in the center of purple and green swellings. "I become like Pierce? Or like you? Or your damn cat?"

"I don't know," she answered, stung by the vitriol in his response. "There's no way *to* know. I've told you that. But I do know what else the elixir can do. I know you wouldn't have to worry about your wound or surgeries, ever again."

David's hands, shaking and trailing the plastic line of the saline, plucked the elixir from his chest. He held it up to the fluorescent lights in the ceiling, staring hard. His eyes closed again, fingers tightening around the glass. Then he was staring at her, and he was holding out the elixir toward her. "Take it," he said. "I don't want it."

"David . . ."

"*Take it!*" he said loudly, which set him to coughing. She took the test tube as his body was wracked with the coughs. He groaned, pressing the button for the morphine drip. When the spasms stopped, he wiped at his mouth with the sleeve of his hospital gown. "Camille, you should go."

His soul-heart was closed, a tight shell inside him that she couldn't touch. Her mind slid around it as if it were slick ice. "All right," she said. "I'll come back again soon. In the meantime, I'll get the apartment ready for you. Mercedes is there right now; she's been helping me." She didn't trust herself to say any more. She rose from the chair, reaching down to touch his hand again. It was like touching a stone. "I'll see you soon."

"Camille," David said as she started to leave. "I don't know how to say this, so I'll just spit it out. When I come home, I don't want you to be there." She stopped. She couldn't look back. "I don't hate you," he continued. "But after all this . . . I can't be with you, either. I'm sorry. I can't."

She forced herself to smile as she turned. "I . . ." she began, then had to start again as her voice betrayed her. "This has been hard on both of us," she said. "I'll do whatever you want; I'll be whatever you want me to be. It's up to you, David. We'll talk later, when we can both look at things more objectively."

He didn't answer her. His eyes closed. She watched the rise and fall of his chest for several seconds before she left the room.

EPILOGUE

SARAH MILES

THE PERCUSSIVE SOUND of the piano swelled in the front room of the house, the intricate twists and riffles of the melody wafting from the open windows to dance above the lawn in the cool Pennsylvania evening and pirouette between the oak and pines surrounding the house. The woman crouched over the keys—a Bosendorfer concert grand, the lid canted to throw the sound back into the room—was Asian, perhaps in her mid-thirties. Her name was Ami Huang. She played with her eyes closed as her right hand coaxed an intricate counterpoint from the shifting foundation of the block chords she played with her left hand. A faint humming came from her throat, just ahead of the melody, as if she were sounding out the path of the notes before she played them. A video foil was unrolled on top of the piano, transcribing the notes as she played them, an eternal double staff rolling across the screen, dotted with the black spermatozoa of quarter and eighth notes.

A younger-looking woman sat on a worn leather couch facing the grand piano, a cat purring on her lap. She was red-haired and short, and the blue light of her own video foil touched the ridges of her face as she listened. She called herself Sarah Miles now, and she suddenly gave a cry as her gaze skimmed the text on the screen. Ami's melody halted in mid-phrase, the video foil recorder on the piano going dark and the chords fading slowly as she rose from the piano bench and came over to sit alongside Sarah.

She touched Sarah's shoulder with long, delicate fingers. The cat looked up at her, its ears flattened, and it hissed warningly. Ami drew her hand back. "I'm not going to leave, Verdette, so you might as well stop it," Ami scolded as the cat leaped to the floor and away. "What's wrong, love?" she asked, and Sarah shivered as if noticing Ami for the first time. Sarah shook her head; she touched the video foil and it rolled into a tight, small scroll on her lap. The cat glared at them from under the piano.

"Nothing. It's nothing . . ." Sarah brushed at her eyes, her hand searching out a cameo brooch around her neck, dangling at the end of a golden chain. "Don't stop. Play what you were just playing," she said to the older woman. "That was a lovely melody."

The pianist smiled. "It's your fault," she said. "You inspire me, dear. These last several years, well . . ." Leaning in, she kissed Sarah, a brushing of familiar lips, a gesture between lovers who were well past the initial heat and flame of infatuation. Ami hugged Sarah hard.

"I want to hear more," Sarah told her. "Go on; I didn't mean to interrupt you."

Ami kissed her again, then went back to the piano. A minor 7th chord sounded, low and resonant and as thick as liquid chocolate, then the melody began again, chasing the chord into brighter places. The foil on the piano began recording the notation once more. Sarah listened, a faint smile on her face. When Ami's eyes closed again as she played, Sarah touched the video foil on her lap, and it snapped open. She glanced at the words, blurred by unbidden tears.

David Treadway, Pulitzer-winning photographer and graphic artist, arguably among the best known of the "Bent Calliope Group" of creative artists, has died at age 83 after a series of debilitating strokes. Treadway is survived by his second wife, Kristin Emerson, who was also a photographer, though not a member of the Bent Calliope Group. Treadway's career blossomed in the years following the death of his first wife Helen (née Meeks), murdered in an apparent robbery. Her suspected murderer then abducted Treadway and attempted to murder him as well, but died in a fire that followed Treadway's rescue by a NYC detective.

Treadway would meet Kristin a few years later, and the couple moved from New York City to New Mexico after their marriage. Treadway is also survived by two children with Kristin: Aaron Treadway, 49, and Michelle Treadway, 46, as well as five grandchildren and one great-grandchild.

The Bent Calliope Group also included among its members the award-winning magic realist novelist Mercedes Vargas, whose longtime partner Camille Kenny had a small reputation as a landscape painter, though the two of them are far better known for their unexplained disappearance. The group was also renowned for the tragically short-lived sculptor Morris Johnson, whose piece "Vengeance" is displayed at the Rockefeller Sculpture Garden at MoMA.

David Treadway himself is best remembered for . . .

Sarah touched the foil again, this time wiping the obituary.

"David . . ." She breathed the name, her fingers scissoring around a sardonyx pendant at her throat.

The two bare syllables seemed to wrap themselves around the melody and the radiance of Ami's green heart, lifting away from Sarah and floating out into the night.

AFTERWORD

As stated in the Acknowledgments at the beginning of this book, please *do not* mistake the genuine historical characters for the fictionalized versions I've presented here. However, I thought certain readers might find it interesting to know some details of what was "true" in the novel and what was not.

PERENELLE & NICOLAS FLAMEL: These two characters really did exist, though the evidence that Nicolas was actually an alchemist is conjectural despite being much repeated (heck, even J.K. Rowling mentions the Flamels briefly in the first *Harry Potter* book). The Flamels *were* wealthy, and there are records of substantial charitable donations as well as several Parisian buildings owned by Nicolas. However, my speculation that Nicolas made himself richer through buying the houses of Jews who were forced to leave Paris, then reselling them for a profit, is exactly that: speculation . . . but then so are almost all of the details of his life. The restaurant at rue de Montmorency is a genuine establishment, and the building it inhabits was indeed built for Nicolas Flamel in 1407. However, it postdates Perenelle's usual death date and was evidently not a house Nicolas built in which to live, but was another of his charitable works—a dwelling for the indigent.

Étienne Marcel, Provost of Paris, was assassinated in July of 1358, but not by Nicolas Flamel and not at a dinner party—he was killed at the Porte Saint-Antoine when he attempted to open those gates for Charles of Navarre's men. The Dauphin Charles, later to be King

Charles V, entered the city a few days later to complete the downfall of Marcel's faction.

The story that Nicolas and Perenelle were alchemists appears to have been started in the 1500s and later—possibly as an explanation for how someone who sold books and served as a scrivener managed to become so wealthy. There is an alchemical book attributed to Nicolas, but the extant copy of that book was published in 1612, centuries after his lifetime. Whether Nicolas and Perenelle really possessed the *Book of Abraham the Mage* is anyone's guess. The tale of Nicolas' tomb being empty is an old one, but again has no definitive proof. I've actually viewed Nicolas' tombstone in the Musée de Cluny in Paris. However, the "arcane alchemical symbols" that many claim are carved on it can also be construed as being straight Christian symbology as well. Want a look without going to Paris? Try here (http://hermetism.free.fr/images/Nicolas Flamel tombe.jpg) or search the web for "Nicolas Flamel tombstone."

And, obviously, there is absolutely no proof that Nicolas and Perenelle lived beyond the usual lifespan, nor that they interfered in anyone else's lives.

Alas, no paintings or sketches survive from the time to allow us to glimpse what Nicolas and Perenelle might have actually looked like.

GIANLORENZO BERNINI: There is indeed a bust of Costanza by Gianlorenzo Bernini, which is considered to be one of his masterpieces, though the date of Costanza's bust varies quite widely: I've seen attributions ranging anywhere from as early as 1633 to as late as 1638; I've gone with 1636-1637 in the novel. Costanza *was* Bernini's mistress, and yes, she was married to one of Bernini's assistants. When Bernini began to suspect that his brother was *also* having an affair with Costanza— Bernini supposedly saw him leaving Costanza's house and kissing her when she was dressed only in her night shift—Bernini hired someone to slash poor Costanza's face and tried to kill his brother. For that, his brother was exiled, while Bernini was ordered to pay a fine. He wouldn't ever pay that fine, since Pope Urban VIII stepped in to save his favorite artist, and forgave the fine provided that Bernini married Caterina Tezio (which is what Nicolas hints at the end of Bernini's trial). Caterina was the daughter of a prominent lawyer who was also friendly with the pope. Bernini agreed to this arrangement, and he and Caterina would remain married for 34 years and produce 11 children.

Of the poor disfigured Costanza, very little is recorded after that horrible incident; she vanishes from history.

If you'd like to see the bust of Costanza, you can find a multitude of images on the web: for instance, here (http://www.wga.hu/frames-e .html?/html/b/bernini/gianlore/sculptur/1630/bonarell.html) or here (http://www.getty.edu/visit/events/mcphee_lecture.html). Or you can go to the *Museo Nazionale del Bargello* in Florence, Italy, where it's on display. That would be the best way of all to see it!

ANTONIO VIVALDI: Anna Giraud (alternate spelling: Giro) was a student of Vivaldi's in whom he took an intense interest, and Anna and her sister did indeed live with him for many years—the evidence that Vivaldi and Anna were lovers is rather convincing. It was convincing enough, in fact, that the Cardinal-Bishop of Ferrara *did* refuse Vivaldi permission to enter the city and revoked the musician's commission to put on operas there. In response, Vivaldi wrote a letter to the Cardinal-Bishop emphatically denying his romantic involvement with Anna; that seems to have ended their public closeness, according to some accounts. Anna and Vivaldi certainly were with each other at various times afterward, but mostly away from Venice.

The playwright Carlo Goldoni, in whose company Nicolas is found in the novel, is also a historical personage—and the Teatro San Salvatore, where Vivaldi and Anna go to see an opera in the novel, was a genuine theater, is still in use, and is now (interestingly) named the Teatro Goldoni. Goldoni's words to his companions about Vivaldi and Anna are a paraphrase of a comment he wrote and which has been preserved: "This priest, an excellent violinist but a mediocre composer, has trained Miss Giraud to be a singer. She was young, born in Venice, but the daughter of a French wigmaker. She was not beautiful, though she was elegant, small in stature, with beautiful eyes and a fascinating mouth. She has a small voice, but many languages in which to harangue." I loved that last line—so wonderfully wicked. And it fits Perenelle, who in this book speaks several languages.

There are a few (very few) paintings and sketches of Vivaldi (for instance, at: http://upload.wikimedia.org/wikipedia/commons/1/1b/ Antonio_Vivaldi.jpg) but I was unable to track down a verifiable image of Anna.

ANTOINE LAVOISIER: Antoine Lavoisier and his wife Marie-Anne are both real characters, and Antoine did die by the guillotine during the French Revolution after accusations were brought against him. It was one of many tragedies of the time. "The Republic needs neither scientists nor chemists; the course of justice cannot be delayed" is an actual quote from the trial by the judge, and his friend Lagrange did indeed say after the execution that: "It took them only an instant to cut off his head, but France may not produce another such head in a century."

I've conveniently ignored the fact that Marie-Anne lived to the ripe old age of 78, ran a scientific salon, and married (evidently unhappily) again.

I have no clue as to whether Marie-Anne and Antoine had a cat.

A wonderful portrait of Antoine and Marie-Anne was painted by Jacques-Louis David (David could have perhaps interceded for Antoine with the leaders of the Revolution, but did not), and can be viewed at http://www.bc.edu/bc_org/avp/cas/his/CoreArt/art/resourcesb/dav _lavois.jpg.

JOHN WILLIAM POLIDORI: I really must apologize to the memory of John William Polidori, for in making him an incarnation of Nicolas Flamel, I also made him rather sinister when there is absolutely no evidence that Polidori was anything more than an honorable physician and writer. Polidori did write the seminal novel of vampires, "The Vampyre," and was indeed Lord Byron's physician, though I have conjectured here that Polidori and Byron were acquainted before Polidori received his medical degree, for which there's no historical evidence. "Emily Pauls" is entirely fictional; there is no one of that name in the historical record. However, Lord Byron, Percy Shelley, Mary Wollstonecraft, and William Blake were all well aware of each other, and Shelley and Mary did run away together in that year.

The "King's Square" mentioned in this section is now called "Soho Square"—and King Charles II's statue still stands there, as I know from having visited London in 2012. The statue is no longer in the center of the square, and has been rather much damaged over the years. The square itself is no longer residential, and only a few buildings survive from the time described in the book. Interestingly (well, to me, anyway) at one point Charles' face was sliced off the head of the statue, though it was cemented back into place when the statue was restored in the 1930s. I couldn't help but stare at it hoping to see Nicolas' face appear in its place.

And there really *was* a Great London Beer Flood in October of 1814. Don't believe me? Here's a link: http://www.bbc.co.uk/dna/h2g2/A42129876—the Great London Beer Flood killed nine people and destroyed several houses. Of course, the Great Beer Flood was actually an accident, not the result of a battle between Nicolas and Perenelle. The British Museum is now only a few blocks down on the same street that was a slum in 1814.

The online National Portrait Gallery of the UK has a Gainsford portrait of Polidori—you can see it at http://www.npg.org.uk/collections/search/largerimage.php?mkey=mw05070

"The Vampyre" is available as an e-book from Project Gutenberg at http://www.gutenberg.org/etext/6087

GUSTAV KLIMT: One of my favorite painters, and one of the darlings of the Art Nouveau movement—in Austria called the "Vienna Secessionist" movement. Emilie Flöge was certainly Klimt's true muse and most constant companion, though he would never marry her, and some historians question whether the two of them were ever lovers in the physical sense. Certainly Klimt had affairs with several other of his models, some of whom bore children that Klimt acknowledged as his own. But when Klimt was on his deathbed, there was only one person he called for: Emilie.

Vienna, at the turn of the century, was indeed a place of grandeur and pomp and gilt, but it was also a place that had perhaps the highest suicide rate in all of Europe. Their society was obsessed with death as much as it was obsessed with beauty.

There was no Gabriele; she is a fiction. Many of Klimt's subjects were well-known women in Vienna, but as many others aren't identified; count Gabriele as among them. And Klimt *did* like redheads . . .

There was also no Anton Srna, though there was a photography exhibition, and Anton Srna's name was plucked from that of two different exhibitors. It seemed to me appropriate that an alchemist would become involved in a process that heavily involves silver and chemistry.

Klimt died of a cerebral hemorrhage (not of a flawed immortality potion) in 1918 at age 55, leaving several works unfinished. Emilie would outlive him by decades; maybe *she* took the true potion?

CHARLOTTE SALOMON: While Anaïs Dereux, Perenelle's incarnation in this section, is entirely fictional, Charlotte Salomon is all too real, all too talented a person, and all too poignant a tale, only a portion of which is glimpsed—as always, greatly altered and fictionalized—in what I've presented here. It's true that suicide ran tragically in her family, with both her mother and her grandmother killing themselves by jumping from a high window; judging from Charlotte's drawings in *Life? or Theater?*, she feared that she might one day do the same. Luckily for us, she did not, and instead rendered her life in the exquisite pictures of her masterwork. If you google her name and look at the images that are linked there, you'll have the chance to glimpse some of these. As for Charlotte herself, there aren't many photographs of her that have survived. If you're curious, you might look here (http://www.ynetnews .com/articles/0,7340,L-3274438,00.html) or here (http://www.jewish-theatre.com/visitor/article_display.aspx?articleID=734).

There was no Anaïs in her life, no relationship with anyone like her, and no attempted rescue of Lotte and Alexander from the clutches of the Nazis. Lotte and her grandfather were interred at the Gurs camp for a few months in 1940; they were released due to her grandfather's ill health and both were allowed to return to Nice—which saved Lotte for enough time for her to create *Life? or Theatre?* However, not long after Lotte married Alexander Nagler (after the Germans took over the Nice region following the Italian surrender), they were both gathered up as so many others were and transported away from France, the majority of them to die in the camps. There is no direct record of Charlotte's death; it seems she was one of the many women culled from the transports as "useless" (because of her pregnancy) and sent directly to the gas chambers upon arrival at Auschwitz, while Alexander was placed in hard labor.

As for Nicolas in this time period: unlike the case with Polidori, in this instance I think I may have done *Nicolas* the injustice by giving him the identity of Alois Brunner, who was unfortunately a very real character and was directly responsible for the death of thousands of Jews, including Charlotte Salomon. I couldn't possibly make Nicolas as vile as the reality: if there is evil in the world, Alois Brunner was a significant manifestation. He vanished for a time after 1945—and in my fictional world, that was Nicolas changing identities once more. In reality, he resurfaced in the 1950s and took refuge in various countries in the Middle East. According to the Jewish virtual Library, (http://www.jewishvirtuallibrary.org/jsource/Holocaust/Brunner.html), he was interviewed in 1987 by telephone for the *Chicago Sun Times,* and said then: "The Jews deserved to die. I have no regrets. If I had the chance I would do it again . . ."

DAVID TREADWAY: It should go without saying that there is no real David Treadway, Camille Kenny, or Timothy Pierce—well, there may well be a David Treadway, Camille Kenny, or Timothy Pierce *somewhere* in the world, but I'm not aware of them and the David, Camille, and Timothy in the book have no connection to them at all. Those characters, and those around them, are made entirely of fictional cloth.

Except for one. The Frenchman named as "Etienne" in the section where Camille walks around early morning Paris and encounters Etienne feeding the birds in the Tuileries—*he* is based on a real person. Denise and I encountered him in Paris, sitting on a chair in the Tuileries and feeding the birds as I describe him in the book. No, I didn't talk to him, and I don't know his story or his real name. I watched him for a long time and took a few photographs. He was the kind of character that you see, and who immediately starts you imagining what his life might be like and why he's doing what he's doing. I knew I would use that imagined person in a story or a novel one day . . . and now I finally have. Here he is, as I saw him that day many years ago:

Books and major articles read in the course of writing this novel which have brought light and vision to the proceedings:

THE LIVES OF THE MUSES: Nine Women and the Artists They Inspired by Francine Prose. Perennial, 2003. A lovely book about a few of the women who inspired (and were inspired by) artists: well-written and well-researched, and worth your effort to find and read! While I didn't actually use any of the muses Ms. Prose outlines, I took away from the book many ideas and a sensibility.

PARIS IN THE MIDDLE AGES by Simone Roux, translated by Jo Ann McNamara. University of Pennsylvania Press, 2009. An entrancing look at Paris in the 13th–15th centuries, in the middle of which Nicolas and Perenelle Flamel were living.

LOST CRAFTS: Rediscovering Traditional Skills by Una McGovern. Chambers Harrap Publishers, Edinburgh, 2008. This is an essential research book for anyone writing of past times, if you want to know how things were actually done "back then."

A DISTANT MIRROR by Barbara W. Tuchman. Albert A. Knopf, New York, 1978. A re-read, actually, since I read this one ages ago. But since a portion of the book is set at the end of the 14th century, and Tuchman was such a wonderful writer, I read it again, especially the section discussing Étienne Marcel.

ARTEMISIA by Alexandra Lapierre. Translated by Liz Heron. Grove Press, 2000. A book on the life of the Italian painter Artemisia Gentileschi. Even though this is subtitled "A Novel," the book is intensely researched and heavily annotated by the author's reading of original texts as well as scholarly research on the life of Artemisia. Essentially, the author has written a biography, but has fictionalized some of the scenes—it reads somewhere between the two genres. Well worth picking up if you're interested in Artemisia.

However, even though a few scenes with Artemisia were written, and though Artemisia is one of the most fascinating artists of the Italian Renaissance, I made the decision to cut her from the book. Still, I'd urge you to google Artemisia and check out some of her paintings. I've always found her "Judith Decapitating Holofernes" (http://www.shafe.co.uk/crystal/images/lshafe/Artemisia_Gentileschi_Judith_Decapitating_Holofernes_c1618.jpg) to be incredibly striking, and far superior to Caravaggio's depiction of the same scene.

And hey, while in London, I was surprised and delighted to find her famous self-portrait in the Georgian apartments of Hampton Court.

THE LIFE AND TIMES OF ANTONIO LUCIO VIVALDI by Jim Whiting. Mitchell Lane Publishers, May 2004. A biography of Vivaldi that gives a good look at the details of his life.

HAWTHORNE: A LIFE by Brenda Wineapple. Random House, 2004. Exactly what you think it is: a biography of Nathaniel Hawthorne, and a fascinating look at an American author who's more complex (and darker) than I realized. The first draft of this novel contained a long (and complete) Hawthorne section with Perenelle as his wife Sophia, but that was abandoned during revision, as it no longer fit.

INTO THE DARKNESS LAUGHING: The Story of Modigliani's Last Mistress, Jeanne Hebuterne by Patrice Chaplin. Virago Press Limited, 1990. The tragic story of Jeanne Hébuterne and Amadeo Modigliani is more tragic than any fiction—I urge you to look it up, even though in the end I deleted my fictionalized version of it. For what it's worth, it was a picture of Jeanne that was the initial impetus for the idea that would eventually become this novel. (That story's here: http://sleigh.livejournal.com/303541.html)

I had to search a bit to find this one . . . The book is less a biography of Jeanne than the author's search for her own obsession, but it's still an interesting volume and a fascinating glimpse of the Jeanne/Modi relationship. As I said above, it was a picture of Jeanne that first sparked the long cascade of serendipitous connections that would lead to this novel.

"Missing Person in Montparnasse: The Case of Jeanne Hebuterne" by Linda Lappin, *Literary Review,* Summer 2002. A long, well-written, and interesting article on Jeanne and her life with Modigliani. A different perspective from the Chaplin book.

A photograph of Jeanne is here (http://esquimalenator.wordpress. com/), and one of Modigliani here (http://cortomalteze.wordpress. com/2007/07/14/amedeo-modigliani/), and an array of pictures of both of them here (http://community.livejournal.com/retroaesthetics/4419. htmlcutid2). Modigliani painted at least two dozen portraits of Jeanne. If you google "Modigliani & Jeanne" you'll come up with tons of images . . .

GUSTAV KLIMT: Painter of Women by Susanna Partsch. Prestel Publishing, New York, NY, 2006. A gorgeously-illustrated short book that contains many of Klimt's paintings and drawings of women, along with a detailed biography of the painter as well as that of several of the women who served as his models, especially Emilie Flöge, who was certainly Klimt's primary muse. I was tempted to have Perenelle be Emilie, except that for the purposes of that section, I needed someone who vanishes quickly and none of the models that Klimt used who are identified really fit the fictional needs—Emilie lived long after Klimt, staying very visible in Vienna. Therefore, I invented a model who could serve as Perenelle. And since Klimt died young and suddenly, it seemed only logical to make him another of Nicolas' subjects for the flawed elixir.

A NERVOUS SPLENDOR: Vienna 1888/1889 by Frederic Morton. Atlantic—Little, Brown, 1980. I've used this book as reference material twice before with other novels, and when I decided to use

Gustav Klimt, well, there it was once again, since Klimt is mentioned several times in the text. I love this book, which is an utterly fascinating view of *fin de siècle* Vienna, with some gorgeous touches of atmosphere. You feel as if you're there, walking along the Ringstrasse.

VIENNA MODERNISM 1890 – 1910 by Isabella Ackert. Federal Press Service, Vienna, Austria, 1999. This is available on the internet as a PDF, and covers Gustav Klimt as well as several other artists, writers, musicians, architects, and thinkers responsible for the flowering of "Vienna Modernism" at the turn of the century. The short book is interesting for its glimpses into the personalities of the era and its speculations as to why such a movement coalesced in Vienna.

TO PAINT HER LIFE: Charlotte Salomon in the Nazi Era by Mary Lowenthal Felstiner. University of California Press, 1997. An intense biography of Charlotte Salomon, murdered in a Nazi death camp, but who left behind a tremendous magnum opus entitled *Life? or Theatre?* Felstiner supposedly dedicated ten years to researching and writing this book—while I wish (for my purposes) that it had been a more straightforward biography, it's a worthwhile read on its own.

I also spent a substantial amount of additional research time on the various historical eras and characters depicted in the book, the majority of that research web-based. The list, I'm afraid, is far too long to give here (even if I could remember it all myself).

CHARACTERS—IN ORDER OF APPEARANCE, BY SECTION

(* indicates a genuine historical character, **bold** indicates an identity used by Perenelle, *italics* an identity used by Nicolas)

—•——•— TODAY—1: CALLIOPE—•——•—

Camille Kenny	**Perenelle's identity during current times.**
Ink	Bouncer at the *Bent Calliope*
Morris Johnson	One of Camille's artistic entourage—sculptor
Mercedes Vargas	One of Camille's artistic entourage—writer/novelist
Tom	A bartender at the *Bent Calliope*
David Treadway	A photographer who becomes Camille's lover
Rashawn	One of Camille's artistic entourage—painter
Kevin	One of Camille's artistic entourage—drummer & composer
Joe	One of Camille's artistic entourage—playwright
James	One of Camille's artistic entourage
Edward Weston *	A photographer in the famous "f/64" group

Ansel Adams *	A photographer in the famous "f/64" group
Charis Wilson *	Model for, and lover of, Edward Weston
Helen Treadway	David's wife.
Robert (Bob) Walters	Private investigator hired by Camille

INTERLUDE ONE, Perenelle & Nicolas Flamel

Perenelle Flamel *	**The POV character, and the "origin" character for all POVs**
Marianne	One of the maidservants in the Flamel household
Cosme Poisson	Perenelle's father, an apothecary and alchemist, died 1344
Marlon Cantrell	Perenelle's first husband, died in the Black Plague in 1349
Nicolas Flamel *	*Alchemist, scrivener, manuscript seller, and Perenelle's second husband*
Telo	Nicolas' apprentice
Benoît Picot	A friend of Nicolas, banker in Paris and minor courtier.
Étienne Marcel *	Provost of the merchants of Paris
Charles Valois *	Dauphin during the captivity of King Jean (John) the Good; later to become King Charles V of France
Verdette	Daughter of Nicolas & Perenelle, b1353—d1398
Élise	Verdette's nursemaid
Marguerite des Essars	Provost Marcel's wife
Yvette Picot	Benoît Picot's wife
Alaine Dubois	Verdette's husband

—•——•— TODAY- 2: POLYHYMNIA—•——•—

Verdette	Camille's cat, a gray French Chartreux
Jacob Prudhomme	Gallery owner who exhibits David's prints

INTERLUDE TWO, Perenelle & Nicolas Flamel

Musetta	Perenelle's apprentice in her later years
Elita Pelletier	Landlady of house where Perenelle flees after taking the elixir
Tremeur Pelletier	Husband of Elita. A seller of manuscripts.
Perenelle Cantrell	**Perenelle's identity with the Pelletiers**
Isabelle Leveque	**Name used by Perenelle with Jean Petit**
Jean Petit *	A miniaturist who was "Isabelle's" lover
Jacquemart de Hesdin *	A master miniaturist with whom Jean studied
Philippe de Vitry *	A musician who was one of the first artists Perenelle "enhanced"
Giselle Boulanger	**Name used by Perenelle with Philippe de Vitry**
Jacqueline Fournier	**Name used by Perenelle when she investigated Nicolas' "death"**
Didier Dubois	Perenelle and Nicolas' grandson

—•——•— TODAY—3: EUTERPE—•——•—

No new characters introduced

INTERLUDE THREE, Costanza Bonarelli and Gianlorenzo Bernini

Costanza Bonarelli *	**Name used by Perenelle with Bernini**

Gianlorenzo Bernini *	Roman artist and sculptor
Matteo Bonarelli *	Apprentice to Bernini and husband of Costanza
Scipione Borghese *	Cardinal in Rome, patron of Bernini
Luigi Bernini *	Younger brother of Gianlorenzo
Antonio Marcello Barberini *	Cardinal and nephew of Pope Urban VIII
Abramo Maroncelli	*Nicolas' identity in this period*
Urban VIII *	Current Pope, member of the Barberini family

—•——•— TODAY—4: ERATO—•——•—

Dr. Timothy Pierce	*Nicolas' identity in this period*

INTERLUDE FOUR, Anna Giraud & Antonio Lucio Vivaldi

Anna Giraud *	**Name used by Perenelle with Vivaldi**
Paolina Giraud *	A companion whom Anna calls her "half sister"
Antonio Lucio Vivaldi *	Musician and Anna's lover
Carlo Goldoni *	A Venetian playwright, a contemporary of Vivaldi
Edward Braddock *	An English musician who was her lover in 1701
Calorgero	Vivaldi's head servant of the household
Tommaso Ruffo *	The Cardinal-Archbishop of Ferrara
Lorenzo Ceribelli	*A Monsignor, and Nicolas' identity in this period*

—•——•— TODAY—5: CLIO—•——•—

Beth Walters	Bob Walter's granddaughter
Gina Palento	NYPD detective who was a friend and former partner of Bob Walters

Sally Treadway   Helen's older sister

INTERLUDE FIVE, Marie-Anne Paulze & Antoine-Laurent de Lavoisier

Marie-Anne Paulze *   **Perenelle's identity in the time of the French Revolution**

Jacques-Louis David *   Famous French painter who painted a portrait of Marie-Anne and Antoine

Antoine Lavoisier *   Perenelle's husband during the French Revolution, executed 8 May 1794

Etienne   One of the Lavoisiers' servants

Josette   One of the Lavoisiers' servants

*Maximilien Robespierre ***   *A leader of the French Revolution, and Nicolas' identity in this period.*

Joseph Louis Lagrange *   A mathematician spared by Antoine Lavoisier's testimony

—•——•— TODAY—6: THALIA—•——•—

Dominique   A clerk at the Hotel de Notré Dame

Etienne   A man who feeds the birds in the Jardin des Tuileries

Charlene   Etienne's deceased wife

INTERLUDE SIX, Emily Pauls & William Blake

Emily Pauls   **Name used by Perenelle during this time**

William Blake *   Poet and artist in Emily's circle

Catherine Blake *   Blake's wife

Percy Bysshe Shelley *   Poet in Emily's circle

Mary Godwin *   Young woman in Emily's circle, and Shelley's lover

Harriet Westbrook *   Shelley's wife

JMW Turner *	Artist in Emily's circle
Lord Byron *	Poet in Emily's circle
Augusta Leigh *	Byron's half-sister, rumored to also have been his lover
John William Polidori *	*The author of* The Vampyre, *Byron's physician, and also Nicolas' identity in this time*

—•——•— TODAY—7: TERPSICHORE—•——•—

Mrs. Darcy	Camille's next-door neighbor

INTERLUDE SEVEN, Gabriele Tietze & Gustav Klimt

Gustav Klimt *	A painter in Vienna during the turn of the century
Gabriele Tietze	**Perenelle's identity during this time**
Pauline Flöge *	Eldest of the Flöge sisters; a dressmaker who runs a school for dressmakers in Vienna
Helen Flöge *	Second oldest of the Flöge sisters, married to Gustav Klimt's brother Ernst.
Ernst Klimt *	Gustav's brother and fellow painter
Emilie Flöge *	Youngest of the Flöge sisters: Klimt's friend, sometimes model, and muse
Franz Matsch *	A friend of the Klimt brothers, who often painted with them on their large projects
Anton Srna	*A photographer, and Nicolas' identity in this period*
Andre	A street urchin Gabriele hires
Franz	Concierge at Anton's apartments

—•——•— TODAY—8: URANIA—•——•—

Roger Compton   Gina Palento's detective partner

INTERLUDE EIGHT, Anaïs Dereux & Charlotte Salomon

Anaïs Dereux   **Perenelle's identity during this time**
Charlotte (Lotte) Salomon *   A Jewish artist and German refugee
Ludwig Grunwald *   Lotte's grandfather, "Grosspapa"
Charlotte Grunwald *   Lotte's grandmother, "Grossmama"
Alois Brunner *   *Nicolas' identity in this time, an*
                                SS-Hauptsturmführer
Alexander Nagler *   Lotte's lover and husband
Ottilie Moore *   Owner of l'Ermitage

—•——•— TODAY—9: MELPOMENE—•——•—

No new characters introduced

—•——•— EPILOGUE, SARAH—•——•—

Ami Huang   A pianist
Sarah Miles   **Perenelle' identity during this time**
Kristin Emerson   David's second wife
Aaron Treadway   David and Kristin's son
Michelle Treadway   David and Kristin's daughter